No one laughed. No one even smiled. Gates took that as a good sign. He continued to describe how for almost twenty years the CIA had gone down to the wire of the scientific frontiers – and had finally stepped over it. There was a haunted tone to his voice when he next spoke.

'There were a number of deaths. Human guinea pigs. Mental patients. Prisoners. They never knew what was happening to them . . . After the deaths there was a cover-up. The front organisations were closed down. Any links to Langley were cut. The silence of those who could be bought was bought.'

A brooding silence filled the Oval Office.

ALSO BY GORDON THOMAS

VOICES IN THE SILENCE

Gordon Thomas

ORION

An Orion paperback
First published in Great Britain by Chapmans Publishers in 1993
This paperback edition published in 1994 by Orion Books Ltd,
Orion House, 5 Upper St Martin's Lane, London WC2H 9EA

Copyright © Gordon Thomas 1993

A CIP catalogue record for this book is available from the
British Library.

ISBN: 1 85797 424 7

Printed in England by Clays Ltd, St Ives plc

To
ELIZABETH KRANER

An Earth Mother without equal.
She knew how to communicate without language.
Hers is truly a voice beyond the silence.

SPECIAL THANKS

The House of Chapman
Each and every one of them for once more making this one possible.

Russ Galen
As always – simply the best.

Victor O'Rourke
He came at the beginning and saw it unfold.

Frank Dolan
For advice freely given and gratefully received.

Sean Carberry
He gave more, far more, than his name.

Giles Montgomery
For making people understand.

Mary and Paul McGrath
Once more they did all that was asked of them.

Julia Martin and Caroline North
Great catches, and gentle with it.

Miranda Moriarty
She again deciphered the almost illegible with a skill that remains unsurpassed. Loyal, discreet and patient, if ever a book has a midwife, she was this one's.

and Edith, Nicholas and Natasha
You saw this one grow and shared the frustrations. I am truly grateful.

Ashford, Ireland
January 1993

1

David Morton watched Tommy Nagier glance over his shoulder, gloved hands in continuous fluid motion in the pilot's cockpit of the F-14D Tomcat. The boy's adrenalin was building nicely and those eyes spoke of determination and total absence of fear. But did he have more to offer than that?

'Catch that report on the radio this morning, Colonel, about those demonstrations in Tokyo?' Tommy asked.

'Some things don't change.' The austerity of Morton's words sounded from the core of time.

There was a moment's silence before Tommy spoke again. 'I was in Japan a couple of years ago. They were pretty bullish then. Kept talking of the need to protect their commercial interests. They see everybody as a threat. Ever been to Japan, Colonel?' The boy had a nice way of trying to draw you out.

'Yes,' Morton replied in a voice designed to discourage further questions.

The ejector seats were high mounted and the key tactical-information display screens positioned to minimise eye movement when manoeuvring against the enemy. More dials and lights came alive. At full surge there was sufficient computer-driven power in this confined space to run a large hospital. But the equipment was solely intended to enable the pilot to kill or avoid being killed. It would be dark soon. Already the carrier's island superstructure, rising like a daunting grey cliff, was lost in the murk. Morton had selected the weather, chosen everything.

Tommy deserved no less. Physically and mentally he fitted the ideal selection profile. He was twenty-six years old, five feet ten and weighed in at 170 pounds in his shorts. He'd run a mile in four minutes and hit a moving target at half a mile. His MENSA IQ rating was 165. With it came fluency in a couple of languages, Mandarin and Cantonese. And he was modest about his skills. But all those plusses would still be weighed against what happened in the next few minutes. The job demanded no less. It always had.

Watching Tommy continue the pre-flight Morton felt an old tug in the stomach. He had been recruited in those dark and dangerous years when the threat was all too clearly delineated. Now nothing was clear. Except that the threat was still there. That reality was finally recognised after a series of particularly horrific incidents in Bosnia, South Africa and Peru. All were failures of intelligence to provide enough advance warning. The Secretary-General of the United Nations had secretly telephoned the leaders of the Western industrial nations, saying it was time for an international intelligence-gathering task force with a strike capability. It would report directly to him. Presidents and prime ministers had swiftly agreed to dip into their own secret funds to set up the Hard Attack Multinational Megaresponsibility Emergency Response Force. It was immediately shortened to Hammer Force.

Its creators accepted without demur that Morton was the only choice as Operations Director because of the universal respect he commanded in the US, British and European intelligence communities. In an anonymous conference room in UN Headquarters, he had spelled out his conditions for accepting: his own choice of team and state-of-the-art equipment, and the unchallenged right to answer to no one on operational details. Acceptance of these conditions was enshrined in the only formal document acknowledging the existence of Hammer Force. The Secretary-General had offered, and Morton had accepted, as headquarters an anonymous building above the north, and less fashionable, shore of Lake Geneva. Once the repository of Switzerland's gold reserves, the building and its hectare of woodland was protected by the most sophisticated electronic perimeter man could devise.

Since then Morton had waited there for a suitable target. That one had now emerged was another reason why he was strapped in the cockpit.

'You think the Japanese are just muscle-flexing?' Tommy asked over the intercom.

'Maybe.'

Japan was only part of it. The collapse of the Soviet Union had thrown out of work entire laboratories of scientists, each a specialist in nuclear, biological or chemical weapons. Many had discreetly accepted unheard-of salaries from Iraq and Iran. Morton knew who and where they were, and the current state of their research. But there was another group whose work had been so secret that even now little about it was known in the West. Those scientists had worked on particle-beam, scalar-electromagnetic and direct-energy weapons, trying to make the world of Buck Rogers finally come true. The discovery was followed by relief in the West that almost all of their research facilities had been destroyed by mobs venting their new-found freedom and hatred for all that Russia's former rulers had represented. Now the scientists who had worked on startling new physics were confined to former prison camps in the Arctic Circle, while in Moscow the new regime decided their fate.

A couple of months ago Hammer Force's Electronic Surveillance Division – Morton's ears to the world – had picked up news that two more specialists in particle-beam weapons had vanished from a camp near Archangel.

Igor Tamasara had also vanished from there.

Professor Igor Viktorovitch Tamasara was to energetics what Barnes Wallis had been to the Dambuster bomb – capable of single-handedly changing the lexicon of warfare. But how close had Tamasara come to producing a weapon capable of making a human brain obey a command, any command, without knowing from whom or where it came? A weapon like that could literally leave anyone without an independent thought of his own. A weapon like that could achieve something no other had ever done. Make man a total, abject slave.

Morton had made discovering everything about Igor Tamasara the first priority of Hammer Force. The technicians at Computer Graphics had once more shown their matchless skills. They used their screens to age Igor Tamasara to what he could now look like; whittling down his face, making his nose appear larger and his chin more pointed. Now aged forty-seven, he could be almost bald, those coal-black eyes staring out at the world from deeper sockets. The Professor and his team in Psychological Assessment suggested those eyes indicated a strong sex drive – though no one could say for which gender.

Nobody, not even Chantal Bouquet's field agents in Foreign Intelligence, was able to discover what had happened to Igor Tamasara after he vanished into the Siberian night.

In his mirror Tommy saw the chin strap drawn tight against Morton's jutting lower jaw, the Colonel's eyes observing everything and revealing nothing – except to suggest if you were not part of the answer, you were part of the problem. His instructor in urban surveillance had said that the Colonel was at his most intimidating when his eyes were on autopilot. And the woman instructor on dead letter-box techniques had told another instructor – small-arms – that she envied the way the Colonel avoided the more obvious signs of ageing, the way his skin was unlined and his body lean and trim.

Here in the confined space of the cockpit the Colonel's height was somehow even more striking. He'd always addressed the Colonel by rank; there was something about him which discouraged familiarity. It went with his reputation as a hard man to please; one who believed totally that knowledge and preparation, coupled to discipline, could face down any kind of danger.

Morton heard the intercom click in his head dome. 'Dad wanted to come today, but I told him he'd know soon enough, Colonel.'

Morton nodded. Tommy was Danny's only flesh and blood, and Danny was Hammer Force's surveillance supremo. He could hide a mike or tracking bug in places no one thought possible. The reports said Tommy had the same single-minded determination. What had happened on that fairground showed that. Fourteen years had not dimmed the memory. Morton had taken Danny with him to London for a seminar on urban terrorism. On that Saturday they'd driven down to Sussex, collected Tommy from his boarding school and gone on to Brighton. The boy, twelve at the time, had headed straight for the amusement rides, inviting them to take turns to accompany him. During its high-speed whirl, the mechanised arm controlling the Combat Fighters had broken loose, leaving the cockpits lurching dangerously high above the ground. Tommy had sat calmly with Morton waiting to be winched to safety. Afterwards Tommy insisted they all rode the rollercoaster. On the way back to London that night Danny had proudly said he had always encouraged his son to play to his strengths.

Tommy continued to work his way through the pre-flight checks. 'The stick feels a little stiff, Control.' There was a moment's pause before the Controller's flat, indifferent question: 'You want to abort, One Zero Zero?'

'You gotta be kidding!'

Tommy's instructors were unanimous in their assessment that he had not been afraid to speak his mind. And in his tradecraft classes he had shown a talent for sifting through a pile of data.

'Two minutes to launch, One Zero Zero,' came the Controller's voice in Morton's headset.

'On the button, Control,' Tommy acknowledged.

Morton heard nothing but quiet certainty. No attempt to impress, no ambition to grandstand. The boy was like his father.

'All set to go, Colonel.'

Morton's ears began to fill with the sound of engines running up to full military power. The instruments pulsed and quivered on the control panel before him. Beneath the analog display indicator screen – which would present all the information Tommy needed to pilot the aircraft – was a small joystick. He'd spent an hour the previous evening reminding himself what the stick could do.

The intercom clicked. 'Let's make it a good one, Colonel. Let's go up, up and away.'

Morton raised a hand towards Tommy's mirror. Everyone had their little mantras and that the boy could share his was good. The job called for a small-team player. Away to his left Morton saw that the yellow pre-launch light remained steady high up on the island superstructure. The engine roar became more deafening. The light turned green.

Tommy felt the muscles in his buttocks tighten involuntarily and he rose a fraction from his seat.

He had felt a similar excitement that first time he lifted a Royal Hong Kong Police helicopter off its Kowloon pad. Perfect tear-gas weather, the patrol leader remarked when they flew in search of another Triad junk running drugs from the New Territories. They'd returned to base without a shot being fired. His time in Hong Kong had been mostly like that, a promise of action almost never fulfilled. Not like today.

Morton saw Tommy's lips move, heard his throat clearance and the repeated murmur 'Go, go, go!' The instruments indicated that the fighter was accelerating past 200 knots. Fuel flow, oil pressure and hydraulics were responding normally to the change in aerodynamics. A steady murmur of electronic mush filled the background. Tommy found the sound reassuring. Here you were on your own, you and the sphinx-like figure in the back seat whom your Dad said was the best friend a man could have, but who now seemed as cold as a radar image. He trimmed the aircraft, allowing the wings to continue retracting. A couple of minutes later the analog screen showed them levelled off at 40,000 feet, flying at one and a half times the speed of sound.

In his headphones, Morton heard the clicking as Tommy switched the radio to attack frequency.

'This is Strike, One Zero Zero. Your target bogey is in vector two-seven-five,' said a new voice, a woman's.

'Roger, Strike,' acknowledged Tommy.

At briefing he had been told the bogey was a boat running a cargo of arms, possibly missiles: another version of Hong Kong. Morton watched a needle on the analog display screen flicker as Tommy pushed the Tomcat into after-burner. A quivering dial mimicked their dropping through the sky. He heard Tommy tap the transmit button on his lip mike. 'Strike, I have the bogey at seventy-plus,' Tommy said. The Tomcat's nose camera had fed the infra-red image of the boat to a cockpit screen which reproduced it as a small dot the on-board computer calculated to be seventy miles away.

Tommy placed his head firmly against his scope hood as he checked the reading. 'Bogey's looking good, Strike. I'm going to make an ID pass.'

A man's voice, cold and pre-emptory, cut in. 'This is Strike Commander, One Zero Zero. We have a positive satellite identification. Your bogey has primed her missiles. Attack at once!'

Morton's hand moved towards his own scaled-down joystick as Tommy placed his face back against the hood. 'Strike. This is One Zero Zero. I've still got time to drop a flare to double check the bogey's ID.' The boy was not allowing himself to be pushed.

On the display screen the small dot representing the Tomcat banked and climbed away from the larger dot, the bogey. The flare-release marker began to fall down the scale to the point Tommy had selected for dropping one of the rack of million candlepower sodium lights. There was a blinding flash beyond the cockpit. In his earphones the woman's voice was filled with sudden urgency. 'Unidentified aircraft heading towards you! Present distance 190 km!'

Tommy thrust his face back against the hood. Nothing on the radars. He adjusted the focus on the nose camera. Still no sign of the unidentified. On his own screen Morton watched the blip of the other aircraft moving steadily towards the Tomcat. He gave the little joystick another jiggle. He heard Tommy swear softly. The Tomcat had just lost the last of its radars.

'Anything on your screen, Colonel?'

'Not a thing.' Long ago Morton had learned that the moment man really separated himself from the other species was when he first used his simple grunting language to lie.

The woman controller was back. 'The unidentified is now at 140 km. We are also picking up activated weapon emissions from your target.'

'Starting attack run on bogey, Strike,' Tommy said. He toggled the stick. The sibilant electronic mush brought him to a level of pure, perfect concentration, a single, totally-focused eye, aware of everything, missing nothing. Morton saw the armament panel light up as the missile-ready lights blinked in sequence, heard the buzzer warning they were ready for launch. He gently moved his joystick to a new setting. He heard Tommy's grunt, then the rapid clicking of radio frequencies being scanned and switched, scanned and switched. Only static.

The intercom clicked. 'Radio's gone, Colonel.'

'Can you still fight the 'plane?'

'I've got a clear steer to the bogey.'

Tommy held the stick firmly, throttles forward against the stops. The Tomcat continued its dive. They seemed alone in this black formless universe. He glanced in the mirror. The Colonel's face was bent forward, watching the armament panel, waiting for the moment when the computer would indicate when to fire. Soon, very soon.

The woman's voice was suddenly clear. 'One Zero Zero. We have your unidentified now at 50 km.'

Tommy glanced at the armament panel. In fifteen seconds he would drop the cluster bombs. But in sixteen seconds he would be in missile range of the unidentified. He toggled the stick trigger, body and brain as one. The woman's maddeningly calm voice was back. 'One Zero Zero, Strike. We have a positive ID. Your unidentified is an Iraqi Mig. Now at 30 km and closing. We show him missile primed ...'

The transmission was once more lost to static. A moment later lights went out on the armament panel. The bombs had gone. Morton moved his stick another fraction. An alarm bell filled the cockpits.

'Bogey's shooting at us!' Tommy yelled.

A stream of tracer reached for the cockpit. Tommy rolled his stick hard left, keeping the turn tight, feeling the pressure build on the controls. The orange fireballs seemed barely to clear the top of the cockpit. Morton touched his stick. The woman's voice was filled with sudden urgency. 'Strike to One Zero Zero! Mig is at nine o'clock.'

Tommy instantly glanced to his left. Nothing. He kept the stick back and the nose up. The gas gauge was close to zero. Morton could hear the rapid breathing in his earphones. On his screen the tiny Tomcat blip weaved and rolled through the darkness. The boy was good, obeying the fighter pilot's imperative – go in fast. But he was getting close to his limit. As the blip began another roll to the left, Morton pushed his own stick to the right. He heard Tommy gasp. Then the blip began to stall, like some wounded bird, its wings waggling helplessly, as the woman's voice called out even more urgently, 'One inbound!'

In a fractional instant Tommy's mind grasped what was happening and sent a hand to the missile deflection chaff button. His fingers pressed twice. Only time for a couple of bursts. He pushed the stick hard left. Morton once more moved his stick to the right. The blip staggered like a drunk. Out of a corner of his eye, Tommy saw the swept-wing fighter hurtling towards them at an angle. 'Eject!'

Even as he reached for the ejector handle between his legs, there was a tremendous flash of light, like a fireball. Then blackness and silence that could not have been more total than death itself.

Above Morton's head a square patch of daylight suddenly appeared in the night sky and a man's face peered down on the Tomcat. He wore a headset and blue overalls. A door opened at the spot where the Mig had appeared and a man wheeled steps to the side of the cockpits. Morton heard the intercom click. 'How'd I do, Colonel?'

'You should have gone for the Mig first.' Morton saw Tommy shake his head ruefully as he pressed the catch to release the cockpits' canopy.

The wall against which the image of the carrier's flight deck had been projected rolled silently back. Beyond sat half a dozen men and a woman at desks equipped with console microphones and keyboards to control the video projectors and loudspeakers that had created an illusion of total reality of combat in the Tomcat simulator. Housed in the basement of Hammer Force's Headquarters, the simulator provided the ultimate test for anyone who applied to join Operations. The unspoken questions that had been asked of Tommy were, as always, the same. Could he maintain control in any given situation? Had he the guts to go in first? But not stupid enough to go in first every time? Morton's skilled handling of his own control stick as he had overridden the pilot's mastery of the aircraft had increased the pressure on Tommy.

He led the way over to the desks where the team were checking paperwork. The Strike Controller looked up at Morton. 'He did okay on responses. The hesitations were all well within the time limits. Initiative, good. Same with decision-making,' she said.

Tommy smiled.

'Thanks Anna,' Morton said.

Anna Cruef worked in Psychological Assessment. There was no one better at avoiding the pitfall of allowing everything to be neatly untangled and tied together again just as neatly. She had produced the psycho-profile of Igor Tamasara. Morton glanced at the man sitting beside her.

He looked at Tommy, waving a hand as he spoke. 'You were right, Tommy. Insisting on going for your ID run. Always check. Be sure.'

Lester Finel, who ran Computers, had a staccato way of speaking and a curious movement of his left hand that mimicked a revolving spool of tape.

'Thank you,' Tommy murmured.

'I take it that's a pass, Lester?' Morton asked.

'Absolutely.'

Morton looked at the technician from Voice Analysis, a large, solid man with the face of a good-natured Great Dane.

'I show a ninety on my graph in the final stall. A little high, but understandable.' The technician grinned. 'Otherwise excellent control.'

Morton nodded to the operative from Covert Action. He had learned the business of killing in some of the harshest corners of the world. The operative glanced at Tommy through steel-rimmed spectacles. 'You did a little too much unnecessary talking during the pre-flight. In my work you keep everything to the absolute minimum. I told you that in class last month.' The operative turned to Morton. 'Providing he remembers that, he'll be okay.'

From a corner of the room a middle-aged man walked forward. Like his son, Danny Nagier was physically unremarkable, with the same fine-boned build. Only when he smiled was his face transformed. His was a gentle smile. He fingered his eye-patch, the way he sometimes did when he was especially pleased. Morton turned to Tommy. 'Welcome to the team.'

'Thank you, Colonel.'

The others made a path for Danny. He stepped forward and clasped his son by the shoulders. 'I'm proud, my boy, really proud of you,' Danny murmured.

Morton spoke to Anna. 'After you've shown Tommy round, find him a desk near you. I want him up to speed on everything we've got on Igor Tamasara.'

'Which isn't much,' she said frankly.

'For sure.' Morton's brief smile almost softened the words. As he stepped back the others crowded around Tommy to offer their congratulations.

Behind them the door to the room opened.

Morton saw Walter Bitburg had again lost control over his eyes; they had begun to carom. His eyes were grey, like everything else about

Hammer Force's Administrator – suit, hair and expression. 'You're a hard man to keep track of, David,' Bitburg said pre-emptively when Morton walked over.

'I called your office. Your secretary said you were in a meeting, Walter, and couldn't be disturbed.'

Bitburg nodded, the light from the room's neon strips catching his thick glasses, enlarging the caroming, once more reminding Morton of balls being repeatedly struck by a cue in Bitburg's head. 'It's budget time. If I took every call I'd never get through.'

It was always budget time with Bitburg. Morton nodded towards the simulator. 'Tommy checked out.'

'Computers, David, that's the future.'

'I need people who can think for themselves.' Morton's voice showed neither impatience nor irritation.

The silence between them was more than distance. It was something wider and deeper. Bitburg's way was to store everything in separate compartments, each labelled with the amount of proof they contained. When Bitburg thought there wasn't sufficient, his eyes led this life of their own. 'Lars Svendsen wants to see you, David,' Bitburg said finally.

'He say why?'

Bitburg shrugged. 'A patient. Somebody called Rebicov. Svendsen wouldn't say more. I really can't think why he called.'

'I've persuaded him we are both on the same side, Walter.' It had taken time to do so. Nor was the psychiatrist a time-waster. And Rebicov was a Russian name. Morton glanced towards the simulator. The others were coming towards them. He turned to Bitburg. 'I'll go and see Svendsen now.'

Bitburg's voice was dry and precise. 'One other thing. I see the CIA's still billing us a quarter of a million dollars a month for a print-out of their surveillance in the North Atlantic. I don't see the point. The Russians aren't suddenly going to send their submarines to sea ...'

'I need to keep the print-out coming, Walter,' Morton said sharply. He strode past Bitburg and out of the simulator room.

What made Lars Svendsen's call especially interesting was that he only treated people who were victims of state-sponsored torture in its many forms, including the kind of scientific experiments in which Igor Tamasara had specialised. A man like that didn't give up. Yet there weren't many with the resources to continue to support him.

Striding towards the elevator, Morton once more ran through his mind a shortlist of likely candidates.

2

The unlit stogey rolled from one corner of his mouth to another as Qiao Peng continued to listen. Though he was not allowed to smoke his doctors had not yet forbidden him the actual taste of tobacco. And he knew they admired the way he accepted impending death with the same cold stoicism that governed his life.

He replaced the telephone without saying a word.

Once more the Director of the Secret Intelligence Service of the People's Republic of China rolled the cigar between his thin, bloodless lips. His suit hung in loose folds, and the unhealthy pallor of his skin confirmed the reality of the advanced state of his cancer. His baldness came from chemotherapy, which had failed after the original malignancy metastasised. A moment ago his chief doctor had told him on the 'phone he had six months at the most, probably less.

It was still enough time to climax his long career with an unparalleled intelligence coup.

The plan hinged on pitting the two great economic superpowers, Japan and the United States, against each other in a titanic struggle which would leave them both crippled. China would fill the vacuum, finally throwing aside the terrible slur of Karl Marx that she was a carefully-preserved mummy in a hermetically-sealed coffin. China would spearhead the world into the twenty-first century. The Pacific century.

Hu – Chairman Hu, China's Supreme Leader – had asked, as always, for the details on a single page. Qiao Peng kept a copy on his desk as a constant reminder of how far he had come and how close he was to succeeding. He picked up the paper, as he had done a hundred times, walked over to the window, and held the calligraphy close to his thick spectacles.

There were moments – after he spent the first million American dollars – when he wondered how far he would be allowed to go. Each time he had been reassured by the bold brush strokes Chairman Hu used to approve expenditure. The first payment had sent a negotiating team to Russia to persuade Igor Tamasara to come to Beijing. His political masters had demanded – and received without demur – ten million dollars to ensure that the scientist and what little remained of his equipment could leave Russia.

In the hills to the west of Beijing, secure from the prying eyes of foreign intelligence agents, Igor Tamasara had purpose built his unique laboratory complex. Later two of Igor Tamasara's assistants had also been smuggled out of Russia in the same total secrecy. Since then his every request continued to be instantly met. In all, a billion American dollars had been spent.

Qiao Peng lowered the paper. Instinctively, he had known he was right not to ask Igor Tamasara for progress reports. A man of such arrogance would have responded badly to such a request. Instead, Qiao Peng had bided his time. Two days ago Igor Tamasara had called to say he would be ready to give a demonstration this evening to Chairman Hu.

The security chief remained at the window, content for the moment to enjoy the heat from the setting sun. Since his last treatment his body had never felt really warm. In a few days he would be sixty-three. There would be no celebration; he loathed any sign of affection. The little shiver that came and went across his lips, the nearest he ever came to smiling, was in anticipation of the mayhem he would create in Langley and in Hammer Force. He had never quite understood what drove Morton. Was it only patriotism? Or something else?

Soon it would not matter. Morton, and the rest of them, as the Americans liked to say, would be history. Despite those years spent in the West which had given him perfect English, as well as a command of several other languages, he had never grasped the American idiomatic use of words. Perhaps it was because they were still a young country. And for all their ruthlessness, the Americans had a threshold they would not – could not – cross. It was something in their psyche. He had no such problems.

This plan had been conceived and nurtured in his office in a corner of the most secret enclave on earth – the Zhongnanhai compound beside the Forbidden City in mid-town Beijing. Within the 250 acres of heavily-fortified parkland, China's aged rulers lived and worked in surroundings as sumptuous as those of any of the dynasty emperors.

But he had deliberately chosen to make this room as starkly plain as possible. Its ceilings, walls and furnishings were a flat white, giving the office a chilling bleakness which even the warming rays of the sun could not lift. White was the Chinese colour of death.

Through the window he saw that down by the lake the evening procession was underway. The survivors of that most epic of feats, one without parallel in the annals of war, the Long March, were taking their evening stroll. There were only a few cadres left now from that unforgettable two-year journey across mountain ranges and provinces larger than most European states. He had himself been a child at the time, clutching his mother's hand, stumbling along towards that moment on October 1, 1949 when Mao Zedong had proclaimed a new China.

The old men would be oblivious to the stench of the protected carp who had long ago turned the lake's water dark with their faeces. No doubt they would be arguing among themselves over the proposal the emissary had brought from Washington, balancing it against its potential to threaten – even destroy – all they believed in. Let them argue. The decision would not be theirs. But it would be taken as soon as Igor Tamasara delivered on the promise he had made in return for fifty million American dollars deposited in his name in a Credit Suisse account in Geneva. At the time he had thought the Russian had sold himself cheaply. He had earmarked a hundred million dollars for Igor Tamasara.

The 'phone rang. Turning from the window, Qiao Peng walked over to his desk to answer it. The voice of Hu's secretary murmured that the Chairman was ready.

Igor Tamasara listened impatiently for the low rumble of the train approaching the railway platform sunk a quarter of a mile beneath the ground.

He wore a wig to hide his baldness and his sunken coal-black eyes were more red-rimmed than usual from long working days. But they had a look of deep satisfaction. In a few months, with a budget and a freedom he never imagined possible, he had driven everyone the same ruthless way he drove himself. And it had worked.

In the first experiments his guinea pigs – Chinese political prisoners – had died in their scores from over-exposure to the electromagnetic energy beams. He had ordered up more guinea pigs and adjusted the settings. When those prisoners also died he demanded still more, and made further adjustments. He had gone on demanding and adjusting. It had been the only way. He had kept a hundred guinea pigs in a magnetic field and bombarded them with a range of microwatt beams. Two thirds had died before the first day was over. But those who lived through the night showed an encouraging inability to make independent judgements before they also perished. High losses, he told his team, were to be expected, especially in the initial electromagnetic pulse experiments. The beams had literally cooked brains.

He had used up a large number of human guinea pigs before that problem was resolved.

There had been hundreds more experiments, all with their quota of deaths. But each one had brought him much closer to proving it was possible to make a human mind believe it was acting on free will – and not under the influence of the invisible beams. Using them was like playing God. Except he did not believe in such divine nonsense. It was not God, but scientists like him, who had always changed the destiny of the world. But he would be the first to create the means of controlling every human being on earth.

To do so he had rebuilt the Gyroton beam machine he had begun to experiment with in Russia. He was now ready to demonstrate its potential to his new paymasters. Even now he did not know exactly where and how they would use his weapon. But it must be someone very important. That fifty million-dollar fee he had demanded proved that; and the way his every wish was immediately fulfilled.

The woman standing beside him spoke. 'Remember, Comrade Tamasara, that while the Chairman speaks a little Russian, try not to be too technical.'

Despite her neutral smile, the unspoken reprimand was plain. Wei had been assigned as his interpreter. She had also turned out to be an inventive lover. He was not fooled, not for a moment, by her reasons for willingly giving herself to him. She was one of Qiao Peng's women. No different to the KGB woman who had been assigned to him in Russia. In the end he had used her and her brother to further his early experiments. Now he could barely remember what they looked like, only their name. Rebicov. He never forgot a surname.

The electrodes he had implanted in their brains had programmed them to kill themselves, the woman first. How they chose to do so had been the only choice he had left them. He had asked Qiao Peng to check they were both dead. The woman had committed suicide in Miami. Her brother had taken her body to be cremated in Haifa. That had been reassuring news. The man's electrode contained an instruction to him to dispose of her body without leaving any trace. Why Rebicov had taken his sister's body to Israel was of no interest. Apparently, he had himself subsequently gone berserk. The problem with those first-generation electrodes was their tendency to develop glitches. But the man would also have committed suicide. The self-destruct command had never failed.

Igor Tamasara looked at Wei and shrugged. 'I will keep it as simple as I can. But I will not minimise what has been achieved.'

Moments later the electrically-powered train that had sped the fifteen miles underground from the Zhongnanhai compound pulled into the platform. The door of the single carriage opened exactly in front of the spot where Wei had positioned Igor Tamasara. A squat and muscled figure in a dark silk suit emerged with Qiao Peng.

Chairman Hu stood impassively while being introduced. 'You speak English, Comrade Professor?' he asked. His voice was surprisingly thin and insubstantial for someone so strongly built.

'Da. Yes, of course. I have been to many international conferences where English – '

'Then you will explain to me in English what you have achieved.'

The group headed for the elevator which would carry them up to Igor Tamasara's complex.

An hour later, coming out of a laboratory, Igor Tamasara said it was an axiom of science that the better an experiment, the more new questions it raised after it answered the one you asked. He glanced at Chairman Hu and Qiao Peng. 'In the beginning the questions came thick and fast. In the end we reduced them to two. Could we induce specific behaviour? Could we make a subject actually do something he would normally be totally opposed to doing? Everything you have seen was designed to answer those questions.'

He had explained electromagnetic coil configurations, wave forms and low-level intensities, explained how randomisers created repetitive patterns to induce symptoms of mental illness. He had explained everything. They had continued to listen intently while he used a human brain in a pickling jar to explain its anatomy, before removing the organ and using a knife to make a cross-section and reveal the specific areas that could be stimulated by electromagnetism: the limbic system, which consists of the hypothalamus, the hippocampus and amygdala. These contained all human emotions.

Walking down the corridor, Tamasara continued to lecture them on behavioural conditioning. 'The most important breakthrough came when we were able to confirm what until now has only been suspected. That in the human brain cortex there is a complex biological comparator. This first identifies every signal the brain receives and then checks it against every other one received in the past. Every one. To replicate that with a computer would need one the size of your Great Hall of the People. And it would probably need several hours to run a check each time. The comparator, which is half the size of a penny, does so in seconds.'

He paused, waiting for another little hiss of air to pass Chairman Hu's lips; it was the way China's leader showed how impressed he was. Qiao Peng's unlit stogey moved slightly, but otherwise he gave no reaction. 'But we have discovered that if the comparator is overwhelmed by the input of unexpected signals, it shuts down. The result each time has been a whole range of behavioural changes, often bizarre or erratic, sometimes producing hallucinations, delusions, personality disassociations, frenzy, perplexity, disorientation and even death.'

Chairman Hu and Qiao Peng exchanged quick glances. 'Have you been able to programme a guaranteed specific response?' Qiao Peng asked.

'Not quite. But we have been able to narrow it down into groups. One set of signals will produce apathy, lethargy and whimpering. Another, thirst, hunger and loss of bodily functions. A third, ranting and raving. And so on.'

Chairman Hu put a question in his faint voice. 'How quickly can this be achieved, Professor Tamasara?'

'Very often as soon as a person is exposed to the beam. A five-second pulse is sometimes sufficient. But to be certain we are using ten-second bursts, four or five given over a short interval.'

How short?' Qiao Peng asked.

'A minute or two.'

'Is there any way these transmissions could be detected or diverted in some way?'

Igor Tamasara flushed. He could not remember the last time someone had even dared to hint he had not thought of everything. 'There is always that possibility. But it would presuppose that prior warning of the beam was known. To ensure that such a warning is not given is not my responsibility, Director. I assume that when the time comes my Gyroton will be positioned in absolute secrecy,' he said stiffly.

Chairman Hu asked another question. 'Is what you are doing a form of what my predecessors called brainwashing?'

Tamasara concealed his irritation with a little sigh. 'What we have achieved here has little to do with what your scientists did to American prisoners of war in Korea in the fifties. That was really quite crude. What we are doing here is infinitely more complex.'

'How so?' Chairman Hu asked politely.

'Our intention is to achieve the maximum effect from the beams after the Gyroton is well clear of the area. We are close to creating this delayed reaction.'

'Close to?' asked Qiao Peng sharply. 'I thought you had reached the stage of being able to provide a successful demonstration?'

'Human behaviour is extremely complex, Director. But I believe you will see enough to satisfy you I have not been wasting my time,' said Igor Tamasara tartly.

Chairman Hu lit another of the Panda cigarettes he chain-smoked.

Igor Tamasara used his door code card to access another room. Motioning them towards armchairs, he walked to a lectern beside a drawn curtain. Close by was a monitor screen. He pressed a button on the lectern's console and the curtains opened to reveal a glass observation panel with a view of the adjoining room. Two young men in convict uniforms sat on the floor, talking quietly to each other in the otherwise empty room.

Igor Tamasara nodded towards the panel. 'They can neither see nor hear us. They are among the last of the Tiananmen Square student rioters. They have been chosen because they are intellectually superior to those we normally use. They are also blood brothers. Their psychological testing indicates that they possess a high resistance to any attempt to alter their perception of what is right or wrong.'

Chairman Hu flicked ash from his lapel. 'I do not see this machine of yours.'

'It's in a building a half a mile from here. You can inspect it later.'

Qiao Peng frowned. 'Half a mile is not a very great distance. It will need to be effective over a far greater space.'

'Director, please be patient,' said Igor Tamasara brusquely. 'In theory the beam can reach anywhere or anyone on earth. That has not been our immediate concern. Our brief was to produce a short-range totally effective weapon. But the theory is the same for a long-range one. I will not trouble you with a detailed explanation now of the physics of how high-energy mass and protons travel through space and how their potency can be mobilised to become lethal only at some predetermined place. That would require more time than I suspect you have, and I detect from your impatience that you are anxious to see something tangible for your money.'

Chairman Hu glanced at Qiao Peng. He had not expected the *waibin* to be so arrogant.

Igor Tamasara was lecturing them once more. 'The Gyroton is intended to fool a human brain into accepting a subliminal command. This is encoded and transmitted as a microwave signal. In other words, the subject subliminally hears and understands spoken words delivered to those parts of the limbic system I showed you.'

'Can this transmission be detected by the person it is aimed at, Professor Tamasara?' asked Chairman Hu.

'All our tests confirm it cannot. At most a subject has complained of a ringing sensation in the ears. But most report hearing nothing.'

'But can't the comparator store the subliminal instruction and later retrieve it for the subject to know he has done something wrong?' Qiao Peng asked.

Igor Tamasara gave him a look that could shatter glass. 'We are working towards transmitting a false story for the comparator to store in a subject's brain. So even if the subject experiences a memory leak in the form of dreams or flashbacks, he will recall it incorrectly.'

'You say working towards ...' Chairman Hu began.

'Yes. In a few months we will have solved the problem.'

Qiao Peng stared at Igor Tamasara without favour or malice, almost without interest. 'You do not have that much time. Now show us what you have achieved so far.' He lifted a hand towards the wall panel.

Igor Tamasara turned to the panel, controlling his anger. Chairman Hu stubbed out his half-smoked cigarette, listening intently as Tamasara continued. 'To understand fully you must know some background about these subjects. A week ago we arranged for them to quarrel with each other over a small matter. Nothing that would not be forgiven in a few hours. Since then we have kept them apart. Normally they are close and protective of each other. The separation engendered – well, let's see ...'

He nodded to the monitor. 'Watch both the screen and what will be happening in the room.' He pressed buttons on the console and spoke into its microphone. 'Start the beam.' On the monitor two separate wiggling lines began to appear.

'What you see are their respective brainwaves. The lower one is that of the brother still seated. The more active wave is for the other man.' One of the men had stood up. His wave pulsed more strongly on screen. Tamasara once more spoke into the microphone. 'Activate hemi-synch.'

He continued to explain. 'Every brain has an individual electrical beat of its own, different in each hemisphere. The hemi-synch is a process by which the Gyroton's computer assumes control over both hemispheres.' On the monitor the top line had altered shape. 'What we are seeing are metabolic changes in our subject's brain. There are leaks in the blood/tissue brain barrier inducing behavioural disorganisation.'

The brother who had stood up moved behind his sibling, still seated calmly on the floor. The upper wave on the screen was coursing faster. Igor Tamasara went on: 'The theta rhythm of the man standing is out of control. And there goes his beta. And with it any hope he has of controlling his emotional or cognitive responses. Now watch.'

The waveform on screen was racing. Igor Tamasara spoke one more time into the microphone. 'Activate alpha block at fifty-plus subliminal input at two-second pulsing.'

The standing figure reached into a pocket and produced a knife. Without interrupting the flow of his movement he drove the blade deep into the neck of his brother, at the point where his spinal cord joined the brain stem. Then, with the knife still vibrating, the killer calmly turned away and once more sat on the floor, his back to the dead man. On the screen the lines returned to their original forms.

In the silence Qiao Peng's voice sounded unnaturally loud. 'You understand it is not killing, but total manipulation that we are after?'

Igor Tamasara flushed and nodded. This man was more unappreciative than those fools in the Kremlin had been.

'Nevertheless, quite remarkable,' breathed Chairman Hu. 'Truly remarkable.'

He now knew what response he would give to the emissary from Washington.

3

Anna inserted her colour-coded plastic card into a slot and, as the elevator door closed, she smiled at Tommy. 'There's a new access colour every day. Without it, no one gets into our elevator. It's one of the Prof's ways to keep out visitors.'

Tommy remembered what little he had gleaned at training school about the Director of Psychological Assessment. How, after thirty years in the Chair of Middle East Studies at Yale, Morton had persuaded him to join Hammer Force and see his theories put into practice. The school's instructors spoke of the Prof with the kind of awe they normally reserved for Morton; one had said the Director was Freud with a killer's instinct. But no one had mentioned that the Prof was quirky about keeping out visitors.

The elevator silently opened on the top floor of Hammer Force Headquarters. Facing them was a solid steel door. Anna spoke into a voice box set in the wall. 'Ochre,' she said firmly, before turning to Tommy. 'Today's password. The Prof is also big on colour symbols.'

The door slid silently open and they stepped into a small vestibule. Tommy looked about him, as curious now as he had been at the start of his conducted tour after leaving the Tomcat simulator room in the basement. For the past hour Anna had taken him in and out of offices, workshops and labs, leaving those who had shaken his hand, a hundred and more times, to explain what went on.

Until then he had primarily thought of Hammer's clandestine role, represented by those sharp-eyed men and women in Covert Action who occupied the ground floor. Anna had smiled sympathetically. 'A mistake we almost all make the first day we join. The fact is we've got more high fliers in engineering and political science than any campus.

The Colonel's very keen on support staff. For every man or woman in the field, there's three to back them up.'

He'd met some of them in the Historical Branch, with its million and more reference books; in Management and Services, who provided all the essential documentation to allow a field agent to move easily around the globe; in Science and Technology; in Computers and all the other workplaces behind uniformly anonymous doors. Half a dozen more led off the vestibule.

She gave another smile. 'Five are today's dummies. The Prof changes the access door every day. It's his way of saying to anyone who doesn't know – let's keep it that way!'

'What about the Colonel?'

'He has an override key. The only one in the whole place.' Anna walked towards the third door on their right and firmly stabbed a toe against a small metal plate set in the lower left-hand corner. The door opened at once. 'Welcome to Psychological Assessment,' she said. 'In the pecking order we're between the Office of Global Issues and Technical Services. Remember? They provide all the gizmos for Covert Action.'

He remembered all those overalled technicians on the third floor, each with a Pandora's box of deadly tricks. Fax paper impregnated with deadly poison; a tubular-framed walking aid that, with a flick of a switch, became a rocket launcher. He'd particularly liked the sleeping tablets which contained enough force to crater a runway or topple a bridge. Tommy stared at the large open-plan room, scattered with desks occupied by men and women, either reading or working on their VDU screens. No one looked up as they entered. An air of absorbed silence permeated the place.

'The Prof has a thing about noise,' Anna whispered.

As if to reinforce the point, a door along the wall opposite the windows opened and a wraith-like figure emerged. He wore a cardigan and corduroys. Tommy thought he looked anywhere between a frail sixty and seventy. Except when he moved. The man strode between the desks to them, the walk of a supremely physically fit man. He gripped Tommy's hand firmly. 'Welcome, welcome,' the Prof murmured. 'If you're half as good as your father, then we're lucky.'

'If I'm half as good as him, I'll be lucky,' Tommy said, lowering his voice to match the Prof's whispered tone.

'Yes, yes, yes.' The Prof had a habit of repeating a word. Tommy wasn't fooled. It was clear that behind the cultivated eccentricity was a razor-sharp mind.

29

'You won't be here long. While you are, make the most of it. Here we think so that others can act.' The Prof turned and strode quickly back to his office, closing the door behind him.

Tommy glanced at Anna. 'What did he mean about me not being here long?'

She smiled. 'After that performance in the simulator, you're field material. Just as soon as you get familiarised, the Colonel will have you on the road.'

She led Tommy through the sepulchral silence to her desk at the far end of the room. She pointed to a vacant one beside her own. 'Use this one. The Prof sometimes likes to sit out here. He says it keeps him in touch with what we're thinking. He's into visual contact in a big way.'

Tommy looked about him as Anna continued her briefing. 'In the far corner we have those who search for hidden motives behind foreign broadcasts. Next to them are the signals analysts. You can learn a lot from the way somebody words a signal. In the middle of the room we have the linguists. Then the guys who scan the media. It always amazes me what they pick up even from a trawl through the tabloids.' She gave him another smile. He really liked her smile.

'And you?' Tommy asked.

'Psycho-profiles. I get all the bits and pieces they send along and try and make sense of what someone in the Kremlin or Beijing, or any other place, is going to be thinking tomorrow.'

'Sounds fun.'

Anna nodded at the room. 'Some of them say it's a glorified form of Trivial Pursuit.'

'Is it?'

'More fun. And I get to peek into some very interesting minds.'

Tommy glanced towards the windows. Through the trees he could see the roof of the training school. Once you were in, there were only two ways out of that compound. Failure and back on the road around the lake, or on up to here. Across the lake he could see Geneva. How many people there had any idea what went on here? How many people anywhere? He turned back to Anna. 'You ever get out of here into the field?' Tommy asked.

'Sometimes. But those are the kind of questions you don't ask.'

'Sorry.'

She smiled. She liked his curiosity and directness. 'Usually people out there aren't as interesting as those I get to study here.'

'Like this guy the Colonel wants me to read up on?'

'Igor Tamasara,' Anna confirmed. She turned to a filing cabinet and pulled out a buff-coloured file. 'As I told Colonel Morton, it's pretty slim.'

She handed Tommy the folder. He settled at the desk and began to read. When he had finished, he put aside the half-dozen foolscap pages and exhaled slowly, shaking his head. 'Sweet Jesus,' he said, his voice unnaturally loud in the crypt-like silence. 'Oh, Sweet Jesus, this guy's a Grade A monster.'

Around the room men and women looked up curiously at Tommy before returning to their work. Anna swivelled in her chair to look at Tommy. 'Igor Tamasara's our number one target. You come up with any idea where he is or what he's doing and you'll write your own ticket with the Colonel,' she said.

But she certainly was not going to tell him that after what the Colonel had also said in the simulator room, they could both soon be working together in the field.

Entering another corridor whose predominant colour was the same soothing green, Professor Lars Svendsen murmured that there were no graveyards in Miami. 'It's because the water table's usually only a metre below the surface. So everyone either gets cremated or buried in some other place.'

'Vitali Rebicov tell you that?' Morton asked.

'No. The Miami Medical Examiner's office …' The psychiatrist's laugh died quickly.

The Medical Director had an indoor face, the skin almost translucent from a lifetime spent working under relaxing lighting. His heavy tortoiseshell-framed glasses made his eyes appear larger than they were when he glanced up at Morton. 'I called Miami to see if they had anything. But there's no report of Rebicov ever consulting a doctor as much as over a cold.'

'And his sister?'

'The ME's office only had her autopsy report.'

'Miami sent you a copy?'

Professor Svendsen gave Morton another swift appraising look. Morton would have sent someone else if there wasn't more to the question. 'Yes. What I would expect on someone who had jumped ten floors. Very general.'

'What about her brain?'

'They recovered what they could. But they were probably more concerned about hosing the area clean. A jumper's bad for business.' The laugh came and went as quickly.

'Anyone know why she was in that building?'

'The police report says she was job-hunting. She had an appointment with an office manager. Then she suddenly got up and plunged through a plate glass window.'

'Anyone see her?'

'Seemingly not. The manager's secretary was away from her desk. He was in his office. Not that either of them could possibly be any help in explaining her brother's behaviour.'

Morton glanced at the psychiatrist. Behind the glasses, the eyes were brown-black, unusual for a Dane. 'Isn't it possible that some sort of delayed reaction to her death could be the reason?'

Professor Svendsen spoke in a soft, certain voice. 'It's possible, of course. Except that he's shown none of the usual signs. No anger, remorse or self-pity. When he's talked about her death, it's only in terms of accepting it. So I think we can rule out a late reaction.'

Once more the laugh came and went. A nervous reflex, Morton decided. In a job like his, there had to be some release. He glanced through one of the corridor windows. Two teams were playing volley-ball on a grass court. Patients? No way of telling. Beyond lay the dull expanse of Lake Geneva. From down there this building blended into the hillside. Lars Svendsen had said he had chosen it for that very reason. He had even hesitated over the discreet nameplate set into the high stone wall at the entrance. Institute For Human Rehabilitation. Any more than the ball-players, the words offered no real clue as to what happened here.

'Is Rebicov on medication?' Morton asked.

'Only the minimum to help him sleep. Part of every patient's therapy is a reality-based coming to terms. Drugs only delay that. And all too often their use evokes deeply unhappy memories.'

'Is that why I haven't seen a white coat around the place?'

A corridor door opened and a couple of women emerged. They were young and pretty enough. One wore a brightly-coloured dress, the other a blouse and skirt. They nodded politely as they passed.

The psychiatrist explained: 'Two of our nurses. I try to choose only the most attractive. Our patients have seen so much that is ugly, especially in my profession. That's why I've insisted that all the other medical staff are women. It helps create a softer image.'

'But women doctors also torture. And they're good at it, too.'

Professor Svendsen nodded but this time did not laugh. 'Nurses as well. But mostly it's my male colleagues who created the trauma we deal with here. Recurring nightmares and phobias, crippling anxiety – medical terrorism can be really terrifying. A doctor who understands how to exploit psychotropic drugs or electro-shock can destroy just as effectively as any car-bomber.'

'How many patients do you have here?'

'Almost two hundred, from sixty countries. We get asked to take many more times that number. Even if we could, we would still only be scratching the surface. Torture is the great growth industry of this century. For all my patients a doctor in a white coat or a nurse's uniform is a reminder of past horror. That's why I insist the staff are careful not to physically touch a patient unless it's absolutely essential – and then only when the reason's been fully explained. To help create the trust, if we're going to be successful in helping them, there are no formal treatment rooms. Nothing that smacks of regimentation or authority. And that includes white coats.'

The psychiatrist nodded towards the volleyball players. 'They look healthy enough because feeding them up is the easy part. Much harder to deal with is their adverse conditioning: a medical ideology which says any individual can be psychologically reshaped. They have all been exposed to forms of mind control that even now we don't fully understand. Too often when they get here they have massive gaping wounds – this is psychologically speaking – and we are still at the bandaid stage as far as treatment goes.'

Morton nodded. The psychiatrist had spoken with the same quiet intensity at a dinner party hosted by Yoshi Kramer, the neurosurgeon. Lars Svendsen had riveted and chilled them with his account of how doctors use their skills for state-sponsored medical abuses of all kinds. Dawn had broken when he described some of the medical experiments which had been conducted in the Soviet Union. It was the first time Morton had heard of Igor Tamasara and his work.

'Have any of your other patients mentioned anything like this machine that Rebicov's described?' he asked now.

'No. But then they don't have his engineering background. Of course the concept is not new. Years ago at Harvard some genius developed a simple transmitter, no bigger than a pager, which enabled a central tracking station to monitor basic physical or neurological signs. It had a range of about half a mile, and was meant to keep track of epileptics in the hospital grounds. Medical staff were supposed to be alerted when a patient's brainwaves changed. The Civil Rights people complained and the whole idea fell out of favour.'

'I thought it was picked up by the criminologists,' Morton said.

The psychiatrist gave another quick laugh. 'I'd forgotten that. But you're right. In the mid-seventies there was a serious move in the US penal system to develop the transmitter as a way of controlling high-risk prisoners when they were released back into society. The idea was that someone would be fitted with one, perhaps even have it implanted. The transmitter would report to a central control not just details of where the person was physically at any given time, but also psychological data. Any increase in respiratory rate, tension in the musculature, a sudden flow of adrenalin. All signs that could be taken as indications that the person was up to no good.

'A computer at central control would alert the police, and at the same time send an electrical signal to the subject's brain, causing him or her to stop whatever they were planning. When the scheme leaked, the Civil Rights people really raised the roof. That stopped things in America. Elsewhere all it did was encourage the psychotechnologists to go on searching.'

'This machine Rebicov said was being developed by Igor Tamasara...' Morton prompted.

Professor Svendsen shrugged. 'It sounds incredible, I know. But the evidence of my patients shows it is possible to use technology to alter memory, mood, feelings and impulses. A machine like that could be the forerunner of a society in which emotions, sensations, desires and the entire range of psychological phenomena could be induced, inhibited, modified and controlled. Computers and radio-telemetry have already changed the classical philosophical concept that the mind is beyond human reach. Someone like Tamasara would have been trying to fine-tune the technology.'

'Does Rebicov know I'm coming?' Morton asked.

'No. I thought it best if he didn't have time to think about it.'

They reached a door at the end of the corridor. Professor Svendsen produced a plastic card from a coat pocket.

'This business of him taking his sister's body all the way from Miami to Haifa,' Morton said.

The psychiatrist inserted the card into a metal slot in the door. 'A need to return to their roots. He's probably telling the truth when he says he was making good on an old promise.'

'But instead of burying her, he had her cremated.'

Professor Svendsen glanced at Morton. He had this way of always coming back to the point. 'Cremated, right. Which rules out any possibility of spotting anything the Miami pathologist may have missed.'

From inside the door slot came a low humming. Morton gave a little sigh. 'No reason, of course, for him to think there was anything to miss.'

'None at all.'

'But it's almost a year since the funeral.'

'Ten months.' Professor Svendsen retrieved the card. There was a click and the door rolled silently back into a wall recess. They stood for a moment in the opening, facing each other. Morton broke the silence.

'And in all that time no one suspected Rebicov had been one of the guards back in Russia, herding Tamasara's human guinea pigs from one experiment to another, while his sister did the paperwork. Then one day Rebicov falls sick. All he remembers is Tamasara and some other doctors around the bed. One of them gives him an injection. When he wakes up he is in another bed, next to his sister's. Their heads are bandaged. When they feel well enough, they are sent home to convalesce

'A few months later the Soviet Union starts to fall apart and they head for Poland. They manage to cross the border into Germany before the shutters go up. The Germans give them papers which get them into the United States, and they both disappear into the Florida sun. Then she jumps. He takes her body to Haifa to be cremated, and goes on as before, for a while. Three months ago the firm he works for posts him here ...Then one morning Rebicov suddenly strips off his clothes in the office and runs out into the street shouting in Russian ...'

Professor Svendsen repeated the process with the card to close the door. They began to walk down another anonymous corridor. 'And, especially in Geneva, you can't do that ...The police arrive. One of them understands a little Russian. So they decide to bring Rebicov here,' Professor Svendsen added.

'But you surely don't admit everyone off the street?' Morton asked.

'Naturally not. And it probably would not have happened this time if I had not been in reception when he was brought in. I went over to have a look at him, so that I could tell the police where they should best take him. That's when he started to talk about Postbox 97. The Soviet research establishment is now familiar to us. So when Rebicov said he had been there, there was no way I couldn't admit him.'

'What's your clinical evaluation?'

'All our usual tests show nothing.'

'You ran a brain scan?'

'We don't do that sort of thing to our patients. But if he's telling the truth he may have been a victimiser before he became one.'

'I'd like to read his medical file first,' Morton said.

Professor Svendsen nodded. 'That shouldn't take you long. In my clinical judgement Rebicov is not really mentally ill. The business of running naked into the street was really no more than his way of getting here.'

Morton looked curiously at the psychiatrist but said nothing.

4

At an hour when only the tip of the Washington Monument was touched by the sun – 6.30 am on the digital clock of his bedside telephone console – the President of the United States dressed in the clothes his valet had chosen: a blue poplin shirt and a darker blue suit. On the day the President had inherited him, the servant had murmured: 'Folks expect you to power dress, Mr President.' Thack said later that the valet had proffered exactly the same advice to the previous three incumbents. As White House Chief of Staff, Thacker Stimpson knew such things.

On the day of his Inauguration *The New York Times* had come closest to defining what else the electorate expected. Under the headline, AN AMERICAN ISAIAH, the newspaper had said the nation would look to him as the nation's conscience, the voice of the dispossessed, the defender of the mute and the prophet who would speak out when others remained silent. The editorial was in a frame on the bedside table.

A light blinked on the telephone console. The President walked over and picked up the receiver.

'Good morning, Mr President.' Even at this hour the Chief of Staff's voice was soft and mellifluous.

'Morning, Thack. Does the Brief get me off to a good start?'

The President's Daily Intelligence Brief was the slim folder handcarried every day at dawn by a CIA officer to the White House. It contained overnight intelligence developments the President needed to know.

'So-so. Bosnia's quiet for once. Another pitched battle in Cape Town. Tokyo's calm after yesterday's riot. Our people say another one is being planned. The Embassy's taking all the usual precautions. Otherwise, it's all as usual in the West Pacific.'

'The lull before the storm, Thack?'

There was a moment's hesitation. 'That depends on how Beijing responds, Mr President.'

'Well, we'll soon know.'

Putting down the 'phone the President fastened a cufflink. He was dressing for a meeting which would never officially happen even though he and Thack would sit down with Cyrus B. Voss. It would not take place in the Oval Office, over in the West Wing, but here in his living quarters, in the oval study a few yards beyond his bedroom door. Few outsiders knew that the White House had two such identically-shaped rooms.

The venue appealed to his sense of history. In the study Franklin Delano Roosevelt had penned his declaration of war after Japan's infamy at Pearl Harbour. Cy would be more interested in the fact that it was where John F. Kennedy had seduced Marilyn Monroe. Cy was an inveterate collector and purveyor of gossip. He was also the Party's single largest benefactor and unquestionably the world's most powerful tycoon since Armand Hammer. Whereas Hammer's special sphere of influence had been the former Soviet Union, Cy was the one American close to the Chinese regime. He even smoked the same foul-smelling cigarettes as Chairman Hu.

The President slipped on his old-fashioned elasticated armbands. A haberdashery in Missouri still made them.

A week ago Cy had taken his proposal to Chairman Hu. No one in Cabinet, in Congress, over at State, out at Langley or in any other Federal agency knew what he had written. Only Thack. They both agreed precedent overrode the risk. Kennedy had sent a personal warning to Kruschev over the Bay of Pigs; Lyndon Johnson had made a direct appeal to North Vietnam to end the war; Reagan had made a similar approach to Iran to open its doors. They had each acted in absolute secrecy.

It had been past midnight, local time, when Cy had called from Hong Kong to say he was returning to Washington. He had given Thack no clue as to how the mission had gone.

There was a discreet knock on the door. A moment later it opened. A tall figure in a black suit stood with a tray holding a cup and pot. 'Tea, Mr President?'

'Thank you, Forbes.'

The valet advanced into the bedroom, put down the tray on a side table and poured a cup of herbal tea.

'Camomile this morning, Mr President. My mother always said it was good for the skin.' The valet handed over the cup.

The President smiled, then began to sip the scalding drink.

'I've set up a light breakfast in the study, Mr President. Juice, bagels and coffee. Jasmine tea for you. Sure you don't want me to serve it?'

'I think I can manage, Forbes.'

'I'm sure you won't forget Dr Barker doesn't want you to eat anything yourself, Mr President.'

'I'll remember.' He had almost forgotten that he had to leave for his annual medical later in the day.

'I'll be in the pantry if you need anything,' Forbes said as he refilled the President's cup.

'Thank you, Forbes.'

Nodding deferentially, the valet left the room.

The President replaced his cup on the tray and glanced towards the bedroom windows. The sky was bright with the promise of another broiler. That would not deter the demonstrators. The first chants were starting again, the same mindless, repetitive slogans: 'Be An American, Mr President!' 'Remember Pearl Harbour!' 'Stand Up To Tokyo!'

Since his first day in office Japan had remained the greatest single threat the United States had faced as they fought for domination of the global marketplace. Across Europe and throughout Africa, Latin America and Australasia, Japanese firms continued to undercut their American rivals. Last year the loss of US contracts had amounted to half a trillion dollars. Within the United States, the Japanese invasion was at flood tide. Its cars had reduced Detroit to a virtual scrapyard. The yen dominated Wall Street. Even that bastion of the American dream, Hollywood, had fallen, joining the ever-growing list of banks and financial institutions totally controlled from Tokyo.

But that still did not mean you physically declared war on them. You found another way to win. That was why he had sent Cy Voss to Beijing with a gilt-edged guarantee that China would become the first new superpower of the next century – with the United States its closest trading partner and protector.

American know-how would ensure sufficient cheap food for China to feed its billion-plus mouths. These increased at the rate of twelve million a year. It was like having to feed every twelve months a new city larger than Los Angeles. American engineers would harness the Yangtze and China's other great rivers to provide an abundant source of low-cost, efficient power. American teachers would spearhead the drive to educate the country's eight hundred million illiterate peasants. American financiers would show the Chinese how to operate a free-market economy in what would be the greatest joint venture in history. A vision even greater than the Truman Doctrine at the end of World War Two which had produced the Marshall Plan to rebuild a decimated Europe.

He had deliberated long and hard over how he should explain what he wanted in return. In the end he had resorted to the directness which always worked for him. In a few sentences he had asked Chairman Hu to lease to the United States for one hundred years the Crown colony of Hong Kong when it was returned to the People's Republic. If China agreed, for the next century Hong Kong would effectively be the Union's newest state, with all the protection that afforded. At the same time China would use the island as a most favoured shop window within the United States.

The President poured himself a near-cold cup of tea. He had lost count of how many pots he had drunk while deliberating just how to phrase the closing part of his proposal.

The Chinese were a proud people. Their recognisable cultural roots went back well over three thousand years. They must not feel that tradition to be threatened. He had promised that the United States would not impose its own value systems on China, and would defend it against anyone who did. By leasing Hong Kong to the United States, China's aged politicians would be ensuring their own survival. Breathtaking in its concept, the plan held the promise of prosperity for both the United States and China well into the next millennium, as well as bringing stability to the West Pacific and beyond.

The President drained his cup and sighed. There would be opposition at first – just as there had been to the Marshall Plan. The isolationists in Congress would scream. So would some of the Europeans, if only because they had not thought of the idea. However, the British would probably shrug philosophically, the way they had after the first loss of Empire. And he was confident that, just as the Marshall Plan had been hailed by Winston Churchill as 'the most unsordid act in history', so would his proposal be similarly welcomed. It epitomised all that was good in the American national character, with its faith in pragmatic solutions.

Knotting his tie, the President sat on the edge of the bed to lace his shoes. The right one had a half-inch medical lift. Roosevelt had worn leg irons and Kennedy a back brace, both impossible to conceal. But a shoemaker had successfully managed to hide his own deformity. Of course, the birth defect formed part of his published medical history. Since Reagan, every Presidential bowel movement seemed to be in the public domain.

The President stood up and looked across the bedroom at his reflection in the stand mirror. He had reluctantly come to accept that the results of his own annual check-up at Bethesda Medical Hospital would be avidly studied across the nation. He still looked conspicuously younger than his sixty-two years. His profile was firm and lean, his eyes clear. Only the grey flecks in his hair and the lines around his mouth suggested that his time in the White House had taken its toll. Nevertheless, the reflection confirmed what Dr Barker had told the White House press corps after his last medical: the President was physically fit and mentally sound. Just a little shorter on temper than when he was first elected. But he had never suffered fools gladly. And Bud Emerson had shown himself to be a Grade A fool.

The day before the then Secretary of Labour had addressed a business club in San Francisco. He had told the gathering he was going to press for the CIA to bug the boardrooms of Japanese corporations. The luncheon was supposed to be private. But one of the guests was the brother of the local Associated Press bureau chief, and the story had hit the wire in an hour. He fired Emerson an hour later after the Secretary refused to issue a retraction.

Now, as the morning light strengthened, from Pennsylvania Avenue came the chant of Emerson For President, followed by more derisive shouting down by the East Gate. That would be for the Oldsmobile he had sent to collect Cy from Andrews Air Force base. Thack said the car would attract less media attention than a helicopter clattering down near the Rose Garden.

For a moment he was tempted to call Cy on the car's secure telephone. Instead he turned back to the window, listening to the demonstrators. What would they chant when they heard of his plan? Part of him could almost sympathise with their anger. They wanted an old-fashioned hell-raiser in the White House, a Reagan denouncing the evil Soviet Empire, or George Bush drawing his celebrated line in the Arabian sands. Or Bill Clinton. But the world had moved on since then. A very different time called for a radically different approach.

Buttoning his jacket, the President walked from the bedroom. Outside in the corridor two men came to respectful attention. One was the duty Secret Service man. The other was the Signals Warrant Officer known as Satchel. He carried a thirty-pound metal suitcase with an intricate combination lock, known as the Football. Inside were a number of bulky envelopes, sealed with wax and the signatures of the Joint Chiefs. Each envelope contained the codes that would enable the President to launch a nuclear attack on a number of targets. With the demise of the Soviet Union, Moscow and other key Russian cities had been removed from the list. But Beijing and other Chinese cities remained.

Nodding to the Secret Service man, the President walked on down the corridor. Behind him, lugging his bag, came Satchel.

Morton flicked back through the green-covered medical file on which someone had written Vitali Rebicov's name, date of birth and date of admission. The man was in his fifty-first year and his vital signs showed him to be physically in good shape. The only significant note was of an intermittent headache. The admitting doctor had written in the case notes: 'Query NTS'.

When he had walked into the adjoining office, Professor Svendsen had explained that the letters stood for Nervous Tension Syndrome. It was a catch-all until the diagnosis could be more specific. Rebicov's personal history in the file merely confirmed what the psychiatrist had said. Details of his hospitalisation at Postbox 97; the brief spell he and his sister spent in Germany; their time in Florida until she committed suicide; Rebicov's own subsequent time in Geneva these past months. All equally unremarkable.

Rebicov's headaches had seemingly started a day or two before he ran into the street. If she thought this to be clinically significant, the admitting doctor had not said so. On a separate sheet Professor Svendsen had written down the details of the machine Rebicov claimed Igor Tamasara was working on in Postbox 97. Rebicov had given the machine a name – 'Gyroton'.

Professor Svendsen had placed the word in quotation marks, but otherwise made no comment. Other descriptions Rebicov had provided were similarly noted: 'force fields', 'pure flux', 'mesoconic effect', 'vacuum compactors', 'mesoscale mystroms'. There were no additional explanations.

There were also two complete sentences. 'The zero-vector scalar EM effect can hold for hundreds of thousands of kilometres. In theory, the Gyroton can reach anywhere on earth and far into space.'

Below the words was a simple sketch of the machine the psychiatrist said he had encouraged Rebicov to draw. It looked like a large square

42

box with several dials and a short barrel at one end. Wheels indicated it was transportable. There was no scale, no way of knowing how big it actually was. It certainly did not look very threatening. But neither had the Hiroshima atomic bomb.

Morton stared at the page once more. He had asked Professor Svendsen whether this could still all be the pseudo-scientific imaginings of a psychopath. Professor Svendsen had repeated that he was satisfied Rebicov was not mentally ill. Morton had asked for a photocopy of the page. He would see what Technical Services made of it. The psychiatrist had gone off to the copier.

Morton continued to leaf through the file. Apart from the daily temperature chart – normal – and a prescription written for Nembutal, there was nothing further of any medical note on Vitali Rebicov.

A faxed copy of the autopsy report on Nina Rebicov was at the back of the file. It was what you would expect from a body hitting the sidewalk after a 300-foot drop. Against 'brain', the Miami pathologist had written: 'Sample recovered too small to fully assess, but no evidence of deterioration or malformity.'

Morton closed the file and walked over to the window. Johnny Quirke, who ran Technical Services, had been frank. None of his scientists had more than a passing knowledge of energetics as a weapons science. They were not alone. Both the Pentagon and NATO had put their money elsewhere. Johnny had said the one man who might know something about energetics was a scientist called Baskin. He had dropped out of sight some years ago. Johnny remembered hearing that Baskin had gone native on some island in Micronesia.

Morton remembered then. Colin Baskin had a daughter, Kate, a neurologist. In the little paperwork available that Johnny had sent over had been a reference to a paper she had written on scalar resonance electrical currents, in which she had cited her father's pioneering work.

From out in the corridor came the sounds of running feet and urgent voices. The door of the office opened and Professor Svendsen stood there; behind him were the two nurses they had passed earlier. Morton had seen that look before on the faces of caring professionals confronted with the unexpected.

'Vitali Rebicov's dead,' Professor Svendsen said softly. 'He's just hanged himself in his bathroom.'

5

The President watched Cy Voss consume another bagel. Everything about Cy suggested an animal, one huge and powerful like a mountain bear. Yet he had delivered his report in a surprisingly gentle voice.

After his private jet had landed at a military airfield north of Beijing he had been helicoptered to the leadership compound in Zhongnanhai, where he had hand-delivered the President's proposal to Chairman Hu. Afterwards he had been kept waiting four full days in the State Guest House. He had taken this as a good sign. On the evening of the fifth day he had been summoned back to Zhongnanhai. Hu had said the proposal contained much merit. But first China wanted a public indication of serious intent by the President.

Cy reached for the last of the bagels. 'Where'd you get these from?'

'The kitchen bakes them from a recipe Nancy Reagan left behind,' said the President. He sat in one of the oval study's chintz-patterned armchairs.

''Bout the only good thing that Administration did leave,' growled Cy. 'What do you say, Thack?' He turned a face dotted with wens, moles and open pores towards Thacker Stimpson.

The Chief of Staff stood with his back to the fake fireplace, with a tall man's way of going loose and gangly when remaining on the same spot. His eyes were startlingly green and topped with a shock of thick red hair. He wore one of the half-dozen suits he ordered every year from Brooks Brothers, an Oxford shirt, burgundy print tie and tan calfskin loafers. The overall effect was as preppy as the Pope in skivvies.

Thack turned aside the offer to criticise a former Administration with a quick hand movement. 'What does Hu want us to do?' he asked.

Cy Voss turned to the President. 'He wants you to go to Manila next month.'

Thack remembered. 'The annual get-together of the non-aligned nations. We were sending Emerson until he went ape.'

Cy walked over to the sideboard and poured more coffee. 'Mr President, the Chinese would also like you to stop over in Hong Kong on the way out. Officially it will be to rest after the long flight, so you arrive in Manila fully refreshed. In reality the two days you spend in the colony will be a testing of the water. You'll make a speech. Meet the local Beijing cadres. It will be an informal declaration of our interest in Hong Kong.'

'And then?'

'Then, Mr President, we wait for formal confirmation that the deal with Beijing is on.'

The President looked at his Chief of Staff. 'Thack?'

Thacker Stimpson moved away from the fireplace. He began to enumerate his points on his fingers as he spoke. 'There are risks. The Japanese could see this as a threat and make some new move themselves. The Chinese in the end could still refuse to step up to the dime. All you could get from going to Manila is a lot of flak from those Third World countries who'll take another opportunity to beat us over the head the way they do in the UN.'

The only sound in the suddenly silent room was Cy Voss gulping his coffee.

The President stood up and looked at both men. 'Thank you both. You're right, Thack. There are risks. But I have to discount them if this is going to work. There's just too much at stake. When is Manila?'

'Four weeks tomorrow.'

The President nodded. 'Then there's no time to waste. Thack, I want you to set up a working committee. Keep it as tight as possible.'

He turned to Cy Voss. 'I want you to go straight back to Beijing and let them know what's happening. I'll give you a note for Chairman Hu in an hour.'

Cy Voss grinned. 'And get your kitchen to bake up a supply of these bagels for the flight.'

In the dim light of the bedside lamp, Leo Schrag lay in the tangled aftermath of sex, the damp sheet rumpled across his legs.

Soon Shaoyen would start again. Reach for the eighteen-carat gold dispenser she wore on a chain around her neck for a few more grains of Ecstasy. Then demand he do it once more. And he would, because she said there was no one like him; because he knew if he didn't continue to satisfy her, he would lose her.

Across the sluggish Anacostia the shadows of the government offices would be lengthening and the flags beginning to limp down their poles. From Foggy Bottom, all the way down to the Jefferson Building, the powerful and the pretenders would be locking away their documents and putting off returning calls until another day. He had not realised how much he despised them all until Shaoyen had convinced him it was not only the exhaust fumes and swampy location that polluted Washington. It was some of the people who worked there.

For the moment she lay on her back, legs splayed, her tangled hair strewn black and shiny across the pillow. Her pubis glistened with perspiration. Her vaginal spray had lost its perfume of spring flowers, leaving only a faintly musky smell. At forty-three, with a twenty-four-year service career behind him, and the makings of a beer belly, he had not believed his luck when she had gone for him. Shaoyen had turned out to have a sexual inventiveness he had found in no American woman. From the beginning, when she had first forced him onto his knees to nibble at her, she had told him that was how she enjoyed sex and he had been relieved.

It had been years since he had managed a proper erection. The Navy doctor had said it was linked to his guilt over the failure of his two marriages. The one with Peggy had lasted three years, Jenny had stayed a year longer. He could barely remember now what either looked like. All he knew was that they were no match for Shaoyen in bed.

He glanced at the alarm clock on the dresser. He would have to leave in an hour. The clock, like almost everything else in the apartment, was a mail-order purchase. When he moved in, Shaoyen told him she shopped as much as possible by catalogue or off the TV screen. It was the same with food. They either ate out or ordered in. She had told him if he wanted a housekeeper he should hire one. But if he wanted the best pussy in town on an exclusive basis, she was his.

It had been six months ago, bored on his day off, when Leo had walked into a bar behind the Washington Convention Center. He had found Shaoyen serving at table. She told him she was from Hong Kong where she had been an aspiring actress. She had come to the United States in the hope of breaking into movies. Instead she had ended up here, working in her brother's bar. It wasn't bad; it wasn't great. But she did get to meet some exciting people. She had looked directly at him.

After a couple more beers she had introduced Li. There was a power in the way her brother moved, a limber, watchful power that was a little

46

intimidating. Li had asked the same questions as Shaoyen about his work. They were polite, interested questions, the kind no one had bothered asking before. A few more beers and Leo explained what he did. Sit at a console for eight hours at a stretch and help track any Soviet subs out on patrol. Only now there were hardly any. The Russkies couldn't afford the fuel. But he still had to sit at his console. They had all laughed and Li had given him a beer on the house, the way it had been ever since.

Shaoyen was stirring, a hand reaching for the dispenser. She had delicate hands, the palest of ivory like the rest of her skin. Her cheekbones were high and wide, in contrast to her chin, which had a spade-like angularity.

She had told him of Li's big disappointment over not being accepted into the Navy. It was their second day in this bed and he had only begun to understand how great was his need for her to desire and admire him. She told him that since being turned down, Li had become an avid collector of all kinds of naval artifacts. She had looked at him through those eyes that were the largest and blackest he had ever seen in a woman, and asked if he could get something from work to give to Li.

Next day he had brought her a paper trace of a Russian submarine's movements. The trace was really a piece of junk he should have shredded. But Shaoyen had yelped in delight over it and later Li had thanked him profusely.

A few days afterwards she had asked him to get another print-out, adding that to give Li a real thrill, maybe he could fax it to him from work. She had given him a number and he had done so. She and Li had been even more effusively grateful. They really knew how to make a man feel appreciated.

Shaoyen's eyes were open. She dropped a few grains of powder from the dispenser onto her tongue. This fool with a sagging belly, hairy chest and balding head thought it was a drug. At the intelligence training school in Beijing they had instructed her how to pretend to be a sniffer and a popper. They had taught her everything she would need to integrate into her new life.

Only weeks after arriving in Washington, she had scored. Once Li had learned where he worked, she had used every trick to dominate and manipulate this *waibin* with his slobbering tongue and protestations of love. But nothing had fully prepared her for the revolting experience of sleeping with him. Somehow it made the success of what she had achieved so much greater, Li had said. He was her controller, the most senior of the Chinese Secret Intelligence agents in the United States.

'Come here,' Shaoyen said throatily. As Leo obediently lowered his head to once more suck at her furiously, she rolled to one side, laughing to hide her disgust.

'No time, no time!' she cried. 'You must go work! And remember you promised Li send him something new today.'

'Okey-dokey.' He liked to mimic her English; it made him feel closer to her.

She got off the bed and looked at Leo. She smiled, keeping her voice light and playing up her accent. She found that always worked best with him. 'You send him something real good now. Maybe you get lucky and see Russian sub? How that cowboy say, make a good day!'

He grinned. 'It's make my day. And Dirty Harry's not a cowboy, but a cop.'

She inhaled deeply. 'Whatever. Cop, cowboy. All same. But you make Li's day, you make him very happy. Okey-dokey?'

'Okey-dokey. Let's see what comes up.'

By the book, what he was doing was a serious breach of security. But that was just because the book hadn't caught up. Russia wasn't the enemy any more.

Leo rolled off the bed and went to the bathroom to shower.

Aboard the train taking them underground back to Zhongnanhai, Chairman Hu and Qiao Peng continued to discuss their visit to Igor Tamasara.

Both men sat in pullman club armchairs, surrounded by burnished wood panelling, their feet on rich red carpeting, their faces glowing in the soft light of Victorian-style chandeliers. A steward in white gloves and jacket hovered in the background.

'This Gyroton machine is larger than I had expected. It will be difficult to transport, let alone hide.' Mandarin gave Chairman Hu's voice a sing-song pitch.

'I plan to use the Russian submarine.' Qiao Peng beckoned to the waiter to bring more tea. Until now he had shared none of the actual operational details.

Chairman Hu lit another cigarette. 'Isn't that too risky? The submarine would have to be in the target area for a little while. If it should be spotted by one of the American satellites ...'

He broke off while the waiter served them. Chairman Hu took his tea English-style, with milk; Qiao Peng preferred the traditional Chinese style of boiling water poured on aromatic leaves. When the servant retreated, Qiao Peng continued. 'The Japanese have recently purchased three Typhoon class submarines. The Russians are selling off everything they can.'

He paused to savour the steam from the cup, before continuing: 'The submarine will act purely as a safe transporter. Close to the target area, the weapon will be transferred aboard a junk which will have been carefully prepared. It will have a powerful engine and a stable launch platform. It will be able to operate even in rough seas and afterwards leave the target area at speed.'

Chairman Hu put down his cup and saucer. 'And the Triads?'

'They will continue to provoke the Japanese and the Americans in Hong Kong, Tokyo and elsewhere, making sure, as usual, that there is enough evidence for each to blame the other.'

Chairman Hu leaned back thoughtfully, his mind considering, analysing, rejecting and then once more coming to focus on the essential. 'There are four weeks to the Non-Aligned Conference. Everything must be in place a full week before then. That will allow for any last-minute adjustments to be made before the American President arrives in Hong Kong.'

Qiao Peng nodded. The timetable exactly matched his own. Chairman Hu lit another cigarette. 'Does our Russian know the time constraints?'

'Yes. But I will remind him again that the timetable cannot be altered – not by a day.'

'Not by an hour,' Chairman Hu said sharply. 'And he must not know until the last possible moment who is the target.'

Qiao Peng's stogey made another traverse of his lips. 'Of course. But in his case it will make no difference to the security of the operation.'

Chairman Hu gave a bored flick of the shoulder. The matter of how the Russian was dealt with afterwards was not his concern. Some details he preferred not to know.

The train pulled into the station beneath Zhongnanhai and the carriage doors opened.

Morton walked across the floor of Psychological Assessment towards the Prof's office. He was flanked by Tommy and Anna, who was carrying the folder containing her psycho-profile on Igor Tamasara.

The specialists at their desks looked up expectantly. Morton's presence was usually a precursor of action. He glanced at Tommy. 'Any thoughts?'

'Only that Igor Tamasara's alive, Colonel,' Tommy said promptly.

'Why do you say that?'

'Because there'd be no other reason for him to vanish from that camp in Siberia. Or for the other two to follow. People like that know their own market value. It would just be a matter of waiting for the right offer.'

'For sure.' He'd thought of that from the beginning. But Tommy was showing himself as sharp in deduction as he'd been in the Tomcat. But he still didn't know who had made Igor Tamasara an offer he couldn't refuse.

'I take it you've got nothing new, Anna?'

'No, Colonel. Not a thing.'

Morton opened the outer door to the Prof's office, then the baize divider and finally the inner door. The office was lit only by a single spot, focused to fall precisely upon the Prof, who reclined on an old-fashioned consulting couch against one wall. Tommy was momentarily reminded of Dracula rising from his coffin as, with a sudden effortless movement, the Prof rose from the couch, vigour flowing into his face.

'I've been thinking since you 'phoned, David. Interesting, interesting, very interesting. Very,' said the Prof.

Morton had called him from Professor Svendsen's office to describe Rebicov's death. The Prof turned on the overhead light, bathing the room in a sudden warm pink. He motioned the others to armchairs as he continued to speak. 'The sister first. Then the brother. Double suicides are rare and usually love pacts between couples. Almost never between blood siblings. Again, there's the time involved. Almost a year between the deaths. I've never known of such a long gap between related suicides. Such a long gap.'

He paused and looked equably at the others, pulling each of his long delicate fingers. A pianist's fingers, Morton thought.

'Anna?'

'I'm sorry, Prof. I don't know what exactly you're talking about,' she apologised.

'So sorry, Anna. So very sorry,' the Prof murmured, looking at Morton. 'David?'

Morton quickly told them what he had learned about Rebicov and his sister and their connection to Igor Tamasara.

Tommy whistled softly. 'Sweet Jesus, you think he did something that could have driven them both to kill themselves?'

'Ah, I sense a disbeliever,' said the Prof, once more pulling at his fingers. His voice suddenly hardened. 'Ju-ju men are still successfully putting curses on people in Africa. And one of my old colleagues at Harvard has just scientifically explained that zombies do exist in the Caribbean. Never underestimate anything just because its mysteries are perplexing.'

A smile, a real smile, and unexpected, crossed the Prof's face. 'But then, Tommy, if you knew what I know, I wouldn't be here, would I?'

Tommy grinned. The Prof certainly knew how to rebuke without giving offence. The Prof squinted at Morton. 'Rebicov's brain may tell you something, David.'

Morton picked up a 'phone on a side table and began to give orders.

6

On the television set of the Presidential medical suite on the third floor of the Bethesda Medical Hospital, the President watched himself arriving by helicopter for his annual physical check-up. He sat in an armchair in a pale blue dressing-gown and pyjamas.

Thack leaned against the half-open door, an ear cocked for anything untoward from the switchboard in the adjoining room. Satchel, with his bag of Armageddon codes, was sitting passively among the Signal Corps technicians who could reach anyone on earth with a telephone.

The President watched himself shake hands with a white-coated figure, Dr Barker, his personal physician, as Thack emerged from the chopper, followed by Satchel. The group strode towards the tower block housing the Presidential suite. On screen Dr Barker smiled discreetly into the TV cameras. From inside a roped-off enclosure, reporters shouted questions.

'Could Emerson cause you a problem over there, Mr President?' It was Todd Harper of Global News Network.

'I haven't given it a thought. But if he does, I'm sure, Todd, you'll be the first to tell me.'

The President used his remote to turn off the set and turned to Thack. 'You think Harper got a sniff I'm going to Manila?'

'No. Absolutely not.'

The President frowned. 'It could still leak. Should we organise our own news release?'

Thack walked over to the window. Out on the turnpike the evening rush hour was slackening. What would the country say when they heard that their President was going to address what amounted to no more than a glorified Third World conference? And how embarrassing could Emerson's presence be? The Chief of Staff gave a quick sigh. No matter how well you planned, there were still some things you couldn't predict. He turned and looked at the President.

'No leaking. We do that and we let the tail wag the dog. We play it like we agreed. Right up until the joint announcement by you and Chairman Hu. That way we keep a handle on things.'

The President stood up and smiled. 'Sounds good to me, Thack.'

He began to walk around the room, gently massaging an arm from which Dr Barker had drawn a half-dozen blood samples. An hour ago, Dr Barker had announced that he wanted to carry out a sigmoidoscopy. 'Why didn't Barker warn me he was going to shove a periscope up my tail? He didn't do that last time.'

'He did it the year before,' Thack reminded him. 'At your age a check every two years for polyps on your lower colon is important.'

'You tell the Vice-President?'

'Yes,' grinned Thack. 'He'll be on tenterhooks for those fifteen minutes you're knocked out in the morning in case someone declares war on us.'

'I'm more worried he'll be the one declaring war!'

Thack knew there was an edge to the joke. Like Emerson, the Vice-President had a bellicose attitude towards Japan.

The President turned and faced Thack. 'And afterwards, Barker does this fancy procedure?'

'A magnetograph. The big brother of a cat-scan. One of only two in the country is here. Programme it right and it'll tell you what you're thinking before you think it.'

Thack kept his tone light. He knew when a man was worried.

'But why do I need the scan?'

The Chief of Staff grinned. 'You don't. But it'll look great on your record. And think what Marty will do with it. "The President underwent a magnetograph and scored better than he would on Wheel of Fortune." Even Todd Harper wouldn't find anything to criticise there!'

The President smiled. 'Where would I be without you, Thack?'

'Where you should be now – getting a good night's sleep before your pre-med. It's set for four-thirty tomorrow morning.'

Shaking his head ruefully, the President walked into his bedroom.

Evening had come when resplendent in the uniform of a Navy Senior Chief Technician, Leo drove across the Frederick Douglas Memorial Bridge in the south-east quadrant of the city. A few moments later, on the corner of M. and First Streets, he stopped the Buick before an electrically-operated gate set in a steel-mesh cyclone fence. He leaned out of the window and held his ID before a small screen on the gatepost. The screen glowed red as it scanned the card. The gate swung open for the Buick to enter, then silently closed again.

A windowless warehouse-like structure loomed in the mist drifting up from the Anacostia River that shrouded the air-conditioning plant bolted to one side. The system cooled the computers inside the building.

Leo parked the car in his designated place, not troubling to lock it. The day he had come to work here the Navy Captain who ran the place had said the only thief they worried about here was time. That was when the Russkies were careering around the ocean as if they were out on the Anacostia freeway. Now you were lucky if you saw a sub a month. The facility which had cost a couple of billion dollars to equip was barely ticking over.

Leo showed his pass to the Marine guard inside the door and took an elevator to the fourth floor. He used a computerised card to access a corridor, waited until the door clicked behind him, then walked the length of the dull green-painted corridor to the workstations in the open-plan area. His was directly beneath an electronic wall map of the North Atlantic.

The daytime operative was already out of the swivel chair, standing and stretching, pulling off his headphones, anxious to be gone. Leo's eyes automatically flicked from the map to the video display unit screen. 'Anything swimming?'

'Not even a tadpole.' A tadpole was a small Russian submarine.

Leo slipped on the headphones and sat in the chair. The screen was on his left, the two keyboards immediately in front. One had a recognisable typewriter layout. The other was covered with anonymous buttons and lights. All were unlit. To his right there was an instrument rather like a microscope. This was the sound-picture scanner. It could match a dot on the screen to its engine noise. At the far end of the curved desk top was a laser printer and a fax machine.

Leo spoke into the console's built-in microphone. 'Station nine reporting changeover effected. No activity.'

'Thanks, Leo,' acknowledged the Watch Commander.

Leo glanced towards the booth. The Commander stood, arms braced behind his back, his uniform gleaming under his ruined face. His mine-sweeper had taken a direct hit during the Persian Gulf war. This tomb-like facility had become a refuge for the living dead.

For six hours Leo sat at the console listening through his headphones to nothing but the faintest hiss of static from the feederline at the satellite ground station in Spain. Then at 2.00 am he handed over his duties to the master console in the Watch Commander's booth and went to the canteen. He was about to eat when the loudspeaker ordered him to return to his station at once.

'Take a look,' the Watch Commander said. He had jacked his own headphones into one of the keyboards. 'She's heading for home, Leo.'

Leo's eyes never left the small white dot on the screen that in shape and size was no larger than a pencil point.

He put on his own headphones, plugged them into a socket, eased himself onto his seat and began to type on the typewriter keyboard. On screen the pencil shape doubled in size. Leo pressed a key, then slid his chair across to the printer. From its maw emerged a hard copy of the image on screen. He skeetered back to the keyboard and depressed more keys. The pencil shape grew larger.

'Does she look familiar?'

Leo squinted. 'Hard to say. Let's check the traces for the past month.' His fingers flew over the second keyboard. Moments later he shook his head. 'Sonofabitch's coming up through the Grand Canyon,' he murmured. 'Guy's got to be nuts risking his boat in that kind of weather.' The Grand Canyon was the largest of the North Atlantic valleys, and the most dangerous to navigate.

'Or just anxious to get home without being spotted,' the Commander said.

Leo turned back to the second keyboard and punched more buttons. While the computer started a new search, checking on every trace for the past three months, he worked at the first keyboard. The shape on screen continued to grow. Leo printed out more hard copies.

The Commander was using the 'phone, speaking softly. 'We have a positive – out of Grand Canyon.'

He spoke first to the CIA's Office of Imagery Analysis at Langley and then to the Analysis Centre at Bolling Air Force Base operated by the Defense Intelligence Agency on the opposite bank of the Anacostia. Both times he was told to fax hard copies.

'Computer's showing no outward trace to match,' Leo repeated.

'If she's coming back she must have gone,' the Commander insisted.

Leo fed further instructions to the computer. The Commander was a real trier. Two minutes later the computer reported it still could not match anything in its memory with the blip on the screen.

Leo slid across to the printer. The copies had grown to a small pile. Pulling his headphones lower on his ears, he took the top copy and placed it under the scanner and his eyes against the eye piece. He manipulated the control with one hand. With the other he worked a key. His headset began to fill with a low-frequency sound, like a truck at a great distance. Leo began to merge the sound with the image so that the rumble was at its clearest when directly over the blip. He punched another key. The computer would do the rest. Search for a match in its memory against the millions of different submarine sounds also there. And it would do it all in seconds instead of the minutes it would have taken a last-generation computer.

'I wonder where she's been,' Leo said.

'I wonder how come we missed her,' the Commander said.

'She sure as hell didn't pass through my watch,' Leo said. 'You'd have to be sleeping to miss her.'

'Someone was,' growled the Commander.

'Day watch. Not your problem,' Leo said cheerfully.

The Commander grunted. Schrag was right.

The VDU screen began to fill with the detailed outline of a submarine and its brief description.

'Typhoon class. Must be one of the Red Banner Northern Fleet's out of Murmansk,' Leo said.

The Watch Commander reached for the 'phone and relayed the news to Langley and Bolling. Afterwards he turned to Leo, smiling. 'Well done, Leo. You want to go take your break now?'

'Maybe later. Let me tidy things away here first.'

The Commander nodded, pleased. Schrag was an old-timer who understood about priorities. He unplugged his jack and, headphones around his neck, walked back to his booth. After he had gone Leo electronically transmitted the hard copies over his fax machine to Langley and Bolling.

He knew enough to know that news of a Soviet sub sneaking back out of the Atlantic would make its way through the intelligence community – the generic term for all US intelligence agencies – until, finally, it could form part of the President's Daily Brief.

Leo smiled. Long before the President learned of the sub, Li would know of its existence. He quickly dialled the fax number Shaoyen had given him. She would be happy he had not forgotten – and when she was happy she was at her most inventive in bed.

*

Igor Tamasara glared across the immense red and gold gilded table which served as his desk. Its ornate magnificence only emphasised how underfurnished and underlit was the rest of the office, no more than a semi-circle of high-backed chairs and a few standard lamps which produced pools of low-wattage light. The surrounds projected the menace and mystery Igor Tamasara enjoyed conveying, fuelled now by the fury he could all but contain.

Qiao Peng had telephoned to remind him again that there must not be an hour's delay in the timetable. Not a word of appreciation of what had been achieved so far. But he knew that to vent it on those sitting before him would be counter-productive. They had met his every demand. And the truth was he should have foreseen the problem that had now arisen.

'We have three clear weeks. The timing cannot be changed,' Igor Tamasara repeated. He turned and looked at the squat, broad-shouldered man at one end of the semi-circle. 'And now you tell me there is a problem, Sacha.'

The others waited in respectful silence. Dr Alexander Fretov was the team's neuro-psychiatrist. He dropped his deltoids like a boxer flexing his shoulders. 'It has only now come to light after I had evaluated all the tests run by Sergei Nikolai,' he said, nodding to the tall, slim man seated beside him.

Sergei Nikolai Petrarova, the Chief Neurologist at Postbox 97, came directly to the heart of the matter. 'The problem is that all the test subjects you have been using are prisoners. To some degree or other they already have been conditioned to respond. That almost certainly has made them more malleable and their comparators easier to override.'

'"Almost certainly" is not scientific!' Igor Tamasara rasped.

'That is exactly why we have raised the matter,' said Dr Petrarova quickly. 'And there is still time to correct the situation.'

Igor Tamasara shifted in his chair. His inquisitorial tone remained. 'Well, what do either of you propose?'

Dr Fretov leaned his heavy upper body forward. 'We have spoken about this and we are of a like mind, Igor Viktorovitch. You could go ahead using the present test results. But there will be a risk. Just as in our very first tests in 97 on animals we knew we had to move on to humans, so now we must move on to humans who are not captive subjects. It may be that the results will be the same as with your prisoner subjects. But we cannot be certain – if you will permit the scientific imprecision.'

Tamasara sat back in his high-backed chair, clasping and unclasping his hands, each movement slow and deliberate to give himself time to think. 'How many do you need?' he asked at last.

Dr Petrarova's sigh seemed to linger in the air. 'It is not just a question of numbers. It is a matter of having subjects who match as closely as possible the brain of the intended target. If the target is a European, for instance, it would be preferable not to use an African. The same with any other ethnic groups with what we neurologists recognise as having distinctive waveforms.'

'Remind me again who they are.'

'Well there are, neurologically speaking, differences between Aborigines and Eskimos. Or Japanese and the Rainforest people of the Amazon. These may not appear to be very great differences to an outsider. But to a neurologist they are significant and need to be taken into account,' concluded Petrarova.

Fretov cleared his throat. His voice was thick with catarrh. 'Different customs, the way of life of each society, produce differing personalities. The basic personality structure is influenced by the roles and habits of a culture. Someone who will be thought of as normal in one society will seem very strange to us. The Americans are a good example. Or, for that matter, our hosts here.

'It is therefore important to include cultural factors in your calculations. The level of aggression, for example, between the Zuni Indians and New Yorkers is very different. Or, for that matter, between our own ethnic peoples. All this needs to be included in the final decisions the Gyroton will be asked to make.'

Igor Tamasara nodded slowly. 'Would it matter if the test subjects were men or women?'

It was Dr Petrarova who answered. 'Ideally, I would like to use men *and* women. There are subtleties in their different wave patterns and it would be interesting to see how the Gyroton exploits them.'

Igor Tamasara leaned forward, his hands on the desk. 'How many do you need? The absolute minimum.'

Dr Petrarova and Dr Fretov looked at each other. The neuropsychiatrist spoke for them both. 'Two. Ideally they should be from the same race as the proposed target. But in the case of the woman that is less important than in that of the man,' said Fretov.

'Why do you say that?' demanded Tamasara.

Dr Fretov spread his hands and smiled. 'It is not difficult to deduce that the target will almost certainly be male. There are still not many women who are sufficiently important to warrant such intervention, now that Thatcher has gone.'

Igor Tamasara led the general laughter in the room.

7

Morton formed one of a group of men gathered over Vitali Rebicov. His body lay naked on a stainless steel table in the necropsy room.

Before coming here Morton had relayed orders from the Prof's telephone to Internal Security to send a team to rummage Rebicov's apartment. Tommy had gone with them; it was as good a way as any to start his field career.

He'd told Anna and the Prof to rework Igor Tamasara's psychoprofile; Lester Finel's operatives to search their computers for anyone else in the memory banks who had worked at Postbox 97 and had subsequently died; Sean Carberry, who ran Covert Action, to put together a team; Johnny Quirke's people to barnstorm their way through paperwork to see what else they could turn up. Danny Nagier had begun to assemble his very specialised equipment.

Shortly before Morton left the building to drive to Geneva's *Privatklinik*, he had telephoned Bill Gates. The CIA's Director of Operations was one of the durables. They had always worked well together because both instinctively understood what was possible in the real world: when to get viscerally engaged and how to control with an easy hand but no negotiations allowed. Gates had immediately agreed to ask the FBI to cast around Miami for anything on Rebicov or his sister.

'So, Colonel, anything special we should be looking for?'

The dark obsidian eyes of Professor Abrahamson, the hospital's Chief of Pathology, glanced across the table. He snugged his surgical gloves down over the sleeves of his smock. Like the room, he smelled of chemicals. His two assistants continued to conduct a careful study of the corpse. One had a weathered brown face and the personality of a wolverine; the other taxidermic eyes, small buttons stitched in folds of skin.

'Anything that could have made him kill himself for no obvious reason,' Morton said equably. Abrahamson was like an endangered species staking out his turf. He was welcome.

Professor Abrahamson turned his beak face to look at Professor Svendsen. 'I would have thought that was more your field.'

The psychiatrist smiled tolerantly. 'The one thing I've learned is not to be subjective. But as I can offer no functional psychosis to suggest cause, I have to hope you can find an organic one.'

'Thank God I'm just a neurosurgeon,' Yoshi Kramer grinned.

Silence returned as they all once more contemplated the body. The skin was waxen under the powerful fluorescent lights. There was a dark bruising on the neck from the belt Rebicov had used to hang himself.

Professor Abrahamson stretched his arms sideways and flexed his fingers. 'Winter stiffness.' He turned to the wolverine. 'Any suggestions?'

The assistant thought for a moment. 'How about a violin solo? Brahms, maybe? Something to get your fingers moving.'

Professor Abrahamson nodded. 'Very well. Nigel Kennedy it is.'

The assistant switched on a cassette player on a trolley in the corner of the room. The music bounced off the ceramic tiled walls.

Suspended over the table were weighing scales and a pair of stainless steel basins. Between them hung an adjustable microphone. On a separate track was a portable X-ray machine. Professor Abrahamson reached up and switched on the microphone. He bowed his head slightly and his movements became more deliberate as he ran his gloved hands over Vitali Rebicov's torso, arms and legs, systematically squeezing muscle and fat. He peered between toes, under the arms and in the groin. He felt over the neck and head. He stopped and parted the hair, lowering his head to peer closer. He looked up at Yoshi Kramer.

'Is this what I think it is?' Professor Abrahamson pulled his right gloved hand down the side of his face, an old man's gesture.

Yoshi peered at the scalp. 'A burr hole,' he said softly, 'an exploratory burr hole.'

The others moved closer to look. Clearly visible in the skull was a small circle, the size of a dime.

'What's beneath that?' Morton asked.

Yoshi stood back. 'Some of the more complex parts of the human brain. But I suspect the bit that'll interest you is the amygdala. That's the little almond-shaped structure which plays a key role in the emotions, especially aggression. I've always said that if someone can successfully tamper with that, he's on the way to creating the kind of monster that would leave dear old Dr Frankenstein looking like a pre-med student!'

Professor Abrahamson looked at the others and sighed. 'Now I'm glad I'm just a pathologist!' He turned to Yoshi. 'It'll be a little while before I get to the brain. Unless you want me to go there at once?'

'No hurry, Isidore,' Yoshi said cheerfully.

The pathologist nodded at his assistants. 'Right, let's turn him over.' When they had done so, the pathologist resumed his methodical physical inspection of the corpse.

Li Mufang wanted tea now. He had a face that never showed what he was thinking. He looked anywhere between thirty and forty, not his fifty-three years. It helped that he was without an ounce of fat and had hair as black as a dragon's colon.

He glanced over at Shaoyen. She was breathing noisily through her mouth. Until the faxes arrived she had been, as usual, insatiable, and they were like animals, locked in a succession of frenzies. Hardly had one climax subsided than she had worked to another one. She was always like this after she had spent a day in bed with Leo; it was her way of expunging his touch and taste.

The first fax had been in the Mandarin reverse-character code with the prefix – Jongjong – indicating it was a message from the Director. As usual Qiao Peng had been brief. When he had read the message, Li tore it into pieces, placed the shreds in a cup and set fire to them. Afterwards he flushed the ashes down the toilet. It was the way he always destroyed all Jongjong's instructions.

Then, with the bedside radio playing in the background – another routine precaution – he had discussed with Shaoyen her part in the new orders from Beijing. They both agreed that what was being asked of her was possible. They had still been discussing the way it would best be achieved when the second fax, Leo's, arrived. Li had brought the length of thermal paper back to the bed and studied it.

A huge Russian submarine had sailed halfway around the world and back again without being detected by the Americans until the last moment. Once again Qiao Peng had been proven triumphantly right.

Even now, Li knew few of the actual details of the operation, code named 'Silent Voices'. But it was typical of Qiao Peng that he had chosen English words as the cover name for the operation. It reflected his deep understanding of the ways of the West. Think like them, become like them, and only then can you succeed in destroying them, he had said at the end of their last meeting in Beijing.

As Li rolled off the bed, Shaoyen passed wind. Li padded, naked and barefoot, across the dark bedroom to the kitchen. He waited for the kettle to boil, then poured water over the sachet of herb tea. Cradling the cup in both hands, Chinese style, he slurped softly, the way his mother had taught him. He continued to think. So far, Silent Voices had been unusually easy. An operation like this could be fraught with difficulties. But from the beginning he had recognised Leo's weakness for sex. Once Shaoyen had hooked him, the rest had been straightforward. Leo was clearly competent at his work, perhaps even outstanding, to have been able to spot the submarine. Otherwise he was naive, as his attitude to Shaoyen showed. But someone like Leo could also be dangerous, could suddenly act out of character. He would have to be handled very carefully, the degree of pressure just right.

Putting down the cup Li walked back into the bedroom. He squatted before the fax machine and dialled the long series of numbers to transmit Leo's fax to Beijing. He wrinkled his nose as Shaoyen once more passed gas. He would order her to curb this passion for pickled eggs.

Afterwards, he tore up the fax and flushed it away in the toilet. Then he showered and shaved in preparation for his meeting with Leo.

In the necropsy room Professor Abrahamson finished his external examination. Vitali Rebicov once more lay on his back and Nigel Kennedy had stopped playing.

'Like to hear something else?' the wolverine assistant asked.

The pathologist shot him a look. 'No. Stiff I may be, but not that stiff.'

Morton grinned at him over the corpse. 'I was just getting hooked.'

The pathologist turned to a surgical trolley. It contained an assortment of scalpels, bone cutters, bowls and pots. The single largest instrument was a small electric saw, connected by a flex to one of the many power outlets in the tiled walls.

Yoshi Kramer nodded towards the X-ray machine. 'Why don't we get some pictures of the head? It should tell us a little more about the burr hole.'

Professor Abrahamson nodded to the assistant with the taxidermic eyes. He manoeuvred the X-ray machine along its track until it was positioned over Rebicov's head. He took a series of pictures of the skull. As he hurried out of the room to have them developed, the pathologist began his external description of the body. While he spoke the assistant took clippings and scrapings from the finger and toenails, as well as snippings of head and pubic hair. These were placed in pots which the assistant labelled.

'You're getting your money's worth today, David,' murmured Yoshi.

The pathologist took a scalpel from the trolley and looked at Professor Svendsen. 'If you want to wait outside ...'

The psychiatrist shook his head.

Professor Abrahamson shrugged and from the trolley selected a long, thin-bladed scalpel. Keeping his fingers spread to hold the skin and flesh taut, he made a Y-shaped incision across the chest, moving the blade in a descending curve, cutting deeply and swiftly through muscle and fatty tissue to expose the breastbone. At the midpoint of the curve he cut downwards with the same certain speed, all the way to the top of the pelvic circle. The skin gaped open. There was almost no blood.

He discarded the scalpel and reached for a shorter blade. With this he pared away the underlying cartilage over the rib cage. Beneath lay the thoracic and abdominal organs. He paused and looked across the table. 'This is the time we get to see how God made man. As long as we remember this is all part of God's plan, then we won't have a problem doing what we have to do here.'

Professor Abrahamson took a pair of bone cutters and began to open up the chest. The air was filled with the squelchy sound of bone and gristle giving way. Morton wrinkled his nose at this dense, miasmic stench which so clearly reeked of mortality. Vitali Rebicov's and everyone else's in the room.

When he had severed the breastplate, the pathologist stepped back for the assistant to expose the organs. Morton recognised the lungs and the liver and the coils of the intestine. The heart, for the moment, was hidden behind the lungs.

Professor Abrahamson resumed his position at the table and cast a searching look over the organs. He addressed the microphone: 'Visual examination of internal organs reveals nothing unusual.' He reached for a clean knife and began to cut out the lungs.

In the living room whose second-floor windows were almost directly across the street from Li's apartment, the two FBI technicians heard through their headphones the sounds of the fax being transmitted and once more the flush of a toilet. Like all the other sounds they had recorded coming from Li's apartment, these had been automatically dated and timed on the tape. The younger agent, a wiry Hong Kong-born Chinese called Teng, glanced at the wall clock.

'Maybe one day we'll get to know what all this is about,' he said.

'Our tickets aren't punched,' said Song. He was a native-born American Chinese, who had learned his hip slang from watching MTV.

'That's typical of Langley.'

Song shrugged. In their business you just did what you were paid for. Speculation was not part of it.

After removing the lungs, Professor Abrahamson inspected them, dropped one on the weighing scales, noted the weight, waited for the assistant to remove it and then weighed the other. He described his findings into the microphone. He glanced across the table as if he expected questions. None came. '... no abnormalities,' concluded Professor Abrahamson.

The dead who came here had no voice except this one, Morton thought. Abrahamson spoke for them, burrowing deep into their bodies, bringing what light he could to bear on their lifestyle. *No abnormalities.*

Professor Abrahamson removed the heart from the body cavity and examined it. He waited for the assistant to remove the lung from the bowl and then place the heart in the receptacle. The assistant secured and labelled the samples. The organs would go to Pathology, the fluids to Toxicology.

Professor Abrahamson squinted into the gaping cavity. 'Last meal appears to have been boiled eggs, cereal, bread, some liquid.'

'He had the same breakfast every morning,' said Professor Svendsen.

'You think that made him depressed?' asked the assistant.

Professor Abrahamson glanced at him. 'If you want to try for a laugh, tell me first.'

The assistant's eyes resumed their fixed look.

The liver, gall bladder, pancreas and kidneys were weighed and drew favourable comment. Vitali Rebicov had been a healthy man.

The other assistant returned with the developed X-rays. He fixed the negatives to the backlit display frame on a wall. Yoshi and Morton went over to inspect them.

'Well, well,' the neurosurgeon murmured after he had studied the X-rays.

The others joined them at the frame.

'What is it?' demanded Professor Abrahamson.

'An implant. It's Delgado's bull updated,' murmured Yoshi.

The others stared at the tiny, dark spot the neurosurgeon was indicating.

Professor Abrahamson looked at Yoshi and spoke in a heavy voice. 'Who exactly is this Delgado you speak so knowledgeably about?'

Yoshi nodded to the display screen. 'When we were still playing at doctors and nurses, José Delgado was doing the kind of experiment that threatened to drive bullfighters out of business. He'd implanted a radio-controlled electrode deep in the brain of a fighting bull. Then he stepped into the ring with nothing more than his little control box. A couple of tons of lethal muscle would come charging at him. When Delgado pressed a button on his box the crazed bull turned into another Ferdinand.'

'Delgado placed his implant roughly where that one is – close to that part of the bull's brain which controls memory, impulses and feelings. Delgado didn't go beyond showing it was possible to exercise remote control over animal behaviour. It seems somebody's been trying to do it with humans.'

Professor Svendsen nodded thoughtfully. 'When I was at Uppsala there was an evaluation of Delgado's work. The conclusion was that it was too dangerous to replicate in humans because it could evoke hallucinations and illusions that could not be controlled. Worse, it could make someone behave completely out of character – like taking his own life.'

Professor Abrahamson smiled in disbelief at the psychiatrist. 'Are you seriously suggesting that someone somewhere pressed a button on his little black box and Rebicov promptly hanged himself? Is that what you're saying?'

Professor Svendsen fixed his gaze on the pathologist. 'I'm not a neurologist, Professor Abrahamson. But I do know that the brain is without doubt the most complex piece of equipment on this planet. Yet we only understand a fraction of its functions, let alone its responses to the philosopher's questions. What happens in the brain when we think? How free are we? How much are we determined by forces we do not control? What happens when we see something in our mind's eye? When a word is stopped on the tip of our tongue?

'There are a hundred such questions we are only on the fringe of understanding. We know there are fifteen billion nerve cells in the

66

average brain, but we still have little understanding, for instance, of which ones influence ageing, depression and addiction. I'm interested in what happens in the brain when a person explodes into violent behaviour. On the effects violence can have on those who produce it. On those at the receiving end. What does science really know about violence? Still very little. Until we know more, I wouldn't write off anything.'

The old pathologist shook his head. 'Now I'm even more glad I only have to worry about the dead.' He turned away and walked over to the table. The others followed.

In complete silence, using a wide-bladed scalpel, Professor Abrahamson peeled back the skull to the bone to expose the crest. He used the electric saw to cut into the bone to make four angled cuts. He took a steel lever, shaped rather like a shoe-horn, and worked it between the first pair of cuts. With some difficulty, and accompanied by a sucking noise, he prised free the crest of the skull. He used a knife to expose the brain covering. Then he took a larger scalpel to cut through the tissue and arteries which held the brain in place. In less than five minutes he had removed the organ.

After minutely inspecting the brain, he held it towards the overhead lights. The others peered at the grey sponge-like object full of dark-coloured liquid.

'I see it,' Yoshi said. 'Between the amygdala and the hippocampus.'

Morton could clearly make out the circular shape of the electrode. 'Let's get some more pictures,' he said.

Professor Abrahamson placed the brain gently on the scales. 'Three hundred grams. We'll weigh it again when that thing's out,' he said.

The others silently watched the assistant take X-rays of the brain. When he turned to leave Morton stopped him. 'I'll have those developed,' he said. It was time to start closing things down.

The pathologist shot him a glance but said nothing. He lifted the bowl off the scales and carried it over to a table. A high-intensity light on an articulated arm provided powerful illumination. The others gathered around.

With a marvellous economy of movement, Professor Abrahamson dissected the brain to remove the pellet-sized electrode. He held it between surgical tweezers under the light. There was no marking on the dull metal surface of the electrode.

No one spoke. Morton picked up a specimen pot on the table and unscrewed the lid. The pathologist gently popped the electrode into the pot. Morton replaced the lid. He looked at the others and spoke in a patient voice. 'I have to formally remind you that what happened here today must not be spoken about to anyone. Your colleagues, your families. Anyone.'

He waited until they all nodded assent, then walked from the necropsy room. He had nothing to support his gut feeling – certainly not the paperwork Bitburg would demand – but it told him that as good a place as any to start looking for answers would be in Beijing. Now that the Russians were out of the frame, that only left the Chinese with the capability of going on from where Delgado had stopped.

At 4.00 am, with the headstones in deep darkness on Arlington's cemetery hill, the Lincoln town car headed northwards of downtown Washington through the flat and partially-wooded countryside on the banks of the Potomac. Gates drove quickly, the radio tuned to an all-night news station.

He was a large man, broad across the shoulders. He had loosened his tie but kept his shirtsleeves buttoned. He had a rail of these shirts at home, each cut from the same cloth. They were one of his unalterable habits.

Listening to the radio was another; he had a low tolerance for silence. And he had a deep affection for radio voices – the way they could convey so much simply by pitch and tone. The Duty Officer who had awoken him an hour ago would never even make it to local radio. He had a nervous speech impediment which had consigned him forever to the graveyard shift in Operations.

He had called with two items that were both on the current Awake Director list: the news that a Typhoon class sub was heading home, and that Qiao Peng's man had sent another fax from his Chinatown apartment. The Duty Officer had stammered that there was no trace of where the sub had been. But the dialling sequence for the fax had been identified as for Beijing. Gates had asked, and was told there was nothing in from Miami. If it was to come, it must come soon.

But what had decided Gates to drive to the office at this hour was a call from Thacker Stimpson to tell him that the President would be going to the Non-Aligned Nations Conference in Manila with a Hong Kong stopover. The security for that would be a major headache. The Brits for Hong Kong; the Philippine Security Service, a clone of the CIA, for Manila. God knows who else would have to be consulted, roped in or just roped off.

Gates gave a friendly wave to the guard at the entrance to Langley. He parked the car outside the Headquarters building and entered the lobby, striding over the agency's emblem set in the floor marble – a sixteen-point star on a shield with the head of a bald eagle in profile. Beyond was the wall plaque that the agency's most celebrated Director, Allen Walsh Dulles, had dedicated. It bore the words of the Apostle St John: 'And Ye Shall Know The Truth, And The Truth Shall Make You Free.' Gates nodded to the night duty man by the elevators, punched a button and the door in the middle of the bank opened. It was programmed to stop only at his floor, the sixth. Seconds later he stepped out onto a corridor panelled in light oak, and carpeted in government-issue olive.

His office was at one end. Reaching its door, he punched his three-digit personal code into a wall keyboard, lighting its small computer screen. Internal Security had said the keyboard was top-of-the-range. What it really was, Gates had decided, was a glorified time clock, keeping track of when he came and went. As he walked into his office the lights came on automatically, another little trick the computer performed.

The office itself was large and airy and three of its walls were lined with bookshelves. The fourth was a single window offering an excellent view of the Washington skyline. Like all the other windows in the building the glass was coated with an invisible substance Technical Services had developed to thwart electronic surveillance. On the old-fashioned partner's desk in front of the window the call-waiting button was blinking. Gates pressed a key to retrieve the message.

'Call me,' ordered Morton's voice.

8

At Zulu 0400 hours – Bethesda Medical Hospital worked on Greenwich Mean Time – a surgeon-commander and Dr Barker approached the door to the President's bedroom. Both wore blue theatre garb. The surgeon had the kindly face of a family doctor who still made house calls. In reality he was a battle-hardened veteran of the Persian Gulf War and had later served for a spell with the United Nations peacekeeping forces in Bosnia. He carried a kidney-shaped bowl containing a loaded syringe and sheathed needle. The syringe contained a light and fast-acting anaesthetic.

Even in his scrub suit, Dr Barker looked every inch the President's physician. He was tall and spare, with silvered hair and a winning smile. He bestowed it upon the Secret Service man seated before the bedroom door. The agent glanced at the kidney bowl before speaking. 'Hasn't been a peep out of Laser since he turned in.'

From force of habit the agent referred to the President by his code name – part of the elaborate security precautions that even here surrounded the nation's leader. His suite was the Castle, the bedroom, Slumber. Dr Barker was Diagnosis, the surgeon, Forceps One. Other key hospital medical staff each had the same prefix, but with descending numbers. The attendants trailing behind Diagnosis and Forceps One were Forceps Nineteen and Forceps Twenty. Satchel, with the Football, the bag with its nuclear launch codes, sat beside the Secret Service man, code name Domino.

'Where's Drummer?' Dr Barker asked, falling into security-speak himself. Drummer was Thacker Stimpson.

'With Watchman in the Communications Room,' replied the agent. Watchman, the Vice-President, would be being briefed by Thack.

Dr Barker switched on the bedroom light and both doctors chorused a good morning to the President.

'Sorry to wake you so early, sir – especially as I'm now going to put you back to sleep,' the surgeon said cheerfully, walking over to the bed.

Dr Barker looked down at his only patient. 'Do you have any questions beforehand, Mr President?'

'Only about this fancy scan of yours, Herb. Have you figured out what you're going to tell the press? You know how they can play up these things. Remember that time George Bush fell off his chair at that Tokyo banquet and the media began to wonder if he had a brain tumour instead of jet-lag.'

Dr Barker smiled reassurance. 'The scan is all part of our policy of preventive medicine. It's really no different to when I shine a light in your eyes or ears. It's a more sophisticated form of reassurance, that's all. That's what I'll tell the press. And even the *Washington Post* won't be able to put a spin on that!'

The President turned to the surgeon. 'If you find anything, what then?'

The surgeon proffered further reassurance. 'A polyp is almost always benign. But to be on the safe side I snip them out. The endoscope's capable of doing that during the examination.'

'How long will that take?'

The surgeon unsheathed the needle. 'You'll be asleep for only a few minutes. And back here in time for a late breakfast,' he promised.

The President gave a little nod, trying to look more assured than he felt.

'Well ... you'd better start,' he said.

Dr Barker took the back of the President's right hand and felt for a vein, trapping the skin with his fingers several times to bring one to the surface. When he succeeded he took the syringe from the surgeon. 'This stuff's faster and lighter than Valium. And there are absolutely no after-effects,' he promised. He expertly threaded the needle into the vein and slowly depressed the syringe's plunger. 'Start counting, Mr President,' he murmured. 'Nice and slow.'

The President's mouth fell slack and he started to breathe more deeply. The surgeon turned to the door and motioned forward the orderlies. Between them they manoeuvred the bed out of the bedroom and into the suite's own treatment room. There the President was rolled on his side, his knees tucked up and a fibre-optic tube fed into the rectum to inspect the inner membrane of the colon. The surgeon conducted the examination by peering through an eye-piece that gave him a hugely magnified view of the tissue.

After a few minutes he lowered the eye-piece and turned to Dr Barker. 'The man's as clean as a whistle. Take a look.'

Dr Barker satisfied himself that this was indeed so. The President was already beginning to stir in the bed.

'Let's move him down to the magnetograph. He still needs to be nice and relaxed for that.'

Preceded by a Secret Service agent murmuring into his mike, the small procession moved out of the suite.

Morton sat in a well-padded chair in his office at the back of Hammer Force Headquarters. He had chosen the corner room because its windows offered a magnificent view of the Swiss Alps. He had always been a mountain man; when this was over he would once more spend a few days testing himself against a peak. An outsized desk and the chair were the room's only furniture. The rest was state-of-the-art communications equipment. He continued to glance at a VDU monitor as he brought Bill Gates up to speed over the telephone. Tommy had called in to report that the rummage squad had found nothing in Rebicov's apartment. Lester Finel's computers had unearthed no one else who had been at Postbox 97. The Prof had left a message on the screen that he and Anna weren't really getting very far in reworking Igor Tamasara's psycho-profile. He turned away from the monitor.

'After Johnny Quirke's technicians stripped down the electrode from Rebicov's brain and subjected it to a battery of tests, Walter said they still couldn't say, for certain, that Igor Tamasara or one of his people planted it,' Morton said.

'So what's Bitburg want?' Gates growled. 'A statement from Tamasara?'

In his mind's eye Morton could see Gates now, sprawled in his easyform chair, 'phone cradled under his chin, staring out over the Langley parkland.

'Ideally signed by two independent witnesses. Since he's discovered what computers can really do, Walter's become convinced that unless it's on a print-out it didn't happen. That's what he said when I told him Igor Tamasara could be in China.'

Gates chuckled. 'Unless you show Bitburg an airline ticket and a room reservation at The Beijing he's not going to buy it.'

Morton glanced out of the window. Cloud was obscuring the Alps. It would be snowing up there; at this time of the year the flakes would turn to slush, making skiing almost as difficult as judging where Igor Tamasara could be. 'China's just about the only place left for him,' he said. 'I've knocked everyone else off my shortlist except Qiao Peng. He's got the money and he's always been interested in mind control. So that makes Beijing the logical point at which to start looking for Igor Tamasara.'

Gates glanced at his desktop computer screen. 'I guess you know all this stuff we've got on him,' he grunted. 'Don't look like a whole can of beans to me.'

Morton listened as Gates read off the details. Bill was right: nothing new there. The CIA had the same sketchy bio that Records had. The details probably came from the same source. Peddling data from the files of the now defunct KGB was a growth industry among Soviet emigrés. He heard Gates suddenly exhale, the closest Bill ever came to expressing surprise. 'No kidding ...'

'Let me guess,' Morton said. 'There's a cross-reference for Colin Baskin.'

'Right on.' When he was genuinely impressed Gates sometimes used phrases that had passed their shelf-life. 'How'd you guess ... ?'

Morton told him about Kate Baskin's paper, with its reference to her father's work.

'Hold a mo, David,' Gates said, reaching forward to press another key. The screen cleared and then began to fill once more with data on Colin Baskin. 'Too much for me to read, David, so I'll fax it to you.'

Gates pressed another key to begin the transmission, and leaned back to watch the text unfolding on screen. 'Even when geniuses in S and T were two a dime, Baskin must have stood out as a genuine off-the-wall maverick,' he said into the 'phone.

Science and Technology had once been the Agency's test bed, capable of attracting the brightest of a year's science graduates, drawn by huge budgets and the promise of being able to publish at least some of their findings in the leading academic journals. Not to forget the appeal of old-fashioned patriotism and the mystique of working towards some covert goal.

'Baskin began working for us on psychotronics, trying to create weapons systems that would operate on the power of the mind theory. Remember SADDOR?'

'For sure.'

SADDOR – Satellite Deployed Dowsing Rod – had been one of the high points of the CIA's paranormal period. A score of psychics had been part of a multi-million dollar a year programme to try to plot the movement of Soviet submarines by using a variety of phenomena such as Tarot card readings, astrology and the supposed second sight of the psychics themselves.

'Now we have that expensive set-up down by the Navy Yard and we're still not getting much success,' growled Gates. He told Morton about the sighting of the Typhoon class submarine. Morton made a note but no comment. This was not the time to get side-tracked.

'What else did Baskin work on?' he asked.

'Something he called "photonic barrier modulation". He wanted to see if his psychics could kill someone by long-range telepathy.'

'He get any results?'

'It doesn't say. But probably not. Even marginal success with something like that would get noted.' Gates pressed the key and the text continued to roll up on screen. He continued to call out items that caught his eye. 'For a while he seems to have been big into seeing if bioenergy could be harnessed. He worked on something called a hieronymous machine. It sounds real comic-book stuff. The theory seems to have been that you needed only a photograph of a target for ammunition. You place a photo of, say, a sub in this machine, press a button and presto! – the sub sinks. Wild.'

In a corner of the office a fax machine had started to receive the data from Washington. 'Did it ever come close to working?' Morton asked.

'Again, it doesn't say. And again, almost certainly not. Something like that would have ended the Cold War sooner. And we'd all have heard about it.'

'He seems to have done a lot of work with little end result, Bill.'

'Spent a lot of money, too. But it's easy to understand why he had little to show for it. To actually prove his point he'd have needed human guinea pigs. And around that time they weren't easy to come by,' Gates said.

Baskin had been working at a time when the supply of anonymous refugees from Eastern Europe suspected of being low-level intelligence operatives had dried up. So had the human guinea pigs from Vietnam.

'What else did Baskin work on?' Morton asked.

Once more he heard that distinctive little grunt, followed by a release of air and: 'No kidding ... the guy worked on brain transmitters.'

'What was he trying to do?'

'Hoping to duplicate some Soviet experiments the Agency had gotten wind of. Least that's what it says here. Let me read this to you. It's a direct quote from his submission proposal to the Director, S and T, "The Soviets believe that one of the possibilities with brain transmission is to influence people so that they conform to the political system. Autonomic and somatic functions, individual and social behaviour, emotional and mental reactions, may be evoked, maintained, modified or inhibited by electrical stimulation of certain specific cerebral structures." And listen to this. Know who the prime shaker was on the Soviet side?'

'Igor Tamasara.'

'Right on, David. Right on.'

'What happened to Baskin's application?'

'Got turned down. We were still reeling from the flak over MKULTRA.'

Morton remembered. The MKULTRA programme had been the CIA's first real plunge into the control of human behaviour. The experiments were a striking example of the way the CIA had been prepared to engage the world at all levels. The research had become more ambitious and dangerous. Even now no one knew its full extent.

Gates sounded sombre. 'Baskin was never directly involved in MKULTRA. But when the intelligence oversight committee pulled the plug, he got caught in the dirt in the bottom of the bath. Enough of that surfaced in the media to end a lot of careers in this place. Baskin's was one of them.'

'What happened to him?'

'Gone from one day to the next. There's nothing on file except the date his contract was ended and details of his severance pay. Forty-two thousand. We were never generous with salaries, so he must have been a high flier.' There was a moment's silence on the line from Washington. 'I wasn't here at the time,' Gates added. He'd been a field agent in the Congo during the MKULTRA purge. By the time he got back to Langley, there had been a clean sweep. There were new men in charge, new rules. One of those was that no one tried anything like MKULTRA again.

'Where did Baskin go?' Morton asked. Micronesia was a big place to start looking.

'You want to go after him?'

'For sure. He's my only way so far to Tamasara,' Morton said. Across the room the fax paper was piling up on the floor.

'There's a note here from Personnel that says all enquiries about

75

Colin Baskin go through his daughter, Kate.' Morton heard Gates laugh. 'And in her case like father like daughter, and yet not. She's into the whole electromagnetic spectrum, especially the low density stuff. But with her, so it says here, she's working on trying to use it to make the blind see, the deaf hear and the lame walk. You want to go and talk to her, there's a number. It's the Department of Neurology at Magill University.'

'Thanks,' said Morton, jotting down the Montreal number.

'Anything I need to know about her?' he asked.

Gates glanced at the screen. 'Only that she's thirty-four, divorced, no children. And it says here, though God knows why, that she's "physically rather attractive". That sounds just like something the FBI would write. "Physically rather attractive" ... Talk about covering your bets.'

'Why would the FBI run surveillance on her?' Morton asked.

'No reason stated. But they'd probably run surveillance on someone like Baskin's daughter just in case anyone approaches her to get to her old man.'

'Anything from Miami on Rebicov?'

Gates snorted. 'They sent a couple of their Ivy League grads just out of that fancy training school of theirs at Quantico. When you cut through the crap about talking to everybody on the block, you're back to first base – none the wiser why she jumped.'

'She may have had an implant like her brother.'

'If she had we'll never know,' Gates said with finality.

Morton shifted in his chair. The fax machine had finally stopped. It looked like a good hour's reading.

'Let me ask you a question, David. If Tamasara's in China, how do you hope to tease him to the surface?'

'Lay some bait. Someone like that is always hungry.'

Gates knew better than to ask a follow-up question. 'Call me before you leave for Beijing,' he said.

Morton promised he would. But first he had a number of other calls to make, to Hong Kong and Tokyo, as well as arranging for an advertisement for a kitchen boy to appear in China's *People's Daily*.

One of the two technicians in charge of the magneto-graphalogram turned to Dr Barker. 'I'm sorry, sir. But to be on the safe side we need to run him through once more.'

The President's physician peered through the observation window.

In his white-walled chamber the President lay strapped in his pyjamas on a slipway before a machine with a hollowed-out centre large enough for his body to enter. The magnetograph scanner looked like an out-sized washing machine. The President lay on his back, eyes flickering. The effects of the anaesthetic were rapidly wearing off. Dr Barker glanced at the bank of monitor screens on one wall of the control booth. Each displayed a different three-dimensional image of the President's brain.

'So far the profiles show nothing. But on the last pass we didn't get a good enough axial tomography of the amygdala.' The neurologist smiled quickly. 'Sometimes even a ten-million dollar machine likes to behave like something you picked off the shelf at the local Radio Shack.'

Dr Barker sighed and reached forward to flick the intercom switch on the control desk. He spoke slowly and clearly. 'Mr President. Just one more ride through the tunnel. You've been doing great so far. Just lie still and close your eyes again.'

The President mumbled and did as he was told.

'Let's shoot for it,' the senior technician said.

The analogy with making a movie was apt. They were creating an action motion-picture of the President's brain. The two technicians pressed buttons and moved switches.

'Sensors activated,' one called.

'Computer running,' confirmed the other.

Behind them the Hewlett Packard computer would once more be ready to accept, analyse and transfer onto the screens the mass of infor-mation the magnetograph scanner would transmit through its sensors.

'Run it,' ordered the neurologist.

The slipway began to move slowly and silently into the machine's innards.

'You'd have thought they'd build in a little noise, just to reassure a patient he's not going to get beamed up like something out of *Star Trek*,' murmured Dr Barker.

The neurologist gave another quick smile but said nothing. He con-tinued to watch the screens. On one the President's head once more appeared as a computer-processed image. 'Hold it,' the neurologist said sharply. He leaned forward and peered at the screen. Dr Barker and the technicians all did the same.

'There, you see it?' asked the neurologist.

'I see it,' said the senior technician.

'Me too. But it's very minimal,' added the second technician.

'What is it?' asked Dr Barker, still trying to distinguish between the variations in tissue density.

'There's a weakness in the amygdala's lower side.' The neurologist pointed to a spot on the small almond shape of the amygdala.

'Is that serious?'

'Serious – no. A lot of people get it around his age. It makes them a tad more tetchy, forgetful maybe. Even a little aggressive. But it's not life-threatening.'

'You're speaking about the President,' Dr Barker reminded the neurologist curtly. 'I need to know if this will get worse, what course it could take, and what can be done about it in terms of treatment.'

'Run him through again,' the neurologist told a senior technician, before motioning Dr Barker to a corner of the control chamber. After watching the President once more entering the scanner, the neurologist spoke to the physician. 'Let me take your questions one by one. There's a statistical thirty per cent chance it will get worse. But the tetchiness, aggression and memory lapses will be a gradual process. They won't really be noticeable until he's into his seventies. By then, of course, he'll be a private citizen and won't have the responsibility of office. In terms of treatment there is none. He has no history of epilepsy, so we haven't got to worry there. And we've seen nothing to show any indication of tissue degeneration as a result of alcohol or drugs. So those are two more plus factors ...'

'Are we talking here about Alzheimer's Disease?'

'Good God, no. Absolutely not.'

The neurologist nodded towards the screen. 'There's nothing there to indicate even the beginning of the onset of atrophy. There's not a single neuron showing fibrillary tangles.'

'Does this affect his decision-making? The President often has to think on his feet.'

The neurologist glanced quickly towards the door. Through its glass panel he could see a Secret Service man and the Marine officer with his satchel talking to each other. 'Of course I'm not familiar with the President's everyday thinking process. But I can see no reason for this to affect him. The weakness is very minimal. In any one else I probably wouldn't have even mentioned it.'

'Are you really saying there's no risk?'

The neurologist hesitated. 'What I'm saying is that the risk is small.

The only problem that might arise is if the President was ever exposed to low-level X-rays. Or some form of electrical radiation.'

'Such as?'

'Well, I wouldn't be too happy if he was to spend a week or two standing close to a high-tension power cable. Or if he felt a need to go and inspect the national electricity grid.' The neurologist squinted at Dr Barker. 'He's not likely to do that, is he?'

'No.'

The neurologist smiled. 'Then there's really nothing for him – or you – to worry about.'

'Should I tell him what you've found?'

'If he were my patient? No. That would only make him worry needlessly.'

In the chamber the President had emerged from the tunnel and was looking towards the control room.

'You all done in there?' he asked.

Dr Barker flicked the intercom. 'All over, Mr President.'

'How'd I make out?'

Dr Barker did not hesitate. 'You did fine, Mr President. Absolutely nothing to worry about.'

Morton sat hunched at his desk, 'phone pressed hard against his left ear, right hand toying with a precise-roller Papermate he always used for note-taking. He had filled several pages with notes on his calls to Tokyo and Hong Kong, and afterwards with Professor Svendsen. The fax from Gates lay in separate piles on his desk: one for Igor Tamasara; a second for Colin Baskin; the third, a couple of thermal pages, for Kate Baskin. He had spent an hour reading the paperwork, underscoring passages, mostly to do with Colin Baskin's work. He'd clearly either been way out on left field or some way ahead of his time.

Baskin had been at the core of the CIA's efforts to match the Soviets in producing exotic new weapons. In his last year at the Agency he had been working on something called electron dissolution. The intention had been to produce a machine capable of transmitting a variety of beams designed to attack biological systems. But before he had been able to try it out on laboratory animals, he had been sacked.

Yet he was no evil scientist hell-bent on creating a modern version of the greatest invincible weapon of legend, the Sword of Excalibur. That much Kate Baskin had made clear early on in their conversation. He had told her who he was, who had told him to call and why he was doing so.

'But you still haven't told me why you want to see him,' she said. She had a throaty voice. And, said the FBI report, she was attractive with it.

'Igor Tamasara,' Morton said, pulling the pages of the CIA biography towards him. 'You ever heard of him?'

'No. But he sounds Russian.'

'He is. And he's in the same field your father was. I want to find out what he can tell me about Tamasara.'

There was silence on the line. 'Like I've said, my Dad's been out of it for some time, Colonel Morton.'

'Maybe I could call him?'

She laughed. He thought it a pretty sound. 'He doesn't have a 'phone. There isn't one on the island. Just a short-wave radio. He uses that when he's got a patient that he can't handle.'

Morton couldn't quite hide his surprise. 'Your father's practising?'

'He began as a doctor, Colonel. He was in his second year as a neurology assistant professor at Parkland Memorial in Dallas when he was recruited. They told him he would still be working in his speciality, the brain, only this time it would be in the national interest. He went willingly. Then, when the national interest gave way to Agency embarrassment, they tossed him out. He just took off, saying he'd always wanted to get back to basics. And there's probably nothing more basic than looking after the medical needs of a few hundred islanders in the middle of nowhere. And they don't come more nowhere than Borakai.'

Using his right hand, Morton tapped on his VDU keyboard: Search – Borakai. 'And your mother? She go with him?'

'Oh, she'd gone years before. Ran off with somebody from the clandestine side of the Agency. My mother always had a flair for the dramatic. We were never very close, and after what she did to my Dad the last ties were broken.'

Morton made a note. There was a tension in her voice he had not expected. Was she still hurting? Or was it something else? The collapse of her own marriage, perhaps? He read as the VDU screen began to fill silently. 'Borakai: island in Melanesian Basin. Latitude 15N 155E; 874 kilometres S-SW of Kosrae. Pop: 425 (est.).'

He punched more keys. The screen told him Hong Kong was 4,900 km from Borakai – a six-hour flight. But probably double that with changeovers and inter-island transport.

'I could go and see your father,' Morton said.

'I don't know,' she said doubtfully.

'Dr Baskin, I wouldn't be asking if it wasn't terribly important.'

In the end it always came down to this. There was another silence on the line. 'Why is it so important?' she finally asked.

Morton glanced at his notepad. 'Do you know Lars Svendsen?'

'The psychiatrist? He used to work here.'

'If I told you he thinks it important I see your father would you agree?'

'Lars is a good man,' she said softly. 'When my marriage broke up he was a great support.'

Morton made another note on the pad. 'Can you arrange for your father to see me?' he asked.

There was silence. He could sense her coming to a decision. 'I'll go one better. I'll come with you. I've still got two weeks' vacation. Can you get to Hong Kong?'

'By tomorrow,' he said.

'I'll need a day to clear up things here. You know the Mandarin?'

'For sure.'

'I'll meet you in the lobby bar. Six-thirty, two days from now.'

He'd be at the airport. But he wouldn't tell her that.

Morton left his office, framing in his mind how he would tell the others about the truly terrifying threat Igor Tamasara now represented.

After studying Li Mufang's latest fax from Washington, Qiao Peng went to a large windowless room adjoining his own office. Li had done well, using the girl brilliantly to entrap such an important asset. A short while ago he had faxed Li instructions on what he wanted the asset to do next.

The room's walls were hung with maps: the United States, Hong Kong, Russia, Japan, the oceans of the world. The floor space was virtually filled by a plotting table. Relaying the co-ordinates on the fax, Qiao Peng watched carefully as the People's Liberation Army officer placed a red-painted model of a submarine on the plotting table at the position where the Typhoon class submarine had been sighted by the Americans. As he turned to leave he looked at the officer, frowning. 'Isn't this normally Captain Wang's shift?'

'Yes sir. But he was taken ill. Central Operations sent me.'

'What is your name?'

'Cheng, sir. Captain, Third Army, Special Signals on attachment ...'

'And you are fully briefed?' interrupted Qiao Peng.

'Oh yes, sir. I am to check with Central Operations every fifteen minutes for satellite reports. These will be updated on the table. Every hour you are to be informed.'

Qiao Peng continued staring at him. 'You are the son of Lizhi Cheng?'

'Yes, sir.'

'Ah, yes,' said Qiao Peng, remembering.

Lizhi Cheng had been military commander in Lhasa when the Lama monks had once more surged out of their monasteries to protest at China's occupation of Tibet. Lizhi Cheng had ordered his troops to fire directly into the unarmed monks. Scores had been killed, hundreds wounded. On his way back to Beijing to receive a medal from Chairman Hu, Lizhi Cheng's military transport had crashed, killing everyone on board.

'Your father was a brave man,' Qiao Peng said, walking from the room.

'Thank you, sir,' said Yaobang Cheng. How could he tell this man the truth? That what his father had ordered was cold-blooded murder. Or that it had taken a stranger to convince him of it.

They had met a full year after the massacre. The encounter had been one of those occasional contacts that sometimes happened on busy Wangfujing Street, the shopping centre of Beijing. The man had asked the way to Number One Department Store. Yaobang Cheng had offered to show him. As simply as that it had begun. They had met several times, strolling through the *hutongs*, the maze-world of alleys and courtyards of the old city, eating dumplings in a restaurant near Coal Hill, riding the cable-lift to the top of the Fragrant Hills; a tourist and his guide.

He could not remember now when he had first begun to realise the truth about the man, who called himself simply David. Was it the way he smiled, a hard, temporary smile? Or his careful questions about Tibet and his father? Certainly David was very well-informed about what had happened. When they had visited the zoo, in between watching the sour-faced gorillas and the Yangzte alligators staring back with burnt-out eyes, David had offered his verdict on the massacre. It had been senseless murder and his father a callous murderer. The judgement had struck a chord in his own psyche. Something he had not realised was there had surfaced in staccato bursts of talk.

When he had finished he knew he had told David more than he had told anyone about his love for his country and the deep anger he felt towards those who controlled it. His father had been only one of the brutal ones; there were many more still alive. Bicycling back from the zoo, two among the huge torpid drifts of bikers gliding *en masse* in a slow tinkling of bells, David had gradually told him what he could do to help change things; to make sure that one day China would be a nation free and ready to take its place in the twenty-first century, the Pacific century, David called it.

Yaobang had accepted without demur that he was being asked to spy on his country. Doing so he had never felt, not once, that he was betraying China – only helping it towards taking its rightful place in the world. The information he had provided revealed the machinations of the despots who had all but ruined his country. Since the advertisement for domestic staff had once again appeared in the *People's Daily* situations vacant columns it had needed considerable skill and risk-taking to arrange for Captain Wang to fall ill from food poisoning so that he could take his shift.

Already what he had seen made the risk worthwhile. But he would do nothing until the next advertisement appeared. That would be the signal for him to go to Tiananmen Square and mingle with the crowds, the headphones of his personal stereo clamped firmly to his ears. The stereo and the tape of songs from the Cultural Revolution looked like any other on sale in the electrical department of Number One Department Store. But David had said they had been custom-made for him in that far away place called Geneva.

9

The secretary in the outer office of Walter Bitburg's suite looked up as Morton entered. 'You can go in,' she told Morton. Bitburg's office was a rich man's library, walled with leather-bound books, self-promotional photographs with princes and Presidents, framed commendations from charities, and the kind of ornate-framed paintings Morton had seen in the offices of other men who paid lip service to culture.

'Aren't you rushing things a little? I mean, shouldn't you get formal UN approval? China's on the Security Council after all,' Bitburg asked, glancing up from his papers, his eyes beginning to carom.

'This isn't the sort of thing to go through channels, Walter,' Morton replied, flopping in one of the armchairs in front of the desk.

'Proper procedure. Sources. The ground rules never vary,' Bitburg said with a perfect symmetry of ambivalence.

'I'll send you a memo. Copy to the Secretary-General. Copy to anyone you like,' Morton said pleasantly. Bitburg had probably already drafted in his mind his cover-your-butt memo.

'The drawback with your memos, David, is that they lack detail.' Bitburg lowered his eyes, as if his own spread of papers would confirm that.

Morton continued to look at the bowed head as he spoke. 'The problem is that some of it's circumstantial, Walter, for sure. You can't put that on paper. But my gut feeling tells me that Igor Tamasara is in China.'

'Proof, proof – where's your proof?' Bitburg leaned back in his chair and looked Morton up and down as if he were inspecting him. The question seemed to have settled Bitburg's eyes. He suddenly stood up, walked over to a bookshelf and took down a leather-tooled volume. 'Have you ever read Macauley, David?'

'A long time ago.'

Morton glanced towards the connecting door to the conference room. 'I'd like to get the briefing started, Walter.'

Bitburg opened the book, riffling the pages, and began to read. '"A perfect historian," Macauley wrote, "must possess an imagination sufficiently powerful to make his narrative effective and picturesque."' Bitburg paused and glanced at Morton before continuing: '"Yet he must control it so absolutely as to content himself with the material he finds, and to refrain from supplying deficiencies by additions of his own."' He stared into Morton's face. 'I've always seen that as the *leitmotif* of Hammer Force, David. In other words, we don't go rushing in until we have proof.'

Bitburg closed the book with a satisfying finality.

'Walter, in counter-intelligence it is the deficiencies we are expected to supply. In this case it is what is the Japanese endgame plan? Is this latest Tokyo riot a prelude to something worse? And these attacks on American installations in Japan and Hong Kong – supposing someone else is behind this? And what about the Chinese? If they have Igor Tamasara working for them – '

'David, David.' Bitburg shook his head almost sorrowfully. 'More of those big "ifs" of yours. I'm not against them as such,' he gave a thin smile, 'but I have to look at the wider picture. If the Chinese spot you in Beijing, there could be serious repercussions.'

He placed the book back on the shelf and faced Morton again. 'Assuming for the moment that Igor Tamasara is in China, that is a long way from being able to say they are using his skills for some nefarious purpose. And any weapon that Tamasara produces – '

'Think what that madman in Baghdad would do with it. Or some terrorist group. Remember Iraq's Supergun, capable of hitting a target a thousand miles away? We know now just how close Saddam came to using it in the Gulf War.'

Bitburg gave another thin smile. 'There you go again, David – more conjecture. There was no proof the gun could do what was claimed for it. You know, you really should read Macauley again. He's very good on self-restraint.'

'That's fine for historians, but a drawback in my job,' Morton said, walking to the connecting door.

After a moment Bitburg followed him.

The conference room was a study in grey – walls, ceiling and carpet in the same uniformly depressing colour. Even the plastic veneer on the table was grey. Built into one wall was a large television screen. Bitburg took his place at one end of the table, distancing himself from the others.

On either side of Danny and Tommy were Anna and the Prof. Lester Finel sat next to Sean Carberry, the head of Covert Action. He had the smile of a talk-show host and the eyes of a homicide cop. Opposite them was Chantal Bouquet, head of Foreign Intelligence. Morton knew she had not attained her fortieth birthday recently without learning a great deal more than most women needed to know about fear and evil. Morton took his seat alongside Danny. A TV remote control was on the table in front of him.

Chantal turned to Morton. 'We haven't found a trace of the Gyroton at what remains of Postbox 97. That's not really surprising. My people say the whole place looked like Sarajevo on a bad day. Nothing's left intact bigger than a rawbolt. They tracked down some of the mob who wrecked the place. One of them remembers a big box on wheels which they took sledgehammers to. But there's no way of knowing if the box is your machine or some other piece of equipment.'

'Keep your people at it, Chantal,' Morton said. He glanced across the table. 'Lester?'

Finel made his habitual curious movement with his left hand as he produced a computer print-out. 'I got one of my people to do a little figuring on the latest North Atlantic trace from Langley. He came up with the conclusion that a Typhoon class sub could have made it to China and back.'

Bitburg leaned forward, his eyes once more on the move. 'Are you trying to say Igor Tamasara made it out of Russia in a submarine?'

'I don't think we can discount anything, Walter,' Finel said.

'Proof, Mr Finel. Where is it?' Whenever Bitburg's anger boiled over he called everyone 'mister'.

For a long moment Morton remained silent. Then in a quiet voice he began. 'I want you all to move forward from the standpoint that Igor Tamasara is in China and continuing with his research. How he got there may have to remain a matter of speculation. But I think Lester's theory is a plausible one. We know the Russians have sold off a number of their subs to the Japanese – '

'But clearly not this one, David!' Bitburg snapped. 'This one was returning to its base.'

Morton ignored the interruption and turned to Chantel. 'Put your best man to keep watch on their Red Banner Northern Fleet. Any sub

86

that moves out I want to know about. I'll get the Americans focusing at their end.'

She made a note.

Morton looked around the table. 'Danny, Tommy and Anna, you're going to form the spearhead of the team I'm taking into Beijing. You'll get detailed operational plans later.' He turned to Carberry. 'Your shooters will provide extra cover.' To the Director of Psychological Assessment he said: 'Prof, you and Chantal will run backstop psycho-profiles of all those we'll need to know about in China. Intelligence assessments. Usual kind of thing.'

Bitburg was halfway out of his chair. 'David, I really must protest. This kind of speculative activity will knock holes in my budget – '

'Hear me out, Walter,' Morton said brusquely. 'It's going to be money well spent.'

He waited a moment longer before continuing: 'To understand why we're going in, I want to give you an overview of the relationship between Japan and China.'

For the next thirty minutes they listened in rapt silence as Morton delivered a concise account of the turbulent history of the two great Pacific powers locked for centuries in conflict. Its root was in colliding ambitions over whose ancient traditions would emerge supreme: China, who had given the region its language and its medicine and five thousand years of the most enduring of civilisations, or Japan, whose imperial lineage extended back through two thousand years, to the Sun Goddess.

He moved back to the present. 'Japan has established itself as an economic and mercantile success without equal. But many Japanese themselves fear they are paying a high price. Japan's extreme Right continues to whip up nationalist feelings. The kind of xenophobia that led to Pearl Harbour. The Emperor is doing everything to check matters. But he's walking a dangerous tightrope in bringing the Throne into the political arena. The extremists are beginning to say he is a puppet of Washington. That kind of thing touches a raw nerve in a people filled with suspicion of all foreigners. The Emperor could get swept aside if he goes too far too quickly. The effects of that could literally be globe-shattering.

'The trigger point for all this could be Hong Kong.'

Those around the table looked at Morton, stunned. He waited for the impact of his words to subside before continuing. 'The British will leave one legacy intact when they depart from Hong Kong – the Triads.

87

And the Beijing regime will continue to do what they have always done, only more so – use the Triads to further their own ends. I am certain that Qiao Peng is the major force behind the recent anti-American feeling that has swept through the Colony and Tokyo.'

He turned to the Prof. 'I want everybody to have a copy of your psycho-profile on Qiao Peng before they leave for Beijing.'

When the Prof spoke his words had a soft tension. 'To get you in the right mind-set, let me just say he is a perfect example of the old Chinese saying that when a man becomes an official even his dogs and chickens go to Heaven.'

Morton gave another smile that seemed on loan. 'Not only could Hong Kong be the trigger factor which could end Japan's Imperial dynasty, it could also bring about conflict between the United States, Japan and China. That could turn into World War Three.'

He told them all he had learned of the secret visit of Cyrus B. Voss to Beijing.

'You are certain ... ?' Bitburg's voice trailed off.

Morton looked directly at him. 'I'm certain, Walter, that the Americans will act, as usual, both from self-interest and a genuine desire to help China, as well as to bring stability to the region. What I was less certain about is how the Chinese will try to provoke a confrontation between Washington and Tokyo in Hong Kong.'

'You said "was", David.' Bitburg's voice was almost a whisper.

Morton told them all he knew about Colin Baskin's work, and how, for sure, Igor Tamasara would have gone beyond the American research. 'If Tamasara has managed to produce a weapon the Chinese would have the means to stage-manage that confrontation,' Morton added.

'But why Hong Kong?' Bitburg asked.

Morton glanced at his watch. He picked up the TV remote and pointed it at the screen. A moment later came the strident music of the CNN global news network, followed by the voice of an anchorman saying they were shortly going over to the White House for a special live briefing by the President's personal physician, Dr Barker.

Marty Fitzpatrick, the White House Press Secretary, stood at the lectern in the crowded press briefing room, exchanging pleasantries with the correspondents, and peered out across the glare of lights. 'For anyone that's new here today the same rules apply as at the President's conferences. Dr Barker reads out his statement without interruption.

Then he takes questions. But I get to choose who asks them. Understand?'

Another chorus came from the reporters.

The Press Secretary turned and motioned for Dr Barker to step up to the lectern.

'Ladies and gentlemen. I have today the results of the President's annual check-up, the laboratory reports and the detailed findings of his physical.' The physician paused and composed his face for the news sound-bite he knew his next words would provide. 'Ladies and gentlemen, I am happy to report that the President is physically fit and mentally sound.'

Then, in a voice filled with what he hoped was the right mixture of patient care and medical authority, Dr Barker read out the results of the check-up. When he finished, Fitzpatrick stepped up beside him. He gave a lazy smile – the signal to the reporters that another of his quotable one-liners was coming up.

'The President scored better on his magnetograph than he would on *Wheel of Fortune!*'

Good-natured groans swept the room. Then hands were in the air, hoping to catch the Press Secretary's eye. 'Right, first question. You, Betty.'

Tradition demanded that the doyenne of the press corps went first. 'Dr Barker, when you said nothing was found to give cause for concern during the President's scan, does that mean something was found that you have decided is of no concern?'

'Good question, Betty,' Fitzpatrick said, glancing at Dr Barker, giving him a few precious seconds to formulate an answer. He looked momentarily floored. Yet in the pre-conference briefing he had said nothing had been found. Why the hesitation?

'Nothing was found. Period,' said Dr Barker finally.

'A supplementary please, Dr Barker. Why did you decide the President needed this examination in the first place? Did you have any cause, any cause at all, to suspect there just might be some abnormality in his brain?'

'There was no prior medical reason for his magnetograph examination. The equipment was there. So why not use it? If we hadn't, I expect some of you would have beefed about the President not getting the best,' replied Dr Barker.

A tall, languid correspondent with the carefully groomed hair of a TV network reporter caught Fitzpatrick's eye and nodded at Dr

Barker. 'Todd Harper, Global Network News. Doctor, as I understand it there are only two magnetographs in the country.'

'That is correct.'

'So they are hardly used for routine examinations?'

'Is that your question, Todd?' Fitzpatrick asked briskly. Once more he had sensed Dr Barker's hesitation. Probably the man's natural reserve made him hesitate. And even for a veteran like the President the confrontation with the press could be intimidating. But Harper did not seem to have noticed anything.

'It's part of it. Here's the other part. Is there any risk at all of any residual effect from such a specialised test?'

When Dr Barker spoke his voice was calm and authoritative. 'Firstly, you are right, Mr Harper. There are only two such machines in the country. And they are normally used only for highly specialist investigations. There is absolutely no risk, either during the scan or afterwards, for the patient. If you like I can let you have the literature. It could help you with your report.'

Harper looked at the Press Secretary. 'How about allowing me to film an actual piece to camera in front of this machine, Marty? It would put your "*Wheel of Fortune*" line into some perspective.'

Fitzpatrick gave a little shrug. 'Let's talk about that later, Todd.'

The Press Secretary peered into the room. 'And now for some more good news. The President has decided to attend the Non-Aligned Nations Conference in Manila. He will be making a stopover in Hong Kong to see for himself the preparations for the handover to the People's Republic of China. During his stay there he hopes to meet with important Chinese political leaders ...'

For a long moment Qiao Peng sat staring at the single piece of paper on his desk. He no longer needed it to reassure him that Operation Silent Voices would go forward. Taking a matchbox from his pocket he set fire to the document. The flames destroyed the fingerprints which would have shown him that the document had been handled by Yaobang Cheng.

Morton turned away from the screen and spoke to the others. 'We now know who Igor Tamasara's target will be. The only question is how does he intend to strike?'

For once Bitburg did not ask for proof.

10

Morning rush hour was over as Li Mufang drove onto Washington's Ohio Drive, which ran alongside the Potomac down to Hains Point. He had arranged to meet Leo there. The radio had promised a breeze. But nothing stirred the trees beside the Tidal Basin and a grey haze hid the sun. Despite its furnace heat he rode with the window down, a form of torture, a test of his will. Slowing down to take a long, deceptive curve, he checked his mirror again. It was hard to see if anyone was following.

For the past hour he had driven a carefully-chosen route from Chinatown. He had stopped twice: at the bank to collect the dollars Qiao Peng had transferred and at a travel agency to pick up the two first-class round-trip air tickets to Beijing. He had paid for them with some of the cash. Passing underneath the Potomac Railroad Bridge he once more checked to make sure that there was no vehicle pulled over to the side. The underpass would be an ideal place for a new tail to take over.

By now Shaoyen should be driving to Hains Point. He had said nothing to her about taking evasive action. There was no point; if anyone suspected her, then they knew too much. He had called Leo from a payphone in the bank lobby. Leo had asked if he knew where Shaoyen was. He sounded upset, which was good. Li had promised he would explain everything when they met. Once more he checked his mirror. There were only a few cars heading down to the Point, tourists probably. Leo had further to drive, so there was time in hand. Li pulled into the kerb and stretched. His shirt was damp and gnats buzzed around his head. Away in the distance 'planes were coming and going from National Airport. He opened the glove compartment and took out the can of iced tea he had put there. It was warm and tasted rancid. He tossed the empty can in the back seat and drove on.

Shortly after noon he reached the Point's parking lot. It was almost empty. Shaoyen's car was already in the far corner. She was leaning against the tailgate, wearing a tight skirt and a jersey halter. Her skin was tanned, but not in the healthy way of the women of his own Yangtze delta.

Li watched Leo's Buick swing onto the lot and stop beside his own car. Overhead, a 737 was descending into National. The constant noise of air traffic would make it more difficult for anyone to eavesdrop. As an extra precaution he switched on the radio to an all-talk station.

Swatting furiously at the gnats, Leo opened the car door. Li smelled the sweat on him as he slid into the passenger seat.

'Why don't you close your window?' Leo grunted.

'It'll take too long for the air-conditioning to cool down.'

'I could do with a cold beer, pal,' Leo said in the vowelly accent Li always found hard to understand.

'Sorry, Leo, I didn't have time to pick up anything.' Li spoke English with the precision of the language laboratory.

Leo squinted at him. 'You said you would explain why Shaoyen's not been home?' He made a belching sound.

'She's over there. By the Chevy.'

Leo glanced to where Shaoyen stood against the car. 'What's she doing there?' He sounded puzzled as he gave another belch.

'That's what I want to talk to you about,' said Li softly. He creased his brow and looked Leo over carefully. 'My sister did not tell you?'

'Tell me what? That she's pregnant, or something?' Leo gave a fat man's wheezy laugh.

'Would it matter if she was?'

'Naw. It would be kind of nice really. A kid with her body and my mind ...' He glanced across the lot. Even from here Shaoyen's nipples could be seen pushing insolently against the cloth.

'No, she's not pregnant,' Li said gently. 'It's worse.'

'Worse? What are you talking about, pal?'

Li watched a United Parcels van drive onto the lot. The middle-aged woman at the wheel wore a company peaked cap. She picked a parking space midway between Shaoyen's car and his own. He reached forward and turned up the radio a decibel. They'd already started to discuss the President's forthcoming trip to Manila. Li gave Leo another careful look and began to speak.

'My sister loves you, Leo. And I take it you love her?'

'Yes. But – '

'Do you love her enough to marry her?' Li asked quickly.

'Marry? Jesus, I've never actually thought of that – '

'It's the only way I can think of to help her.' Li's voice grew more urgent. 'My sister's visa has expired. I have tried to have it extended. But they refused. Yesterday, the police came to the bar looking for her. They said unless she leaves the country in twenty-four hours she will be arrested. After she goes to prison she will still be deported. I called a lawyer. He said this was all part of a big new clampdown on illegals, and that the only way my sister could escape was to marry an American citizen.'

Li made a slow, sad movement with his hand. The van driver was eating a sandwich, staring fixedly ahead. Washington was full of lonely women like her. He turned to look at Leo. 'My sister loves you,' he whispered. 'Before you, there was no one. We Chinese are very careful whom we give ourselves to, especially our women.'

Leo looked across the lot. Shaoyen looked as if she had been crying. A familiar excitement began to course through his body. If they were married she would be his twenty-four hours a day. The sex would be even more unbelievable. 'Marriage ... ? Don't you think I ought to ask her? I mean – '

'It is the Chinese custom for the senior male member of the family to settle such matters,' Li said quickly.

Leo looked at Shaoyen. Why not? They'd have a terrific time. And God knows, he loved her.

He nodded. 'Okay, pal ... and I'm glad to have you as my brother-in-law.'

Li smiled.

'Not brother-in-law, brother. I love you like a brother – pal!' He reached over and gave Leo an embrace.

'Okay,' said Leo. 'I can get a licence in a couple of hours. But we're both going to have to get the usual medical checks. That could take a day, maybe two.'

'Too long, brother! Shaoyen will be deported by then!'

'Jesus, pal! I can't buck the whole system,' Leo protested.

Li reached under the dashboard and produced the wallet containing the air tickets. Still smiling, he handed the wallet to Leo. 'Part of my wedding gift to you,' Li said formally. From his trousers pocket he produced a roll of bills. 'The second part. Two thousand dollars. For your honeymoon.' He thrust the money at Leo and waved to Shaoyen. She started to walk towards the car, a tote bag in one hand.

'I don't understand,' Leo said, holding the tickets in one hand and the money in the other.

Li smiled at him. 'You have a furlough, right? You use it to fly to Beijing with my sister and have a traditional Chinese wedding which will be registered at the American Embassy there. Then you fly back here with your bride and continue your honeymoon. As Mrs Leo Schrag she will be as much an American citizen as you are. The first in my family! We will have a big party!' He leaned forward and gave Leo another embrace. Over his shoulder he saw Shaoyen smiling. Beyond, the woman in the van was eating an apple.

'Jeez, pal!' Leo said, disengaging himself. 'You have it all planned!'

'For my sister I would do anything. And from now on, for you as well,' Li said with total sincerity.

Shaoyen opened the near door and tossed the bag on the seat. She leaned forward and kissed Li on the cheek chastely and Leo on the mouth, forcing her tongue into his mouth.

'When do we go?' Leo asked.

'Today, in two hours. In the morning you will be in Beijing. I will call our family to make all the wedding arrangements.'

'And what about a visa?' Leo asked.

'No problem. Our family is very powerful. Your passport will be stamped in Beijing.'

'But I'll need clothes – '

'I have everything you need.' Shaoyen indicated the bag. 'And we shall both buy new clothes in Beijing.' She giggled and said something in Mandarin to Li. He laughed.

'My sister says you don't need any clothes on honeymoon!'

'You sleep on 'plane,' Shaoyen said. 'Then you big and strong for honeymoon!'

'Okey-dokey,' Leo said happily. He shoved the tickets into one pocket, the money in another as Li started the engine.

In the United Parcels van the FBI agent behind the wheel spoke quietly into a throat mike. Her name was Marjorie, and she was divorced and a grandmother.

'I got some good pictures,' Marjorie said.

94

The camera was mounted in a corner of the windscreen and was remote-controlled. All she had to do was press a button at the end of a flex attached to the steering column.

'We got only snatches of sound to match them,' grunted Song, one of the agents in the back.

'And it's going to take days to piece them together,' added the other agent, Teng, pulling off his headphones.

Song called to the driver. 'You recognise the woman or the other guy?'

'No. But this is only my first day on the case,' Marjorie said. She started up the van. 'They're pulling out. The woman's left her car over at the long-stay area, like she's going to be gone for a while.'

'I'll call in and have somebody check it over,' said Teng.

Keeping a distance, Marjorie drove back up Ohio Drive behind Li's car.

Qiao Peng had already made two telephone calls.

The first alerted all those on duty along China's separate borders to be on special watch; particular attention should be paid to anyone claiming to be a tourist. Foreign intelligence agents favoured tourism or educational visits as a cover. Morton would send someone, of course, but even he would be unable to change the course of events. No one man could.

The second telephone call was to Hong Kong, to an apartment block on Hennessy Road, where Tung Shi had been waiting. He had told the Triad Supreme Dragon head to have his men keep a similar watch on flights and ships arriving in Hong Kong. They had then discussed what more needed to be done by the Triads to foment further trouble against America.

He was about to make a third telephone call now. Vice-Premier Oleg Kazenko of Russia had special responsibility for the former Soviet Navy. In that afternoon spent together in the total privacy of the Zurich headquarters of Credit Suisse, he had learned that Kazenko was a Mongol. Mongols had been wheeler-dealers long before Kublai Khan had pitched his tents on the site of the Forbidden City. They had bargained into the evening before a deal had been struck. Every time a Typhoon class submarine was sent on a secret voyage, two million American dollars would be lodged in Kazenko's account in Credit Suisse.

Qiao Peng glanced at his watch. It would be close to midnight now in

Moscow, but Kazenko would still be at his desk immediately below the large dome of the Council of Ministers Building in the Kremlin. From there the new rulers of Russia uneasily governed and took every opportunity to line their own pockets with secret deals. The 'phone was answered on the second ring. Qiao Peng immediately put down the receiver, waited a full five seconds and dialled again. The pause was to enable Kazenko to activate his scrambler system. After the Zurich meeting the state-of-the-art apparatus had been couriered to Moscow. The director of Qiao Peng's Technical Services Division had said that the equipment was sophisticated enough to defeat even American scrambler-breakers.

'Good weather, Vice-Premier,' Qiao Peng said when the 'phone was answered again.

'Here we have snow,' intoned the voice from Moscow. The exchange was their pre-arranged confirmation that the scrambler was working.

Qiao Peng came straight to the point. 'I need another delivery. But this time the boat must remain in the area longer, and bring a cargo south to a rendezvous with a junk off Fujian Province.'

There was silence on the line. Kazenko would be consulting a map, calculating how much more he should ask. 'That is close to Taiwan. The Americans have a satellite tracking station there. The risks will be far greater than before. So must be the price.' The Vice-Premier was not quite able to disguise the greed underpinning his words.

'And I have calculated accordingly. Six million American dollars will be deposited in your account, one third now, the balance on completion.'

'Seven million. Two thirds now. A third on completion.'

Qiao Peng sighed. 'Very well.'

There was no time to haggle. He continued: 'This time you will send the Typhoon by the northern route, under the polar ice into the Sea of Japan. Between Korea and the southern island of Japan, it will surface long enough for the American satellites to detect it. Then it will continue to Quingdao. I will arrange for your captain to receive further orders there. But he must be told as little as possible, except this is a joint training exercise between our respective navies.'

'This cargo, will it be accompanied?'

Qiao Peng shrugged. Kazenko would find out anyway. And later it would protect China's involvement if Kazenko realised he was an accomplice. 'Yes. By some of your countrymen.'

'Who are these people?'

96

Qiao Peng felt his brow crease, but his voice remained impassive. 'They are Professor Tamasara and his assistants.'

A pair of spectacles perched on the end of his nose, the President read the briefing notes Thack had prepared on how much to say to whom – and why.

The British Ambassador, the saturnine doyen of the Washington diplomatic corps, was the first outsider to learn a still closely-guarded secret: the true purpose behind the President's stopover in Hong Kong, and the encouraging response of Chairman Hu.

During the constant coming and going from the Oval Office, the President's secretary, Madeleine Masters, remained a silent figure in a corner, taking notes of what was said. They recorded, among much else, the President's scrambled telephone call to the American Ambassador in Tokyo, Hershel Lincoln. The President had instructed Ambassador Lincoln to seek an urgent private audience with the Emperor to fully brief him. The Emperor's support would be critical.

'Hersh, I don't want a war, a trade war or any other kind, with Japan or anyone,' Madeleine Masters noted the President had said.

Dusk gathered over the Rose Garden and the steady pace continued. Thack ushered people in and led them out, a restless, tireless figure, gliding across the thick rug, a veritable powerhouse, always ready to speak to the President, but never for him.

In between meetings and 'phone calls, the President removed his spectacles and rubbed the bridge of his nose and ate another of Forbes' exquisite tray meals. Afterwards the work resumed. A trip to Texas for a spot of informal politicking was rescheduled, a visit to Florida cancelled. A charity film premier in Los Angeles brought a grunt from the President to send the Vice-President.

'It's got a war-in-space theme,' Thack said.

The President smiled. 'Better he says we should declare war on the Martians than on the Japanese!' He stood up, stretched and moved his neck in the exercise Dr Barker had suggested as a tension-breaker. 'Anything else? It's been a long day.'

'You've got a seven o'clock with Bill Gates. He wants to give you a run-down on Langley's who's who in Hong Kong and Manila.'

Thack turned to a bank of television sets in a corner. 'Want to see how your day played for the big hitters? Marty says they're leading on your trip. Second item's Herb Barker's fifteen seconds of fame. Global News have done a piece with Todd Harper being fed through the magnetograph. It's a change from his usual stand-up-and-be-counted routine on our front lawn.'

The President frowned. 'Harper still worries me. He's smarter than a rattler. If he even got a sniff of what's cooking he'd build a fire that could send everything up in flames.'

'Stop worrying! That's why Marty gave him his little exclusive. There's nothing like that to keep Harper in line. If he thinks there's more where that came from he's not going to foul his nest,' Thack said.

The Chief of Staff walked over to the sets and turned them on.

In the control centre bunker Igor Tamasara supervised final preparations for another test.

In the centre of the floor, its outer casing made from milled steel and painted matt black, the Gyroton was on a flat car. The rail track extended beyond a sliding door. Inspection hatches in the side panels allowed access to its interior. A snub-nosed barrel, resembling an outsized telephoto camera lens, was calibrated and pointed towards a narrow wall opening to one side of the observation window. The controls were at the back of the machine. The operator sat on a bucket seat. Igor Tamasara stood beside him.

He turned to one of the other technicians holding a clipboard of papers. 'We must reduce the machine's physical size, but without any loss of power.'

The man consulted his clipboard. 'The energy fall-off will still remain the same over the distance travelled,' he pronounced.

'How long will it take you to complete the reduction?'

Once more the technician riffled through his worksheets. 'A couple of months – '

'You have two weeks!'

'Yes, Comrade Professor.' The technician knew better than to argue. Igor Tamasara ordered the test area to be evacuated.

A mile away down-range, Dr Fretov reported that the area was clear of everyone except the human guinea pigs. His jeep disappeared behind the mound which concealed the necropsy centre with its autopsy rooms and attendant pathologists.

Igor Tamasara joined Dr Petrarova at the window. The building chosen for the experiment was protected by sandbags and barrels filled with water.

'Activate hemi-synch,' Igor Tamasara ordered.

The Gyroton operator manipulated a toggle-switch. Tamasara and Dr Petrarova walked to a bank of wall-mounted monitor screens. Cameras concealed in the building provided a view of every guinea pig. Each cell contained an electric bell.

Dr Petrarova nodded at the screens. 'We have two Kazakhs, one a woman. Three Miao. Two Moslems, a married couple. A Han and a Buddhist Dai. It's the best I could do, neurologically speaking, to get a cross-mix of ethnic groups. But it should provide useful data until those foreigners arrive.'

'They look very relaxed,' Igor Tamasara said.

'Each one has received a mild sedative. There will be absolutely no effect on their neurological output,' Dr Petrarova said.

'Hemi-synch at full strength,' reported the operator.

Dr Petrarova pressed a wall button to activate the bells. On the screens the prisoners began the routines they had been given. The Buddhist monk squatted cross-legged in prayer. The Moslem couple rolled out a sleeping mat and curled into one another. The Han tribesman stood at his window, peering into the gathering dusk. The Kazakh and his woman began to pace around the cell. The three Miao tribesmen started to talk volubly among themselves.

'Start alpha block at forty. Subliminal input at one-point-five pulsing,' Tamasara ordered.

The Gyroton's barrel began to traverse. Only the click of the calibrations moving through their settings broke the total silence in the control room. On a screen, the tribesman at the window suddenly thrust his hands to his head and screamed. A moment later he collapsed on the floor, writhing and moaning. Next the Buddhist Dai keeled over.

Igor Tamasara spoke urgently. 'Reduce setting to thirty, input to one-zero pulsing!'

The Moslem couple were prostrate on the ground. The Kazakhs man and woman had collapsed against one another. Finally the Miao tribesmen fell on their faces.

'Stop the pulsing!' shouted Tamasara.

The terrible silence was broken by Dr Petrarova. 'Igor Viktorovitch, the problem may be – '

'I know what the problem is! The Gyroton still cannot control their minds in matters of everyday routine! It's these damned scalar resonance electrical currents, Sergei Nikolai. They are swamping the brain cell membranes, destroying their fibrous cover and cell structure.'

Struggling to control his sudden, savage fury, Tamasara turned back to the screens. Soldiers were removing the bodies. He turned to a technician. 'Tell Dr Fretov that I want him to conduct each autopsy personally and that I want a full report on each brain on my desk by this evening!'

The technician hurried from the bunker.

Calmer now, Igor Tamasara continued to lecture Dr Petrarova. 'Until we get the balance right between the scalar resonance currents, making sure they both sum to zero, we will have this problem of only being able to kill! Not control!'

He nodded towards the Gyroton. The technical crew were hooking up the rail car to a small diesel engine which would tow it back to the workshops. 'We must ensure that the scalar resonance moves in the right mode,' Tamasara said. 'Without that we cannot guarantee mind control.'

Dr Petrarova briefly touched him on the arm. There was something close to excitement in his voice. 'Do you remember that report, Igor Viktorovitch, the one KGB sent us some years ago? You had just come to 97 and we were all concerned that the Americans could be ahead of us in mind-engineering?'

Igor Tamasara frowned. 'I remember some people being concerned. I never was.'

'Of course,' murmured Dr Petrarova quickly. 'But the report mentioned that the one CIA scientist who could be a threat was the neurologist, Baskin.'

'So?'

'In a follow-up report, the KGB said this Baskin had either resigned or had been fired by the CIA.'

'And? Did the KGB offer him a job?' Tamasara asked witheringly.

'I've no idea, Igor Viktorovitch. But what I am saying is that we should find Baskin.'

Tamasara gave a short, icy laugh. 'And how do we do that? Baskin could be dead. Or living quietly in some corner of the United States. He could have changed his name. He could have done anything, could be living anywhere! I have less than three weeks, not the rest of my life to solve our problems. I'm not going to waste time – '

'Read this,' said Dr Petrarova triumphantly. He removed a sheet of paper from his pocket and gave it to Igor Tamasara.

'What is this?' Tamasara demanded.

'A clinical report Baskin's daughter wrote last year on the potential of scalar resonance currents as a healing medium in cancer. It's pure theory, of course …'

Igor Tamasara scanned the paper as Dr Petrarova continued: 'This Dr Kate Baskin works at Magill University in Montreal. Surely it would be an easy matter to check with her whether her father is alive and, if so, where he is now?'

Igor Tamasara read the paper a second time, more slowly. It *was* theory: this idea that scalar resonance was capable of preventing the formation of cancerous cells in the human body by enabling the mind to exert a control powerful enough to ward off the onset of malignancy. But the argument was well presented and showed not only a sound grasp of cellular histology but also of brainwave theory. At the end of the paper, a reprint from the respected *Journal of Ultramolecular Medicine*, Kate Baskin paid tribute to her father's earlier research.

Igor Tamasara looked thoughtfully at Dr Petrarova. 'You are right, Sergei Nikolai. Let's see if this Colin Baskin is alive,' he said softly.

He walked to a wall 'phone and dialled the direct line of Qiao Peng.

In the Hammer Force conference room on the ground floor, the Prof continued to address the team for Beijing. Danny and the shooters listened intently. No matter how many times they had heard the set lecture, the Prof's words were a salutary reminder. For Tommy the lecture was a masterful exposition of the psychological pressures they would all be facing soon. Anna, despite working closely with the Prof, felt almost a sense of disappointment as she sensed he was coming to the end.

'… it is an axiom of behavioural psychology that no one "owns" his or her identity. Never is this more true than in your work. Each of you belongs to the environment that nurtured you. But to survive in China you must – and this is an imperative – assume the psychological identity of the Chinese. Physically, you cannot. But mentally you must think like them. That means being as paradoxical as they are.'

He paused, looking into each face, as if seeking reassurance that they would, indeed, do this. 'Remember, they are masters of agriculture, but have to import grain. They have the world's oldest musical tradition, yet now write the worst kind of music. They are child-loving to a fault, but make it a crime for a couple to have more than one child. They turned a man, Mao, into a god, and have now besmirched his memory. They are admirable and infuriating, humorous and priggish, modest and mendacious, loyal and mercenary, sadistic and tender.

'If you remember all this, you will come a little closer to understanding the Chinese.'

He stopped abruptly and, without another word, strode from the conference room. Danny stood up and began to distribute the air tickets for the long flight to Hong Kong.

11

Fifty-five thousand feet above the Dnieper River as it flowed through Central Russia, Morton was linked to the communications complex in the former KGB headquarters on Moscow's Dzerzhinsky Square. The aircraft was Hammer Force's flying battle headquarters. In charge was the Concorde Communications Officer, CCO.

On a screen in the communications centre were Professor Dimitri Zakharov, Russia's foremost expert on bioelectrics, and General Yuri Savenko, the Deputy Director of Russia's new security force. Physically, they looked ill-matched. The Professor's flesh was stretched and as frail as tissue paper over his nose, cheekbones and high-domed forehead. The General's features were florid, his hair still thick and dark. A strong, robust peasant's face which Morton knew hid one of the sharpest minds in Russia. He had worked with Yuri in the past and trusted him, the way he trusted Bill Gates. There were few he was nowadays prepared to say that about.

Morton glanced at his notes then looked at the screen. 'What you're really saying, Professor, is that Igor Tamasara's work in Postbox 97 had not really gone beyond crude behavioural tests.'

Dimitri Zakharov gave the slightest nod. 'This is my opinion, yes. What little I have been able to glean about Academician Tamasara's work indicates he was having the sort of problem we have all faced – controlling the effects of electromagnetism on the endocrine, metabolic and cardiovascular systems.'

The Professor paused and stared fixedly from the screen, the gifted lecturer imparting complex information to a bright student. 'All living things have a built-in capability of distinguishing between electromagnetic data and filtering out input they have not encountered before. At their simplest the bioeffects can be seen from how animals and humans adapt to unfamiliar surroundings. A common effect is stress. They become nervous and stay close to familiar objects they have brought with them, until they make the necessary adjustments to their new environment.

'This is especially common in those who are suddenly removed a considerable distance from their surroundings. Businessmen encounter it after long-distance trips. They put it down to jet-lag. In fact it is the effect of entering unfamiliar electromagnetic fields. Companies recognise this, even if they do not understand the biomechanics involved, by insisting executives should rest for a day or so after a long flight before starting important business discussions.'

Savenko gave a sour little smile. 'Oh to be a businessman ...'

Professor Zakharov continued in the same controlled voice. 'But when stress is too strong or persistent, the results become obvious and often serious. Sometimes they are even irreversible. The thyroid gland and the basal metabolic rate are the most commonly affected. But the worst damage is to the cardiovascular system. In Academician Tamasara's research papers appear the same changes in blood levels of glucose, globulin, lipids and haemoglobin concentration that other Soviet scientists have reported in animals exposed to extremely low-frequency electromagnetic fields. The most common effects were changes in the relative number of various types of white blood cells.'

Morton glanced at a folder before him on the desktop. Embossed on the cover was the Hammer Force logo of intertwined bolts of lightning. The file contained the Prof's psycho-profile of Qiao Peng. 'If someone had cancer would exposure to those waves worsen it?'

'Most certainly, yes.'

'Even if there was not direct exposure?'

Professor Zakharov gave a ghostly smile. 'If someone was within, say, five kilometres of a properly focused electromagnetic beam, the residual effect would almost be the same as direct exposure. But that is a long way from saying that Academician Tamasara achieved such a result.'

'How can you be so certain?' Morton asked.

There was a brooding silence from Moscow. Professor Zakharov sat in his chair, staring bleakly out of the screen. 'I cannot be certain,' he said finally. 'There was much done in my country that was dark. To scientists like myself who tried to remember that our first principle is to do no harm, men like Academician Tamasara were a disgrace. But as I have tried to indicate to you, there is nothing I have read which shows that Academician Tamasara achieved any real success in his prime area of research.'

On an adjoining screen Morton saw Bill Gates lean forward in one of the cubicles on the communications floor at Langley. Both screens were interlinked, enabling Morton to run an audio-visual conference call.

'Bill?' Morton prompted.

Gates shifted in his seat. 'Even a year ago, Professor, we wouldn't have been having this conversation – right?' Gates began.

Professor Zakharov gave a little nod.

Gates leaned further forward, his face almost filling the screen, causing the image to distort. The CCO made an adjustment to bring Gates back into sharp focus as he continued in the same flat, emotionless voice. 'Professor, you could be wrong about how far Igor Tamasara has gone. In the last few hours I've learned how far some of our own people had gotten before they had the plug pulled.'

Like Morton, they all sensed the effort this was costing Gates. More implacable words came from the screen hooked up to Washington. 'They began by trying to find out the effects of electromagnetic energy produced by a nuclear explosion.' Gates gave a tight smile. 'Those were the days when we thought you were going to nuke us, Professor.'

From Moscow came a swift nod.

'Our people discovered that certain pulsed microwave beams that accompany an explosion could be turned into an effective weapon to enhance the effects of drugs on the brain, especially the psychotropic ones, the so-called mind-benders. They then went on to see if they could dispense with the drugs and still produce the same effect.'

Morton was making notes.

'Our people found that when microwaves of between 300 and 3,000 megahertz were pulsed at specific rates, animals could "hear" them.

'Next they tried it out on humans.'

Gates paused and stared into the camera, and there was cold anger in his voice when he continued: 'I'm proud of my country, as proud as any man can be. But I'm not proud of what was done in her name by those scientists.'

He looked down for a moment.

'We have all done things we cannot be proud of,' Professor Zakharov murmured with surprising gentleness.

Gates continued as if the interruption had not occurred. 'Our scientists secretly used mental patients and prisoners in their experiments to try to establish whether the microwaves could be sensed somewhere in the temporal region just above and slightly in front of the ears. They thought the best results could be obtained by making their guinea pigs face the beam. That also created the greatest damage.'

Gates glanced down at a piece of paper. 'In one experiment an attempt was made to beam a pulsed microwave into a human brain. The intention was to deliver undetectable instructions. To see if it was possible to create a programmed assassin.

'That's when the plug was pulled.'

Morton broke the lengthening silence with a question. 'Who were the people who did this work, Bill?'

Gates smiled grimly. 'When the plug was pulled, it was the night of the Shredders' Ball. The stuff I told you about got misfiled, and so escaped going into the maw. It's not much, but it's enough for me to be pretty damned convinced that if our people travelled that far down the road to producing a zombie, then Igor Tamasara would have gone the extra mile.'

The silence returned.

At a little before ten o'clock, US Ambassador Hershel Lincoln drove past another one of Tokyo's art galleries specialising in the latest Japanese craze for holography. On either side of the wide-lane carriageway Japanese limousines were taking senior executives to the exclusive restaurants around Akasaka and Ginza. None of the passengers gave a second glance to the foreigner at the wheel of a modest Mazda.

Hershel Lincoln had chosen to drive the family car rather than be chauffeured in the stretch Continental which came with his post as the United States Ambassador to the Imperial Court of Japan. In direct contravention of his own instruction that no Embassy staff member was to travel in public without an armed Marine escort after the continued attacks on Americans, the Ambassador was alone and unarmed. He had told no one of his destination or of the call from the President which had prompted him to drive across the city to keep his appointment with the Emperor. It had taken the best part of a day to fix the meeting. He knew his tone-perfect Japanese had once more surprised the flunkeys who manned the 'phones in the Palace's outer office.

He was confident that the Mazda would provide the necessary anonymity against the marauding gangs who had once more taken to the streets chanting anti-American slogans. Their behaviour was part of a phenomenon few in Washington really understood even now. As the Japanese had continued to widen their commercial bridgeheads in the United States, it had led to a fear back home that such massive investment would inevitably lead to the 'Americanisation' of Japan by its business community, eager to make further profits by promoting for domestic consumption what was being attacked as America's 'cola and hamburger society'. These feelings were being exploited by the powerful xenophobic force behind the mobs.

The Ambassador drove carefully, listening to All-Nippon local radio broadcasting live reports of renewed disturbances in several parts of the city. He slowed to pass the crowd watching the huge video screen above Shimbashi Rail Station, which relayed live pictures of a mob attacking one of Tokyo's most famous landmarks, the Ashai Beer Hall. The multi-floored tavern was now one of the few places where American beer was available.

The hall's curvaceous pillars and rippling walls had been designed by a foreigner – just as he himself had contributed to the city's forest of Manhattan-ish towers when Tokyo had decided to imitate New York. That had been thirty years ago, when he was an architect and Tokyo his ever-expanding sketchpad for fantasies which became stunning visions in glass and concrete: buildings with spires or topped with bubbles, or shaped to resemble sharpened cleavers. It was then that he had first come to love the city and admire its people. When the President offered him the ambassadorial post he had jumped at the chance to return and continue his love affair with them. He spoke their language fluently, and understood their customs. He understood why it was that the old citadel of the Shoguns – Japan's military rulers – had become a great distorting mirror reflecting the good and bad. Shaken to pieces in the earthquake in 1923, carpet-bombed in 1945, the Japanese had been severed from their history – except for the forested acres of the Imperial Palace.

He could see it now, an oasis of darkness in a manic light show. More even than Las Vegas, Tokyo had become a heaven for aficionados of neon trash. Even the capsule hotels, whose accommodation consisted of a version of high-tech coffins, had their vulgar flashing displays. He loved it all. It was that understanding, offered without arrogance or anger, which had brought him into the Imperial presence.

The Emperor had read his article proposing a dramatic solution to Tokyo's overcrowding: buildings should not be fixed, permanent entities, but capable of growing like plants to meet changing requirements.

He had called it organic architecture. He had been summoned to the Imperial Palace and spent an entire afternoon outlining his ideas. So had begun a deep and respectful friendship between the Emperor and himself.

Driving through another smoked-glass-and-concrete canyon, the high buildings faced with movie screens and electronic display hoardings, the Ambassador wondered again how long the Emperor would be able to maintain their relationship. The extremists were getting more volatile by the day. Yet, Hershel Lincoln simply did not believe that Japan was girding itself to launch another war – let alone against the United States – despite its renowned commercial aggression and a need to dominate everyone and everything it touched. Filled with optimism he drove up to the guard house above the outer moat of the Imperial Palace, presented his diplomatic passport, waited for the sentry to carefully inspect it, acknowledged the salute and drove across the moat's bridge. The sounds of one of the world's most congested cities gave way to a peace unchanged over the centuries.

The guard posts cut into the trunks of trees or concealed in shrubbery were from the days when the Imperial sentries carried swords. Now there were sensors, trip-wires and remote cameras to protect the Imperial Presence. Minutes after entering the heavily-wooded grounds, the Ambassador parked before the newly-refurbished east wing. A chamberlain in full morning dress waited in the doorway. He bowed formally but, in the tradition of court etiquette, offered no verbal greeting. The chamberlain led the way through a series of corridors on whose walls hung a stunning combination of traditional and contemporary Japanese art. From time to time they passed open doors, offering glimpses of gracious rooms. One was furnished with a white grand piano, another with display cases for the Emperor's collection of rare butterflies. A third room contained a spinning jenny, reflecting the Empress's own interest in textiles.

As they crossed the marbled floor of a small gallery, Hershel Lincoln paused to look at the four large photographs hung one on each wall. They were of buildings whose sweeping, curling and configurated lines echoed traditional temple architecture. They had been the first structures he had designed for the city. He felt a surge of pleasure at the tribute the Emperor had paid him. It might also explain why he had not been more closely questioned by Ko Matzuda, the Emperor's principal private secretary, when he had sought this audience. Matzuda's anti-American feelings were barely concealed behind icy manners. He had told Matzuda the reason for the meeting was to discuss a matter close to the Emperor's heart. He suspected that the secretary assumed it was once more architecture.

The chamberlain finally knocked at a door halfway along another corridor. When a voice spoke from within the room, the flunkey fell to his knees and opened the door. Head still bowed he shuffled into the room as custom demanded servants must enter the Imperial Presence. Hershel Lincoln walked into the Emperor's study, while the chamberlain, still on his knees, slowly and carefully backed out of the room and closed the door behind him. The Emperor came forward from the fireplace. In the glow of the flames he had delicate features which were almost feminine; a small, well-shaped nose and wide, dark eyes that held the fire's light. His jet-black hair was close cut. He wore a *yakata*, a simple one-piece garment, and sandals. He used a remote control in his hand to switch off the TV set in a corner.

'Welcome, Hershel.'

'Thank you, Your Majesty. I am sorry to call upon you so late.'

'It is never too late for a valued friend,' the Emperor said. He motioned the Ambassador to an armchair, then sat opposite him.

Even when seated the difference in their physical appearance was marked. Hershel Lincoln was altogether a bigger man, wide-shouldered and heavily muscled. His large bald head was freshly shaven. His suit fitted him tightly.

The Emperor motioned to the TV. 'You had no trouble getting here? I saw the latest pictures. Sometimes I wonder if our technology has not gone too far in bringing disasters into our home as they happen. Surely it only encourages more violence – like in your Los Angeles riots?'

He looked searchingly into the Ambassador's face. He trusted this man, he valued his opinion.

Hershel Lincoln smiled. 'In my country there's this inalienable belief that everyone has the God-given right to point a camera where they want.'

'Ah, the American media ...' The Emperor laughed, almost softly. 'But I forget. A drink? I have a new malt I would welcome your opinion on.'

He stood up and walked over to a cabinet. For a moment he busied himself pouring whiskies, then returned with the tumblers. They sipped in silence for a while, savouring their drinks, and agreed that the whisky was excellent. For a moment longer they exchanged pleasantries. Then the Emperor's features composed themselves.

'I am sure you have not driven halfway across our city to keep me company, Mr Ambassador.'

The switch to formality was the signal for Hershel Lincoln to come to the true purpose of his visit. He set down his glass and stared at the Emperor.

Beyond, from the Palace gardens, came the cry of a peacock. The Ambassador waited a moment longer and then began to explain in a careful voice the reason behind the President's visit to Hong Kong.

General Savenko had arranged for the Concorde to land and refuel at a military airport twenty miles north of Moscow. He was waiting on the tarmac when the 'plane landed, dressed in fatigues, a pistol at the hip. He led the way to an office in the control tower. Through its smeared window panes Morton saw the tankers preparing to pull away from the aircraft. He continued to listen to Yuri making another 'phone call, this time to the Naval Station at Gremikha, on the shore of the Barents Sea. Gremikha was where Russia's Typhoon class submarines were berthed.

'I don't care if he's got amoebic dysentery – haul him out of there!' Savenko roared into the 'phone. He did not bother to cup his hand over the mouthpiece as he glowered at Morton. 'This damn fool captain is going to find himself commanding a fishing boat if he doesn't get off the toilet!'

Morton smiled. Patience had never been one of Yuri's virtues. In the past thirty minutes what little he had had swiftly evaporated as he tried to learn from where the *Rodina* – the Motherland – had returned to the submarine dock of the Red Banner Northern Fleet. Morton had told him the *Rodina* was the Typhoon class boat the Americans had spotted in the North Atlantic and had asked him to discover the purpose of the voyage and who had authorised it. The chief assistant in Vice-Premier Kazenko's office had directed him to telephone the Admiralty building on the opposite side of Red Square. There, the Commander of the Strategic Submarine Flotilla referred him to Red Banner Northern Fleet Headquarters in St Petersburg. The Admiral-in-Charge told him to call Operations at Murmansk. When the Vice-Admiral First Rank (Submarine) at Murmansk had said there was a standing order that all Typhoon movements were still restricted, Yuri's wrath had boiled over. He had warned the senior officer he had more to lose than his Hero of the Soviet Union's Silver Star. The audibly shaken Vice-Admiral had told him to call the Base Commander at Gremikha.

Morton heard a click over the speaker-phone. Then a formal voice. 'Captain Malenko, Base Commander, speaking. How can I help you, General?'

'You are a line officer, not a *zampolit*?' barked Savenko.

A *zampolit* was the political officer attached to each naval base.

'A line officer, General,' Malenko confirmed.

'And you have taken your new oath of allegiance to the Republic?'

When Russia had wrested control of the former Soviet Union Navy for itself, its members had been asked to swear new allegiance.

'Of course. Why do you ask? Is this a political matter you are calling about? If so, I must refer you to the Captain *zampolit* – '

'It's an operational matter, Captain,' Savenko said, crouching over the 'phone.

'Then how can I help you?'

Morton saw Yuri's face relax. A stern closed-mouth smile lightened his face. 'The *Rodina*, where has it returned from?'

There was a moment's silence on the line. 'I fear in this instance I cannot, after all, assist you,' apologised Malenko.

Savenko's smile had gone, the growl back. 'Why not, Captain?'

'The *Rodina* has effectively been detached from the flotilla.'

'On whose orders?'

There was another silence.

'Vice-Premier Kazenko's,' Malenko finally said.

'Savenko glanced quickly at Morton.

'How long has the *Rodina* been detached?'

'Six months this week.'

Morton nodded. Gremikha was only a short distance from the camp where Igor Tamasara and the other scientists had disappeared.

'What were the detachment orders?' Savenko asked.

'They allow the *Rodina* to request fuel and supplies to travel anywhere without explaining her mission. It is my understanding that she is supposed to test the NATO sonars and American satellite capabilities.'

There was a hint of sarcasm in Savenko's next question. 'You believe that, Captain? That we are doing this now when we need the West to help us?'

'That sounds like a political question, General.'

Savenko laughed. This Malenko was no fool. He clearly understood that serving your country meant staying clear of the political minefields.

'What is your personal opinion, Captain? Not for the record. Just for me to not have to trouble you again,' Savenko said softly.

This time there was no hesitation. 'I don't think *Rodina* is on anti-sonar or surveillance work. To do that she would need a refit. There hasn't been one,' Malenko said.

'Who is her captain?'

'Marlo. He was the *zampolit* at Archangel Naval Base before he was given this command.'

'Marlo? I know this name,' said Savenko.

'Josef Marlo. He is the son-in-law of Vice-Premier Kazenko. Some of us feel he would never have been given his command but for the family connection.'

'Now I remember. Was there not some scandal involving a sailor ...?'

'Nothing was ever proved, General. And before a court of enquiry could be convened the sailor had hanged himself.'

'Or someone hanged him,' murmured Savenko.

'Like I said, General, rumours. Is this why you have called – something new Marlo has done?'

Savenko ignored the question and put another of his own. 'Is he a good sailor?'

'He sails his boat like a *zampolit* – by the book. If his father-in-law told him to sink it with all hands on board, he would probably do so, General.'

Savenko chuckled appreciatively. 'You do not like this Marlo, Captain?'

'Frankly – no.'

'Where is Marlo now?'

'Red pennanting.'

'What? What is that?'

A laugh came from the speaker-phone. 'Sorry. When a Typhoon is ready for sea, she flies a red pennant. Marlo has just hoisted his. He'll be out of here in an hour.'

'Can he be stopped?'

'No. Not without Vice-Premier Kazenko's written order.'

'Do you know what his sailing orders are?'

'No. They would have come directly from the Vice-Premier's office.'

Morton made a gesture to Savenko. The General nodded.

'Captain, I have someone here who wishes to ask you further questions. You can speak to him as freely as you have to me.'

Morton moved closer to the speaker 'phone. 'Captain, how many trips has the *Rodina* made since being detached?'

'Two.'

'Did she carry any passengers?'

'On the first trip there was one. He arrived here shortly before sailing time. His papers said he was an engineer from the Admiralty.'

'Is there any record of the man's name?'

'No. Because the *Rodina* was detached, the usual record-keeping in her case was not followed.'

'And the second time?' Morton asked.

'Two passengers. They were also listed as engineers.'

'Did any of them return with the submarine?'

'To here, no. But they could have gone ashore at Murmansk. The *Rodina* stopped there first.'

'Is that usual?'

'Malenko hesitated.

Savenko leaned towards the speaker. 'It's okay, Captain. You don't have to mention anything classified,' the General said quickly.

'Murmansk has special facilities to check if certain ... sensitive equipment on each Typhoon has been exposed to ... well, let's call it unfriendly surveillance.'

Morton waited a moment to let Malenko settle. He continued in the same careful voice.

'I know you have said her special sailing orders are not known to you. But could they, for instance, have involved sailing to China and back?'

'Well ... yes. Except that she returned from the Atlantic both times. The normal route to Chinese waters is the polar one and down through the Sea of Japan.'

'And this new trip – ' Morton prompted.

'Yes, that's polar. Though she's officially detached, the *Rodina*'s still had to file an exit route from here. It takes her past the Kanin Peninsula and north past Novaya Zemlya. From there it's under the polar ice,' Malenko said.

'How long would it take her to reach Chinese waters, Captain?'

'In the old days, when we had to keep a watch for the Americans, it could take a week or more. There'd be a lot of ducking and weaving. But now that the Americans have only a few Hunter class subs in the area, the *Rodina* should make it in a few days.'

Morton had a last question. 'These Typhoon class submarines the Japanese have bought from you. Could they be mistaken for the *Rodina*?'

'Yes, of course. They are identical in every way. You'd have to listen to their engine noise to tell the difference.'

'Maybe that's what those engineers were doing, Captain. Running engine tests,' Morton said pleasantly before thanking Malenko.

Out on the tarmac Concorde's engines had restarted. Morton stood up and moved towards the door. Savenko was thanking Captain Malenko for his help and reminding him that his oath of allegiance extended to cover the confidentiality of this call.

12

In the Emperor's study there was silence when Ambassador Lincoln finished. Small tongues of flame flickered in the fireplace, casting shadows. The Emperor put down his glass on a side table, walked over to the hearth and lifted a log from a copper urn. He turned the wood in his hands, studied the whorl of the grain at its ends and looked at the Ambassador.

'At least five hundred years old. A tree already a sapling before our two countries knew of each other's existence,' the Emperor said gently.

He carefully placed the log on the glowing embers. The fire flared up again. The Emperor watched for a moment longer then picked up their glasses and went to the drinks cabinet. He poured whisky, then returned and stood by Hershel Lincoln's chair. Handing him a drink he broke the silence.

'Thank your President for having me briefed.'

'What will you do?' The Ambassador sipped his drink.

The Emperor tilted his head slightly as he considered. Then he sighed. 'You are aware more than anyone of the pressures being exerted on me to remain apart from the political scene. What your President is proposing could cause the greatest crisis this country has faced since my father was forced by our militants to support their war against your country in 1941.

'Since succeeding him I have done everything I can to ensure that my people are not dragged into another terrible conflict. But once more the spirit of Bushido burns fiercely in the hearts of those who wish to exploit its code of chivalry for their own base ends.'

The Ambassador nodded. The ancient code of the Samurai had become a clarion call for the Right. These new Knights of Bushido were far more dangerous than their World War Two predecessors. By appealing to the growing number of young Japanese unemployed – themselves a recent but growing problem – the extremists had cut deep into the ranks of the Liberal Democratic Party which, since 1945, had struggled to give Japan a manageable democracy.

The jingoistic potential of the proposed economic alliance between China and the United States would give the extremists a powerful platform from which to rail that the time had come to redraft the Japanese Constitution, the bandage that protected the country's already bruised and confused national psyche. From there it would be a small step to tearing up the international treaties, conventions and protocols which kept Japan as a vitally important member of the international community. If that happened, the Emperor and the Imperial Throne would be swept away. The Knights of Bushido would do this without a moment of moral concern, a second's pause to consider the ultimate consequences for their nation.

The Emperor spoke again. 'I want you to convey to your President my clear and unequivocal response to what he is proposing.'

'May I please take a note, Your Majesty?' the Ambassador asked softly.

'Of course.'

The Emperor paused to frame his words, watching the Ambassador fish from a coat pocket a small notepad and pen. Hershel Lincoln looked up. The Emperor's face had changed subtly; the patina of courtliness remained, but behind it now lay something harder and more determined that carried into his voice.

'Tell your President that I understand what he wishes to do and why he is doing it. That I know it will not be easy for him – just as he must know it will not be easy for me to support this. But tell him I am prepared to use all my influence to ensure that my people will understand the true value of what is being proposed. That, too, may not be easy. In many ways our two countries have grown far apart. There is misunderstanding in your country, and often misrepresentation, too. Tell your President I am sure he will do everything possible to end such distortion.

'For my part I will continue to do all in my power to end these senseless attacks on your people and property here. Finally, please tell your President that I see what he proposes for China also as a new bridge between our own two nations.'

The Ambassador blinked, not trusting himself to speak for a moment. When he did it was in a whisper.

'Thank you, Your Majesty. I will make sure every word reaches the President.'

The Emperor nodded. The die was cast. There would be no going back.

The Ambassador put the pad and pen back into his pocket as he spoke. 'Your government will receive confirmation of our plans once we have a formal response from Chairman Hu. That will not come before the President visits Hong Kong.'

Hershel Lincoln looked directly into the Emperor's face. 'Will you need to inform Secretary Matzuda at this stage?'

Something quickly came and went in the Emperor's eyes. When the Emperor spoke his voice was low and icy-cold. 'Secretary Matzuda will no longer be a factor in this or any other matter. An hour ago I approved the order for his arrest after the head of our Security Service showed me incontrovertible proof that Matzuda has been closely involved for many years with the Triads. He has received substantial payments for betraying his country. Almost certainly he has other connections ... to the Chinese Secret Intelligence Service. Our Security Service believes he passed important information to the Chinese through his Triad connections. No doubt it will take time for everything to emerge. But be assured that nothing I have heard about the Chinese involvement changes my position over what your President is proposing.'

Ambassador Lincoln did not bother to hide his relief.

The Emperor smiled for the first time. 'You are a good man, Hershel. Your country should be proud of you.'

He glanced at the fire. The log had almost burned away. He turned back to the Ambassador, a troubled look on his face. 'But what does China want? For them the Middle Kingdom was always the core of the human world. My one fear is the very one many of your own people now have about us. That China will swallow us.'

The Ambassador gave a little shiver, not out of fear or cold, but from some deeper and more complex response, one he could not himself explain.

'I hope you are wrong, Your Majesty,' he finally said.

From time to time the President or Thack glanced at the copy of the briefing document Bill Gates had handed each of them. Occasionally they made a note, but otherwise they listened raptly as Gates continued to describe the key players in Hong Kong.

'... Governor Sir Alan Wingate is a Chinese scholar and a Mandarin speaker, and a widower like yourself, Mr President.'

Thack made a note.

'What about the Colony's Executive Council?' asked the President. 'Any one there I should pay special attention to?'

'No. It's a shambles since Dame Lorna Bell resigned over Britain's refusal to give right of entry to millions of Chinese who hold its passports.'

'Where'd she go?' Thack asked.

'To Manila. She's set up some sort of anti-British movement there. She's independently wealthy enough to indulge her colonial-bashing. The only other thing worth mentioning is that she's pally with Emerson. She's putting him up during the conference – a suite in the best hotel, and some of her private bodyguards watching over him.'

'What's she getting out of this, Bill?' Thack asked.

'She thinks Emerson can give her a voice over here. And he's a useful man on the masthead to beat the Japanese with. You know how sensitive the Filipinos are about Tokyo. Emerson's tomfoolery will go down big in Manila.'

The President sighed. 'I only wish it was just tomfoolery, Mr Gates. CNN's reporting that a poll shows thirty per cent think Emerson was right in what he said in San Francisco and almost twice that number say I was wrong to sack him.'

Thack shrugged. 'The polls were wrong about your election. They're wrong this time. And anyway, Emerson's a spent force.'

'I'll still have someone keep an eye on him in Manila,' Gates said. The Chief of Staff looked down at his document. 'This Tang Ming ...'

Gates nodded. 'Ming's the man Beijing has designated to replace the Governor when the Colony reverts to China.'

'Is Tang Ming based there?' asked the President.

'Officially, no. But there's an understanding between London and Beijing that he can come and go as he pleases. The Governor's not actually thrilled. But there's not much he can do about it. Tang Ming will certainly be on hand to meet you.'

'What about that creepy Prime Minister of theirs?' asked Thack.

Gates have a tight little smile. 'He's officially on sick leave. In reality he's in Beijing's equivalent of our Betty Ford Clinic. The Prime Minister's got two problems. A taste for opium and little girls.'

The President shook his head. 'If this deal goes through,' he said softly, 'the first thing Hu's going to have to do is clean up the act of those around him.'

Emerging from the Imperial Palace grounds, Ambassador Lincoln turned on the radio. A minor riot was in progress around the National Museum of Modern Art. A week ago he had opened its exhibition of American Indian paintings. The museum was on his route home.

Rather than risk encountering the mob, he decided to make a detour. In moments he had driven off the interlinking grid of highways onto the narrower city streets. At this hour they would normally still be busy, but the violence had sent most people home early. The Ambassador drove in the centre of the street, just below the speed limit. After a while, he turned down the radio volume and reached for a small dictaphone under the dash. It had long been his practice to record impressions of important meetings.

He switched on the machine and began to record everything he had been told by the Emperor. 'The discovery of Matzuda's treachery is a major blow for the Emperor. But it confirms my own fear of how far the extremists have penetrated. Matzuda is almost certainly not the only one. Their network of influence extends deep into the National Police and the Military, especially the Navy. His arrest will either cause the others to cover their tracks more effectively until they feel the time is right to move – or they may decide to do so now.'

He paused as he passed one of the great anomalies of Tokyo – a ramshackle wooden shack clinging like a barnacle to one side of a modern department store building. The hut's owner had stubbornly turned down a sizable fortune for the few square metres of ground which had been in his family for centuries. Outside the hut a group of youths straddled powerful motorcycles. They wore bandanas, studded leather jackets and wraparound sunglasses, the uniform of the *Kosuzuka*, Japan's even more violent version of the Hell's Angels.

Careful not to make eye contact, the Ambassador drove past the bikers. A block on from them he resumed his dictation. 'There is little doubt that the Bushido mentality finds a ready response not only with the young unemployed, but also among their elders, especially those in the middle classes, where there is growing disenchantment and xenophobia, the two elements which in the past have led this country down a path of self-destruction. If the Emperor is to sell his people our China plan he will have to carry the middle classes with him. No easy task, given that the extremists have made their bed there.'

From ahead came the sound of glass breaking. A group of men were looting another shop window a couple of blocks away. They stopped to watch the car approach. He increased his speed. Out of the corner of his eye he saw one man pick up a display dummy and run towards the car. He accelerated and the plastic effigy shattered on the road behind the car.

After a few blocks he slowed down and resumed his dictation once again. 'If the present unrest continues there will be no alternative but for the Embassy to recommend that all our dependent and non-essential staff should leave the country. There may also be a need for the Marine presence at the Embassy to be increased. But any such moves will have to be taken in conjunction with what the Emperor will be doing to assist us in getting acceptance of our China plan. Nothing must be done to allow its opponents to undermine him – or accuse us of threatening behaviour ...'

In the mirror he could see the bikers coming up behind, spread across the road in formation. Steeling himself not to increase speed – the Mazda could never outrun them – he searched for an intersection. As he passed another city landmark – the Nakagain Capsule Building, two towering black steel shafts on which were bolted freight containers, converted into pieds-à-terre for rising executives – he again switched on the radio, which reported that trouble had broken out around the nearby Spiral Building. A number of US companies had offices there.

Away to his left he glimpsed the towers of mid-town, so tightly packed they looked like one great glittering mass. Down here, close to the bay, the buildings looked abandoned, their loading bays steel-shuttered. The spray-painted anti-American graffiti came and went in the car's headlights. The bikers were coming closer. He began to accelerate, his eyes searching more anxiously for the first turn-off. He turned up the radio, seeking comfort from the voice. A police spokesman was reporting that control had been re-established at the National Museum. If he could find an intersection he could turn and double back. He gripped the wheel with both hands, head forward and shoulders hunched as he concentrated.

A shadow roared past his near side, forcing him to swerve instinctively. Another couple of bikers hurtled past. He swerved again. He felt the perspiration cold on his skin. He had heard about the *Kosuzuka*'s kamikaze-style manoeuvrings.

The Ambassador gunned the Mazda forward. There *had* to be an intersection. The bikers were on either side, keeping pace, steering with one hand, using their free hands to smash their gauntlets against the car windows. One was twirling something over his head. Suddenly the front passenger window shattered and the object smashed into the Ambassador's shoulder.

He screamed in pain. A moment later another object smashed his own window, showering glass over him. Blood streaming from his face, Hershel Lincoln drove on. The roar of the motorcycles drowned out the radio, drowned everything. Ahead he could see an intersection. Some of the bikers had already reached there. With their helmet visors lowered, they looked like combat troops.

Desperately, he looked for another way out. There was a gap between the buildings ahead. A loading bay. Maybe he could turn there, reverse and escape back up the street.

There was a sudden flash from the intersection. The windscreen shattered, blinding him in one eye. He was disorientated, his body twisting in agony, out of control. Another shot hit him. He heard the shouts of excitement, felt his hands leave the wheel, sensed the car careering towards a wall, heard his own scream – an awful, unnatural high-pitched sound, that died as quickly as it came. Then darkness, complete and total.

Ambassador Hershel Lincoln fell forward against the steering wheel, his ruined face pressed hard against the car's horn.

The biker who had killed him wrenched open the nearside door. The others crowded round, staring at the body, laughing among themselves. The gunman reached into the car, silenced the horn by shoving the body aside, prised free the dictaphone and dropped it into a pouch pocket. He expertly riffled through the Ambassador's pockets and removed his personal belongings. The red diplomatic passport, embossed with the eagle of the hated enemy, drew a cheer from the others. Still laughing and talking among themselves, they roared off into the night.

They called to each other not in *putonghun*, the slang of the Tokyo street gangs, but in higher-pitched Cantonese. The bikers were one of several Triad groups who had arrived in Japan from Hong Kong in the guise of the Japanese *Kosuzuka* and were under orders to attack foreigners.

Captain First Rank Josef Marlo watched the tug nudging the *Rodina*'s spherical bow further out into the channel at Gremikha Naval Base. A thin crust of ice partly covered the water and a chill north wind blew directly off the icepack against the squat, black-painted sail – still called the conning tower in diesel-driven submarines.

The Captain, like everyone else on the bridge, was dressed in several layers of thermal underwear, windproof woollen jerseys and water-resistant oilskins. His protective clothing only reinforced Marlo's ape-like appearance. He had the long, dangling arms and the jutting jaw of a Mongol. His eyes were close-set, and surmounted by shaggy eyebrows. People said he was a clone of his father-in-law, Vice-Premier Kazenko, even down to the habit of expelling gobs of spittle.

When the tug stopped nudging the Captain grunted into the bridge telephone, 'Engine ahead slow.' Beside him Lieutenant Boris Tarinski continued to sweep with his glasses the seaway beyond the harbour.

The navigator was a tall, well-proportioned man, and deeply tanned, with a strong chin and deep-set blue eyes. In the two days he had been ashore after the last trip, he had celebrated his thirtieth birthday. Marlo had made a formal appearance at the party and left; the carousing had continued for almost another full day. There was nothing else to do at Gremikha except get drunk. And you needed to be very drunk to bury yourself between the thighs of one of the local whores.

'The *Rutka's* on station, Comrade Captain,' Tarinski called out.

The icebreaker would butt a channel free of the chunks of frozen water that could damage the submarine's hull.

'Tell me something I can't see,' snapped Marlo.

The navigator flushed. This had all the makings of another bad trip. At the briefing in the wardroom, Marlo had been as unforthcoming as usual. He had said no more than that the mission orders required a navigation course under the North Pole down to the Sea of Japan, where they were to surface briefly and then submerge and head on under the Yellow Sea. At least this time there weren't any damned civilians on board. On both trips he had been made to give up his cabin to accommodate them. But if they were naval engineers, then he was a whore's douche. Lieutenant Tarinski grinned. That last one had known her business. He would have to pay her another visit. By the time he got back from this trip, he would be ready for anything.

The seamen look-outs spread their feet a little wider on the bridge deck of the submarine, which began to reverberate under its own power.

Marlo lifted the bridge 'phone. 'Order the *Rutka* to come in closer. Time she earned her keep.'

He put the 'phone back in its cradle, hawked and sent a gob of spittle over the side of the bridge. Above the sail a radar antenna twirled on its shaft. The wind had started to moan through the aerials which enabled the submarine to communicate when surfaced. The tug slid out of the way as the *Rodina* passed, its crew staring impassively at the vast bulk of the submarine. The only gesture was a wave from the bridge. Marlo ignored it.

'Copters at port ten, Comrade Captain,' one of the seamen sang out.

The others swung their binoculars to watch the pair of anti-submarine helicopters sweep low over the water. Beyond the harbour the choppers would drop the first of their sonobuoys. The instruments would automatically transmit the presence of any lurking foreign subs. The Americans still liked to snoop up here.

'Unless those buoys can pick up a satellite, they're a waste of time,' said Tarinski.

The captain glared at the navigator. 'Is that what they taught you at navigating school – to denigrate our equipment?'

'No, of course not, Comrade Captain. But we were given a course on hostile surveillance, and that included satellites.'

'Did they teach you anything about the velocity of sound through water?'

'Of course, Comrade Captain.'

'And did they teach you anything about how it depends on relative temperature and salinity?'

'Yes, certainly they did, Comrade Captain.' The look-outs kept their backs to the two men. Tarinski was popular among the crew. They could think of several other officers more deserving of the public humiliations in which the Captain regularly indulged.

'Then you will know that as soon as we submerge there will be no way for even this wondrous Amerikanski equipment you seem to either fear or admire to locate us.'

Marlo gave an ugly smile and turned to watch the icebreaker forcing aside the floes. The sea had begun to lap over the *Rodina*'s bow, surging back down the flat, wide missile deck. There were no nuclear weapons aboard. The Amerikanski had threatened to attack any Typhoon carrying them. Moscow had once more capitulated, another insult to endure.

The Captain turned and glanced aft. If they were going to be ordered back to base, the order must come in the next few minutes before they submerged and went under complete radio silence. Through his glasses he peered at the seascape of foam and blinking buoys that indicated deeper waters ahead. The *Rutka* had taken up station two hundred metres in front, and the noise of her crunching the ice carried clearly.

'Ahead by one third, Lieutenant,' barked Marlo.

Tarinski relayed the order to the control room fifty feet below where they stood. The sea surge increased, sending spumes of icy water flying towards the bridge. A moment later the bridge 'phone rang to announce that the helicopters had reported no hostile contacts.

'Tell that damned *Rutka* to get a move on,' the Captain ordered.

A few moments later the icebreaker began to pick up speed, the surge of its bow wave making the submarine rock. It would take another thirty minutes to reach the open sea.

Marlo reached for the 'phone. 'Increase speed to two-thirds. Come left fifteen degrees. Inform *Rutka* of our course change – and tell him to get out of the way.'

Tarinski reached under the bridge coaming and unhooked the small blinker light. He began to transmit the morse message. An acknowledging light blinked from the icebreaker's bridge. The *Rodina* began steadily to accelerate, her 30,000 tons moving effortlessly under the power of her reactor.

Marlo lifted the 'phone again. 'Depth under the keel?'

'One hundred and fifty metres, Comrade Captain.'

The start of deep water. The *Rutka* had fallen away to starboard, and the shore itself was a distant blur.

'Signal to base, Control. "Diving at" – ' he checked his watch, ' "sixteen hundred hours".'

'Sixteen hundred, Comrade Captain.'

Marlo turned to the others on the bridge. 'Secure and clear the bridge!'

He watched the look-outs press buttons to retract the radar and radio masts. The seamen disappeared through the floor hatch, eager to be out of the cold. Tarinski took a moment longer, taking one last look at the sky. He had never quite grown used to the moment of disappearing beneath the waves.

'Comrade Captain! What's that – starboard ten?' The navigator pointed away to his right, high in the sky, instinctively bringing his glasses to bear.

'Vapour trail,' Marlo growled, lowering his glasses. 'A commercial airliner.'

'Too high, Comrade Captain,' Tarinski ventured. 'Unless it's a Concorde.'

Marlo shook his head, the ugly smile back on his lips. 'You missed your vocation. You should be in air traffic control.'

Tarinski dropped down the hatch. Marlo swept the sky one more time. The trail had faded. But how could anyone tell from this distance what kind of aircraft had created it? Tarinski was too quick with his mouth. The Captain reached for the bridge 'phone one last time.

'Dive!'

He slammed the receiver back in its cradle and entered the hatch to descend the sail ladder. By the time he reached the control room Tarinski was spinning the locking wheel to seal the hatch against the enormous pressure which would soon be exerted upon every inch of the *Rodina*. Its hull was filling with the rush of air being expelled as vents in the ballast tanks opened to allow water to flood in, causing the deck to tilt forward as the Barents Sea swallowed the submarine.

As the vapour trail burned off when the Concorde reached its cruising height, one of the electronic specialists in the Communications Centre turned to Morton and grinned.

'A near perfect reading,' the technician said. 'Wherever he goes, providing we are within a couple of hundred miles – we'll find him.'

On his oscilloscope was a computerised soundwave of the *Rodina*'s engine noise. Like a genetic fingerprint, it was like no other.

Morton told the CCO to organise another conference call.

13

After the short night the sun rose on a landscape of a beauty that only increased Leo's feeling of unreality. Twenty hours ago he had been in Washington, leading Shaoyen to their first-class seats. Now the China Airlines 747 was beginning its leisurely descent into Beijing, coming down through pillows of cloud, glowing pink and flowery in the climbing sun, the aircraft's shadow magnified as it passed over a landscape of subtle colours. They were the only two passengers in the front cabin, and throughout the long flight they had been pampered and fed delicacies he had never known existed.

The only discordant note was Shaoyen's behaviour. Towards him she had been cool, almost distant, yet with the cabin crew she had been animated, talking to them in her own language. He had finally put it down to pre-wedding nerves. She breathed noisily beside him through her half-open mouth.

When the flight attendant arrived with breakfast trays, he nudged Shaoyen. She shoved her eye mask up onto her forehead and said something to the stewardess in Mandarin. The attendant nodded.

'Good sleep?' Leo asked.

'Okey-dokey.'

The stewardess was back with a glass of water. Shaoyen fished from a pocket the vial Li had given her and carefully shook two capsules into her palm. She handed them to Leo.

'Take these now. Then you have no problem with the water. *Waibin* always sick when they drink our water.'

Her mouth curled in simulated pain and she leaned forward with her hands tensed over her stomach and let out a constricted groan.

'You've never called me a *waibin* before,' he said reproachfully. She had once told him the word was pejorative, like calling a black a nigger.

'In my country all foreigners are *waibin*,' she said, picking at her breakfast tray.

Leo swallowed the capsules with the water. 'Will your family be at the airport to meet us?' he asked.

'Yes.'

'Will they like me?' He realised he knew nothing about Shaoyen's family.

'Of course.'

'Is there something wrong, honey? Something I've said or done? You've not been yourself since we left home.'

Shaoyen checked herself. Home was down there, somewhere between the Yellow River and the hills.

'I guess it's just all the excitement ... coming here, bringing a new face into the family ... all that ...' Leo speared one of the savoury dumplings on his tray and shoved it into his mouth.

Another immeasurable silence fell. She used her chopsticks for the noodles and ate noisily. *Waibin* never showed their appreciation for food; they just assumed it would always be there. They knew nothing about real starvation. She looked at him at last.

'Yes. It's all the excitement of coming home.'

Leo reached across for Shaoyen's hand, his face coming closer to hers. 'I wish we could stay a little longer, honey. But maybe there's still time for you to show me that place where the old monster lies in his coffin?'

She looked at him quizzically. 'Monster?'

He laughed. 'Old Mao. Isn't he on display like Lenin in Moscow?'

The ferocity of her response astonished him. 'He was not a monster! Not like your Reagan or Bush! Mao Zedong never wanted to make war like America, to conquer. He only wanted to give us a better life. For that we had to work, work hard. Of course, he made mistakes. But that is not a reason for you to call him a monster!'

He held his hand against his chest. 'Hey, excuse me, sorry and *mea culpa*! I didn't mean to insult Mao. And I had no idea you were a fan. Forget I spoke – okey-dokey?'

She laughed unexpectedly. 'Okey-dokey.'

After a moment Leo asked Shaoyen penitently, 'You promise if I say anything stupid about China you will put me right?'

'Okey-dokey.'

The PA system announced that they would be landing in a few minutes. They both fastened their seatbelts.

Shaoyen turned to Leo. 'When we land, we will be met by members of my family who are quite important officials. Because you do not have a visa they will drive you directly into the city to the Ministry where you will be given one.'

'What about you? Can't you come with me? I mean, I don't speak Mandarin and supposing something goes wrong? They're bound to do things differently here.'

She waited until the stewardess had removed their trays. 'You will be fine. I will see you at the hotel.' She smiled quickly. 'Anyway, I have to claim our luggage.'

A frown settled between his eyes and wrinkled upwards. 'But can't I wait and then we could travel in together?'

'No.' She shook her head in emphasis. 'This is China. We have a different system.'

She was looking at him with barely concealed contempt. But he felt too sleepy to ask why.

Two hundred flying miles east of the North Polar Cap, Concorde's Communications Officer informed Morton that the links to Hammer Force Headquarters and Washington were back in place. Crossing Siberia, the hook-up had broken down several times due to electrical storms. The static cleared and the faces of Professor Lars Svendsen and Yoshi Kramer appeared on one screen, that of Bill Gates on another. The psychologist and neurosurgeon, like Bill, would be able to hear and see him and each other.

Professor Svendsen and Yoshi were in Morton's own office: he had asked Chantal to bring them there. He glimpsed her in the background. Bill was in one of Langley's communications cubicles. One of the Concorde's technicians was monitoring the call, checking the security of the link to Hammer Force's own satellite high above the Equator. Others were sampling the radio traffic en route. Voices from the independent Moslem republics of the old Soviet Union, the Koreas and Japan came and went in their headphones. One radio man had established a link with the US Air Force Base at Kadena in Okinawa.

'I'll cut to the chase in case this hook-up goes down again,' Morton said briskly.

He told them what he had learned from the call to the Base Commander at Gremikha. 'The bottom line is that almost certainly the sub, Igor Tamasara and those two sidekicks of his who have vanished from their Russian camp, are all part of the same scenario,' Morton added.

'I can live with that, David,' Gates said. 'But where does that leave us?'

'With the President in the frame.'

Gates spoke softly. 'That's one hell of a leap, David. One hell of a big leap.'

Morton clasped his hands on the desktop. 'Everything points to an attack on the President, either in Hong Kong or Manila. Either would provide Igor Tamasara with a perfect demonstration for his weapon.'

Before anyone could respond Morton spoke again. 'Igor Tamasara may or may not be working with the full sanction of the Chinese regime. But that doesn't really matter. The power-brokers are Chairman Hu and his Security Chief, Qiao Peng. He's always used surrogates to stir trouble.'

'But that would wreck any hope of China and America getting together,' Yoshi said.

Before the link had broken down Gates had told them of the President's plan. Now Gates spoke again, like a man regaining his wind. 'Qiao Peng would make sure there's no trace back to Beijing. He managed that in Afghanistan and Cambodia.'

Morton shifted forward onto the edge of his seat. 'The Triads are already fronting for him. It would make absolute sense for him to go on using them.'

For the next few minutes he spoke without interruption, his voice low and almost monotone, as he described the link between the Beijing regime and the Triads. When Morton finished there was complete silence from both screens. From the console around him came the low mash of radio traffic.

'Killing the President would lead to a war in the Pacific,' Yoshi Kramer finally said.

'And beyond, Yoshi. Far beyond,' Morton said softly.

He watched Professor Svendsen adjust the tortoiseshell frame of his glasses.

'There are some people who would almost welcome such a conflict, both in Japan and the United States,' the psychiatrist said quietly.

'That's a fact we've got to live with,' Gates grunted.

Morton watched him draw out his silver cigarette case and light up, each movement deliberately slow to give him time to think. He'd thought Bill had quit smoking.

'Emerson,' continued Professor Svendsen. 'Could he somehow be involved? He was on our television again last night. The man sounds almost a fanatic. But the reporter in Washington said there was growing support for his views.'

There was another grunt from Washington. 'Todd Harper's only too willing to provide free air-time for anybody who kicks the Administration,' Gates said wearily. He told them about the former Secretary of Labour's forthcoming trip to the Non-Aligned Conference and Emerson's relationship with Dame Lorna Bell.

Yoshi glanced at Professor Svendsen before speaking. 'How can we help you, David?'

Out of the corner of his eye Morton saw the Communications Officer standing over a technician, his own headset jacked into the operator's console. The CCO was frowning. Morton addressed the screen linked to Geneva.

'I need you, Professor, to try to read Igor Tamasara's mind. Your own patients have shown you what someone like that is capable of.'

The psychiatrist nodded. In Washington Gates stubbed out his half-smoked cigarette.

Morton continued: 'I want you to see things from Tamasara's point of view. I need to know how he would react in any given situation. Even if he's got his machine up and running, there's still bound to be pressure on him. Qiao Peng wouldn't have it otherwise. I know how he's likely to react. It's Tamasara I need to know about. His strengths and weaknesses – anything at all. I need you to get into his head, to try to read his mind-set. That means thinking like him. Can you do that, Professor?'

The psychiatrist's nervous reflex laugh came and went. 'I try to do that all the time, Colonel. It's part of my work. But if I'm to treat Igor Tamasara as a patient, I'll need to know everything that is possible to know, given I'm not going to actually meet him.'

'You'll have it, for sure.'

Morton saw the CCO was writing on a scratchpad as he continued. 'Yoshi, you're the best man I know who understands the mechanical functions of the brain. It certainly helped in getting a fix on Saddam.'

'I think clinically speaking someone like Tamasara can also be called a psychopath, David. As a rough rule of thumb, a psychopath will say he shouldn't do something, but he doesn't *feel* he shouldn't. The emotional or affective compound – conscience, if you like – is absent in the psychopath. We saw that in Josef Mengele and the other Nazi doctors, and those who worked in the old Soviet system.'

The CCO was at his elbow as Morton spoke. 'You'll have others to help you. Chantal will introduce you to our own experts. Anything you want from them, you'll get. What I want from you both is to tell me what is going on in Igor Tamasara's mind.' Morton smiled his temporary smile. 'It's good medicine versus the worst kind.'

The CCO placed a sheet of paper before him.

'It's still unconfirmed,' murmured the CCO.

Morton looked up and stared into the screens.

'A Tokyo radio station's reporting that the American Ambassador has been assassinated. There's no other confirmation – '

'NHK's just reported it as a fact,' called out the technician. NHK was the Japanese government radio system.

Gates' cursing made even the technicians and Morton blink.

Li Mufang stood under the plastic bubble of a payphone in the main concourse of Washington's Union Station. He had used a credit card to make the call to Montreal. The card was in the name of Gary Summers, one of his several aliases; the billing address was a mailbox in a shopping mall out on Rhode Island Avenue. He had earmarked the station payphone when he first reconnoitred the city. The booth was in the centre of the concourse, making it easier to spot if he was being observed. The departure of Shaoyen and Leo had increased his watchfulness.

As he listened, the 'phone pressed tight against his ear, hand cupped over the mouthpiece to reduce the station noise, he could not believe how easy it had been. Kate Baskin had accepted without challenge his reason for calling. He had told her he was a post-graduate student at Georgetown University, and doing research into the positive use of artificial energy. He had spoken knowledgeably after a morning spent in the public library reading what was available on bioelectrics as a healing medium. Some of the books had cited Kate Baskin's research. But there had been no mention of her father's work. This had given him the opening he needed.

'Dr Baskin, may I ask you a personal question?' Li asked politely.

In her office in Magill University, high up on Montreal's Mount Royal and with a magnificent view of the St Lawrence seaway, Kate glanced at her watch. She was used to students calling her from all over North America; her reputation for never turning away a genuinely enquiring mind was deserved. She had never forgotten the debt she owed her father for the time and trouble he had taken to lead her down the byways of scientific research. But in a few minutes she would have to go if she was to catch the flight to Hong Kong.

As usual she had told no one where she was going; she liked to make her breaks from campus total. She smiled: how would she explain to anyone that she was taking a detour to Hong Kong to meet a man she had only spoken to briefly on the 'phone? But there had been something quietly persistent about Morton that had both intrigued and disarmed her. Rather like this student who had called out of the blue.

'Go ahead, ask your question.' She managed to keep any trace of impatience from her voice.

Li once more glanced quickly around the concourse. At this hour it was not busy. A soberly-dressed businessman, burdened under a suitcase and shoulder bag, was staggering towards a quick-snack cafeteria. He looked Chinese; probably another Hong Kong Cantonese who had run out before Beijing imposed its own order.

'Thank you, Dr Baskin. My question is: are you the first member of your family to work in your field? I only ask because I myself come from a medical family.'

'My father was also a neurologist,' Kate said.

The Cantonese had flopped on a chair outside the café, baggage at his feet.

'Ah-ha. That explains it. But I have not come across your father's work.'

'He didn't publish much. In his days bioelectrics was still something new and outside mainstream scientific enquiry.'

Li paused. He wanted to give her time to think he was digesting her reply. Across the concourse the businessman had gone inside the café, leaving his baggage unattended. Only a stupid Cantonese would do that.

'So much of medical biology is still affected by tunnel vision, Mr Summers. We know everything we need to know about the genetic code, the nervous system and so on. But we still only know life itself by its symptoms. Most doctors and biochemists aren't much closer to the truth about life than my father was when he started. We still know virtually nothing about such basic functions as pain, sleep and the control of cell differentiation, growth and healing, especially when it comes to diseases like cancer.

'Mechanistic chemistry rules everything. So only a few of us study the enigmas of life, like the role even a single cell has to play in such things as human instinct, choice, memory, learning – the whole shooting-match of human responses.'

She paused. A 'plane was climbing out of Mirabel. She would really have to go.

'And your father led you to all this?'

'Yes. He's a wonderful man,' Kate said.

'He is still alive? Again, I only ask because my own father died a year ago ...'

The Cantonese was back at his table, sipping from a plastic beaker.

'I'm sorry about your Dad. I'm lucky. Mine's not only alive, but still working.'

'Working?' He managed to give the word the right amount of surprise and pleasure. 'That is wonderful.'

Kate smiled. Despite his American name, Gary Summers was no Caucasian. Only the Japanese were usually this polite.

'Where are your family from?' she asked, thinking how she could end the conversation without giving offence.

'Seoul. I am second-generation American,' Li lied.

He sensed her good manners struggling with her impatience. Maybe she had a class to teach. He would have to move things along more quickly. 'I always feel we students only learn from our books,' he said.

'My Dad would be really glad to hear you say that, Mr Summers.'

'I would very much like to speak to him,' Li said quickly. 'Maybe he would let me visit him?'

She laughed. 'I'm afraid that's not possible. He is a long way from Washington.'

He sighed, not bothering to conceal his disappointment. 'I could write to him.'

Kate glanced at her watch again. Time really was running out. But it wasn't often she came across a student who was so polite and eager to learn. She came to a decision.

'Here's my Dad's address,' she said. 'It may take a little while before you hear from him. He never was a good correspondent.'

'Thank you, Dr Baskin,' Li said, writing down the address. 'I shall certainly be writing to your father ...'

But she was already saying her goodbyes and hanging up.

Li hurried out of the concourse.

FBI agent Song put down his beaker, picked up his baggage and walked to the payphone. The suitcase contained a built-in camcorder which had videoed the 'phone call, and the shoulder bag's parabolic mike had picked up Li's words and recorded them on the cassette machine in the bag.

He called the payphone number into the FBI telephone tracing unit. A technician dialled the telephone company security office on

Eighteenth Street. A clerk fed the number into a computer bank, instructing it to isolate all the calls made from the payphone over the past six hours. There were ninety-seven, forty-four to numbers in the Washington area. Thirty were toll calls, the remaining fourteen long-distance, three of which were credit card calls.

The clerk faxed all the details to the FBI unit. The technician processed the information through his computer. The second call-trace triggered a Code Red, the highest form of security in its memory. The call-trace showed a report-and-watch number in Montreal. Against it was a boldly printed instruction: Inform Deputy Director (Surveillance). The technician immediately did so on a priority fax line to FBI Headquarters across the city.

The Deputy Director was on the 'phone to the Agent-in-Charge of the FBI Bureau in New York, settling a minor administrative problem. He broke off to 'phone Bill Gates in Langley and tell him what had happened.

Gates immediately called Kate Baskin. The Magill switchboard said she had gone on a vacation. Shortly afterwards Song rejoined his partner, Teng, in the apartment opposite Li's bar. Once more they heard him dial the sequence on his fax machine that they now recognised as a Beijing number. Then came the flush of a toilet.

After transmitting Colin Baskin's address, Li had torn up the paper and sent it on its journey through the city sewers. He then went downstairs to the bar and began a normal working day.

Entering the suburbs of Beijing, Leo grew increasingly tired. His eyes ached and he had a throbbing headache. Those tablets Shaoyen had given him had done nothing to ease his feeling of lassitude. He stared blearily out of the car's rear window. There was something impersonal and vaguely hostile about this city. Its broad roads and massive buildings all appeared to have come from the same drawing-board. Everything seemed as intimidating as the two men in the front seat.

They had been waiting on the tarmac when they had disembarked and Shaoyen had briefly introduced them as her cousins. She had said a quick goodbye to him and hurried into the terminal. The men had led the way to a car. Driving out of the airport he'd heard the rear doors lock. When he tried to lower the window, the man in the passenger seat had turned and looked at him. The warning in his eyes was unmistakable. Since then, whenever he tried to engage them in conversation, using the few words of Mandarin Shaoyen had taught him, they ignored him.

Leo slumped back against the hard leather seat and watched the flow of traffic. There seemed to be thousands of cyclists, pedalling solemnly in regimental shoals. The men had tobacco-stained teeth and the women sallow faces, their plaits and ponytails bound in elastic bands. They all had the same inscrutable look as Shaoyen's cousins.

Leo tried again to make conversation. 'You come to wedding – okey-dokey?'

He spoke slowly, lapsing into the imperfect grammar of a foreigner trying to make himself understood, his voice louder than usual. The men ignored him. He tried a different approach.

'Can you please open window? Very hot in here.'

The man beside the driver turned in his seat and shook his head. The sonofabitch understood English. So what was he playing dumb for?

'Stop the car. I want to get out and take a leak,' Leo said.

'Wait,' said the man.

'So you do speak my lingo, pal!' Leo said, feeling foolish at his relief. The man had turned his back on him.

Leo felt suddenly irritated. This was not the welcome Li had promised. If all Shaoyen's relatives were like this, the sooner he got the hell out of here with her, the better. But he just wished he didn't feel so damned tired. Yet he couldn't go to sleep until he got that visa. He struggled to remain awake by concentrating on the passing scenes.

There were more billboards than on an interstate – advertising soap, hand lotion and even fireworks. The eight-lane highway had been sliced through a mesh of alleys and courtyards. The buildings had the same curved tile roofs, garishly-painted doors, grimy windows and walls made from strips of wood. The structures were fragile enough for a breeze off the Potomac to blow them away. Shaoyen had said they built like this because Beijing was on an earthquake belt. It somehow made the place seem even more alien.

The pressure on his bladder was increasing. He leaned forward and tapped the man's shoulder. 'Look, I gotta go,' Leo said.

The man turned and looked at him then said something to the driver. The car pulled into the verge. There was a click of the rear doors unlocking. The driver remained behind the wheel, while his companion followed Leo out of the car.

Leo urinated on the road. A passing shoal of bikers did not give him a second glance. The man motioned for Leo to get back into the car. When he had done so, there was the sound of the doors locking once more. Leo tried to fight down a feeling of alarm.

The city which had appeared to be directly ahead was now on his left and receding into the distance. Ahead were hills. The car picked up speed. Only a few other cars drove along here. Leo leaned forward and tapped the man on the shoulder.

'Is this the way to the visa office?' he asked.

There was no response.

Leo came to a decision. 'Okay, pal. Turn the car around. I want to go to the American Embassy. Right now, understand? Right now!'

The man turned and looked at Leo. In his hand he held a pistol.

'Be quiet,' said the man in excellent English.

'What the hell – '

'Be quiet, *waibin*,' repeated the man more forcibly.

Leo slumped back in his seat, silent with sudden panic. He began to whimper softly.

It was the only sound in the car as they drove into the Western Hills. A mile further on it stopped at a checkpoint. A soldier stepped forward and examined the driver's papers. Three more times over the next mile the checks were repeated before the car stopped at a gate in a chain metal fence. Leo saw that the gate was guarded by a squawkbox and remote camera. Just like the entrance to his own workplace.

His panic gave way to sudden hope. Maybe this was a special place where foreigners like him in sensitive work collected their visas. But he knew he was kidding himself. The man with the gun proved that. The gate swung silently open. Two jeeps with armed soldiers were waiting inside the perimeter. One led the way, the other fell in behind. The small convoy drove onto the test range of Igor Tamasara's research complex.

The night was dark and foul as the 747 descended across the New Territories, part of the Chinese mainland, towards Hong Kong. The captain announced that a thousand miles to the north a typhoon was sweeping towards the Chinese coast. Here the wind was no more than tropical storm strength. Nothing to worry about. Tommy grinned; only an Australian would offer that with such cheerful conviction.

After dinner he'd fallen asleep remembering what Anna had said on the way to the airport: this mission was so highly classified it couldn't be classified. They hadn't spoken since then. The others had taken the travel security precautions he'd learned at training school, checking in at different desks at irregular intervals. Some time during the night he'd dreamed the Colonel had faced him with the ultimate challenge: killing a man. If it was Igor Tamasara, he wouldn't hesitate. Not after what he'd read in Anna's file.

When he knew her better he must ask her what effect knowing all that had on her. In many ways she reminded him of his mother. Anna had that same way of appraising you, that same sense of readiness to meet a challenge head-on. Mother had literally met hers in a road crash, overtaking a second too late. He'd been ten at the time. Dad had woken him with the news. Years later he'd learned why she'd been speeding – hurrying back from the doctor to tell Dad she was pregnant. Was that why he'd never married again?

Had Anna ever been married? Was there anyone in her life? At training school the instructors had made a point of stressing that agents shouldn't carry any emotional baggage. He could understand that when it came to a place in Covert Action: anyone who ended up there was probably like a boxer forgoing sex while training for a tilt at the title. But he was assigned to Operations. And Anna was only detached from the Prof's outfit. Where did that leave her? Or him, for that matter? Should he even be thinking like this? Or maybe he should – maybe it was all part of what Dad had said about the Colonel expecting you to work things out for yourself?

The questions drifted through his sleep, though not the answers, until he was awoken by the captain's announcement. Around him came anxious whispers as the cabin lights dimmed for landing. The closer they came to the ground the more furiously the rain beat against the fuselage. As they broke through the cloud Tommy saw the wind sheeting across the vast bay which made Hong Kong Harbour one of the most well-protected on earth. A handful of ships rode with their anchors full out. The sea was surging over the walls along the water-front while the rain lashed against the Golden Ferry Building and the towering banking houses. In the hillside shanty towns the storm would further increase the misery of the thousands of dwellers. The Triads drew their foot soldiers from among them.

Tommy tightened his seatbelt as another furious eddy rocked the plane as it swept low over the high-rises of Kowloon. Then the wheels hit the tarmac at Kai Tak Airport, and a spontaneous cheer came from passengers. Tommy watched a stewardess pull back the curtain dividing off the first-class cabin.

Danny was already on his feet, removing his attaché case from the overhead bin. He knew the case, like everything else about him, bespoke respectability. His light tropical suit was of a dark cloth, the tie marked him as a member of one of London's oldest clubs. Even his eye-patch, which usually gave him a somewhat rakish appearance, now reinforced the impression of serious sobriety. His diplomatic passport completed the image, confirming him to be an inspector with the United Nations.

He had spent the night reading a history of the Riley, his favourite motor car. Now that the operation was underway he knew that, for the moment, there was nothing he could do. Besides, he loved driving as much as he hated flying. Not even Simone's death had changed that. And there was something about the bucket seat of a Riley that was far more comfortable than this cantilevered, under-padded and over-priced airline seat.

Anna was seated a dozen rows behind Tommy. She did not have the benefit of Danny's diplomatic cover – only a Canadian passport and a letter from her publisher announcing that she was a travel writer gathering material for a book. During the flight she had eaten sparingly and sipped orange juice at regular intervals. She had sprayed her wrists and face with water. It was the best way she knew of avoiding the skin fatigue of long-haul travel. And she'd thought a great deal about what she was going to do. Like everyone else, she had memorised her operational details before leaving Hammer Force Headquarters. As usual the Colonel had left everyone an amount of leeway. The best plans on paper were the ones not written in stone.

After a while she'd started thinking about Tommy. From back here his head rose above his headrest and had hardly moved from that position. But what was he thinking? The same thoughts she had had on her first field trip – a little excited, a little nervous? No matter what they taught you at training school, nothing really prepared you for the first time in the field. Or the second, either. This was her third trip, and there was still this feeling of disorientation, as if the huntress were also the prey.

The engine came to a stop and passengers were scrambling to their feet. Among them were members of Covert Action. They were also travelling on various diplomatic passports, allowing them to carry the weapons of their trade. Hammer Force routinely moved them around the world under such cover. The surveillance team's equipment had gone directly to Beijing under diplomatic seal on a separate flight.

In the scramble for the coaches to ferry them to the arrivals terminal, the passengers were drenched. Tommy did not mind: he loved storms. Not like Dad: he was a desert man. Danny was being led to a separate arrivals desk for first-class passengers by a uniformed girl. She was smiling at him the way Cantonese always did to a foreigner. A mixture of fawning insolence and contempt. But she had nice teeth, and an even better figure in the sleek, clinging *cheung-sam*, and he briefly wondered what she would be like in bed.

The cold-faced uniformed immigration officer behind the desk took his passport, saw its red cover, glanced at the photograph, glanced back at him and returned the document.

'Welcome to Hong Kong, sir,' he said formally.

As the girl led him into the customs hall, the immigration officer picked up a 'phone and dialled the information desk beyond the restricted area. The clerk handed the receiver to the uniformed police officer leaning against the counter.

'One diplomat,' murmured the immigration officer. 'Surname, Nagier. First names, Daniel Frank.'

The policeman used the 'phone to call a number on Hong Kong side and repeated the details. Soon the policeman received similar calls from other desk officials announcing the arrival of Tommy, Anna and the Covert Action shooters. Each time the policeman called the number across the bay in Hong Kong. Like the immigration officers he would later go to a barber shop on Connaught Road and collect his sealed envelope of American dollar bills. The shop was one of the Triad's paying-out points for its informers.

The information was relayed to the apartment on Hennessy Road.

An hour later, Tung Shi, the Supreme Dragon head, arrived at the apartment for his daily 'phone call from Beijing. As he let himself in the 'phone was ringing.

The woman who used the place for her work as one of the Triad's high-priced call-girls smiled prettily; white teeth, raven hair, dark sloe eyes, ivory skin. No one knew her real name; to everyone she was Suzy. She offered him the 'phone and withdrew to the kitchen, closing the door behind her. Suzy did not need to eavesdrop. In the greatest secrecy the foreigner Suzy still knew only as David had sought her out and said he would place one million Hong Kong dollars in her name in a bank in Switzerland and provide her with a passport of her choice, in return for allowing him to install a number of button-sized listening devices and a recording device small enough to be hidden in the base of the kitchen's dishwasher she never used.

The *waibin* had told her he was gathering information about the activities of business rivals. The explanation was plausible: blackmail was a regular spin-off from her own profession. Not that she cared what the *waibin* did. All that interested her was that the money, and the passport, were her guarantee she could leave Hong Kong well before the cadres of Beijing arrived and put an end to prostitution, at least officially.

There would no doubt be a way around such a restriction for clients of hers like Tang Ming. She could well imagine that when he became Chief Executive of Hong Kong, he would make sure his needs were still fulfilled. Not having to indulge his particular depravities was one more reason to go.

Unknown to Suzy the contents of the recorder's spool of tape were regularly electronically retrieved by one of the Hammer Force technicians in Electronic Surveillance. All he did was to press a button on his console. The cleaned tape automatically rewound itself to once more begin recording. The technician became the first to learn that Tung Shi had reported to Qiao Peng the arrival in Hong Kong of the surveillance team.

Flanked by Dr Alexander Fretov and Dr Sergei Petrarova, Igor Tamasara stared through the observation window at Leo. They sat in the viewing room where Chairman Hu and Qiao Peng had witnessed the murder of one brother by another.

'He is more frightened than I had thought,' said Dr Petrarova, nodding towards the window.

'That is good,' murmured Dr Fretov. 'He will respond all the better.'

The neuro-psychiatrist turned to Igor Tamasara.

'When can we expect the other foreigner, Igor Viktorovitch? The woman?'

'Soon, Sacha. Very soon now.'

They continued to watch in silence the abject figure on the other side of the glass.

14

The crisis meeting in the Oval Office following news of the assassination of Hershel Lincoln had begun with Marty Fitzpatrick reporting that the White House press corps was clamouring for a briefing. The President quickly drafted a statement. It began with a rousing declaration: 'Ambassador Lincoln died trying to preserve, protect and defend the Constitution of the United States.'

America, for its part, would continue to try to resolve its differences with Japan. There would be no down-grading of US representation to the Imperial Court. A new Ambassador would be announced as soon as possible. Meanwhile, American citizens in Japan should remain calm but take all prudent steps for their personal safety. The state of readiness of US forces remained as before the assassination.

The Press Secretary hurried to deliver the statement. Secretary of State Robert Collins announced that the Japanese Ambassador had hand-delivered a telegram from his Foreign Minister stating that the murder bore the hallmark of a street gang killing, with robbery the motive. The envoy had also presented a message of condolence from the Emperor.

The President told those seated before him why he had sent Hershel Lincoln to the Imperial Palace. He wanted the body flown home for a State funeral. After that it would be buried in Arlington, alongside those of the other Americans who had died serving their country. Thack nodded; the funeral arrangements would fall to him. FBI Director Charles Wyman said a team of agents was on its way to Tokyo to work with the Japanese police in tracking down the killers. Other FBI units were travelling to US Embassies in the region to beef up existing security.

Before entering the Oval Office, Gates and Wyman had spoken

briefly about what the FBI had discovered, and what Gates had been told by Morton. Wyman had said that the Chinese Security Service could be involved in the disturbances in Tokyo. Wyman now paused: he had the trick of the successful trial lawyer of looking around the room, double-checking that everyone was listening. He told them there was another matter. A Navy rating in a sensitive post had left the country in the company of a woman who was almost certainly in the employ of the Chinese Secret Service.

In sentences as choppy as the hand gestures accompanying them, the Director explained how his agents had found Leo Schrag's name on an envelope in the car the woman had left in the parking lot at Hains Point. Computer checks had turned up Schrag's Navy records and his present place of work, and confirmed that his was the name on the first-class ticket of the man who had flown out of Washington with the woman.

'By the time these facts were discovered the 'plane had already landed in Beijing. FBI agents attached to the Embassy there are now trying to trace Schrag. In the meantime, the woman's associate in Washington, a known Chinese intelligence officer, is being watched. He will be arrested when no further information comes from this surveillance.'

The shocked silence in the Oval Office was broken by a Texan drawl. 'All very fascinating, no doubt. But I don't quite see what any of this has to do with Ambassador Lincoln's death. Surely you should be concentrating on Japanese culpability and not this somewhat esoteric diversion?'

The speaker was a tall, sun-tanned man in his early forties with movie-star good looks and a fine grey suit. Twice a year the Vice-President flew to London to see his tailor in Savile Row.

The Director smiled bleakly. 'Why not hear the rest before you rush to judgement?'

'I think that's a very good idea,' the President said firmly.

Wyman glanced towards Gates. 'Bill.'

Gates described Leo Schrag's work. He then explained how a Typhoon class submarine had been spotted returning from the Atlantic. The same sub was once more at sea, somewhere under the polar ice, heading towards the Pacific, to where it had made previous journeys, bringing important Russian scientists to work for the Chinese Intelligence Service. That same service had now persuaded Leo Schrag to go to Beijing, admittedly for reasons as yet unknown –

'How do you know any of this is a fact?' snapped the Vice-President.

Gates stared at him coldly. 'Whether you personally accept it is a matter for you. But don't try to punish the messenger. I've been too long in this business to have to take that.'

'Hang on a second, Gates. You're talking to the Vice-President – '

'Let's all listen to what Mr Gates has to say without interruption!'

The President glanced over his spectacles at the Vice-President, the flash of anger plain in his eyes. It was hard for him to believe now how he had been persuaded to accept this insufferable playboy as his running mate. The Party and the media had called it a dream ticket: the respected legislator from California and his preppy partner, the scion of old Texas money. Everyone said that despite obvious differences in style and temperament they would be united by a common passion to use the political system to make the country a better place in which to live. Everyone had been wrong. The Vice-President only had one interest: himself. The man's behaviour now only confirmed that he had been right to decide not to have the Vice-President as his running mate next time. He would make the announcement after his return from Manila.

The President turned and looked at Gates. 'You have something else?'

'Yes, Mr President. It's history of a kind that's also relevant to your trip.'

The silence was absolute as Gates took them on a journey into madness, describing how the CIA had tried to find the solution to mind control. The search had begun in the fifties, at the height of the Korean War, when the Chinese had persuaded captured US fliers to publicly recant their actions in broadcasts which had sent shock-waves through all listening Americans. Discovering how the airmen were brainwashed became the CIA's most secret and important scientific investigation. Distinguished scientists had been given unlimited research grants to discover how the human mind could be influenced and surreptitiously controlled.

Gates paused and looked at the others, then continued in the same quiet voice.

'You have to remember the mood in this country at the time. There were hundreds of red-blooded Americans, the cream of the nation's youth, many of them graduates of our finest military academies, who were suddenly sounding like die-hard Communists. They were expressing political views they had never held before and writing articles attacking their country. When the Chinese and North Koreans began to send some of them home, they took to our streets, urging people to support Communism – and even to emigrate to North Korea!

'There was bewilderment, and then a growing sense of fear. Everybody agreed that what was happening was evil, and the greatest threat this country had faced. Period. It seemed the enemy had managed to change the minds of a generation – and could be about to change the minds of future generations of Americans. Serious people said there would be no future for this country, for the free world, until we found a way to defeat this mental enslavement.

'When the Agency took on the job of finding out how it was done, and coming up with an antidote, it quickly found that not just the Chinese and North Koreans, but also the Russians, were into mind control in a big way. To try to catch up, the Agency spent, in one month alone, over four million dollars on research projects that sound off-the-wall now, but at the time were treated with the utmost seriousness.

'Neurologists tried to build a machine to hypnotise people from a distance. Chemists consulted old almanacs to see if potions existed to control minds. They mixed together the blood of bats with mushrooms picked in the Andes. Behaviourists poured over the records of the Inquisition for clues to how the priest-interrogators had made victims confess.

'Orientalists searched their books, Arabists theirs. The psychiatrists, psychologists and trans-culturalists all agreed that what had happened to our fliers was psychologically rooted. But how? Drugs? Hypnosis? Or something else? The neurosurgeons who examined the prisoners on their return from North Korea reported no evidence of surgical intervention. Yet it appeared part of their brains had been interfered with.'

Gates looked directly at the President. It was hard to know what he was thinking, just as it was difficult for himself to describe this dark period in the Agency's life.

'A real rift developed at Langley. There were those who believed the prisoners were latent Communists and their beliefs had simply surfaced under some pretty good probing by their captors. Others pointed out that the prisoners were often pillars of their communities. God-fearing, church-going youngsters filled with their parents' old-fashioned values. And that something very peculiar had happened to them in North Korea which had turned them into zombies.'

Gates paused. How far should he go? But how far could he not go if he was to convince the President?

'A decision was taken, I believe in this very office, that anything could be done in the search for an antidote. That's when the journey into madness became a flat-out race into the insanities.'

He told them how a group of engineers in Los Angeles had tried to develop a radio wave capable of entering a human brain to change a person's emotional state. An electronics team at Harvard had spent several million dollars creating headphones which could be installed in the United Nations debating chambers. After each session the headphones were to be recovered and subjected to laboratory analysis to extract details stores within the sets of each user's brainwave patterns.

A group in Chicago had worked on producing a device capable of being fitted into a radio or TV set, enabling a listener's or viewer's vital signs to be recorded and transmitted to a monitor station. From the station an undetectable electromagnetic signal would be sent back to the device, causing it to emit a pulse capable of affecting the target's heart, either producing a panic attack or slowing down the heart to the point of lethargy.

Gates paused again, not for questions, but to give them time to digest before he continued to describe how far the Agency had moved into the realms of the bizarre.

'When conventional science failed to come up with answers, the Agency turned to other areas. Psychics and palmists were put on the payroll. And, finally, demonologists. We spent a fortune funding courses in sorcery. We had a whole team of the brightest and best watching fertility rites and attempts to raise the dead. And not in some jungle clearing in the back of beyond, but only a few blocks from here.'

No one laughed. No one even smiled. Gates took that as a good sign. He continued to describe how for almost twenty years the CIA had gone down to the wire of the scientific frontiers – and had finally stepped over it. There was a haunted tone to his voice when he next spoke.

'There were a number of deaths. Human guinea pigs. Mental patients. Prisoners. They never knew what was happening to them. It happened here. But mostly in Canada at Magill University. We had a professor there who would try anything. After the deaths there was a cover-up. The front organisations were closed down. Any links to Langley were cut. The silence of those who could be bought was bought.'

A brooding silence filled the Oval Office.

'But all for nothing?' the President finally asked. 'I'd heard stories ... but this ...'

Gates stared at him. There could be no holding back – not after what Morton had told him. 'As far as success for the Agency? Yes, nothing. The consensus of the investigating committee was that one hell of a lot of money had gone into thin air,' Gates said.

The judgement broke the spell. Heads were shaking and nodding. Only the President remained perfectly still.

'That was the problem out at Langley – accountability,' said Secretary of State Collins.

His face confirmed the theory that your sins start to show after fifty: there were broken veins in his nose; the skin around his eyes was pouched and had started to sag under the chin.

'Some of us think it's still a problem,' snapped the Vice-President.

'Let's not go into that,' Thack said sharply.

He looked at Gates. 'You said this history lesson has a relevance to the President's trip? And maybe also to the disappearance of this Naval rating ...?'

Gates nodded slowly. 'I believe it has.' He glanced around the room, then directly addressed the President.

'Director Wyman mentioned the Chinese intelligence officer his people have under watch. That man has just made a call to Montreal, to a Dr Kate Baskin. She's a neurologist. So is her father. And he worked for the Agency until he was one of those purged – unfairly in his case. But there was a need for sacrificial victims and he happened to be handy. I don't think we should regard the agent's call to Baskin's daughter as a coincidence. It could be connected to Igor Tamasara's work.'

Earlier he had told them all he knew about that.

'Where is Kate Baskin now?' the President asked.

'On her way to see her father. She's also arranged to meet Colonel Morton in Hong Kong.'

The President's surprise was genuine. 'How long has Hammer Force been involved?'

Gates told them everything Morton had told him. They listened in rapt silence. When Gates finished, the President stood up and walked over to one of the windows set in the curved walls. Across the lawns drifted a new chant, as mindless as all the others.

'Stay in Manila, Mr President! Let a new man stand up to the Japs! Emerson for President!' came the repeated call.

The President turned back into the room. When he spoke his voice was sombre. 'If I don't go to Hong Kong, the Chinese deal is dead. I can't allow any other considerations to influence me – let alone this Professor Tamasara and any weapon he may have developed. And nothing I have heard convinces me that he has gotten any further than our own scientists did all those years back. As far as Dr Baskin and her father go, they don't sound the kind of people who would do anything to harm this country.

'But even if they were, what could they do? Baskin has been out of the field for years. An he's hardly likely to have kept abreast of technological advances, practising missionary medicine on that island. Again, everything I've heard about his daughter suggests she's true to her oath not to harm anybody.'

He walked back to his seat, glancing to where Dr Barker sat. The President turned to Gates, frowning. 'You asked for Dr Barker to be here?'

'Yes, Mr President.'

He turned to the physician. 'I understand that when the President underwent his scan a weakness was discovered in his brain?'

Dr Barker glanced quickly at the President. 'It was so small that there seemed no point in telling you, sir.'

The President nodded; he understood the ways of doctors. Dr Barker turned back to Gates and spoke stiffly.

'May I ask how you discovered this information? Clearly there's been a breach of the patient-doctor confidentiality.'

'Doctor, it's simple enough. When you allowed Todd Harper to play Dr Kildare in front of that scanner he tried to sniff out the scan findings from one of the technicians. The technician had the good sense to report that. In an hour the news was on my desk. Be glad that technician didn't try to sell the story to the *Post*.' Gates smiled pleasantly.

'I still don't see the relevance of this – ' the Vice-President began.

'Then let me spell it out,' Gates said, his voice suddenly steel. 'Professor Tamasara's main research work has been into how to manipulate the amygdala and the adjoining hypothalamus and hippocampus. Between them they control how we think, react and respond.'

Gates turned to Dr Barker. 'Can you categorically assure us that the beam, if properly directed, cannot harm the President?'

The physician's voice was a bare whisper. 'No, I can't.'

'Thank you, Dr Barker.' There was no satisfaction in Gates's voice. He addressed the President. 'I must ask you, Mr President, to reconsider your trip.'

147

All eyes focused upon the upright figure seated behind the desk. The silence was a long, tangible thing. From beyond the window the demands of the demonstrators carried clearly. Slowly, then with growing certainty, the President shook his head.

'I have to go.'

Concorde dropped out of the Pacific sky, slammed and slapped by the wind which came in short, violent bursts off the sea, sheeting torrential rain across the runway of the United States Air Force Base at Kadena on the island of Okinawa. Morton knew these were only the peripheral winds. The typhoon proper was still some distance away, moving on a thousand-mile front over the Pacific towards the Chinese mainland.

The vast mass was swirling in a clockwise motion which kept pace with the rotation of the earth. All the time it drew millions of tons more of heavy, moist air from the Pacific. The air expanded and cooled as it rose, forming clouds which turned ever darker before rupturing and dumping their loads with increasing volume and violence as the great storm grew stronger. The unstoppable spiralling effect of the front's progress created a vortex into which tremendous amounts of latent heat were also continuously released, causing the air to rise even faster. This provided sufficient force to propel the air mass at speeds of up to 200 knots at its centre – the roaring wall of wind and rain around the typhoon's eye.

Minutes after landing, Morton stood in the office of the base meteorologist. The Major looked like he had stepped out of a recruiting poster. He was tall with black wavy hair and just the right number of lines around his eyes and lantern jaw. His gleaming white teeth enhanced his tan. With him was the Base Commander. He looked at Morton with awe as he glanced up from the signal he had received from Washington.

'I've been thirty years in the Air Force and it's the first time I've received one of these. You got some pretty powerful friends in high places, Colonel. Pity they couldn't fix the weather for you.'

'For sure.' But Bill had still done a good job.

The Commander turned to the Major. 'Anything he wants, he gets.'

With another sidelong look the Commander walked out of the office. A signal from the Chief of the Air Force, and now this Concorde parked on his doorstep. It had to be something very big. Best with that sort of thing to keep well away.

As the Major tore off a sheet of paper from the telex machine behind his desk another gust of wind smashed against the windows. The Major shook his head. 'Hong Kong's just closed down for all commercial air traffic, Colonel. So's Manila. And every other airport between here and Bangkok and Singapore. It could stay this way for some days. Our Cindy's one bad typhoon. A real bitch who is going to give the Chinese one hell of a hard time when she finally gets there.'

'Major, I've got to get to Hong Kong.'

Shortly before landing Chantal had come on screen with the news of the latest Electronic Surveillance pick-up from Hong Kong. He would need to brief Danny and the team.

The Major shrugged. 'You can't even get a 'phone call into the place. Cindy's knocked out all the sat links.'

He picked up a satellite photograph from his desk. 'This is the last one before the weather closed down. Cindy's one hell of a twister. See for yourself.'

Morton glanced at the print. It showed a mass of deep black cloud, swirling in a violent eddy, ragged at the edges but solid-looking around the centre. It reminded him of the water whirling out of a bath.

'Where's Cindy now?' Morton asked.

The Major turned to a large-scale map of the Pacific. 'Somewhere about here.' He jabbed a finger at a point south-east of Okinawa. 'On her present course she'll pass over Taiwan and track on up the Chinese coast, sucking and shedding all the time.'

He smiled, his teeth white, even and perfect. 'That's why we now give typhoons female names. There's something very sexual about them.'

Morton smiled. Maybe that's all there was to do out here – think about sex until the next weather front.

'You primarily use a sat to keep track?' he asked.

'Hell, no. We still get observations from land stations all over Asia. They're radioed to us. Then we get more data from balloon-borne instruments. Close to six hundred go up every day around the Pacific Rim. They measure pretty well everything up to cloud-top level. Then there are sea-level observations from ships. On an average day there are up to a thousand criss-crossing the Pacific. Not now, of course. They'll all have run for the nearest typhoon shelters. Finally, there are our own reconnaissance 'planes. They fly right into someone like Cindy, to goose her.'

'Where's your nearest recce plane?' Morton asked.

'Right here.'

Behind him the telex machine had started to clatter.

149

'Can that 'plane get to Hong Kong?'

'No sweat, except the airport's closed.'

Morton pointed to a flag positioned over Hong Kong on a map.

'What do you have there, major?'

'That's the *USS United States*. She's our latest, as well as our biggest and best carrier. But she's still pulled into Hong Kong bay rather than tangle with Cindy.'

Morton smiled. 'I've got myself a runway. Let's get that weather 'plane tanked up.'

'Rather you than me, Colonel.'

The Major led Morton into the adjoining room. The walls were lined with racks filled with weather maps and in the middle was a large draughtsman's table. An Air Force captain and a couple of other junior ranks were bent over a map. They were drawing sweeping lines with little flitches on them which spiralled inwards to a centre point. They looked up briefly, then resumed their work.

The Major pointed. 'Cindy's eye. Right now the wind around there's over the 200-knot mark. It's probably going to increase.'

'Where will it be when we're up there?' Morton asked.

The Major studied a dotted track across the Pacific. Against each dot was a time check. 'On her present hourly speed, she's between here and Hong Kong. You're going to have to fly right into the eye and out the other side. You still want to go?'

'The sooner the better, Major.'

The officer walked over to a side table and picked up a 'phone. Outside another gust of wind hit the building with sledgehammer force.

Leo looked up with sudden hope as he heard the key turn in the lock. Since he had been brought to this bare room he had seen no one. He had given up banging on the door, trying to stop his mood altering between despair and anger. This still had to be some dreadful mistake and somebody was going to have to pay. The thought of revenge gave way to another. If this was no mistake what did they want with him?

An imposing figure stood in the doorway, holding a tray of food. He had coal-black eyes and the kind of badly-fitting wig Leo had seen in some of the bars down on Third Avenue. The man wore a doctor's white coat. So this was some sort of hospital. Leo's hope grew. 'Hey, pal!'

'Good evening, Mr Schrag,' Igor Tamasara said pleasantly in English. 'You must be hungry.'

'Are you a doctor? Maybe you can tell me why I'm here?'

Igor Tamasara stepped into the room. 'All in good time, Mr Schrag. Just eat your food now.'

He courteously offered the tray. Leo glanced beyond the open door. A soldier with a rifle stood in the corridor. Must be a military hospital.

'I want to know what's going on,' Leo said, not quite succeeding in keeping the fear from his voice.

Igor Tamasara spoke more firmly as he thrust the tray at Leo. 'Your food, Mr Schrag. Take the tray!'

Leo did so. It contained his favourite beanshoot soup, dishes of noodles and a plate of sliced duck. A knife and fork were provided. Shaoyen must have told them he could not use chopsticks. Maybe this man knew her and would bring her here. She would explain everything.

'Eat now,' Tamasara said in a stern voice. It was important to establish the correct relationship. That was more effective than drugs. Leo squatted on the floor and drank noisily from the soup bowl, realising how hungry he was. He had not eaten since breakfast on the 'plane.

'What is this place?' he asked, forking slices of meat into his mouth.

Tamasara watched impassively. During the day he had questioned the woman agent of Qiao Peng who had brought this American from Washington. He now knew all he needed to know about the fool.

Leo spoke between mouthfuls. 'Does Shaoyen know I'm here? I'd like to see her. She'll tell you who I am. Is this some kind of military hospital? Is that why the soldier's out there? I felt a bit queasy on the 'plane. But I'm fine now.'

'Good, good,' soothed Igor Tamasara. 'And you'll feel even better after a good night's sleep.'

'I don't want to sleep here! I want to go to an hotel!'

'You must stay here.' The firmness was back.

'Why? I'm not sick. You're a doctor. You can see that.'

'Please don't argue, Mr Schrag. You will stay here.'

A new thought occurred to Leo. 'Shaoyen gave you my name, right?'

'That's correct.'

'She tell you we're getting married and I've got to be back in Washington by the end of the week? Otherwise a lot of important people will start looking for me. That could cause you a few problems!'

'I don't think so, Mr Schrag.'

Leo put down the tray and struggled to his feet. 'What are you saying, pal?' he asked, sudden anger forcing his voice higher.

'Nobody knows where you are, Mr Schrag.'

'Shaoyen does?'

'Yes. She does.'

'You mean she's letting you keep me here?' Leo's anger gave way to panic.

'Pick up your tray, Mr Schrag. Always remember to do that,' Igor Tamasara said.

In conditioning it was the small things that mattered. Controlling the conversation. Instilling uncertainty. Having the tray picked up. Leo stooped and picked up the tray.

'Leave it outside the door.'

Leo did as ordered. He glanced at the soldier. The guard stared back. Leo returned to stand before Igor Tamasara. He was sweating slightly. 'Please ... why am I here?' he asked again.

Igor Tamasara studied him for a silent moment. How had the Americans ever come to dominate the world?

'Why am I here?' Leo asked one more time.

Tamasara turned and quickly stepped from the room, locking the door behind him. Leo sank to the floor, suddenly too frightened to even cry.

Morton thought that from 3,000 feet and twenty miles away Typhoon Cindy did not look like her satellite photograph. The vast black violence spread as far as he could see, reaching down to touch the white spume whipping off the swell. He sat behind the US Army pilot, the roar of the engines in his flying helmet almost drowned by the sound of the wind.

'We're going down,' yelled the pilot over the intercom.

Before they had left Okinawa he had given Morton a brief description of what to expect. They would fly in low, no more than a couple of hundred feet above the mountainous waves, going with the wind, allowing it to carry them towards the eye. Morton cinched his straps tighter, feeling the harness cut into his flying suit. He had not bothered with a life jacket. There was no hope of surviving if they ditched. The great wall of whirling cloud rushed towards them. The sea was like a pot boiling out of control. Waves crashed together and were sucked upwards until they seemed as if they were going to swamp the fuselage. The wind was doing its best to tear off the wings. The 'plane nosed down still lower. Morton could see the individual columns of spume, towering geysers of foaming white as tall as a house, hurtling across a sea almost as black as the sky.

Still the 'plane descended.

'I'm going to try to get a little lower,' yelled the pilot.

Morton glanced upwards. It was like being at the base of a moving mountain. The whirling clouds seemed to rise for miles.

'One-fifty feet,' yelled the pilot. 'We've got a wind speed of one-seventy plus on our tail. You okay back there?'

'It's not exactly a rollercoaster.'

'It certainly isn't, Colonel. I sometimes think I should have been a tank driver.'

The winds were increasing. Great gusts that twisted and turned, looped and doubled back. The 'plane lurched upwards, then sideways, then down and up again in a non-stop maelstrom.

'Hang on! The fun's just beginning!' yelled the pilot.

Morton felt as if his body would tear through the harness as the 'plane continued to turn and slew as if rudderless. One moment his head was slammed with sickening force against the canopy, the next it was hurtled against the back of the headrest. They roared on into the blackness. The engines screamed like banshees. The wings seemed about to sever themselves from the fuselage. The aircraft staggered and plunged towards the white caps, then rose again. The rain hammered on the canopy with a noise like millions of rivets being driven home by piledrivers.

'Radial distance from the eye twenty miles!'

The 'plane drew even closer to Cindy's black core, protesting and bucking every mile of the way. The winds had taken on demonic force – a solid black roaring, a sound Morton had never before heard. He clung to his seat, head hunched into his shoulders, and wondered how much more he could endure. The 'plane was spun helplessly about a sky totally black.

Suddenly the terrible night lifted and a strange yellowish glow filled the cockpit. The air abruptly became still.

'The eye,' shouted the pilot, his voice suddenly unnaturally loud. 'Take a look. Few people see this.'

Morton stared around him. They were moving across a great walled area, bathed in sunshine. The black cloud banks spiralled ever upwards all around them. But the air in the eye itself was perfectly still.

'Wind speed all around us is over two-fifty knots. And the barometer pressure's dropping. It's going to be an even rougher ride to the other side.'

The pilot nosed the 'plane downwards into the black wall. Moments later they were out of Cindy's eye and back into her body, being tossed and battered. Morton sat braced in his seat, the sweat running down his neck. He did not know how long the 'plane battled against the blackness, how many more times he was viciously jolted, his head flying forward and backwards, the straps cutting deeper into his skin, the roar of the wind threatening to burst his eardrums.

Then the pilot's voice was back in his headphones. 'We're out!'

The fury gave way to mere storm winds. Behind them the vast wall of black receded.

Up front the pilot was calling up the radio room on the *USS United States*. Twenty minutes later, in poor visibility and falling rain, he made a perfect landing on the carrier's deck. In fifteen minutes one of the carrier's tenders had brought Morton ashore on Hong Kong island. Dressed in borrowed foul-weather gear, he looked like any other seaman.

15

Captain Yaobang Cheng pedalled along Changan Avenue, the broadest and largest of Beijing's majestic boulevards. From either side the city's early-morning workers poured out of the alleys, shouting to make themselves heard above the loudspeakers strung from street lamps. Between bursts of martial music, the tannoys broadcast news bulletins. Yaobang nowadays thought everyone shouted because noise meant knowing you were not alone in facing the next misery.

Since meeting David he had come to look at China through different eyes, as a dictatorship like no other, operated by the most perfect of all control systems: the people watching the people. Reporting any deviation from the Party line – there was one for everything, from sex to marriage, from birth to the actual form of approved funeral – was rewarded with extra food, permission to shop in special stores and the privilege of sending your children to better schools. This was the China he had come to hate, and was determined to help try to change, to give all those around him a chance to enjoy the meaning of the one word for which their language had no translation. The word was democracy. Here on Changan, he knew why people glanced quickly at his shoulder tabs and moved out of his way. Those two silver stars embossed with a lion's head meant he was on special security duty. Someone to be truly feared.

At an intersection a policeman waved him forward, holding up the cross traffic, saluting smartly as he passed. Such fawning behaviour was a symptom of a system in which the Army and the Party were in symbiotic relationship, each feeding off the other, supporting one another against the people. Now he had a further chance to stop that. At the end of his last shift Qiao Peng had put him in charge of the map room. For one fearful moment he had wondered if the promotion was some devilish trap to test his loyalty. But Qiao Peng had explained he needed a quick mind to keep track of developments.

Yaobang turned into a street market. The air was pungent with spices and roots. He dismounted and pushed his cycle past butchers, displaying frogs and snakes from the valleys of the Yangtze, turtles and tortoises from the coastal deltas, caged cats from the city suburbs. Customers poked at them with sticks, trying to judge how much meat lay beneath the fur. The stallholders expertly wrung the neck of each selection. He paused to watch a chef preparing elaborate cold delicacies. The cook looked away. Yaobang moved on, past stalls offering wine made from bamboo leaves, cassia flowers and ginseng.

Outside a teahouse he placed his cycle against a wall and went into the crowded smoke-filled room. A record player blared out traditional music competing with a transistor radio broadcasting continuous news. Oblivious to the noise, most customers read their newspapers. A copy came free with each pot. Since the first advertisement for a kitchen boy had appeared in the *People's Daily*, he had come here every morning to glance through the newspaper while drinking tea.

Today the entire front page was devoted to a speech Chairman Hu had delivered to the Politburo on Chinese aspirations for peace. Yaobang smiled briefly. He now knew that was a lie. He turned the pages and felt his heart begin to thump. In the middle of the columns of advertisements for domestic staff vacancies was another for a kitchen boy.

He paid his bill and left the café, running over in his mind the instructions David had given him about transmission.

Minutes later Yaobang cycled past the guards at the entrance to Zhongnanhai and disappeared behind the red lacquered lattice-work screen intended to ward off evil spirits attempting to enter the leadership compound. On the far side of the lake he could see Chairman Hu and Qiao Peng performing their *taijiquan*, the traditional martial arts exercise with which almost all Chinese began their day.

The *Rodina* had settled into the familiar routine of a submarine at sea. Cut off from the surface by ten-foot thick polar ice, time was measured in watches: four hours on, four hours' stand-down. At the start of another forenoon watch, Marlo continued his daily Captain's inspection. He had already checked the officers' cabins and the bunks and hammocks of the crew slung in the missile room. Now that no torpedos were stored there, he had given permission for some of the enlisted men to sleep in the cavernous, cylindrical compartment.

When he entered the wardroom, several officers around the dining table drinking coffee and smoking sprang to their feet. He looked around the cabin. Nothing to complain of here.

'Who has the conn?' Marlo asked.

'Navigator Tarinski, Comrade Captain,' said a warrant officer, who was on his first voyage.

'Navigator *Comrade* Tarinski,' corrected Marlo. 'On this boat we still use full titles!'

'Of course, Comrade Captain.'

Marlo grunted, closed the door behind him and continued along the central corridor which led to the control room. He paused before the ship's library, a closet-sized room, its shelves crammed with approved books and periodicals for the crew to read. He had chosen the material himself. He was about to turn away when he spotted a magazine wedged between two political digests. He pulled out the periodical, his face darkening. The cover displayed a nude. He riffled through the pages of erotic photographs.

Holding the offending magazine between two fingers Marlo hurried forward to the control room. The control room was a brightly-lit area and crammed with monitors, oscilloscopes and other electronic equipment. A dozen men were at their stations, responding to the data from the sonar men. They were listening through headphones to information from the transducers mounted on the hull. Lieutenant Tarinski stood before a bank of dials displaying the *Rodina*'s present position, speed and distance from the sea-bed.

'Lieutenant Comrade Tarinski!' Marlo said sharply. He held the magazine before him.

'Comrade Captain!' The navigator turned and came to rigid attention.

'Explain how this got into the library!'

Tarinski glanced at the magazine. 'I have no idea, Comrade Captain.'

'You're the officer of the watch! It's your business to know!'

'May I see it, Comrade Captain?' Tarinski politely extended a hand.

Marlo handed over the magazine. The navigator glanced at the cover. 'The date, Comrade Captain. It's three years old. It could well have been here when you took command.' Tarinski handed back the magazine.

'Be careful, Comrade Lieutenant! I conducted a full captain's inspection at the time!'

'Of course, Comrade Captain.' Tarinski was once more at attention.

'Then explain how it got into the library!'

'I can't. But I would remind you, Comrade Captain, that you also conducted a full inspection immediately after we submerged. At the time I was on duty here. And I have remained here, apart from a short sleep.'

'Right now *you* are in temporary command of this vessel! The safety – in every sense of the word – of the crew is at this moment *your* responsibility. And that includes their moral safety.'

'Yes, Comrade Captain.'

The oppressive silence was broken by Tarinski. 'Permission to speak, Comrade Captain?'

'Speak.'

'As acting commander, I would like to suggest that the magazine be destroyed.'

Out of the corner of his eye, Marlo saw several of the ratings struggling to remain solemn. He strode over to one of them. 'You! Take this to the head and flush it away!'

The seaman took the magazine, saluted smartly and trotted from the control area. After a moment Marlo left to resume his inspection. Tarinski had wriggled out of it this time. But he had better watch his step. Just because he was good at his job, it didn't mean he could ignore the rule book. Instinctively, Marlo touched his breast pocket. He never went anywhere without his own copy. There was a rule for everything and Tarinski had damn well better remember that.

Staring down from the hotel window onto the waterfront of Hong Kong, Morton could still hear the roar of Cindy's fury in his ears and it felt as if the bedroom floor was heaving up and down. But already there was a break in the cloud as the typhoon turned north along the Chinese coast. Over the New Territories he glimpsed airliners once more circling, waiting to land.

Behind him Danny was speaking again, his voice raw and constricted. 'I saw no reason to change her operational plan ... '

Danny had just told Morton that some hours ago Anna had left Hong Kong by train for Beijing. Now she would be across the border and heading towards Canton. Morton turned from the window. 'Don't blame yourself, Danny. There was no way I could reach you.'

Hong Kong's telephone links with the outside world, which Cindy had disrupted, had only been restored after Morton reached the hotel. By then he had told them that their arrival in the Colony was known.

'Anna can take care of herself,' Tommy said.

Morton looked at him, a swift, probing, questioning glance.

'We had dinner together before she left. She was fine, Colonel,' Tommy added. He'd seen in Anna a confidence, a sense of control. And something else he couldn't be sure about, but would not tell the Colonel if he was. 'Maybe Qiao Peng will think we're here as part of the President's advance protection force,' he suggested.

Morton dragged a hand down his face. 'Let's hope so.' The last few days had brought him to the verge of his physical endurance.

'Savenko's clearance came through for us to use the Russian Embassy in Beijing as our base,' Danny said.

Morton turned back to the window. The wind had eased, and the rain no longer fell in continuous black furls. Cindy had done no more than give the Colony a good soaking. Another 'plane was coming into Kai Tak: Kate Baskin's flight from Montreal, which had been diverted to Bangkok, was expected in the next hour. Junks and *sampans* were moving out of their shelters. In the bay the USS United States loomed like a grey cliff. He turned back into the room when Danny spoke again.

'I can use Bosstars to call the Russians in Beijing. They can have Savenko's security men fly down and meet Anna's train at some point. Anna's going to be on it for another twenty hours.' Bosstars was the totally secure battery-operated solid-state transmitter/receiver with a built-in scrambler in Danny's briefcase.

Morton shook his head. 'With this typhoon about to hit the mainland there's no guarantee their airports will be open. Tell the Russians to put a team into the Beijing rail terminal. If Qiao Peng knows she's on that train, that's the most likely place for him to try something.'

He looked around the room at the Covert Action shooters. 'Who went with her to the station?' Morton asked.

'I did.' It was the bespectacled shooter who had helped test Tommy in the simulator. 'I checked the train and waited until it left. It was right in the middle of the storm. There was no one hanging around,' he added.

Tommy looked up from the airline timetable he'd picked up from a table. 'There's an Air China scheduled to leave here for Changsha in a couple of hours, Colonel. Anna will have to change trains there. I could join the train there and ride on to Beijing with her.'

Morton saw the clenched muscle at the corner of Tommy's jaw and the look in his eye. The boy would kill for her. He hoped it wouldn't come to that. 'I need you to go direct to Beijing with your father. We've only a limited time for the pick-up on Tiananmen Square. Yaobang will try for three successive days and then abandon.'

Morton turned to the shooter. 'You go to Changsha, hire a car, pick up Anna and drive to Beijing.'

The man left to prepare for the journey. Morton turned to the other shooters and told them to start staking out the apartment on Hennessy Avenue from which Suzy, the high-priced Triad call-girl, operated. When Danny finished his call, Morton nodded for him to leave too.

After the door closed Morton turned and faced Tommy. In so many ways he reminded him of Simone, the same compassion in the eyes and also his mother's slight stiffness and reserve. Morton momentarily wondered whether if Simone hadn't been killed, she would have encouraged her son to join Hammer Force, the way Danny had. But the boy was here, and there was no easy way to say what he had to. 'I'm going to say this only once, Tommy. Whatever you think you could have going with Anna, forget it. Too much has been invested in her to risk losing that investment. Besides, I have an absolute rule there are no liaisons between members of Hammer Force. The job doesn't allow for it. If you can't accept that, now is the time to pull out.'

Morton reached forward and placed a hand on Tommy's shoulder, smiling his on-loan smile. 'I probably should have spelled it out for you even before you climbed into the simulator. But I'd assumed your father had told you.'

The smile had gone as Morton stepped back, watching Tommy's face, until finally he saw that something in Tommy's eyes had been extinguished.

'Understood and accepted, Colonel,' Tommy said gruffly.

Morton turned back to the window. The frustrating part about his work was not knowing if you had covered everything.

Their morning exercises beside the Zhongnanhai lake over, Chairman Hu and Qiao Peng walked towards the compound's bath-house. As they approached the windowless building with its green-tiled, shrouded roof, the Supreme Leader waved to a group of frail figures. The sounds of their querulous argument carried clearly.

'Listen to them,' he murmured contemptuously. 'Once they ran their country. Now they can just about remember Mao's phrases. "The

Marxist-Leninist praxis", "Ideological flexibility". The Great Helmsman was well into his paranoia when he said that.'

Qiao Peng remembered. Mao's madness had led to massive population dislocation, violence and famine. Economic blight swept the land. Over twenty million people had died. Mao called it the Cultural Revolution.

'As long as they argue, they'll have no time to unite against the plan,' Qiao Peng said as they walked up the gravelled pathway to the bath-house.

Chairman Hu frowned. 'In the end they combined against Mao.'

Qiao Peng grunted. 'His mistake was to mobilise the youth. He gave millions of teenagers power far beyond their understanding. They turned on their teachers, on everyone. I still remember that night when they destroyed every household pet in this city. Every dog, cat, bird, fish was killed by the Red Guards because Mao said keeping pets was bourgeois. The next day he announced chess-playing to be the same. There were millions of bonfires as the guards burned boards and pieces. A week later he ordered them to burn stamp collections. After every fire people hated him more and more. This time it will be different. The people will be behind us because they will see the opportunity for themselves to benefit.'

The revolution he envisaged would be very different from Mao's. In one brilliant move Japan and America would be at each other's throats. And afterwards China would be master of all she surveyed. No longer would she have to beg for foreign investment. Or send her brightest and best to study abroad. The world would come to China as supplicants. It would be a sweet moment, far far sweeter than having to accept that scheming plan of the American President. That was no more than self-serving manipulation.

'How is Tamasara progressing?' Chairman Hu asked as they entered the bath-house.

'He is running more tests. But he assures me he will be ready,' Qiao Peng assured him.

They entered a locker room and began to undress.

'And Kazenko? Will he really place his nuclear submarines at our disposal?'

'I am certain he will see the opportunity to be gained from aligning Russia and, it is to be hoped, some of the other republics to form part of a Greater China,' Qiao Peng replied.

It would be a new Mongol Empire, greater than anything the mighty

Khan had achieved. The only boundary left to conquer would be the limits of space itself.

After soaping themselves they went to an adjoining room and submersed in the first of three connected tanks, leaving only their heads above the surface. Qiao Peng lay back, his feet floating from under him, allowing the water's heat to calm the forces of Yang and Yin which always struggled for domination of his mind. Yang was the male, the bringer of violence. Yin, the female, provided the covert deviousness essential to his work. Through half-closed eyelids he watched Chairman Hu heave himself out of the tank and allow an attendant to scrub dead skin off his feet with a black pumice stone.

Afterwards Qiao Peng allowed the attendant to minister to him. Then he lowered himself back into the water of the adjoining tank. The heat made him gasp. He felt the perspiration run out of his bald scalp. As his body adjusted to the temperature he once more relaxed, his eyes closing. From a long way away he heard the soft splash as Hu lowered himself into the third, and hottest, of the tanks, and began to swim through the steaming water. Qiao Peng joined him, circling the tank, an emaciated shark to the Chairman's sleek porpoise.

After a while they lifted themselves out and allowed the steam to evaporate from their bodies. Attendants stepped forward and wrapped them in robes. The tiles cold under their feet, they walked to a room where two masseurs in white uniforms and galoshes stood beside wooden forms. The attendants waited in respectful silence as the Chairman and security chief slipped off their robes and lay face down on the forms. Then the masseurs set to work, scouring the bodies with wood blocks covered in cloth. Finished, they bowed deeply as the attendants wrapped both men in fresh robes and led them to the next room.

Chairman Hu and Qiao Peng chose adjoining beds. Wrapped in sheets so that only their faces appeared, both men quickly fell asleep.

Some time later one of the attendants extended a cellular 'phone. 'The Director insisted,' the man murmured, before retreating.

'Yes,' Qiao Peng said into the mouthpiece.

'Macau border control reports a Canadian woman is on the train to Changsha,' said the Director of Public Security.

With no acknowledgement, Qiao Peng broke the connection and lay back on his pillow, listening to Chairman Hu's snoring. Then he used the 'phone to give instructions.

Inside the airport terminal at Kai Tak the air was hot, humid and redolent with sweat despite the air-conditioning. The concourse was filled, as always. Men, women, children and babies. Wealthy Cantonese mostly, off to a new start. A few more Europeans who had liquidated their holdings and were doing the same. Morton had taken up a position which gave him a good view of the sliding doors leading to the customs hall. A few minutes ago a loudspeaker had announced that the delayed flight from Montreal had landed. Kate would be a little while yet.

Over by the information desk another policeman waited impassively. A few minutes ago he had used the counter 'phone. Since then he had kept his eye on the customs exit. One of Morton's shooters had picked up the call on his lapel sensor mike and relayed the details through his throat mike to the tiny button fixed behind Morton's ear. That was Tung Shi's style. Bribe a cop to keep an eye out for passengers. Bribe the whole damned Hong Kong police force if he could. No class. Not like Qiao Peng. He was class A authentic evil. He had to be to have Igor Tamasara on his side. You needed an especially evil kind of mind to justify doing that.

Tommy and Danny were in separate queues shuffling towards the ticketing counters for the Beijing flight. So far no one had taken an interest in them.

'Go,' Morton murmured into his throat mike.

Two shooters walked over to the policeman and raised their voices, saying that their baggage had been stolen when they had arrived at the airport. They waved towards the terminal, tugging at the cop's arm and demanding he investigate. Soon a small crowd was urging him to do something. Baggage theft was commonplace at Kai Tek. The furious policeman was led away from his observation spot by the ever more voluble shooters.

Morton walked up to the entrance of the customs hall and rapped on the closed door. It opened a few inches and an officer peered at him suspiciously.

'United States Navy. Movements,' Morton said curtly. 'I've got some sailors coming in on the Bangkok. I want to get them straight on a flight to Manila.'

He thrust the pass he had picked up before leaving the *United States* at the officer.

The man nodded and opened the door for Morton to walk through.

16

Carrying her tote bag, Kate Baskin walked wearily across towards the ladies' washroom. The long flight had left her feeling dehydrated and wrung out. At the immigration desk the officer had stared intently at her, as if he could see she was not wearing a bra and her breasts were large and firm, the nipples brown against the white. She had fixed him with her pale blue eyes and murmured a Cantonese obscenity. The officer had looked discomfited. That was always the way with men out here; challenge them and they backed off.

She was tall – a head above most of those milling around the baggage conveyor belt. With her height came blonde hair, cut at the shoulders, and an easy, athletic stride, a reminder she had been the campus middle-distance track star. Out of the corner of her eye she spotted a tall broad-shouldered man standing by the belt. He had not been on the 'plane. But he looked as jaded as she felt.

She had spent most of the flight reading again the dossier containing details of Dad's research she always carried on trips to see him. Dad liked nothing better than to spend an evening going over those pioneering years. Though she could never bring herself to tell him, she knew that most of that early work was outdated. No one bothered any more to expose lab rats to microwatt bombardment. Or used dogs to demonstrate how ultra high-precision beams could induce muscular weakness. Electromagnetism had gone well beyond that.

Yet some of Dad's research was still a benchmark. Like the time he'd placed himself in an isolation chamber and was bombarded with a pulsed microwave beam sending him pre-taped subliminal instructions. Dad had reported hearing disembodied voices in his head telling him what to do. The weirdest thing was that during the experiment he couldn't remember he had made the tape himself.

Shortly afterwards the Agency had dispensed with his services. Now the dossier was all that remained of those seminal years. He had given her the papers before he moved to Borakai in the hope his work would help her with her own research. In the file she had come across Dad's assessment of a phenomenon which had plagued the United States for years: a radio that sounded like an electronic woodpecker. Thousands of people in scores of US cities had complained of pressure and pain in the head, feelings of anxiety, fatigue, a lack of co-ordination and an inability to make decisions after they heard it.

Dad had suggested that the signal was some kind of mass brain-washing weapon. Underneath this conclusion he had written the name of Igor Tamasara, underscoring and ringing the name for emphasis. Colonel Morton had mentioned that name. She had wondered several times what he would be like. She had formed no impression from her 'phone call of his physical appearance. But his voice sounded strong and decisive.

Kate walked into the airport washroom. The place was empty apart from an old Chinese woman mopping the floor. Kate smiled at the crone and went to the end of the row of basins. Placing her bag on the floor she ran water in a basin. The attendant had stopped mopping and was watching. Smiling cheerfully at the old woman Kate closed her eyes and immersed her head. She dipped her head twice more, then ran her fingers though her hair to brush it back until it formed a mane. Tearing off paper towels from another dispenser she patted her face dry. She looked in the mirror over the basin. The vitality was returning to her skin. She felt human again – or at least enough to meet this Colonel Morton. By the time she reached the Mandarin she might even feel ready for dinner. Kate picked up her bag and, with another cheerful smile for the crone, left the washroom.

Halfway towards the baggage belt, she saw the man she had noticed earlier coming towards her. He was carrying her suitcase. She stopped, looking quizzically at him.

'You don't look like a bellboy from the Mandarin,' she said.

Morton shook his head. 'Not even the front desk manager.'

'So you have to be Colonel Morton?'

'David Morton.' He smiled. 'I'm not one for the ranks.'

'But you try to surprise people by meeting their flights instead of sticking to the original arrangement?' She smiled.

'Only in your case.'

They were both smiling.

'Why so?'

Morton told her. And then told her what they were going to do.

The long journey north had become one of endless frisson for Anna. At the border, her papers had been taken away by a soldier and only returned just before the train moved slowly out of the coastal delta and into the mountains. The act of departure had served as an invisible barrier to her recent past, as if it had made her withdraw into her true self. Immediately she had done so, she realised that kissing Tommy had been a mistake. There had been a momentary look in his eyes she'd regretted being responsible for. The Prof had once said she was a born enchantress, but she hadn't meant to exercise her charm on Tommy. When they met up in Beijing she would tell him the truth, that she never combined business with pleasure. In the meantime she would put him out of her mind, put everything out of her thoughts except her immediate surrounds and the role in which she had been cast: the travel writer absorbing everything around her.

She was travelling soft seat class, the most luxurious. The carriage seats were covered with lace antimacassars and the floor in bamboo matting. A potted plant and porcelain mugs stood on a narrow table beside the window. Although she had bought all four seats, it had made no difference. After the border crossing three Chinese Army officers had occupied the others and sat, marinated in cigarette smoke, talking loudly among themselves, completely ignoring her. Several hours later they left the train at a wayside halt, still not acknowledging her presence.

Outside in the corridor, standing class travellers, the women dressed in the same shapeless trousers and jackets as the men, continued to peer into the compartment, proudly holding up their purchases from Hong Kong: television sets, radios, kitchen equipment. They were going home with a veritable cornucopia. Above their conversational roar came the sounds from the loudspeakers at either end of the corridor: music and songs interspersed with announcements. Along with her ticket had come a route map. But it was hard for her to tell where she was in this maze of valleys and mountains.

The map was like the Chinese themselves. A puzzle of paradoxes, the Prof had called them when he had supervised her training for Psychological Assessment. Part of it had focused on Chinese methods of interrogation. The Prof had said many of their techniques were probably over a thousand years old, yet as effective today as the most sophisticated drugs. China had made mind-bending an art, he'd said. The only way to beat it was to stop thinking like a Westerner. He had made her read Confucian philosophy and master the physical discipline of *taijiquan*. In between he'd kept her hooded and handcuffed in a solitary cell, exposed to intense cold and heat, starved and forced to listen to a barrage of taped monologues interspersed with endless music. By remembering what he had said, she had survived. The Professor had said that next to Morton, he knew of no one better prepared to cope with the Chinese. Certainly it had prepared her to cope with her travelling companions.

The train halted at the most unexpected of places. A solitary factory beside the track. A hamlet which seemed to have no visible means of support apart from the maize drying on the rooftops. Once a great silence fell over the passengers as the crew unloaded a coffin and left it at the gate of the graveyard in the middle of nowhere.

Late in the afternoon the train stopped beside a wayside café. A man came to Anna's window with a tray. She selected several dishes in plastic containers and paid for them. The beancurd, strips of meat wrapped in cabbage leaves and slices of sea-urchin were excellent. Afterwards she closed her eyes and meditated. In those long periods of isolation ordered by the Prof, she had learned to concentrate and make her mind and body function on a new level. At first she had only been able to do so for a short while. But gradually she had been able to sit for many hours in a state of relaxed awareness.

When Anna opened her eyes, the train was pulling into a small town and passengers boarded in the usual scrimmaging rush. Three men unceremoniously barged into the compartment, taking the spare seats. When she smiled at them, they continued to talk animatedly among themselves as if that would somehow banish her from their presence.

A ticket collector opened the door and blinked when he saw her.

'Why you travel alone?' His English was surprisingly clear.

'I'm a travel writer, collecting material for a new book.'

'What is your group?' demanded the collector, as if he had not heard.

'Writers don't have groups.'

'All writers belong to *danwei*,' he insisted. 'Must have *danwei* number!'

'Not a Canadian writer,' Anna fished in her bag for her passport and her papers. She handed them to the collector. He held the documents so close to his face that she thought he was sniffing them. He handed them back.

'You alone?' he asked again, baffled.

'Alone. Absolutely alone.'

He looked at the others, shaking his head, then looked at Anna's ticket. 'Why you need four seats one person?'

Anna smiled. Now she understood. She pulled from her bag a small cassette recorder. 'I like to record my impressions on tape. It's easier when I'm alone. And that way I don't disturb anyone.'

One of her fellow passengers plucked the machine from her hand. He inspected it carefully, then handed it to his companions. One by one they studied it equally thoroughly, then spoke among themselves, their faces clouded in perplexity. The collector looked at Anna in growing bewilderment.

'Why you use this?' he finally asked, pointing to the recorder.

'There is so much to see and remember. Taping helps me do that.'

She nodded towards the window. The sun was setting, bathing the landscape in a buttery light. The encircling mountains seemed to be drawing closer. She smiled again at the collector. He shook his head, determined to get back on familiar ground. 'How you work without *danwei* number?'

'I'll get one when I get to Beijing,' she promised.

The response was immediate. 'Aa-eeh! Beijing!' he said, as if everything suddenly made sense.

The collector turned to the others and spoke rapidly. They all looked at her intently. The man who had taken her recorder reached for her route map and using a stubby finger began to trace the line to Beijing. When he finished he turned to the others, as if proud of his map-reading.

'Aa-eeh!' chorused the others. 'Aa-eeh, Beijing!'

Anna smiled. It was not every day they met someone going to the capital, let alone a foreigner and a woman who was travelling alone without a *danwei* number.

The ticket collector handed her back the recorder. 'Aa-eeh, Beijing!' he repeated one more time before leaving.

Todd Harper prided himself on being the kind of TV news reporter who always looked the part: piercing grey eyes that could subdue a lens or a difficult interviewee, a jaw which always seemed ready to do battle. Washington's powerful and pretentious usually avoided him.

That was why he had been mildly surprised when Bud Emerson had called the bureau an hour ago. On that morning's *Today* show, the former Secretary of Labour had been given a thorough work-over for his constant sniping at the President. Todd knew Fitzpatrick was behind Emerson's come-uppance. There was no better political assassin than Marty in this town. Emerson should be lying low instead of coming up for more. Yet he'd insisted he had something important to share.

Driving to their meeting Todd tried to remember what he knew about Emerson. His public persona was of a tight-lipped, unsmiling figure. But he had a sharp, calculating mind, at times positively devious. Was that why he'd selected the parking lot at Hains Point for the meeting? During Watergate, Deep Throat had met Todd's alter egos, the *Washington Post*'s Woodward and Bernstein, there. Maybe Emerson had something new on the President's failure to come down hard on the Japanese? Certainly the White House response to the assassination of Ambassador Lincoln was classic knee-jerk.

When Todd pulled into the parking lot, he saw that Emerson had parked his Lincoln Continental on the far side, and was sitting behind the wheel. He turned and watched Todd pull alongside.

'Mine or yours?' Todd called through his window.

'Mine,' said Emerson.

As Todd slid in beside Emerson he squinted professionally. 'You don't look too bad for someone who's just been eaten alive in front of the nation,' he said cheerfully.

'When the President casts you out with a crown of thorns, one more prick doesn't matter.'

'May I quote you?'

'No.'

Emerson glanced sharply at Todd. 'I thought I made it clear that this is off the record?'

'Only kidding, Bud.' Todd gave him another squinted glance. 'Okay to call you Bud?'

Emerson continued to stare at Todd. He had thought long and hard about who he would telephone. He knew a dozen Washington reporters who would know how to handle what he had to say, but none would have asked to call him by his first name. He had settled for Harper because he could give the facts that extra spin. And he had chutzpah.

Emerson nodded. 'Sure ... Bud's fine.'

Todd settled in his seat, knees pressed against the dash. 'So what's the scoop? The Japanese about to invade Hawaii?' He kept his voice light.

'China,' Emerson said flatly. 'There's something going on over at the White House. It started before I got canned. And it's been going on ever since.'

'Like what?' The banter had gone from Todd's voice.

'Cyrus Voss has made a couple of trips to Beijing in the past week. And Thacker Stimpson's got some sort of adhoc committee operating out of the White House basement, co-ordinating everything.'

Todd did not bother to disguise his disappointment.

'It's probably to do with the President's stopover in Hong Kong. You know what Thack's like. Always one for over-briefing. By the time they get to Hong Kong, he'll make sure the President knows more about the Chinese than they do themselves.'

Emerson shook his head. 'It's not Hong Kong. The stuff Thack's putting together is about the mainland. It's a huge shopping list of all the things China lacks now.'

Todd's interest had still not been rekindled. 'Maybe the President's planning to make an announcement at the Manila conference about increasing trade with the People's Republic?' he suggested.

Emerson waited until a 'plane had climbed out of National Airport. The evening rush hour in the sky was about to begin. 'It's more than that, Todd. It has to be the way they're keeping it under wraps. Everything's on a need-to-know basis. And only the absolute minimum personnel involved. It has to be more.'

'How much more?' Todd kept his voice neutral. No point in getting excited again.

Emerson turned and stared at him. He knew that inflating a story to someone like Harper was the quickest way to kill it. 'I think the President is planning some sort of deal with China to try to stop Japan stone dead in its tracks,' he finally said.

Todd allowed his breath to expel noisily. 'You mean like a new treaty? That would have to go to Congress. And there would be one hell of a dog-fight. The chances are the whole thing would be tossed back into the Oval Office.'

'Not necessarily, Todd. Not if it's sold properly.'

'Like?'

'Such as China and us against the Japs,' Emerson said.

Todd stared at Emerson for a long moment. 'If the Japanese thought that was going to happen, they could move first.'

Emerson nodded vigorously. 'And where better to move than Hong

Kong? There's a vacuum there. Supposing Tokyo decided to stir things up a little? Rattle Beijing's cage?'

Todd's excitement was not quite under control any longer. 'You're not suggesting the Japanese would stage some incident while the President's in Hong Kong?'

'Why not, Todd? If they can murder an ambassador on their own streets, what's to stop them trying to kill the President when he's in Hong Kong?'

'You got anything to back this up, Bud?' Todd's voice was his familiar inquisitional.

'Only the facts I've given you. But they should be enough to get you started. I suggest you begin by working your contacts over at the CIA or FBI.'

'Thanks,' Todd said drily. He'd need a lot more than intelligence sources before going with this story. A thought struck him.

'Why the FBI?'

Emerson smiled for the first time. 'Then you haven't heard about our mysterious Navy surveillance specialist? He took off for Beijing a couple of days ago. Now the FBI are looking for him.'

'Why? What's he done?'

'He seems to have gone with a Chinese woman who is supposed to be involved with their secret service – '

'Holy Christ! You got a name?' Todd abandoned any attempt to keep his excitement under lock and key.

Emerson shook his head. 'No. But she's supposed to have worked in a bar in Chinatown – '

'Him! You got a name for him?'

Emerson fished in his pocket and pulled out a small notebook. Harper was hooked. Just feed him the facts. He'd know what to do. 'Schrag. Leo Schrag. He's a senior chief technician working out of some submarine surveillance unit down by the Navy Dockyard. That's all I know.' A little legwork would sharpen his nose for a story.

'Holy Christ!' Todd said again.

'That's what happens when you have a weak man in the Oval Office, Todd. You get a knock-on effect – '

'I'll be in touch,' said Todd. He opened the door and ran to his car.

On the far side of the parking lot, the agent Gates had assigned to tail Bud Emerson put down his stick mike and pulled out his earpiece as Todd's car swept past his own parked van. He had recorded the conversation. But he decided the matter was sufficiently important to dial Gates' direct line number on the van's 'phone.

Anna's train rattled through the darkness, in and out of gorges and across ravines: on and endlessly on, her compartment full of the snoring of her new travelling companions. Once more Army officers. Out in the corridor people dozed on their feet, leaning against each other. Even the loudspeakers had fallen silent.

The silence reminded her of those nights the Prof had left her trussed in a cradle lowered into a tank so only her head was above the water. When she had been in Psychological Assessment for a year, and was helping him run the test on other potential recruits, she discovered the experiment was to gauge their vulnerability to prolonged hypnosis.

As dawn crept across the landscape, the music started again. Out in the corridor people shook their heads as if they were emerging from a collective dream. Maybe they had their own in-built cradles? The train began to slow until finally, at a snail's pace, it entered the industrial city of Changsha.

Collecting her bag, Anna joined the scramble to leave the carriage. The train to Beijing was on an adjoining platform. She settled in her compartment before the now familiar routine of departure was underway – a great waving of flags and blowing of whistles by the train guards. Then it was north towards the next great feature on her route map, the Yangtze River.

Fifteen minutes after the train departed the shooter parked a hired car outside the station and ran inside. An official told him the train had left. Two men were waiting when he returned to the car. One held up a warrant card. 'Security police,' he said to emphasise his authority. The shooter reached inside his jacket pocket for his diplomatic passport.

Perhaps mistaking his intention, perhaps knowing it would make no difference if they killed him here or later, the security men shot the shooter dead. A truck with soldiers drove out of a side street. The soldiers jumped down, picked up the body and dumped it in the back. The security men drove away in the rented car.

The plotting table that was Yaobang's responsibility was now covered with models of ships representing China's three fleets either already at sea or preparing to leave their bases once Typhoon Cindy had passed. The Naval High Command had suddenly publicly announced it was bringing forward this years's naval war games by a week. The announcement was the result of another call Qiao Peng had made from the bath-house in Zhongnanhai.

On a wall map was a solitary red flag. It represented the estimated position of the Soviet submarine *Rodina*. In this room her role was a closely-guarded one known only to him. He glanced at a second wall map, displaying the disposition of the country's military aircraft. Most were still on the ground, waiting for the weather to improve. But an H-6 long-range bomber had taken off from a base near Yan Luna. The latest position showed the 'plane to be south of Kosrae, heading towards one of the Outer Micronesian islands.

Yaobang remembered that in World War Two the Japanese had built airfields there. During last year's war games several of these long-abandoned bases had been used as staging-posts.

Another map showed the progress of the Hong Kong to Beijing train after it left Changsha. The latest report from Public Security headquarters showed that it had reached the Yangtze River.

17

Igor Tamasara stood on the gantry which enabled him to see the entire workforce. An area the size of a tennis court was filled with the noise of rivets being hammered, the arc of welders' torches and the deeper flashes of energy particles undergoing electromagnetic testing. Working round-the-clock shifts, they had been driven to achieve what even he had sometimes doubted possible: in days they had done what normally would have taken weeks. In one corner welders were riveting casings for the scaled-down model of the Gyroton. Each casing was no larger than a domestic refrigerator and made from different metals and thicknesses. He would make a final selection once he received the results of tests being conducted in the centre of the work area.

Descending the gantry steps he paused at each workstation to observe the electronic assemblers, photo-cell technicians, the specialists in stolhastic gravitation, photon-structures and scalar engineering. Men were testing stimulus waves, passing them through a vacuum to check they left no trace. At an adjoining station another law of thermodynamics was being redefined as technicians checked the spatial energy density of beams. Nearby, the magnetohydro-dynamic effects of soundwaves were being measured.

He felt his excitement intensifying. The technology being developed here would eventually make it possible to produce a beam weapon powerful enough to shake loose the foundations of the skyscrapers of Manhattan and collapse the pillars of the Golden Gate Bridge. It would be possible to target any structure in the world and shatter it to pieces. When that happened he would be looked upon with awe and proper fear. And yet the Americans could have beaten him! One of them had discovered directed energy as long ago as 1898. But the man who gave the world alternating current had been ignored when he tried to show

174

the full potential of that force. It was bewildering that a country like the United States, which had produced so many other original thinkers, could continue to discard them.

It would be interesting to discuss such matters with Professor Colin Baskin. He may have come closer than any of them to understanding how to harness scalar resonance electrical currents. He might even have understood how to deal with the woodpecker radar that had relentlessly bombarded North America with its endless signal. Soon there would be infinitely more powerful and terrifying electronic weapons able to control the weather, create hurricanes over deserts and produce sandstorms capable of burying forests. Through electromagnetism, the sun and the very air itself would be turned into weapons!

In a mood of growing pleasurable excitement, Igor Tamasara reached Dr Petrarova's laboratory. A dozen white-coated assistants were busy at their benches, microscopically examining tissues from the brains removed from the prisoners who had died in the last experiment. Dr Petrarova came forward, a lab pickling jar in his hands. It contained a complete brain.

'This is interesting, Igor Viktorovitch. It's the brain of that monk who collapsed just before you ordered the pulse setting reduced.'

Dr Petrarova held up the jar for inspection. 'There seems to have been a depolarisation of his brain tissue. That would explain the soldier's report that when he shot him the monk had actually regained consciousness and was even smiling at the prospect of death.'

Tamasara frowned. 'It could have been his Buddhist training about not fearing death.'

'It could, of course. Except the other monks we used in earlier experiments didn't show such control. One of them was so frightened he induced a brain haemorrhage. But let's see if I'm right that the depolarisation's caused by reduction.'

The neurologist led the way over to his bench. He set the jar down on the worktop and tipped the brain into a laboratory colander. The spongy mass of pinkish-grey tissue gleamed wetly as Dr Petrarova placed the organ on a dissecting board. He began to insert fine steel probes connected by leads to a small cabinet whose open front revealed wires in intricate groupings. The neurologist nodded at the cabinet. 'It's an improved version of the one I used back in 97 for those experiments on conscious patients undergoing brain surgery. Remember them?'

Igor Tamasara smiled. 'I remember.'

Sergei had shown it was possible to tap the master recordings of a person's memory by stimulating the temporal lobes with an electrode to recall incidents of special interest because they still contained the emotions of the original experience. It was as if Sergei's probings had stumbled upon an original strip of film, complete with soundtrack and the feelings and reactions that had formed the actual event.

'You remember that as soon as an electrode was removed, the induced memory was lost. Unlike voluntary memories, which are a composite affected and changed by the passage of time, the artificial experiences were reproduced exactly as the patient experienced them at the moment of occurrence.'

The neurologist explained as he inserted a probe into the monk's brain, 'What I'm looking for here is evidence that the beam disturbed specific sensory functioning. To see if it made the monk forget the mortal danger he was facing. If so, it means the beam changed his memory trace. You get that with someone who has had a severe blow to the head. The whole trace goes out of kilter. People behave crazily, like not being frightened of fire and traffic – or even death.'

Dr Petrarova pressed one of the buttons on the cabinet. The brain gave a little movement. The needle on a phase-meter dial twitched. 'Polyfrequency is interesting,' he murmured. 'Especially given the swelling and distension of the nerve cells.'

Igor Tamasara wondered whether when he reduced the pulse force of the beam he may well have induced a form of brainwashing before the brains themselves were once more physically cooked by electromagnetism. Dr Petrarova pressed the button again. Another needle twitched. 'There's a significant calcium efflux present in the brain tissue around the emotional areas, which means he was pretty confused in his last moments. That would confirm the soldier's report.'

Dr Petrarova continued to speak as he worked. 'One day I keep hoping to discover what changes actually take place in the brain when memory takes place. When I was a student doing my first dissection I had this idea that maybe memories are stored in code form in individual cells. Discover which cells and I'd crack the code. Now, a couple of thousand brains later, I'm still no closer! When computers became more sophisticated, I used to think the answer lay there. But computers are logical. The brain isn't. And the bigger the computer, the more you get out of it. But the largest human brain actually belonged to an idiot. Stalin's brain was below average weight, yet he could think twice as fast as anyone around him.

'When I was at the Academy, we did tests on his brain to see if we could begin to understand the physical submicroscopic structure of his brain cells. We were trying to discover the one great secret Stalin, like the rest of us, took to his grave – how we think. We gave up none the wiser.'

Igor Tamasara nodded. The more you probed this vast jungle of nerve cells, the more mysteries they threw up. The brain insisted that about one third of human life be spent asleep, yet we still did not know exactly what sleep was. Just as we didn't know how the brain created feelings of boredom, happiness, excitement, fear and terror. Just as he knew he enjoyed the growing sexual stirring in his body, but could not say exactly which of his brain cells was creating it.

Dr Petrarova turned to Igor Tamasara and said apologetically: 'It's a pity we have no more live subjects to test. Then we could be more certain. If we could expose just one to your last beam setting and then explore the subject's memory, that would be very interesting.'

Igor Tamasara smiled. 'How long do you need to prepare the theatre?'

'An hour. No more than two.'

'Prepare it.'

Igor Tamasara walked out of the laboratory. An hour would give him time to satisfy this now almost uncontrollable urge for sexual fulfilment.

Kate felt wide-awake and her brain clear. Only the lines of fatigue around her eyes showed she had flown several thousand more miles since leaving Hong Kong. Morton had led her from the terminal at Kai Tek to a US Navy helicopter, asking if anyone had recently made enquiries about her father. She had told him about the call from Gary Summers. How had he obtained her name? Had Summers mentioned anyone he knew at Georgetown University? A professor or tutor, a student? She had shaken her head.

When they reached the *United States* she had waited in a wardroom while he made a call to Washington. They had flown to Okinawa in separate Navy jets. The flight was the most exhilarating experience she could remember for a long time. They had landed right beside the Concorde. Morton had shown her to a small but comfortably furnished cabin behind the flight deck. That was the last she had seen of him during the flight. She had stretched out on the day bed and tried to sleep. But the adrenalin was still running.

Morton had told her probably no more than he needed to. But she had grown up with secrecy when Dad was at Langley. He'd had the same cool and deliberate way of using the power of understatement and saying as little as possible. Unable to sleep, she had stepped out of the cabin. A steward had politely barred the way, suggesting he bring refreshments. She understood: beyond the cabin was off-limits. Just as she understood why Dad's study had been.

Now, sipping tea, she stared out of a window. The sky was once more bright and blue and, far below, she glimpsed what looked like a toy armada spread across the ocean. She wondered if they were anything to do with what Morton had explained to her.

After seventy minutes Concorde landed at the US Air Force Base at Guam, the only airport in the region with sufficient runway length. Morton led her across to a military transport which flew them to Truk Island, on the edge of Micronesia. He spent the time in the cockpit, using the radio. Landing at Truk, she knew they were getting close. You don't get this kind of air anywhere else, perfumed with a combination of rotting vegetation and pollinating insects.

There was an hour's wait for the three-hour flight to Kosrea. Morton used the time on the 'phone in the airport manager's office, while she sat in the frond-roofed terminal. As they boarded the Cessna for the final leg of their journey, he said that trying to call Washington from a place like this was harder than reaching the moon.

She turned to him, smiling. 'You should talk to my Dad. Last time I was here he was thinking of patenting his persophone. He reckons the telephone companies could buy him out for enough to realise his big dream of building a hospital that would serve the whole of Micronesia.'

'How's this persophone work?'

'By reproducing sound and information directly in the mind and brain. It's based on the principle that all sounds can be reduced to a defined pattern of what are called squarewaves. Dad's been working on an electrode you place on the forehead which picks up the ones your brain tells you it wants to receive.'

She smiled again. 'Like you get this sudden urge to talk to someone in Washington when there's no Ma Bell to oblige you. All you would do then is stick on your electrode and the guy you want to talk to gets the message and does the same. Ergo: you have your persophone.'

'Sounds like your father's still pretty inventive.'

'He is. And don't ever forget that!' Her sudden ferocity was unexpected.

'Sorry. I didn't mean to sound patronising.'

She nodded, mollified. 'It's okay. But lots of people think that because he's out here, Dad's out of touch. No way. He still gets papers sent to him for referring.'

The pilot said they were the only passengers for the thirty-minute flight to Borakai, as he handed them each a can from a small ice-chest behind his seat.

'Last time I got prickly pear juice,' Kate said, opening her can as they rose off the earth strip.

'This one tastes as if it's all prickles and no pears,' Morton replied.

He swigged a mouthful and turned to her. 'Summers, could he have been Chinese?'

She considered. 'I suppose so.'

Kate looked at Morton directly. 'Is there a problem with giving him Dad's address?'

'It's okay.' No point in alarming her, even though she was not what he had expected. Not bookishly academic at all. Only bright. And those eyes. Emotion there, and something else. They were watching him now.

'So why don't you ask?' Kate asked, in her throaty voice.

'Ask?'

'About what went wrong. Most men do when they discover I've been married.'

'So what went wrong?'

'He was one of the great Savers. Save the Elephants. Save the Whales. Save the Arctic. He was so busy trying to save everything else that he didn't bother to even think of saving our marriage.'

'Is that why you went to Professor Svendsen?'

'Lars was wonderful. He said the hardest thing is hanging onto a fantasy. He's right, of course.'

'For sure.'

'Are you married?'

'Was. But she wasn't a Saver. Just a Taker. When I hadn't enough to give she just took off.' Now he could barely remember what Shola had looked like. The memory, like everything else about her, had faded.

'How much did your work have to do with it?' she asked. He liked her directness. 'It was a factor. Probably the same as it is in most break-ups.'

'Probably,' she said, turning to look out of the window.

After a while Morton leaned forward and spoke to the pilot. 'You fly over any foreigners coming in these last few days?'

'The last one was a World War Two veteran. That was about six months ago.'

'American?'

The pilot shook his head.

'No. A Jap. He'd been stationed on one of the islands round here in 'forty-four. Then MacArthur's boys drove them out.'

'I didn't know the Japanese had bases this far south,' Morton said.

'Oh, sure. Nearest one's just the other side of Borakai. You want to see? Cost you no more.' The pilot grinned.

'Why not?'

Minutes later Morton saw ahead an island. Beyond the cliffs was a plateau, its surface scarred in long straight lines.

'Borakai's big brother, Boradin,' said the pilot. 'That's why the Japs chose her. They put down half a dozen runways in parallel. It became the largest aircraft carrier in the Pacific.'

'Dad says the place reminds him of St Helena,' Kate said. 'Hard to get on, harder to get off.'

The pilot banked and climbed slightly to clear the cliff face. Beneath the port wing stretched broad swathes of concrete. The 'plane descended until they were flying less than fifty feet above the old runways. On either side derelict buildings were all but buried in the dense overgrowth. The pilot explained: 'Curtis Le May's bombers used this as their launch pad for the Tokyo fire raids until that other B-29 took off from Tianian one morning and changed everything over Hiroshima. There's probably enough memories down there to run a whole festival of reunions.'

Morton peered down. Those tyre scorch-marks on the concrete were not old enough to have been made in 1945. 'Anybody use this place now?'

'Not really. Last year the Chinese were here for a few days during their war games.'

That would explain the tyre marks.

The Cessna began to climb and head towards the north end of the island. Borakai was immediately ahead. Moments later they swept over a fringe of beach and touched down on a grass strip.

'Welcome to paradise,' Kate said formally. 'But don't drink the water. Not unless you want to spoil Dad's whisky.' She pointed through the window. 'That's his place over there.'

Morton could see a couple of low-roofed buildings about a mile from the strip, on the edge of the jungle. Beside the larger one was a radio mast. Away to his right was a collection of tin-roofed houses and huts. That had to be Borakai Town.

A battered old car was bumping over the ground towards them as they stepped out of the 'plane. Kate waved and turned to Morton. 'Luke runs the island taxi service and buries the dead. He tells everybody he takes over where Dad's failed. They're really the best of pals.'

The car wheezed to a stop beside them. A huge dark-skinned, middle-aged man dressed in shorts and sweatshirt, with a baseball cap on his head, poked his head out of the window, smiling cheerfully. 'Hi, Dr Kate. Visiting long?'

'A week, Luke.'

Luke looked at Morton. 'You with Dr Kate?'

'Yes.'

'Then I'm with you. Any friend of Dr Kate's a friend of mine, Mr – '

'Morton. David Morton.'

'I isn't one for formalities. So I'm Luke, you David, okay?' He spoke as if he had learned English at mission school.

'For sure.'

Morton tossed their bags on the roof-rack and climbed in beside Kate. 'How's Dad?' she asked Luke.

'Last time I saw him, he was fine. Right now is a slack time. Dying season doesn't start for another month.' Luke squinted at Morton in the mirror. 'That's when the nights get damp. People here very susceptible to colds, David.'

'So what do you and Dr Baskin do until you get busy?' Morton asked.

Luke gave another broad smile. 'Fish a little, eat a little and talk a lot. Dr Colin's best talker I know. More stories than a ju-ju man. Isn't that right, Dr Kate?'

She laughed. 'You're not so bad yourself, Luke.'

The car moved into a green tunnel of creepers. At its end were the buildings. 'The bigger one's the clinic. It's got beds for half a dozen patients,' Kate explained.

Luke honked the horn as they stopped before the house. 'When he's full, I come over and make beds, empty the pans, cook. But most of the time Dr Colin does everything. He says that's what he trained for,' Luke said, honking again. He got out of the car wheezing a big man's wheeze. 'Guess he's out back in the radio shack.'

Luke led the way onto the verandah which extended around the house. There were a couple of rockers by the front door, which was ajar. 'Can't have gone far,' Luke said, pushing open the door.

Behind them came the sound of an aero-engine running up to power. Morton glanced up as the Cessna roared overhead. Its wings waggled, then it was gone. The silence of the house seemed all that much deeper.

Beyond the front door was a hallway, the floor covered in rattan, the walls hung with a few paintings of what Morton took to be island scenes.

'Dr Colin's pretty good artist,' Luke said. 'He teaches me pretty good to do that!'

'Dad?' Kate called out.

There was no response.

She led them down the corridor, poking her head into doors as they passed. The rooms Morton glimpsed were simply but adequately furnished.

'Dad?' Kate called again when they entered the kitchen.

The back door was open. A narrow path led to a small building beside the radio mast. Beyond was the jungle. The path disappeared into the undergrowth. Luke walked to the door and shouted, 'Dr Colin? Dr Kate's here.'

There was no reply. Luke walked over to the radio hut. Its door was padlocked. He turned to the others.

'Maybe he's gone fishing?' Morton suggested.

Kate shook her head. 'Not at this time of day.'

Morton followed her down the path to the hut. At the back was a small window. He peered in. The short-wave radio stood on a table. Kate was behind him. 'With that he said he could be anywhere in the world at the touch of a dial. Not that he wants to be. He's had his fill of grant applications and steering committees.'

He turned and faced her. 'Do I detect a little disenchantment?'

She shrugged. 'With university life? Sure. Even a place like Magill is not what it used to be. There's a form for everything. I spend more time arguing with the department Chairman and the resource committee than anyone should. To get a few more feet of workspace or an extra assistant needs more paperwork than I once needed to get a year's research funding. Every time I come here I think Dad's right that universities have become so enmeshed with bureaucracy that they are no longer the front-runners where it matters.'

Kate paused and glanced towards the jungle. 'Dad says you could just as easily build a lab in a place like this and make the next big discovery. Look at the transistor, the microchip, the personal computer, the hologram, that fancy scanner they have at Bethesda. None of them were discovered on a university campus. They all came out of private funding. One of Dad's great dreams is to see something really big come out of this part of the Pacific. And he reckons you don't need to have a university to make it happen.'

Kate looked at him and smiled. 'Sorry. I didn't mean to harp on. Anyway, you'll get enough of this from Dad. He's a one-man anti-university campaign. That's another reason he came here.' She turned and led the way down the track. In moments the foliage closed on them. But the path itself seemed well trodden.

'Where's this go?' Morton asked.

'The beach. Dad likes to come down here in the evenings.'

When they reached the strip of sand there was no sign of Colin Baskin. But there were imprints in the sand, close to the water's edge. Morton stooped and examined them. 'Who else comes down here?'

'Sometimes some of the older kids from town. They sneak down here to learn about sex,' Luke grinned. 'Dr Colin now leaves out a few packets of condoms.'

Morton stood up and looked out across the sea at the island of Boradin. The throb of marine diesels carried across the water. Moments later from behind a headland appeared a fishing boat.

'That's John the fisherman,' Kate said. 'He supplies the whole island.'

'Maybe your father's with him?' Morton suggested.

Luke stepped to the water's edge and waved. When the boat came closer he yelled. But they could already see there was only one person on board.

'Anywhere else your father could have gone?'

Kate shook her head, the dread she had felt when Morton first spoke to her in Hong Kong was returning. 'You think something could have happened to him?' she asked in a low voice.

'Let's just keep looking,' Morton said.

An hour later they had checked every building in Borakai Town. No one had seen Colin Baskin. Luke drove them back to the house and they had conducted a thorough search of all the rooms and the clinic. They found no clue as to where Kate's father could have gone, or why.

'I need to use the radio,' Morton finally told her.

18

Parking the buggy, Igor Tamasara hurried into the complex's main building. His excitement was a living, throbbing thing. The longer he was from his last sexual release, the more urgent it became to find satisfaction. He pushed open a door and entered a room dimly lit by Chinese lanterns. Along one wall was a bamboo bar and several stools. There was a strong smell of incense and cheap perfume in the air. A number of girls sat watching a video. They were the whores Qiao Peng provided for the scientists and technicians. They smiled at Igor Tamasara professionally.

One of them walked over to the bar. 'You like drink, Professor-san?' she asked sweetly.

'No.'

Igor Tamasara turned to another girl. She wore a skimpy blue dress. The last time she had surprised even him with her skills.

'You like Meila again this time?' she asked.

He never understood why whores felt it necessary to pretend they needed a modicum of personal contact, like reminding him they had a name.

'Come with me,' he ordered.

Meila obediently followed him, hurrying to keep up, all the time smiling coquettishly under her false eyelashes. When they reached the end of the corridor she began to turn into the one which led to his private office.

'This way,' he said abruptly, taking another corridor.

Meila felt suddenly apprehensive. No girl was ever allowed into this area. From behind the closed doors came the sounds of machinery and the murmur of voices. Igor Tamasara stopped outside a door and opened it. 'Come,' he called into the room.

Shaoyen emerged. She glanced at Meila but said nothing. But she knew a whore when she saw one. Igor Tamasara led them down another corridor and into the observation room. The women looked around, mildly curious. Meila sat down experimentally in one of the armchairs. Shaoyen glanced at the drawn curtains along one wall.

'Why we here?' Shaoyen asked. She had expected by now to have been gone from this place and this *waibin* who, when he questioned her earlier, had looked at her the way Leo did, the way all men looked at her. Igor Tamasara walked over to the lectern and pressed a button on the console. The curtains covering the glass observation panel slid open.

Shaoyen blinked, not quite taking in what she could see. Finally she whispered: 'Leo.'

On the other side of the glass Leo sat morosely on the floor. His face was puffed from lack of sleep, he looked dishevelled and disorientated. Meila glanced at her in surprise. 'You know this *waibin*?'

'Leo,' Shaoyen called out again, moving towards the panel.

'He can't hear or see you.' Igor Tamasara started to undress.

Shaoyen stared at him for a moment, then threw back her head and burst out laughing. 'You kinky sonofabitch! You want to get off in front of Leo! You're really something!'

Igor Tamasara looked at her, not quite understanding her Americanisms, but sensing she would not object. 'Hurry! Hurry!' He nodded at Meila. 'You too. Both of you!'

Meila smiled. Nothing surprised her any more. She slipped out of her dress and stood in her black stockings and panty briefs under a red suspender belt. Igor Tamasara glanced towards the glass panel. Leo was staring vacuously about him. Shaoyen looked at Igor Tamasara. Qiao Peng had told her to do anything this *waibin* wanted.

In moments she stood in the expensive silk underwear she had bought in Washington. 'All off!' cried Igor Tamasara. 'Hurry! Hurry!' Shaoyen bent an arm behind her back and unclasped her bra. Meila released one stocking, then the other, from the belt's suspenders. Igor Tamasara stepped out of his trousers. He stood in his shorts and socks. Shaoyen was eyeing him, her smile mocking. He'd remember that. But for the moment all that mattered was that both women obeyed him totally. They now stood completely naked, facing each other, as if they sensed what he wanted from them.

He glanced at the panel. Leo had risen to his feet and was once more hammering on the door of his cell. The gesture seemed even more futile because no sound carried to this room.

'Which of us would you like to play the man?' Shaoyen asked coquettishly.

'You.' Later he would show her how a man treated someone like her.

He heard Shaoyen say something in Mandarin to Meila. She turned and looked at him. The way the *waibin* had spoken. Was there more than lust? An unspoken threat? You could never tell with a *waibin*.

Leo had stopped beating against the door and was pacing around the room. 'Start now!' Igor Tamasara ordered. The women lay on the floor. Shaoyen slowly kissed Meila on the mouth. She responded and they began to explore each other with increasing urgency. He had known it would be like this! That the hormones overrode everything! His own excitement grew.

Meila paused to look up. 'Come,' she called out softly before Shaoyen covered her mouth with her own. Then Meila gently pulled him down, drawing him to them.

Shaoyen moved her mouth away from Meila and looked at him. 'You take me first,' she said.

'I take you both at once,' Igor Tamasara replied.

He looked once more at the window panel. Leo was sitting on the floor silently rocking back and forth.

As Igor Tamasara worked his way between the women he imagined he could hear Leo screaming. Then he realised the wild, uncontrollable animal sound was his own.

Leaving Arlington National Cemetery, Gates was once more struck how a State funeral is essentially high theatre. When Air Force One arrived from Tokyo with Hershel Lincoln's body, the protocol managers had taken over. There had been a lying-in-state on a catafalque beneath the Rotunda on Capitol Hill, followed by a mass at St Matthew's Cathedral. Then the horse-drawn caisson made its slow, measured journey across the Potomac to Arlington. At the cemetery gates the President and his Cabinet left their cars and walked the last distance to the grave.

The President had made a point of beckoning forward the Japanese Ambassador from the ranks of the diplomatic corps. The gesture was shown worldwide on television.

The closing rites followed quickly: the transfer of the casket from the caisson to the mechanical hoist which lowered the coffin into the grave; the last prayers followed by the singing of the national anthem; the three volleys. As he turned away, Gates saw that the Ambassador would lie forever overlooking the distant columns of the Lincoln Memorial.

The initial fury of the American people had given way to something close to a national mood of forgiveness, as a carefully-controlled campaign to convey the President's view that the murder was the work of street thugs gained momentum. The clear message from the White House was: steady at the helm; Hershel Lincoln would have wanted it no other way. Gates understood. For perfectly legitimate political reasons the Ambassador had been turned into a national hero. In Japan itself the murder had been similarly exploited, in this case from the Imperial Palace.

The Emperor had driven out to Narita Airport to see off Air Force One, an unprecedented gesture. That night he made a second one by appearing on Japanese prime-time television to denounce the murder in a speech that was also a plea to end the violence against Americans. He concluded with eloquent simplicity by reminding his audience of the great debt Japan owed the United States. Americans had given them something they had never before fully enjoyed in their own long history of nationhood: democracy. Stop this senseless violence now, the Emperor had urged one final time, and live up to the meaning of that most precious of words.

And the violence *had* all but stopped. In the past twelve hours there had only been reports of sporadic incidents, not the sustained campaign which had culminated in Hershel Lincoln's death.

Walking out of the cemetery, Gates wondered if the concert masters behind the killing really had heeded the Emperor's plea. Or merely retreated to plan some new strategy. Tokyo Station said it was too early to say. The good news was that the Japanese were co-operating fully with the Agency's operatives and the FBI team from Washington. That said, the investigation was stalled: the killers of Hershel Lincoln had vanished. Nothing new in that, Gates reminded himself. Just as there was nothing unusual in the way Washington was already shrugging off its funeral mood.

Driving along the gentle curve of Arlington Boulevard, he could see flags being raised to full mast. The radio had just announced that public tours of the White House would resume after lunch. At the same time Congress would reconvene and continue its debate on the President's trip to Hong Kong and Manila. The radio promised a lively session.

Gates smiled ruefully. How much more charged it would become if Todd Harper managed to get someone to confirm Emerson's story that the White House was cosying up to Beijing at the very time the electronics surveillance specialist had gone there for a reason no one had yet worked out. Charlie Wyman's people had gutted Schrag's apartment. Another team had questioned everyone where he worked. Again, nothing. The FBI agents at the Beijing Embassy had so far failed to discover his whereabouts. The time to really panic would be if Schrag failed to show up from his furlough. The attempted reassurance had not fooled Gates. The FBI director was as worried as he was.

The continued surveillance on Li Mufang had produced nothing new. He had not left his bar or apartment for the past twenty-four hours. That could mean anything.

Gates had stopped Wyman calling in Emerson and threatening to throw away the key for talking to Harper. If Harper got wind of that, it might just be enough to make him go with the story. But Gates had agreed that the FBI should tap the 'phones of the reporter and the former Labour Secretary. Harper had been working his own 'phone non-stop, calling and recalling his contacts. But so far the line had held. Marty Fitzpatrick had seen to that. He told everyone to say the story was just too ridiculous to even comment upon. Along the way he had begun to tarnish Harper's name discreetly. But Marty had said that he would only be able to slow down the reporter in the short term. Gates had seen Harper in the press pen near the grave. The reporter had spotted him and started to cut through the crowd, but he had turned away and hurried down the hill to his car. Smiling and ducking was part of his game.

He glanced in the rear-view mirror. Only government cars behind. Ahead loomed his destination, the five-sided concrete façade of what was still the world's largest office building: the Pentagon, the prime military headquarters of the nation. Those on the top floor would have read his briefing paper.

After showing his ID to the Marine at the main entrance, he crossed the lobby to the Secretary of Defense's private elevator. An Army Major who looked as if he had been newly burnished was waiting when the door opened. He led the way to an empty conference room. From behind a closed door at the far end came the sound of voices.

'I'll tell Mr Secretary you're here,' said the Major, leaving. He walked like a butler. Another Major appeared, carrying a tray of coffee. He offered Gates a cup and withdrew with the same butler's gait. Round here they used majors as flunkeys.

Gates strolled over to the electronic map covering one wall. It displayed the latest positions of the Chinese fleets. Each ship was marked with a little flag bearing its name, speed and tonnage. How many hours had gone into painstakingly placing these flags? Maybe that's what majors did when they weren't butlering. Interspersed among the flags were tiny models of the submarines of the US Seventh Fleet, in all a dozen, each proudly carrying the name of an American city deep beneath the Pacific waves. The subs formed a loose arc extending from the Formosa Strait on up into the East China Sea, where the *USS Seattle* lurked in the waters separating Korea from Japan. To the north of *Seattle*, about to enter the deep undersea valley of the Kuril Trench, was a solitary model submarine. Pinned to its conning tower was the tiny hammer-and-sickle flag of the old Soviet Union. The emblem bore the name, and marked the latest estimated position of the *Rodina*.

Gates frowned. That assumed Ivan had held her course and cruising speed. But, just as the flag was out of date, so could be her plotted position. A larger model, with its identification flag pinned to the flight deck, showed the *USS United States* still in Hong Kong harbour.

Behind him the door opened and the Secretary of Defense led in the others. The civilians were dressed in sombre blue suits, the officers still in their funeral rig of the day. The Secretary of Defense waved the others to the oval conference table. He was a short, slightly-built man with an intensity that compensated for his lack of inches. While they settled, Gates finished his coffee, left the cup on the windowsill and took his place at the far end of the table.

The Secretary of Defense sat halfway up, a placing which marked the division in the room. To his left were the Chairman of the Joint Chiefs and the other Service Chiefs: the policy-makers. On his right sat the policy implementers, aides of various ranks. The Secretary of Defense looked around the table. Satisfied that everyone had their briefing paper open, he nodded to Gates. 'We've all read this. Nothing you want to restate or pull back from? Now is the time.' He had the voice of a martinet.

'No sir,' Gates said.

'Then I take it the situation remains basically as stated? That the Chinese Security Service has brought forward their war games to give them cover to bring in a Russian sub? Correct?'

'That is correct, Mr Secretary,' Gates said. Eyes were turning to study the wall map.

'And you remain convinced that this submarine will be used to

189

mount some sort of attack on the President, with Hong Kong the most likely venue?'

'Yes, sir.'

The heavily-built figure of the Chairman of the Joint Chiefs turned his bulldog head away from the map to look down the table at Gates. 'Can you be a little more specific?' For a man so physically powerful, his voice was high-pitched and querulous.

Gates quickly sketched an account of the previous trips the *Rodina* had made, and what else he had learned from his conversation with Morton and Savenko in Moscow. He concluded with a summary of Morton's subsequent telephone calls from Okinawa, Truk Island and finally, from his short-wave radio message from Borakai. In the silence eyes once more swivelled to the map to see where these remote places were.

The Secretary of Defense resumed his questions. 'The Russian sub is not armed with nuclear or any weapons? Is that correct?'

'Yes, sir.'

'Then by itself it could not mount an attack?'

'It could be supplied with weapons by the Chinese,' Gates said.

'Wouldn't that point the finger at them?'

'It would – if we could prove it, sir.'

The Secretary of Defense looked to his left. It was time to widen the questioning. The Chairman of the Joint Chiefs tapped his briefing paper. 'This Baskin character. Have you still no idea what's happened to him?'

'No, General. Only that he's disappeared.'

'Any reason? Domestic unhappiness? Financial problems?'

'None that we know of, General.' Morton had said he had questioned Kate Baskin and pretty well everyone else on the island on these very points.

The Chairman of the Joint Chiefs probed again. 'He could have gone swimming, got into difficulties and drowned. That been eliminated?'

'Yes, General. No sign of that.' Morton had checked that, too.

'A character who took off like that into the wilds of beyond could have done so again.'

'All the islands in the area have been searched. There's been no trace of Baskin, General.'

The Chairman of the Joint Chiefs tried for a laugh. 'You're not suggesting he's been spirited away by aliens?'

Smiles came and went. The Chairman of the Joint Chiefs had been a life-long opponent of efforts to have a full-scale congressional investigation into Unidentified Flying Objects.

'No, General, I'm not. All I'm saying is that Colin Baskin has disappeared, so far without trace.'

'Any possible Japanese involvement?'

'Nothing so far points to that. Nothing points to anyone being involved. Baskin's just gone.'

The Chairman of the Joint Chiefs glanced at the Chiefs of the three Services. 'Remind me, didn't your people send out a report a while back that the Japanese have been buying up Russian Typhoon class subs?' asked the Chief of the Air Force, a grey sere man with gold-rimmed spectacles.

'That's correct. Three so far,' Gates said.

'So why can't this Russian sub be another one Moscow's sold to Japan?'

Gates once more told them all he knew, adding that he hoped to have conclusive proof soon. Morton had promised him that.

The Chief of the Navy frowned. 'Okay. But aren't you still rushing to judgement?' He was a career officer approaching retirement with a reputation for never acting in haste.

'No sir, I don't think I am,' Gates replied firmly. No point in being less than firm now.

The Admiral considered. 'I could call Vice-Premier Kazenko and tell him to recall that sub pretty damn quick, and tell him why,' he finally said.

Gates shook his head. 'There's no way for Kazenko to call the *Rodina* back. She'll be running on total radio silence.'

'So what do we do? Or rather what do you want the Navy to do?' There was a testy note not there before in the Admiral's voice.

'How long will it take your subs to get into position to intercept the *Rodina*?'

The Admiral laughed drily. 'There's a few things you seem to be overlooking, Mr Gates. Those subs are on what we call a run-silent, run-deep mission. They're there to get as much information as possible about the Chinese Navy. I start moving them now and a lot of my people in Seventh Fleet Headquarters will start hollering. But the short answer to your question is this. It would take several days to get them into position. By then the *Rodina* could be anywhere. And there's a lot of sea out there that we just can't cover at the best of times. Right now if we even start trying to do that, the chances are the Japanese will say we're threatening them.'

'How about the *Seattle*? She's right up there on the heel of Japan. Is there any way at all she could at least be alerted that the *Rodina* could be coming her way?' Gates asked.

The Admiral looked down the table at a Navy Captain who nodded. 'We could get a signal to her. But that's still a lot of sea space for one sub to cover, Admiral.'

The Secretary of Defense looked at the Air Force Chief. 'How about air support? When I was out there last year your people were telling me they could find a dime in a rough sea!'

The Air Force Chief digested the words with the hesitation of a politician asked to go back on a promise. He put on his best crying-face voice. 'Since you were there we've cut back on our Pacific capability for budgetary reasons,' he said.

'Satellites?' the Secretary of Defense pressed.

'We've got a couple of K-iis in the area. But they'll take time to reposition.'

The Secretary of Defense nodded brusquely. 'Do what it takes.'

The Chairman of the Joint Chiefs put a new question. 'Why should we do anything? We have one unarmed Russian sub. But that's all we have! Plus a missing scientist whose been out of the mainstream for years.' He looked directly at Gates. 'I appreciate that your business is adding up two and two and seeing if they'll make more than four. But do you really believe the Chinese would try something like this?' A small humourless smile hardly softened the question.

Gates glanced across the table. 'What I *believe* doesn't matter, General. But everything I *know* tells me that Qiao Peng is going to try something. And I also try to make two and two never anything but four,' Gates said calmly.

The policy-makers fixed Gates with cold stares. Suddenly the Secretary of Defense gave a little smile.

'You've got balls to say something like that in this room! But I'll go with you. So what do we do?'

Gates relaxed. 'Thank you, Mr Secretary. What I suggest we do is this. After the Chinese war games we pull our subs back around Hong Kong. Create a sort of defensive perimeter. If the *Rodina* comes anywhere close, our boats drive her away. Meantime, the *United States* becomes our base for the President when he's in Hong Kong. It's got everything he'll need in the way of communications. When he has to go into the Colony he flies in by Navy helicopter and out again once he's finished. The Brits will understand.'

'And the Chinese?'

'They'll understand as well, Mr Secretary,' Gates said.

'I agree, Mr Gates.'

Around the table heads were nodding. The Secretary of Defense put a further question. 'What can you tell us about this beam machine this Russian – ' he glanced at his briefing paper – 'this Igor Tamasara is working on?'

Gates meditated for a moment. Should he try to offer bland assurance? A long time ago his lawyer father had told him that juries love facts; speeches just confuse them. 'Very little, sir. There's no use pretending otherwise.'

The Secretary of Defense laughed. 'At least that's honest – if hardly what I wanted to hear!'

Gates looked around the table.

'Gentlemen, we are in a best-hope situation. All I know is what Morton has told me. And I believe him absolutely. Just as I don't believe that this earth is flat, that Einstein got it wrong or that Igor Tamasara's in China for his health. But if you ask me here and now to say what exactly he has achieved there, then the answer stands. I don't know. Not even Morton knows. But we both think there is every chance we are going to find out soon enough!'

In the map room in Zhongnanhai, Yaobang waited until the changeover of shift, when for a few minutes there was a milling of officers around the plotting table. In those moments he quickly noted down the current position of as many of the models as he could. Turning from the wall maps he saw Qiao Peng standing in the connecting door to the room, then he walked back into his office, closing the door behind him.

All day the train had steamed northwards through China. Beyond Anna's window an immense panorama of isolated valleys, their villages filled with a rude poverty, had come and gone. Now, late in the afternoon they were travelling slowly through a patchwork quilt of cotton, sugar and wheat crops. After crossing the Yangtze, the compartment had once more been invaded, this time by a young couple. They had only one small bag between them. They nodded pleasantly to her and when the train once more resumed its journey, the woman introduced them. Her name was Lilina, her husband's, Bing. They were teachers on their way back to Beijing. Her English was excellent.

Once, when an Army officer tried to enter the compartment to take the one remaining free seat, Bing blocked his way and spoke quickly in Mandarin. The officer backed out, apologising profusely.

'My husband's brother is an important cadre,' Lilina murmured to Anna.

Coming out of another valley Anna returned to a conversation she had begun earlier with Lilina. 'What effect has the end of European Communism had on your students?' she asked.

'There are still some good students, of course, but most have given up the habit of hard work. Not like when I was a student in the Cultural Revolution. Then we all worked hard.'

Anna wondered whether the Cultural Revolution was still the major event in her life. 'Do you think socialism can still survive in China?' Anna asked.

'Of course! We are not going to end up like the Soviet Union! That is why it is important that our students accept what the Party wants to do, and do not challenge it all the time,' Lilina said in her soft, girlish voice.

'Challenging can be good, Lilina. It helps give you a different perspective.'

'Do you allow uninformed challenge in your country?'

'Yes, of course. And wasn't it Confucius who said that out of ignorance comes knowledge?' Anna asked.

She became aware that Bing was staring at her. He peeled the glasses from his eyes. 'Why have you read Confucius?' he asked.

Anna laughed. 'Why? The same reason, I guess, I read anyone. To learn.'

'Why do you want to learn about us?'

Anna explained once more that she was a writer.

'Why do you write about us?' Bing persisted.

'Your country is very beautiful. But not many people know that, or anything about its peoples,' she said.

Bing put his glasses back on and stared fixedly out of the window. Anna wondered what she had said to offend him. Lilina leaned forward and said that soon they would reach Qufu. 'That is the birthplace of Confucius. His home is now a guest house. Would you like to see it? I can show you.'

'We have time?'

'Of course. The train waits one hour in Qufu. Plenty of time,' Lilina assured her.

The corridor loudspeakers delivered another burst of taped music, and then a voice began to sing. It took Anna a little while to recognise the words as a Mandarin version of *Danny Boy*. Lilina smiled as if she had personally arranged for the song to be played.

The sun was low when the train reached Qufu, so that its crumbling walls and bastioned gates appeared to be bathed in stage lighting. Leading Anna from the train, Lilina kept up a continuous commentary. 'The people here all say they are the first family under heaven and insist they are all directly descended from Confucius. But all the treasures he hoarded have long gone. Others were destroyed by the Red Guards.'

'What a terrible loss,' Anna said, glancing back to where the train stood in a siding. She could see Bing staring out of the compartment window, as blank-faced as ever. They had walked a little further, keeping to the edge of the town when, far ahead, came the crash of finger-cymbals and drums being banged.

'Come,' Lilina said, gripping Anna's arm more firmly. 'There's a procession. We go this way, otherwise we will never reach the palace in time.'

She led them towards a grove, almost a small forest. 'We go through there and reach the palace from the other side,' Lilina explained.

'You have been here before?' Anna asked.

'Yes, many times. I met my husband here. We both came on different tours. We left together.'

'How romantic.'

'Yes.'

Away to the left the sound of the dry, shrill music was fading. Then, above the noise came a more familiar one – the deep mournful hooting of the railway engine signalling departure time. Anna stopped and turned. In the distance she could see the train slowly moving out of the siding. Coming down the road towards them was a car. Anna turned to Lilina. 'Do nothing foolish,' Lilina said softly, keeping her revolver steady in one hand.

The car stopped. From behind the wheel Bing motioned to Lilina. 'Get in the back,' Lilina said in the same soft voice.

Igor Tamasara looked at Dr Petrarova and the team around the operating table. Like them he was gowned and capped in surgical garb. The neurosurgeon and his assistants were Chinese, loaned from Military Hospital Number One, the country's leading centre for the practice of *Qi*, the vital force at the very centre of Chinese Traditional Medicine. To one side of the table stood a trolley with Dr Petrarova's cabinet. The neurologist was busy connecting electrodes. The operating team watched impassively.

Igor Tamasara walked to the door of a changing room. 'I'm glad you found a suit to fit. Most of them are a little on the small side for us non-Chinese,' he said apologetically.

A tall man with a shock of white hair and a deeply-tanned autocratic face came slowly forward. He was lean and very fit. He wore a scrub suit. 'I think you might find the preparation as interesting as the procedure itself. So come and take a look,' Igor Tamasara continued courteously. He turned and led the way over to the operating table.

Strapped onto the table, fully conscious but showing no sign of fear or concern, lay Shaoyen. She wore an operating gown. Her head was supported by a padded horseshoe-shaped frame. Igor Tamasara smiled down at her. Knowing he had already chosen her for the experiment had given their sexual encounter a piquancy which had driven him to surpass himself. She looked up at him without trepidation.

Tamasara turned to the white-haired man at his elbow and explained in the same courteous voice: 'We use an acupuncture analgesic. It's slow-acting and she remains fully conscious. But we have to wait a little longer before we can actually begin. Already she feels nothing, including any fear. Here, let me show you.'

Igor Tamasara picked up a needle from a steel bowl. He leaned over Shaoyen and firmly drove the needle into the pupil of her left eye. 'You see – no response,' Igor Tamasara said, withdrawing the needle. 'We've come a long way since your research with lab mice, Professor.'

Colin Baskin looked at him wordlessly.

19

On Beijing Central Station Tommy had discovered that Anna was not on the train that had arrived from Changsha. 'The next one's tomorrow. She could be on that,' he said, turning away from the last of the disembarking passengers. Describing Anna to them his body had felt stiff with uncertainty. There must be something else he could do. But he couldn't think what.

'Anna's not the sort to miss her connection,' Danny said gently, seeing the pain pass like a cloud across Tommy's eyes. He'd seen that look in others when someone had gone missing. There was no easy way to deal with it except to let Tommy talk his own way through.

Driving back to the Russian Embassy compound, their Beijing headquarters, Tommy shook his head, as though desperately trying to deny the reality. When he spoke his voice was a raw whisper. 'She could still be coming on by car with the shooter.'

'They would be here by now. If they had broken down, the shooter would have used the Bosstars in that briefcase I gave him.'

Tommy's throat seemed to have closed, grown together like a painful wound. He should have persuaded the Colonel to let him go to Changsha. When he spoke his voice was a stranger's, harder and coarsened by the knowledge of failure. 'We've got to do something, Dad. We've just got to!'

'We'll do all we can, Tommy.'

They did not speak again until they reached the Embassy compound and Danny took Tommy's shoulder in a surprisingly powerful grip. 'If anyone does, Anna knows how to take care of herself. You said so yourself. But you're not going to help her, playing what-if in your mind. What we need are facts. No better place than here to get them.'

He turned and walked into the Embassy.

*

An hour later the Ambassador's formal enquiries to the police in Changsha had been politely referred to the Foreign Ministry. An official painstakingly took down Anna's description and details of her Canadian passport. When he was told her profession he gave a long constricted 'Eyuhh!'

'A writer,' he repeated, as if the word explained everything about the foolish duplicity of all *waibin*. The official gave another low moan of lament to stretched belief when he came to the shooter's stated profession. 'Diplomat? Why does a diplomat fly first to Changsha to meet this writer woman's train and then come on by car? That is not a normal way for a diplomat to behave.'

Working with the cover story Danny had provided, the Ambassador explained that the missing couple were friends and had probably taken the opportunity to see more of the country. He had managed to imply romantic undertones. But even in Mandarin the fiction sounded fragile.

'A writer and a diplomat,' the official said one more time. The increasing disbelief in his voice gave his clear, beautiful Mandarin an unnerving tone.

An hour later he called back to say there was no evidence that either missing person had entered China. The official's voice on the Ambassador's speaker-phone struck Danny as no longer intense, only relieved at a job well done. Danny used the Embassy's scrambler phone to call Morton on Concorde.

It took a few minutes for the Embassy communication room to locate the aircraft out over the Pacific. On the scrambler Morton's voice had a metallic sound. Danny briefly wondered if someone in the communications room was recording it. Not that it mattered, they were all on the same side now.

'We're starting a grid search for the *Rodina*,' Morton began. 'The techno-boys want to keep all communications down to the absolute minimum. So you'll have to keep this short, Danny. What's up?'

Danny told him.

'Let me get things up and running this end, and I'll be in Beijing. Meanwhile you and Tommy concentrate on the pick-up. That's more important than ever now,' Morton said, hanging up.

'Is that all?' Tommy asked, abruptly closing his hands into fists, as he paced around the Ambassador's office.

'Priorities,' Danny said harshly. 'The Colonel knows his. You'd better get yours, son!'

*

Danny and Tommy made their separate ways to Tiananmen Square to receive Yaobang's transmission. Tommy had borrowed one of the Embassy's bicycles and wobbled through the maze of lanes, attaching himself to one pedalling group after another. People looked at him briefly then continued their shouted conversations. Behind The Beijing Hotel Tommy joined a group of young women workers. Beneath their split skirts he glimpsed knee-length stockings, and spangled hairnets under straw hats. They giggled and spoke behind their hands as he cycled alongside them onto Changan Avenue. On the sidewalks groups were performing their exercises: arms and legs lifting and rotating in controlled movements, faces wearing the same dreamy expressions.

. Outside the Museum of Chinese History and Revolution on Tiananmen Square Tommy parked his bicycle and allowed his motions to unfurl in a rhythmic flow; he had learned to perform *taijiquan* during his time in Hong Kong. Like many of those around him, Tommy wore a personal stereo headset as if, like them, he was listening to the translated instructions on how to perform *taijiquan* correctly. His stereo was identical to theirs in every way except that built into the player's motor drive was a tiny receiver which would be automatically activated once Yaobang began to transmit. As each exercise was completed, Tommy moved further into the vast square.

The square could hold over a million people. Today, Danny estimated there were probably only a hundred thousand dotted about its paved expanse. The place looked almost empty.

Danny had arrived there on board a tour bus. The tourists set about photographing the Great Hall of the People and the other architectural monstrosities. Many listened to an oral history of the square on the cassettes of their personal stereos. Danny's was identical to Tommy's. He picked his way through those engaged in graceful shadow play towards the Monument to the People's Heroes. The obelisk reminded him of a Confucian memorial stele. He walked past the friezes of long-forgotten heroes which adorned the monument's terraces and headed towards the mausoleum of the man they had given their lives for – Mao.

A serpent of pilgrims, six abreast, coiled around the cenotaph of their dead god. They stared at him impassively, not even by the smallest gesture showing they knew the *waibin* was there. Danny turned and began to walk up the centre of the square, towards Tiananmen Gate, on which hung Mao's enormous painting. After photographing it, the tourists reboarded their bus. Removing his headset, Danny joined them. There had been no contact.

Across the square he saw Tommy push his cycle onto Changan and begin to pedal slowly away. There had been no contact in his headphones either.

Two hundred air miles out from Okinawa, the Concorde's Communications Centre Officer told Morton that Lars Svendsen was about to come on screen. They were heading back to refuel; until they began their next grid search, external communications were permitted. Morton turned to Kate. 'There's a five-second delay between them speaking and us hearing him. You have to allow for that otherwise the transmission gets fouled up.'

The CCO looked away from his own screen at Kate. 'The delay's nothing to do with our equipment, Dr Baskin. It's purely atmospheric.'

She smiled. The technicians had the dedication of a medical team, and she realised that the CCO was fiercely protective of his equipment. He tapped a key on his board. 'We've locked on.' Picture and sound were pristine clear.

Morton gave Professor Svendsen an update.

'I'm sorry about your father, Kate. But all I can say, and it's not much comfort right now, is that nothing I have read about Igor Tamasara suggests that kidnapping is part of his style,' said the psychiatrist.

Morton liked the way he had come straight to the point. 'What's your evaluation?' he asked.

Professor Svendsen waited a moment before he said:

'He's not mad. For him, almost certainly, his work is both a creative and self-protecting act. He probably sees himself as a veteran of a thousand battles in the laboratory. His mind challenging the frontiers of science. Just as a soldier feels no remorse for those he kills in battle, so Igor Tamasara feels none for those he destroys. It's the search for answers which drives him. And he is not interested in profit. Only power. In some ways, he's also a revolutionary.

'Kate, if your father is in Igor Tamasara's hands, the chances are he will only wish to debate, and of course, justify, the vile work he is doing.' Professor Svendsen paused and leaned into the screen. 'I think we both learned as students how the Nazi doctors of Auschwitz instructed the parents of those they had murdered how best they could raise their surviving children.'

Kate shook her head. 'And you say he's not mad?'

Professor Svendsen blinked. 'I don't like labels, Kate. But if I had to choose one, I would call him a doubler, like Josef Mengele and the other Nazi doctors were.'

Morton nodded, remembering. Those doctors had represented a kind of omega; central to their ethos for what they had done was their claim to logic, rationalising and experimenting for the advancement of science.

Professor Svendsen spoke again. 'Those doctors successfully divided themselves into two functioning wholes, so that a part-self acted as an entire self. That enabled them to actually totally believe that what they were doing was not in any way evil, but was for the greater glory of the Third Reich. They would spend a day selecting those they wanted to die in their experiments and go home and be good husbands and fathers, showing a proper respect for authority and yet maintaining a total belief in the future they hoped to create.

'Igor Tamasara has the same mentality. It has enabled him to embrace a wide range of evils with a moral certitude, however distorted that certitude seems to us. For him it systemises his behaviour, gives it an absolute positivism and, of course, enables him to eliminate any capacity for what we see as normal feelings. But that does not make him mad, only someone who has developed what we psychiatrists call a thickening of the psychic skin to an unusual extent. Nothing, or no one, can sway him from his path. His is the self-righteousness of the true fanatic. He sees what he is doing as a sacred duty. If he believes your father can help him to better perform that duty, he will treat him with respect.'

Kate leaned towards the screen. 'And if my father refuses, Lars?' she asked softly.

Professor Svendsen was silent for a moment. 'Primarily a personality like Igor Tamasara's is not driven by malice or sadism. The motive forces within him have created a numbing which allows nothing to intrude upon his concept of being a doctor. Conversely, if your father refuses to co-operate, Igor Tamasara will see him as not behaving like a doctor.'

'And then?' Kate moved closer to the screen.

'I don't like to speculate, Kate ...'

'He will kill my father.' It was not a question.

'Kate, I don't think – '

'You must kill this monster first!' Kate said with quiet ferocity, turning to Morton.

In the communications centre there was complete silence after Morton spoke.

'For sure.'

Qiao Peng picked at another stogey from the humidor on his office desk and continued to study the display on a side table. Behind it stood his Chief of Technical Services, Professor Wu. He was small and thin with sad eyes in a face which had a shiny sheen from psoriasis. The scaled skin gave the Professor a reptilian look. When he spoke his voice was a high-pitched whinny.

'A belated birthday present, Director,' said Professor Wu, spreading his hands over the contents of the table as if he was about to perform a feat of magic.

Qiao Peng shoved the stogey between his lips. He briefly wondered how Wu knew his sixty-third birthday had come and gone earlier in the week. Then he remembered they both shared the same birthdate.

Professor Wu's hands hovered over an open briefcase. 'A Bosstars,' he said proudly. 'Their very latest model. But then Morton always ensures that Hammer Force gets the very best.' Professor Wu identified the items. 'The woman's tape recorder is also a receiver/transmitter. The man's weapon is standard issue for Hammer Force's field agents.'

The Professor swept his hand over the table. 'The rest is really only personal effects. The woman's clothes were bought in Paris. And her Canadian passport is an excellent forgery. As you know, that is another speciality of Hammer Force.'

Qiao Peng picked up the briefcase and tested it for weight. 'Can you duplicate this?'

'Yes, of course, Director. In a year we will be able to mass-produce them.'

Qiao Peng put the briefcase back on the table and walked to the picture window. The lake, as so often at this time of day, was covered with smog drifting into the compound from the city's millions of coal-fired domestic and industrial ovens. The light was as pallid as the colour of his skin. The doctors had given him the latest results of his blood tests on his birthday. Three months was their latest prognosis. His cancer had started to spread far more rapidly than even they had expected. He walked back to the table and stood before the briefcase. 'Show me how this works,' he instructed.

Professor Wu gave a little whinny of laughter, a nervous response to the unexpected. 'Once we realised that the scrambler was pre-set, the rest was easy to understand. It's like any other satellite-linked 'phone. The system has been automatically programmed to connect with a series of numbers. Here, let me show you.' Professor Wu pressed a button on the handset.

They listened in silence to the lengthy sequence of numbers being dialled. A moment later a voice came from the speaker. 'Good morning. Russian Embassy, Beijing.' A *waibin* despite her tone-perfect Mandarin. Professor Wu broke the connection and gave another whinny of pleasure.

'Have you tried the other numbers?' asked Qiao Peng.

'Yes. One is an unlisted number we know belongs to Hammer Force's Electronic Surveillance. One we tried was a complete surprise. Our engineers were puzzled that the call did not seem to fit into any of their bands. You know the way we have divided up all the time zones and 'phone systems into various groups – ?'

'Yes, yes, what happened when they dialled this number?'

'They discovered it was ringing out in something moving at high speed.'

'An aircraft?'

'Exactly. An aircraft. It has to be their Concorde,' Professor Wu said.

'Did your engineers actually connect?'

Professor Wu shook his head. 'There is clearly a voice-activated security device that stops any unauthorised contact. Almost certainly the voice of this dead agent of theirs was the one that could unlock the device. Without him I fear there is no way of doing so. In any event, by now they will have changed the access code to their Concorde frequency.'

Qiao Peng walked to the far end of the table. Two identical personal stereos were displayed side by side. Professor Wu quickly moved to join him and picked up both cassette players in his hands. 'They are quite remarkable, Director. Between each song on the tapes there is sufficient space to receive and record information. It is transmitted by the standard short-burst method. Five seconds a thousand characters. The receiver can be changed to a transmitter by a single press on the rewind button. Really very ingenious. The choice of Cultural Revolution songs is also clever. There is actually space inside them to record. My voice analysis experts calculate that on a single tape you can record 40,000 characters. Or several documents.'

'Which is the woman's?'

Professor Wu studied both personal stereos for a moment, then looked up.

'This one.' He offered the one in his right hand.

Qiao Peng pointed to the personal stereo in the Professor's left hand. 'Return this now to where it was taken from. It has a little more work to do yet. But your people have done well. Please thank them.'

When Professor Wu bowed and left the room, Qiao Peng walked over to the connecting door to the map room. For a little while he stood in the doorway watching Yaobang and the other officers going about their work. Then he turned and closed the door behind him. Only then did Qiao Peng shake his head, almost as if he was saddened. Long ago he had learned that human frailty was the greatest enemy in his work. But it had been a long time since he had made such a mistake.

Seeing the needle driven into Shaoyen's eye by Igor Tamasara and then removed with still no sign of pain from her increased the feeling of disbelief in Colin Baskin's mind.

'She really feels nothing,' Igor Tamasara assured him one more time. 'But soon you will see what we can really achieve. And I would very much welcome your comments. But for the moment, you can relax after your long journey.'

The words and solicitous tones of a colleague seeking the valued opinion of another had only deepened the chill of fear in Colin Baskin. At the Agency they had said Igor Tamasara was mad. That was too simplistic. The man was evil incarnate. Those curiously deadened eyes said it all. No better were those others grouped around the table. Igor Tamasara had courteously introduced them, beginning with Sergei Petrarova. He knew the name. Any neurologist would. Petrarova was to research into the brain what Christian Barnard had been to the heart: bold and innovative. But unlike Barnard, Petrarova had long ago made what his CIA file had called a 'Faustian bargain'. He had sacrificed ethics for success. Gifted and immoral had been the Agency judgement. Petrarova's presence only confirmed Colin Baskin's foreboding.

The names of the others around the table meant nothing to him. Professor Wang, the neurosurgeon, and his assistants nodded politely as if this was a lecture theatre demonstration and he was the distinguished visitor to be treated with respect, not someone who had been abducted.

He had been preparing breakfast when the Chinese commandos had burst into the kitchen, bound and gagged him and carried him to their rubber boat on the beach. They had crossed to Borakin and he had been hauled up a cliff face by more commandos and bundled on board a 'plane. They had taken off at once. Coming in to land, he had seen a large city away to his left. From his memory of aerial reconnaissance photographs he recognised it as Beijing.

A closed truck had been waiting on the tarmac and he and his commando escort had been driven here. He assumed the place was a research facility. But he still had no real idea why he had been kidnapped until he reached the operating table and Igor Tamasara explained. 'You are here, Professor Baskin, because you have knowledge we would like you to share with us. But first, we will show you how far we have advanced, so you will see we are worthy of your co-operation.'

Since then Igor Tamasara had spent his time with Dr Petrarova, talking quietly with him in Russian. It was Professor Wang who gave a little bow and politely motioned Colin Baskin to stand beside him at the head of the table.

As the surgeon spoke, the anger, fear and sense of disbelief gradually gave way to professional curiosity in Colin Baskin.

'There is an old Yuan dynasty proverb which says that a teacher for a day is to be respected like a father for a lifetime. I hope that what you will see here today will allow you to respect a medical system very different to yours,' Professor Wang began.

Baskin sensed that if he was to have any chance of leaving here alive he must pay attention to what was being said. Professor Wang was an excellent lecturer and made his points by showing the limitations and differences between the traditional methods he practised and Western medicine.

'Western medicine depends, almost totally, on specific therapies. Traditional medicine does not. Western medicine can only claim about a thirty per cent cure rate. Traditional medicine aims at seventy per cent success, and often higher. Western medicine depends largely on causal factors, structures and quantitative changes in the human body. Traditional medicine is based on three thousand years of observation and philosophy, in which the body, like the universe itself, is a complex system of Yin and Yang.'

Professor Wang smiled, displaying a row of gold-capped teeth. 'You are familiar with Yin and Yang?'

'I fear not.'

The surgeon sighed. *Waibin*, even as brilliant as he'd been told this one was, really had regrettable gaps in their knowledge. 'Yin and Yang are the two great forces in all of us. They are both opposing and complementary. Yin is cold, Yang hot. Yin is night, Yang day. They are present in every object, and every action. In everything. Always.'

Professor Wu glanced up at the ceiling. 'They are both up there, for example. Yang, because the ceiling is relative to the floor on which we stand. And Yin because the ceiling is relative to the sky. You accept that?'

Colin Baskin nodded. 'I can see that. But I still don't understand how it applies to the human body.'

Professor Wang gave another patient smile. 'All organs are Yin or Yang. The solid ones are Yin. The heart, the liver, kidneys, brain and so on. The hollow organs, blood vessels, the circulation system, are Yang. When Yin and Yang work in harmony, the body is healthy. But Yin and Yang are also old enemies. So they fight for control. That creates the imbalance we call disease or illness. It is really very clear.'

'Not to me, it isn't,' Baskin said.

'Be patient, dear colleague. Everything in the universe, including man, is also made up of five basic elements: wood, fire, earth, metal and water. In addition, each element has its corresponding parts: sound, colour, weakness, and so on. With that as our guide, we can deal with any sickness.'

Baskin remembered those long-ago days at medical school, trying to absorb information which made little sense but would, he hoped, one day make him a good doctor.

'It's quite simple, once you accept,' Professor Wang continued as he soaped and began to shave Shaoyen's head with an old-fashioned cutthroat. 'Wood destroys earth, earth destroys water, water destroys fire, fire destroys metal, and we come full circle: metal – in the form of a saw, for instance – destroys wood. Like everything else in nature, the balances and relationships become clear when you study them.' He whetted the razor and continued to shave the scalp.

He looked up and smiled. 'I see you are still confused. But it is really very simple. Wood generates fire. You accept that?'

'Yes, of course.'

'But in our medicine wood also compares to the liver, while fire compares to the heart. We know that the liver has a general influence over the heart. We call that the inter-relationship between mother and son organs.'

Baskin shook his head. 'I'm sorry, you've lost me again. How do you get to linking wood and fire to the liver and heart. I mean there's just nothing in the textbooks – '

'Not in your textbooks, Professor. Only in ours,' Professor Wang gently admonished. 'For three thousand years we have understood that there has to be a full relationship between man and nature. Man cannot exist in a vacuum. Surely you know that?'

Baskin looked around the table. The others were looking at him with polite amusement. 'I accept that man has a relationship with his environment. But I don't see that as a diagnostic tool.' He glanced down at Shaoyen. She stared back at him, alert and yet indifferent to the pieces of hair which had fallen on her face. An assistant took a small brush, the kind pastry cooks use, and brushed away the snippets.

Professor Wang sighed and continued to lecture. 'I think you have never been taught the true relationship between man and nature. The best way to see it is to watch what we are going to do here.' Professor Wang turned to Shaoyen and carefully inspected her forehead. Her eyes followed his hand movements.

'Can she speak?' Baskin asked.

'Of course. But she has no need to unless we ask a direct question.'

Professor Wang reached for a tray containing a selection of gold acupuncture needles. Igor Tamasara and Dr Petrarova now stood beside him. Professor Wang chose a six-inch long needle. He held it up to the high-intensity light suspended over the table. 'To induce deep analgesia we have six points,' he said. 'First we start here, here and here.'

He used the needle to touch the middle of Shaoyen's right eyebrow, the inner point of her left eye and finally the skin across the top of her nose. Moving with incredible swiftness he drove the first needle into the right eyebrow. He inserted the others in the places he had indicated. He quickly placed more needles in the skin covering Shaoyen's temples and behind her ears.

Professor Wang glanced up at Colin Baskin. 'Do they tell you about *Qi* in American medical schools, Professor?'

'No, I fear they don't,' Colin Baskin said truthfully.

'So much to learn ...' The surgeon sighed. '*Qi* is vital energy. Now watch.'

He began to work the needle inserted in the right eyebrow between his thumb and forefinger, rolling it back and forth three or four times per second. He swiftly repeated the process with each needle. He looked down at Shaoyen. 'Do you feel the vital energy?'

'Yes, yes,' she murmured.

Around the table the assistants were nodding.

'Yes, yes,' they repeated. 'She has the vital energy.' Professor Wong continued to stimulate the needles.

'How do you feel now?' he asked Shaoyen.

'Very full. But relaxed,' she replied.

'No fear?'

'No.'

'Good. Soon we will open your head,' Professor Wang promised.

Anna counted under her breath: nine ninety-eight, nine ninety-nine, one thousand ...

She opened her eyes and slowly rose from her squatting position on the floor to walk around the bare room. At the locked door she resisted any temptation to hammer on its metal surface for attention. Her abductors would see that as a sign of weakness. She also knew the only help she could expect must come from within herself. For the moment they would be assessing her, either through a camera concealed in the ceiling's recessed light or in an observation panel hidden in one of the walls or in the door itself.

The Prof had warned her about rooms like this: drab and lustreless, the floor, like the walls and ceiling, painted a flat grey. They were the same the world over – designed to intimidate. In coping with this one, the important thing was to remember everything he had told her.

Colours have an important effect on the human psyche. Red stimulates energy, yellow relaxation, blue a sense of peace. Grey is the colour of depression. But depression is a chemical event, an electrolytic imbalance in the brain, an *inner* reaction which leeches out the spirit. The way to avoid that happening was to accept that depression is formed, always, through the deposit of tiny poisonous crystals on the template of experience. In her case the train journey.

No point in saying she should have known. That the guard at the border who had inspected her passport, the Army officers and the officials who sat with her on the journey, even the ticket collector, that they had all kept her under surveillance. For Lilina and Bing it had been an easy assignment. In the back of the car Lilina had removed her watch before blindfolding her. She had known then she was in the hands of professionals.

Anna leaned against a wall. The first thing they would do, the Prof had said, would be to take away her means of keeping check on the time and her surrounds, so as to destroy her initial disbelief that what was happening was actually happening to *her*. He had also told her the first hours after being abducted were always the most critical, when people felt a compulsion to talk. That was the time when their captors set out to show they were all-powerful and resistance was pointless.

To help overcome this she'd been taught to create in her mind's eye a clock with a sweeping hand. When it had gone around sixty times she must add a notch to the clock face. When she had twenty-four notches a day had passed. She must see each completed day as bringing her that much closer to freedom. She'd estimated that Bing drove for an hour before they stopped close to the clatter of helicopter rotors. The flight, she thought, took about two hours.

When they landed she had been put in a truck. From the sound of clanking weapons, her escorts were soldiers. They had spoken quietly among themselves in Mandarin. When the truck stopped there had been other voices, Russian voices. Igor Tamasara's men. Gripped firmly at the elbows on either side, she had been half-marched, half-dragged into a building. From time to time there had been the sound of a lock clicking open and shut behind her. Finally her blindfold had been removed and she was pushed into this room. The door had slammed shut behind her.

She estimated that that was now ten hours ago.

The door had opened twice, each time to admit a Chinese guard. The first time he carried a bowl of noodles.

On the second occasion he motioned her to follow him, leading her to a lavatory adjoining the room. She had smiled at him gratefully. But when she tried to close the door, he had kept it open, threatening her with his rifle.

The knowledge that she was unusually well-equipped to deal with such psychological pressure continued to help her. She must keep her mind alert and healthy. That required rest. Anna went to a corner of the room and curled up on the floor, cradling her head in one arm, draping the other over her face, which she turned to the wall, away from the light, away from the door.

In the adjoining observation room, Dr Fretov rose from his armchair and crouched so that his face was only inches from Anna's. He knew she could neither see nor hear him.

After a while he rose to his feet and returned to the armchair, making further notes on a pad. She was behaving differently from what he had expected. That made her a far more interesting subject than the American in the next cell.

20

The Hammer Force Concorde technicians continued to quarter the North Pacific, using laser, radar and electronic-intelligence gathering systems to methodically scan the ocean in fifty-mile wide tracts for the *Rodina*. The distinctive pinging of returning signals was the only sound. Two hours into the search the CCO turned to Morton, frowning. 'I've got Langley on the line. Gates is insisting on talking to you. The hook-up's going to slow down what we're doing.'

Bill wouldn't be calling unless it was urgent. 'We'll go into a holding pattern on the grid search while I take the call,' Morton said.

Moments later when Gates came on screen, his face was as grim as his voice. He spoke without preamble. 'Our Beijing Embassy people say Leo Schrag was driven away by a couple of Qiao Peng's operatives. He seems to have gone voluntarily. His knowledge could be invaluable to help that sub avoid detection.'

Morton shook his head. 'My bet is they need Schrag for something else.'

'Like what?' Gates demanded harshly.

'That's the damnedest part. I can't think of anything.'

Gates smiled bleakly. 'There's nothing to show that Schrag's another of the disillusioned. Quite the contrary. He was a Reagan and Bush activist. He was even on a Rehabilitate Oliver North committee, for God's sake!'

Morton shifted in his chair, frowning with concentration. 'This woman he went with. Do we know anything about their relationship?'

'Only that they'd been shacked up for a while. Given Schrag's broken marriages he was probably glad to sleep with anybody. The FBI's spoken to both ex-wives. Each said the same thing: he was impotent.'

Morton raised an eyebrow slightly. This was getting nowhere. 'Why don't you squeeze Qiao Peng's man in Washington?' he asked.

Gates shook his head. 'I still need to keep Li Mufang out there. For one thing he may lead us to Colin Baskin. That's the other thing I wanted to talk to you about.'

There was no smile on Gates's face now. His mouth was clamped in a grim line. 'One of our satellites monitoring those Chinese war games picked up an H-6 taking off right in the middle of that typhoon. Given the weather, the Chinese had nothing else up at that time, which made the sat's computer decide that the bomber was up to something unusual.'

Morton's smile came and went as quickly. Sometimes a computer came close to thinking like a human.

'The sat's cameras tracked her right to the edge of their resolution, just beyond the Marianna Islands. The computer projection suggests that the 'plane landed at that old Jap base right next door to Borakai. It's the only suitable spot in the whole of Micronesia. On the way back the sat followed her into a military base close to Beijing. If there was a snatch squad on board they could have gone across to Borakai and been back here before our people got the images processed.'

Bill was prickling a little. Probably thought he should have done something before.

'Did the sat keep looking after the H-6 landed?' Morton shot in quickly, authoritatively.

'All the way until she rolled into a hangar. The images from in there are useless.'

'Any sign of anything leaving that hangar?'

'A truck. It had gone before the sat cameras could switch to a higher definition. There's just no way of knowing if Baskin was inside. Assuming, of course, that Tamasara had him snatched in the first place.'

'I think we should assume that, Bill.'

They were silent until Gates nodded grimly. 'I think you're right. But there's certainly nothing on Baskin's file to suggest he's up to speed. Logically, Igor Tamasara must be light years ahead.'

'But supposing he doesn't know that?' Morton spoke quickly.

'He's bound to find out.'

'But probably not at once. And time is critical here. The President will be setting off for Hong Kong in a few days. If Igor Tamasara's grabbed Baskin there's just a chance he can't be absolutely certain his weapon will work. Maybe he wants Baskin to check something. Run a few tests. That sort of thing.'

Gates shook his head. 'Baskin would never co-operate.'

'We're not talking of co-operation, Bill. Coercion more likely. Or maybe Igor Tamasara will appeal to Baskin's vanity. You know: science transcending all the other barriers. It's happened before.' Morton leaned into the screen. 'How quickly can you retune that satellite back over Beijing?'

Gates smiled wolfishly. 'Already done. We're using it to try to locate Schrag.'

'My bet is that find him and Baskin won't be far away,' Morton said. And nor would Igor Tamasara.

Gates sighed. 'Even with a sat it's still a lot of looking. Greater Beijing's now bigger than Los Angeles.'

'Unless I'm badly mistaken, Igor Tamasara isn't operating in some alley around the Forbidden City, Bill. He needs space and security. The only place Qiao Peng can guarantee that is out in the Western Hills. The PLA has a number of facilities out there.'

'You're still talking of a ground area of several hundred square miles, David.'

'Have the sat start looking for a rail spur, Bill. Igor Tamasara's going to have to move his Gyroton down to the coast. The easiest way to do so is by rail.'

Gates was silent for a moment. 'Say we find his machine, what then? We can hardly bomb the facility. And if we try to do something diplomatically, it'll be too late. When it comes to delaying tactics, the Chinese make *mañana* sound like Spanish for sprint.'

'When you find it, I'm going in,' Morton said softly.

He had done it before, many times, and each time it became no easier to overcome the enemy as it crouched out there in ambush, waiting for him as Igor Tamasara would be waiting now. 'I'm going in, Bill. It's the only way,' Morton repeated.

His soldier's instincts urged him to engage this enemy as soon as possible – but something else cautioned him to hold back his fighting man's instincts for a little longer.

In the operating theatre Professor Wang rummaged in a tool box on the floor and selected a spanner. He began to tighten the nuts on the frame supporting Shaoyen's head. The lack of asepsis astonished Colin

Baskin. Instruments seemed to have undergone only cursory sterilis-ation and, in the case of the spanner, none at all.

As he worked, Professor Wang questioned Shaoyen. 'Do you still feel the *Qi*?'

'Yes, I still have it.'

He gave a nut a further turn. 'You feel no unpleasant pressure?' the surgeon asked.

'No. Only a little tightness.'

Professor Wang turned to Colin Baskin. 'It is important we hold her head as tightly as possible without creating undue pressure.'

'Why?'

'Pressure tells us exactly how alert she is and that she is always feeling the *Qi*, and therefore no pain.'

Once more the surgeon twisted the needles inserted under Shaoyen's skin. 'What I am doing here is controlling the level of acupuncture analgesia,' Professor Wang said.

'But how?'

'How? By three thousand years of experience, dear colleague.' Pro-fessor Wang tried to control his asperity. *Waibin* could be very stupid. 'Would you like to speak to her? Ask her anything you like.'

Baskin stepped up to the table and looked down at Shaoyen. She stared at him calmly, her eyes clear and alert. 'Do you understand what is going to happen to you?' he asked gently.

'I have been told.'

'And you know the risks?'

'There are always risks, Professor Baskin, in any kind of surgery,' Igor Tamasara said sharply. Baskin felt the anger and hatred rise from some hidden place in his soul. But he could not now afford the luxury of gut emotion. He turned back to Shaoyen.

'You are certain you are not frightened?'

'No.' She felt no fear, only this curious pressure in her head. It had begun after she had been left alone in a room with a grille in a wall before being brought here.

'I am not frightened,' she repeated.

Tamasara smiled. 'She has been exposed to electro-magnetic impul-ses, Professor Baskin. Something, of course, you know a great deal about. We shall speak about that later. But be assured she is telling the truth. She is not frightened.'

Baskin turned back to Shaoyen, the feeling of dread once more rising in him. Now he knew why he was here. Igor Tamasara thought that he could – or would – help him with the currents the Agency had insisted were too dangerously unpredictable to ever harness. He looked at Tamasara. 'Are you telling me you have removed her fear by scalar resonance?'

Tamasara gave a little smile. 'Yes.'

Despite his loathing Baskin felt a stirring he had not experienced for a long time. It was the excitement only another scientist would understand. His own research had shown that the tiny electrical currents running through the nervous system affected all the vital processes of the body. He had called this kindled thought energy and had identified its seat as the unconscious mind. He had been about to begin work on exposing the kindled thought energy of lab rats to scalar resonance when the Agency had pulled the plug.

Baskin looked at Shaoyen. Was it possible it was not acupuncture analgesia which had produced this unnerving calmness in her, but scalar resonance? If so, Igor Tamasara's knowledge far surpassed his own. In that case, Igor Tamasara would probably kill him as casually as he had driven the needle into Shaoyen's eye – unless he could still bluff him. He began to apply his formidable intellect to recalling all he remembered and putting it into the context of what Igor Tamasara's own research appeared to have achieved.

Morton began to take notes as Yoshi Kramer spoke from the screen. The Concorde was once more headed back up the Sea of Japan to continue searching for the *Rodina*. The neurosurgeon looked as dejected as he sounded. 'I've been trying to see what defence can be constructed against beam-energy weapons. Short of creating a contra-electromagnetic field around the President, there's nothing.'

'What happens if we put him in such a field?' asked Morton.

'There's no saying he won't be even worse off. To be effective the field would have to be weaker than the earth's field. The problem then is that you risk exposing him to a whole Pandora's Box of problems. After a few moments the President could find himself trapped in his own electromagnetic madhouse.

'I've dug up all that work José Delgado did back in the sixties. When he placed his lab animals in an electromagnetic tent, his cats compulsively licked the floor of their cage, and the monkeys kept turning their heads and smiling crazily for days on end. Delgado actually got one chimp to do it up to twenty thousand times before the animal smashed its head against the bars.'

Morton looked up from his note-taking. 'They're planning to keep the President on the *United States* and use the carrier's own defence system to throw an electronic net over the area,' he said.

Yoshi shook his head. 'Even if they kept the President in a lead-lined vault with walls a couple of feet thick, the chances are that an electro-magnetic beam would still get through.'

After the screen had cleared, Morton felt the weight of dread bearing down upon him like a physical burden. The more he knew, the more he realised that this enemy was like no other. If this enemy was allowed to triumph, then the world would be forever a darker place.

Dr Fretov continued to observe Leo Schrag from the other side of the observation window. There had been small but significant changes in the American's behaviour. His isolation was creating a traumatic psychological infantilism. That was evident from the way the American unconsciously moved his hands across his private parts. A fear of castration was a common response to someone in his situation.

Dr Fretov made another note. The way the American walked, the REM movement of his eyes, their growing dullness, the slackness of the lips: all were clear signals of the growing terror the American was experiencing. Isolated and engulfed, he was like a child unable to cope; experiencing the same foreboding, mental disintegration and sense of being on the edge of the abyss. Someone in that situation would do anything to survive.

That made him an interesting clinical contrast to the woman. When the time came for them to confront each other it would be fascinating to see how her well-attuned defence system would deal with the American's altogether more unpredictable one.

Professor Wang's assistants were fixing cuffs onto Shaoyen's wrists and ankles to monitor pulse and blood pressure. Igor Tamasara and Dr Petrarova had completed their own preparations and stood with folded arms beside the trolley holding the neurologist's purpose-built cabinet. Colin Baskin did not recognise it from the medical literature.

He nodded at the apparatus. 'What's that box?'

'It's a memory stimulator,' Dr Petrarova said. He glanced at Shaoyen and continued. 'Surely you have not forgotten that by her age she has stored at least ten times more information than is contained in all the books in your Library of Congress? The cabinet is intended to help us search for specific memories.'

'How?'

'Be patient, Professor Baskin,' Igor Tamasara said.

Professor Wang picked up a marker pen and outlined a three by four-inch rectangle on the right side of Shaoyen's skull, above the ear. He made an identical marking on the other side. 'These will be our entry points to her secret world,' he said, glancing at Baskin. 'The next part of the procedure will be familiar to you,' the surgeon added.

'Except that she will be fully conscious,' Colin Baskin said, a note of incredulity once more in his voice.

Professor Wang sighed. 'In Chinese Traditional Medicine we have a simple rule. What you imagine, you feel.' He selected a scalpel from an instrument trolley and made an incision along three sides of the first rectangle he had marked out. Shaoyen showed no sign of pain, even though the knife had cut to the skull bone. What was just as remarkable was an almost total absence of blood.

'What you imagine, you feel,' murmured Professor Wang once more.

'Are you seriously saying the mind can influence physical factors like bleeding?' Colin Baskin asked.

An assistant began applying gauze pads to the incision to soak up a trickle of blood.

'Show me your tongue,' the surgeon commanded Shaoyen.

She stuck out her tongue. It was redder than normal, with a thin white coating. Professor Wang inspected the tongue carefully, pinching it between his fingers and feeling the surface. He nodded, satisfied. 'The acupuncture has done its work well. For the moment she has a deficiency of Yang, which means that she will not suffer much blood loss.'

'But how ... ?'

Colin Baskin once more struggled to conceal his bewilderment. Everything he was being told flew in the face of all he knew. It was like trying to use two completely disparate formulae to solve a problem. Professor Wang reiterated a now-familiar reminder. 'We have used acupuncture for over three thousand years. But we still do not know exactly how it works. It is enough that it does.'

'But don't you want to know?'

The surgeon sighed. *Waibin* had the strangest ideas. 'There would be no point. Each patient and his symptoms are unique.'

Professor Wang spoke quickly in Mandarin to an assistant. The man handed him a high-speed bone drill, then took up another. Standing on opposite sides of Shaoyen's clamped head they began to bore holes through the four corners of the outlined rectangles. Next they each inserted a wire saw through two adjacent holes and pulled back and forth until they had cut through the bone. In a surprisingly short time they had exposed two openings in Shaoyen's skull. Her brain was now covered only by a membrane. She lay completely still while this was happening. Not so much as a murmur had passed her lips.

'You still have the *Qi*?' Professor Wang asked her.

'Yes.'

Using a pair of surgical scissors he snipped away the membrane. The exposed brain pulsed wetly under the light. Dr Petrarova and Igor Tamasara wheeled forward the trolley with the cabinet. The neurologist picked up an electrode and looked at Colin Baskin. Then he carefully drove the probe into the right side of Shaoyen's brain.

Once more Baskin felt an involuntary thrill of excitement at how far research had progressed since his own pioneering work. He had only been on the brink.

Dr Petrarova turned to him. 'What we are doing here is filling the gap left by the collapse of philosophy and theology as major influences in people's lives. Those disciplines have failed to answer such basic questions as "how do we know what we know?", and that cornerstone of Christianity, Pilate's question to Jesus: "What is truth?" We are coming closer to the answers with psychobiology.' He began to connect an electrode to the lead of a pulse-meter.

Igor Tamasara looked at Colin Baskin. 'We have come a long way since those crude experiments in stimulation by Wilder Penfield in the very department at Magill where your own daughter now works.'

Baskin stiffened at the mention of Kate. There had been a hint of menace in the way Tamasara had spoken. Fear now joined the hatred he already felt for this man.

'Wilder Penfield,' Dr Petrarova murmured, as he tested the electrical circuit to the pulse-meter. 'A man before his time ... and like so many of your brilliant scientists, never properly appreciated ...'

Penfield had been a neurosurgeon in the fifties who had electrically stimulated the brains of his patients during surgery. Though deeply anaesthetised, they had recalled long-forgotten incidents under his probing of their temporal lobes. The experiment failed to excite lasting interest; many of Penfield's peers felt he was violating the patient-doctor trust. Colin Baskin turned to Dr Petrarova, his professional curiosity once more momentarily overcoming his other feelings. 'Is that what started you off – Penfield's idea that the mind is really a clockwork mechanism in the brain itself?' he asked.

Dr Petrarova nodded. 'Partly, yes. But Penfield did not really grasp that even the deepest memory can be recalled with a complementary experience. He was content to use his probing merely to stir surface memories. What you see here is proof of a deeper form of recall. Of conversations and emotions she felt at a certain time, even the thoughts she thought.'

Baskin nodded. That much had already been amply demonstrated to him. Under Igor Tamasara's skilled questioning Shaoyen had revealed a great deal about herself.

Dr Petrarova inserted the probe into the left-hand side of Shaoyen's brain. The needle on the pulse-meter flicked briefly. He nodded to Igor Tamasara to resume his careful questioning.

'A little while ago, Shaoyen, you told me about that time you went to Li Mufang's apartment, and you made love until you received the faxes. Who were they from?'

'Li gets first fax from Jongjong.'

'Who is he?'

'Jongjong, Qiao Peng. You know that.'

'Yes, I know that. And the message?'

'It is in reverse characters. So, very important.'

'What did the message say?'

'Kidnap Leo,' Shaoyen said matter-of-factly.

Igor Tamasara and Dr Petrarova exchanged glances. Professor Wang and his assistants looked on impassively.

'Why kidnap Leo?' Igor Tamasara asked gently.

'Jongjong says he needs a *waibin*.'

Baskin was mesmerised by the droning questions.

'Did Jongjong say why he needed a *waibin*?' Igor Tamasara asked.

Shaoyen continued to look up at him. Those coal-black eyes seemed able to see into the very recesses of her mind, making her recall things she had only overheard and barely understood.

'Jongjong says it is for Silent Voices.'

'What is that, Shaoyen?'

'Li thinks it will change the world. Make China more powerful than United States or Japan.'

Colin Baskin sensed the tension in Igor Tamasara. Whatever this Silent Voices was, he hadn't know about it until now! He felt a sudden irrational hope. The monster wasn't completely invincible!

'Did Li say how?' Tamasara asked.

'No ...'

One of the assistants checked the pressure cuffs. Shaoyen's vital signs were stable.

'And the second fax?' Tamasara asked.

'From Leo. A *Dai Feng* had sailed long way and back under the sea to Russia before the Americans find out.'

'*Dai Feng*?' Tamasara asked.

'Big wind. You call typhoon. A submarine.'

'What did Li do with the fax, Shaoyen?'

'Send it to Jongjong. But first he goes to kitchen to make tea. Then I go to sleep ...'

'And that is all you remember?' Tamasara asked.

'Yes.'

'Can you tell me any more?' he asked quietly. 'Anything at all?'

'I want to help you,' Shaoyen said. 'My head says I have no choice.'

'But ...'

'I do not know any more,' said Shaoyen softly. 'And I am afraid because of this.'

'Do not be afraid, Shaoyen.' Once more he quickly touched her face, watching her eyes carefully. Then she lowered the long curled lashes shielding them from his scrutiny.

Colin Baskin saw Igor Tamasara glance quickly at Dr Petrarova. There was something in that look – perhaps a momentary and unfathomable regret. But it was hard to say. Dr Petrarova walked over to the cabinet and studied the pulse-meter. The needle had returned to zero. He looked at Igor Tamasara.

'Her memory circuits have been fully explored, Igor Viktorovitch.'

Igor Tamasara nodded to Professor Wang and said, 'You may now proceed.' He beckoned to Colin Baskin as he turned away from the table. 'Come, Professor. We have shown you a little of what we can do. Now it is your turn to share your knowledge with us.'

Accompanied by Dr Petrarova, they walked towards the surgeons' changing room.

'Your daughter ... Kate. She would have found this fascinating, I think?' Igor Tamasara said.

Baskin stopped and looked at Tamasara.

'What do you know about my daughter?'

Igor Tamasara smiled briefly. 'A great deal, Professor. For instance, I know she has gone to Borakai to see you. Perhaps soon we will see her here.'

To hide the fear gnawing at him, Baskin looked back at the group around the operating table. Igor Tamasara took him firmly but kindly by the arm. 'Come, let's get changed. There's really nothing more to interest you there. They're just tidying up.'

He led the way into the changing room.

On the operating table Shaoyen stared as Professor Wang selected a long broad-bladed scalpel. The surgeon looked down at her impassively for a moment. Then, with none of the finesse he had shown earlier when inserting the acupuncture needles, he drove the scalpel through the left-hand skull opening to her brain and out through the right-hand one.

With brute strength he twisted the blade. For a moment there was a stunned look in her eyes. He twisted harder. The looked passed. He twisted again to finally destroy Shaoyen's brain.

21

Qiao Peng's eyes remained unblinking after Chairman Hu read out the telegram from the Chinese Ambassador in Moscow announcing that Vice-Premier Oleg Kazenko had been among those killed when their military transport crashed on its final approach to Archangel. General Yuri Savenko, who was in charge of the investigation, had ruled out sabotage.

'Almost certainly another case of pilot error. The break-up of the old Soviet Air Force has led to a distressing number of such fatalities,' Qiao Peng finally said.

'Have they all been investigated by Savenko?' Chairman Hu asked.

'Almost certainly not. But given that it's the Vice-Premier, I'd have been more concerned if Savenko had not taken charge. If he's ruled out foul play, we can take it there wasn't any.'

'But coming now ... when we are about to move ... ?' Chairman Hu's pensive voice trailed off. Once more he glanced at the Ambassador's message on the desk.

It was the only item on the lacquered surface almost large enough to accommodate the Red Flag limousine that had brought Qiao Peng the short distance from his own compound in Zhongnanhai to the Supreme Leader's on the far side of the lake.

Qiao Peng used his tongue to work free a piece of tobacco between his molars. The important thing now was to remain calm, to do nothing to increase the anxiety in the Chairman's voice. Human frailties made people feel vulnerable, an emotion unaffordable at a time like this. He continued to think. With Kazenko dead, almost certainly the Typhoon submarines would no longer be available. It was now more important than ever for that other arrogant Russian and his team to succeed. Igor Tamasara had asked that another snatch squad be sent back to the island, to kidnap the American's daughter. But she had already left Borakai. Was she like Morton's woman, the Canadian: clever, well-trained, resilient?

He had been in Hong Kong. Now he was out there, somewhere over the Pacific on his Concorde. Let him find the submarine. Qiao Peng settled in his chair, beginning to enjoy the silence, the sheer opulence of the salon. The size of a small ballroom, the salon's coffered ceiling was supported by twin rows of columns. Stuffed cranes and tortoises, symbols of longevity, stood on marble plinths, their bodies darkened with age and the needlework of the taxidermists coming apart. A pair of outsize lion-dogs were cast in bronze, their manes raised in fury and their mouths agape with fearful fangs.

Chairman Hu sat on the grandest of all the pieces of furniture, a sedan chair raised off the floor on its own dais. The chair had belonged to the last Emperor. The Supreme Leader leaned forward. 'How can we safely proceed without Kazenko's submarines?' he finally asked.

Qiao Peng spoke firmly; it was now important to take control. 'I had always intended that they should primarily be a protective measure. Our own Navy and Air Force have just demonstrated that they are more than capable of defending our shores and carrying the fight to wherever it is needed. Not that I expect much opposition after the Americans and Japanese have fought each other.'

Chairman Hu picked up the piece of paper off the desk. He scrutinised it once more, as if seeking reassurance. The look on his face showed he had not found it. 'There is another matter,' he began. 'Shortly before this news from Moscow, the Emperor of Japan telephoned.'

Qiao Peng's eyes never left the Chairman's face. 'What did he want?' he asked finally.

Chairman Hu considered for a moment, then sighed. 'First he wants to reassure me about the safety of all our nationals in his country. He has issued an order placing all foreigners under Imperial protection.'

'Of course. That is to be expected after recent events.'

For a moment there was quiet in the room. From a long way away came the sound of a telephone ringing.

'There is more,' said Chairman Hu in a low voice. 'The Emperor wanted me to know what he was going to say to the American President.'

Qiao Peng remained perfectly still and silent. Chairman Hu continued in the same intense voice. 'The Emperor said he would tell the President that Japan welcomed any help the United States could provide. He said all our countries could benefit from the situation. And he made it absolutely clear he would guarantee that Japan has no hostile intentions against us, or anyone else.'

'We must not forget that he has been trained in the art of evasion,' Qiao Peng replied in a reproving voice.

'But this could change the situation – '

'It changes nothing!'

Qiao Peng's words brought him to the edge of his seat.

'It changes nothing,' he repeated more calmly.

Chairman Hu frowned. 'But if the Emperor convinces the President that Japan will not oppose the proposed American alliance – '

'It will later be seen as calumny by both the Americans and the Japanese! The Americans will say that the Emperor's call to the President was a smokescreen. Remember what happened before Pearl Harbour? The Japanese Ambassador in Washington was still promising peace when the Japanese battle fleet had actually launched its 'planes. The Americans said then that that was Japan's day of infamy. They will say the same again!'

'And the Japanese?'

Qiao Peng felt the tension easing in his throat. When he spoke his voice was once more completely controlled.

'The Japanese will say that the Americans were seeking war no matter what the Emperor had promised. It will make them fight that much harder.'

He sat back in his chair, silent and watchful.

After a while Chairman Hu began to nod, finally reassured.

Immediately aft of the *Rodina*'s control room was the domain of Surgeon Yuri Borikov. He was thirty years old, with a Slav's high, broad cheekbones. His cropped hair, barrel chest and rippling biceps made him look more like a wrestler than a physician. His medical facility consisted of a cubby-hole office, a small but well-equipped operating theatre, a three-bed infirmary and another cubby-hole which served as a laboratory.

The crew liked him. He cursed with the best of them, cured their clap – catching it was still a punishable offence in Russian submarines – and for those who contracted HIV, he arranged a swift but discreet transfer to shore duties. He had also achieved what everyone on board agreed was nearly impossible – keeping on the right side of Marlo. He did so by knowing exactly when to win or lose their endless games of chess. They had again pursued each other's pieces as the *Rodina* raced out of the Japan Trench. Once more sensing the captain's mood, Borikov had let him win. A victory always lifted the anger never far from the surface in Marlo. And the Captain had almost a pathological need to win.

Borikov sat back from the chessboard and looked across his desk at Marlo. One day he would write a paper about behaviour in submarines. Like Marlo's reaction to the girlie magazine. What would the Captain say if he told him he had brought the magazine on board simply to provide a little relief for the crew – and to observe how the Captain would respond when he found it? There'd be no surprises there.

Marlo began to lay out the pieces on the board. Borikov shook his head. 'You're too good, Comrade Captain.'

It was not true; he could have defeated him a full thirty moves back. 'Your last two moves were worthy of a grand master,' Borikov added.

He saw that the outrageous flattery had once more worked. Was there something about a submarine command, with its long periods of being removed from the world, which made a man more susceptible? Marlo's hands hovered above the chessboard. 'You can't be persuaded into one more game?'

The surgeon shrugged apologetically. Another game and he might be tempted to win. Which would be no fun for everyone else on board. He glanced at a wall clock. 'It's coming up to badge-testing time, Comrade Captain.'

One of the surgeon's duties was to routinely check every crew member's radiation badge.

'After dinner, then?' the Captain said, standing up.

Borikov rose to his feet. 'Of course, Comrade Captain.'

Not for the first time he wished something would happen to get him out of the game.

Igor Tamasara walked over to a side table filled with bottles of vodka. He didn't really need another drink, only time to prepare his next move to discover how much Colin Baskin knew. He was certain that so far the American had answered his questions truthfully. He had spoken knowledgeably on scalar resonance and wave formation; about vectoring and the superimposition of their linear values. And he clearly knew a great deal about virtual state and kinetic energy. The American may have chosen to bury himself on that island, but his mind remained sharp.

Tamasara pretended to concentrate on which bottle to choose. Playing the tipsy host was a role he had long ago perfected. It always relaxed people. Then he was at his most dangerous. He studied a label and put it down. A Minsk vodka, never the smoothest. The experiment with Shaoyen had come tantalisingly close to success. Yet in their last conversation Qiao Peng had told him the time for experimenting was almost over. In three days the Gyroton must be ready to show its beam could force a subject's mind to obey without question. Always.

Igor Tamasara toyed with another bottle. He still did not know who the target was. But the code name Shaoyen had mentioned – Silent Voices – had an American connotation. He put down the bottle; a Georgian vodka, raw and spicy, to be drunk before sex. Could the target be an American? Qiao Peng would not have spent so much money on controlling just any American. On last night's TV news there had been a report about Hong Kong preparing to receive the President of the United States. To actually be able to control the mind of the most powerful man in the world would be the absolute proof that the Gyroton was the ultimate weapon!

Tamasara turned and looked at Colin Baskin, another bottle in his hand. 'This is a really excellent vodka. From the Urals. Would you like some?'

Colin Baskin shook his head. In the last hour he had drunk several shots, partly to help settle his fear and partly because he did not want to offend his intimidating host. Igor Tamasara's mention of Kate had been particularly scary. If he brought her here, God only knows what he would do with her. Kate could be very stubborn. And he had seen enough to know what would happen then. This man was one of those dangerously malevolent creatures their profession occasionally threw up. Mengele of Auschwitz. The Iranian doctor who had tortured the Beirut hostages. The German who looked after the kidnap victims of the Italian Red Brigade.

Another drink would blunt his mind. From there it would be a short step to getting himself killed. This monster knew his subject. It had been years since he had heard anyone discourse so authoritatively on pulse modes, phase conjunctions and wave anenergies. Only by remembering where his own research was heading had he been able to bluff. But for how long? Yet he sensed that behind Igor Tamasara's confident manner, something was unsettling him. Whatever had happened in the operating theatre had not turned out quite as planned.

And he wasn't fooling him with his little game with the bottles. At Langley they'd called that Buying Time. See it as a sign of uncertainty, the tradecraft instructor had said. He watched Igor Tamasara pour another large measure into his own tumbler. The man had wooden legs. Tamasara gulped a mouthful, his eyes on Baskin.

'Our KGB people said that those early electrographic experiments of yours were part of Project Bluebird.'

Colin Baskin shifted in his armchair. In the sixties, Bluebird had been the top of all top secrets. But the programme was long past its classified date. He grinned mirthlessly. Share a little, live a little longer. 'It was pretty basic stuff really. We thought you were working on developing a machine that would put subjects to sleep without electro-shocks so that you could explore their twilight zones.'

Igor Tamasara shrugged. 'We gave that up the time your people started Operation Artichoke. It took us a little while to work out that your CIA Director Dulles liked to name all his projects after fruits or vegetables.'

Baskin nodded, remembering. Artichoke had quickened the Agency's search of how to take possession of a man's mind.

'How far did you get with Artichoke?' Igor Tamasara asked, his interest genuine.

'A few yards beyond the start line. I was able to demonstrate that scalar resonance can produce lethal effects over a distance.'

'How far?'

The experiment had not moved outside the lab. But why not give him something to think about?

'Half a mile.' Colin Baskin was surprised how convincing a liar he had become in the past few hours.

Tamasara nodded and refilled his glass to conceal his surprise. The Americans *had* been ahead. So why had they stopped?

'We were at the same stage,' he said. Lying was second nature to him.

'You were only using rats, of course?' he asked turning back to face Colin Baskin.

'Never got beyond that,' Baskin replied.

Tamasara frowned. 'That's not true, Professor! What about all those people killed in Germany in your Operation Sunflower? Or Operation Lettuce?' Why had the American lied?

Colin Baskin's jaw tightened. What else did this bastard know? But he was wrong there. 'Those weren't CIA operations, but projects run by our Naval Intelligence people. We only heard at Langley a full year later what a debacle they had been.'

The Navy had flown a team to Germany at the height of the Cold War to conduct its own experiments in brainwashing. They had used captured KGB officers and suspected double agents. No one ever knew how many had been killed in secret safe houses all over Bavaria. 'When Dulles found out he insisted that all experimental work on mind-control was done by Langley,' Colin Baskin continued. 'Anyway, what the hell were your people doing out in Siberia with all those so-called psychiatric patients?'

Igor Tamasara suddenly smiled. No point in antagonising the American. But he had shown him how much he knew. It would make Baskin think twice about trying to mislead him. 'What happened, happened,' he said, the sharpness gone from his voice. He drank from the tumbler before continuing. 'While you were working with your lab rats, I'd gone back to Maxwell's original unified theory of gravitation.'

Colin Baskin nodded. A logical step. Maxwell's work, published in 1864, had paved the way for Einstein's law of physics. But like those of so many pioneers, Maxwell's theories had fallen from favour.

Tamasara put down his glass on the table. 'I superimposed Maxwell's theory onto the one Hebb postulated in 'forty-nine.'

Baskin's surprise was genuine. Ronald Hebb's theory was that electrical activity held memory in place on a temporary basis; more lasting memories were stored after protein synthesis took place in the brain. The brilliance of what Igor Tamasara had done was its simplicity. Successfully combining Maxwell and Hebb would indeed be a cornerstone of modern memory science.

'And that led you to scalar resonance?' Colin Baskin was not able to conceal his own excitement.

'Yes, though it took a while. I kept failing because I was using vector analysis instead of magnitude only.' Tamasara walked back to his armchair and sat down, his eyes never leaving Colin Baskin's face. He had totally caught the American's attention. He must have been working on magnitude himself!

'And then you combined magnitude *and* time?' Baskin asked.

'Yes.'

'And it worked?'

'Very nearly.'

'Is that when you started those energy taps?' Baskin asked.

Igor Tamasara blinked. The energy taps had been ultra-secret; probably less than a hundred people in the entire Soviet Union had known about them. Each tap had consisted of an electromagnetic probe designed to extract energy from the molten core of the earth. The result had been an abundant supply of scalar energy which had been stored in Postbox 97's endothermic tanks. Like everything else these had been destroyed in the ransacking of the research facility. If this American knew about energy taps, what else did he know?

Igor Tamasara waved his hand. 'We sent down over thirty taps. The last one was on the day Gorbachev resigned. Yeltsin ordered the programme stopped. The trouble with politicians is that they will never put their mouths where their money is! They spend and then pull back when things become really interesting.'

Colin Baskin nodded. 'It was the same in Washington.'

Igor Tamasara suddenly leaned forward. 'Is that why you left?'

Baskin smiled. The monster was playing his little games again. 'They sacked me. Your people must have told you that.'

'For doing your job too well? Do you miss it?'

Baskin shrugged. 'Not really. I was happy on Borakai until I was kidnapped – '

'Please, not kidnapped. Let's say you are on loan from your patients,' Igor Tamasara said quickly. He paused and looked at Baskin speculatively. 'Of course, you don't have to go back. They can find another doctor, Professor.'

Baskin gave another shrug. This was getting onto dangerous ground. 'Is this a job offer?' he asked lightly.

'If you like, yes,' said Igor Tamasara in a serious voice.

At the gift kiosk inside the gate of the Forbidden City, where he had been sightseeing for the past hour as part of his cover, Tommy bought a cassette describing the palaces of the old dynasty emperors. After crossing Changan Avenue to reach Tiananmen Square, he clipped in the cassette from his pocket, the one designed to receive Yaobang's transmission. Once more he began to stroll past the groups of tourists, pausing from time to time to look back at the Forbidden City, as if he were trying to pick out various buildings described on the tape he had just bought.

A moment ago he'd spotted Dad, walking past the People's Monument. In his light cotton suit, he looked like any other distinguished foreign visitor standing in awe in the presence of such monolithic power. And, despite the dust eddying across the square, Dad's shoes would be burnished to a gloss none of the shoeshine boys around the square could achieve. They'd looked at his own scuffed shoes and thought him another tourist on a tight budget. The square was dotted with them, carrying their backpacks and with Walkmans over their ears. Mostly they were Chinese. Could one of them be the pick-up? Apart from his name, Yaobang, he knew nothing about him. Working on a need to know basis had been one of the lessons drummed in during training. That way everyone's butt was covered. Not that it had helped Anna. He couldn't quite shake off the thought that she was here. Somewhere close by. He hadn't told Dad; he'd probably have growled that such speculation wouldn't get anywhere.

Tommy reached the People's Monument and strolled passed the patient lines waiting to view Mao's open coffin. He glimpsed the back of Dad going into the mausoleum.

Danny entered a vestibule where a marble colossus of Mao gazed down from behind a forest of flowers. The air was sickly sweet. Shuffling slowly forward with the other pilgrims towards the soldiers with fixed bayonets guarding the entrance to the tomb itself, he wondered if Tommy had made contact. The lad was keen, the best he'd seen, David had said. Tommy had shown that in the way he'd gone on pushing for more to be done to find Anna. He just couldn't accept that nothing more was possible. He hadn't meant to rip into him in the Ambassador's office, but in this business priorities –

'Excuse, please,' said a soft voice in accented English at his shoulder.

Danny turned to face a pock-faced man, pointing at his headset and wagging his finger. 'Not allowed, please,' the official said.

'My apologies,' Danny said, removing the headset.

He entered the mausoleum, completely unaware that from behind the bank of flowers one of Qiao Peng's agents had photographed him.

Out in the square, from his vantage point on the People's Monument, another agent had taken a snapshot of Tommy. Shortly afterwards he and Danny left the square separately, still without having made contact with Yaobang.

When the Concorde landed on Guam to refuel, Morton made one more call to Washington, to Bill Gates. After the aircraft had taken off to continue its search for the *Rodina*, Morton went to the Base Commander's office to await the arrival of the plane bringing what he needed to enter China undetected.

22

Night came like a warning as Todd Harper drove eastwards on New York Avenue, heading back into Washington. Although the dash clock showed a few minutes after eleven, the road was almost deserted. He glanced in the rear-view mirror of the Chevrolet Caprice he'd rented after deciding that his own Network car was too conspicuous. Now he knew he need not have bothered. A truck was coming up fast, a Christmas tree of lights. It could be a driver in a hurry to get home or another drug delivery; the beltway was an entry and exit for traffickers. Sometimes they were ambushed by foot soldiers of rival dealers. This past month there had been a half-dozen more killings along this arrow-straight length of road. As the truck swirled past, he glimpsed the logo: a giant bottle of baby food. You could get a lot of cocaine into a bottle like that. He shook his head, mildly irritated with himself. In this city the further you were away from your last bout of paranoia, the closer you were to the next.

Todd kept in the left-hand lane, the speedometer needle steady on the fifty mark. He'd been booked twice already for speeding. The first time he had been on his way out to Leo Schrag's apartment. The traffic cop had acted like he was auditioning for the lead in a remake of Attila the Hun. When he reached the apartment the door had been opened by an FBI agent he recognised. Usually she tolerated reporters. This time, not. He'd been sticking out his hand to shake when she closed the door. There had barely been time to glimpse the rummage squad taking apart the place. If Schrag was important enough for that, then the rest could be true.

A small convoy of cars swept past on the other side of the central divider. Commuters heading home, clinging to each other. It had become bandit country out here. The second booking had come when a

Maryland state trooper pulled him over on the way back from Bud Emerson's. The cop made it sound as if he had turned Wisconsin Avenue into a race track. It had been late evening when he'd reach Enerson's home, an end one in a row of old-money mansions. Emerson had been waiting with a brandy and coffee and a staggering piece of evidence. It was a copy of the Bethesda brain scan report and contained a full description of the slight weakness found in the President's brain. The report was signed by the hospital's chief neurologist and Dr Barker and bore the bold red letters NFC. With his knowledge of an Administration preoccupied with acronyms for sensitive intelligence or policy information, Todd recognised that the classification stood for Not For Circulation. He had not asked how Emerson had come by the report. The man almost certainly still had moles buried in all sorts of woodwork.

The bottom line was whether the President knew about his weakness, and how serious was it? Emerson had 'phoned a surgeon friend, who had explained that someone could live with the condition with no ill-effects, although if he were subjected to stress there could be a real problem. Afterwards, Emerson had said that refusing to stand up to the Japanese and then cosying up to the Chinese in return for a pimple-sized piece of land on Beijing's rump could cause a lot of stress in a man. Sometimes Emerson could be very obvious.

Todd glanced in the mirror. Another truck was coming up in the fast lane. It swept past, horn honking. But the headlights he'd spotted a few minutes ago had not made any effort to overtake. An FBI trail? They had probably been dogging him since the visit to Schrag's apartment.

He continued to do what he always did when a story was starting to crack: arrange and re-arrange the known facts. Schrag's disappearance; the President's brain weakness; Marty Fitzpatrick's clampdown, even to the point of refusing to issue a denial; the White House and pretty well everybody else gone to the mattresses. Schrag was a submarine surveillance specialist. Was the President planning to sell some of our subs to Beijing? Was Schrag on some top-secret mission related to that? He'd driven over to Schrag's workplace. The building had spook written all over it, and those working there he had tried to buttonhole had been as tight-lipped as a Boston clam. He had driven over to Bethesda. When he had asked to see the neurologist he had been politely but firmly turned away.

Another small convoy of cars passed on the other side of the beltway. Concert-goers, probably, from that recital at the Kennedy Center. A

Japanese violinist, all of twelve. He had been on *Today* that morning, plugging his latest album like a veteran. Todd glanced in the mirror. The car had come closer. If it was a tail, they were being rather obvious. He shook his head, irritated. He could not see if there was one or more people in the car. He had just assumed 'they'. That sort of thing really fed a person's paranoia.

A couple of hours ago he had driven all the way up to Sallmudet University. Herb Barker lived on one of the streets behind the campus. He'd opened the door himself, in pyjamas and dressing-gown, and Todd had remembered that the doctor was a widower. He'd smiled winningly, said he knew it was late, but he had something to show him. In the living room he had produced the scan report. Dr Barker had looked at it wordlessly, his face paling. There had been a tremor in his voice as he insisted that the President was in no danger, no danger at all. Barker had asked how he had gotten hold of the report. He'd smiled another winning smile. Just as the doctor would not expect him to reveal a source so he could be guaranteed that anything he said would never be attributed. The 'phone had rung in the back of the house and Dr Barker had excused himself. Moments later he was back, his face flushed, saying he had nothing further to say. Todd had guessed that the call had been from his FBI watchdogs. For once they had been a little late.

He checked the mirror again. The car was a couple of hundred yards back. Maybe they were trying to intimidate him. The thought brought a wolfish smile. Someone was starting to panic. He wouldn't do anything stupid, like jumping on the gas. Besides, fifty was his thinking speed for those times driving back from an assignment when he shaped a story in his mind's eye, selecting the sentences which always gave his reports the bite that kept everyone glued to their screens. This time the forty million who watched the national nightly news would be transfixed. So would everyone at the Desk, that bastion of the Network's New York headquarters where a reporter's worth was constantly judged by senior news executives. No one knew what he had been working on. And, right until that moment in Barker's living room, part of him had wondered if he could pull off the biggest single story to rock an Administration since Woodward and Bernstein had nailed President Nixon.

Todd's eyes once more flicked to the mirror. The car was closing. It was now fifty yards behind. A Saab. He had not heard that the FBI were using imported cars. He checked the mirror one more time. There was nothing behind the Saab. On the other side of the median barrier a truck was heading out of the city. The Saab had moved up to only a few yards behind his rear bumper. He had been right: he could make out the silhouettes. A two-man team. Todd reached under the dash shelf for one of the blank radio tapes he kept there. He fed it into the maw of the cassette player, pressed the record button and began to speak in the deep voice which enthralled his viewers.

'This is a story about a secret the President of this nation carries in his head ... perhaps unaware it is there. A physical weakness in his brain that could explain some of his otherwise inexplicable decisions ... and of a Chinese-born barmaid with connections to that country's secret intelligence service ... a few days ago she returned there with a US Navy technician employed in a sensitive intelligence-gathering post ...'

Todd paused. The Saab was moving up and slightly out of lane. The passenger was lowering his window. What the hell ... if they flagged him down, he'd keep on driving. No regulation said you had to stop for anyone except a police cruiser. Todd continued to formulate thoughts for his commentary. 'Seemingly disparate facts ... but they may well prove to be the real reason why the President is making a journey to Asia that many find inexplicable ... unless those who have been close to this Administration are right ... that the White House has embarked upon a momentous co-venture with the People's Republic of China ... one that could affect the lives of every American ... could alter the balance of power not only in the Pacific, but the entire world ...' He pressed the replay button and glanced sideways.

The Saab had dropped in beside him. Todd's mouth sagged. The figure in the passenger seat wore a balaclava and was resting the barrel of a sawn-off shotgun on the rim of the open window.

Todd opened his mouth to scream. But no sound came. He moved to press the accelerator pedal. But his leg seemed frozen. He heard his own voice coming from the car's speakers.

'This is a story about a secret the President of this nation ...'

He saw the finger begin to tighten on the trigger.

'... otherwise inexplicable decisions ...'

The finger continued to curl.

'... a Chinese-born barmaid with connections ...'

He felt for one fleeting second the glass of his own shattered window showering into his face. In that same moment he tasted the blood, the fear, the reality. Todd's head exploded as two more shells removed

233

most of it from his shoulders. His taped voice continued to speak with the same compelling control.

'Seemingly disparate facts ... but they may well ...'

The car had begun to veer out of control towards the central median.

'... that the White House has embarked upon a momentous co-venture with the People's Republic of China ...'

The Saab was already accelerating as the gunman pulled in the shotgun. He peeled off his balaclava, then pressed the button beside the gear shift to roll up his window. He turned to the driver. 'Gonzales didn't look Colombian.' The gunman's Spanish was soft almost feminine.

The driver glanced in his wing mirror. Flames were beginning to light up the beltway a quarter of a mile back. 'It was Gonzales's car,' he said. 'Had to be the *puta*.'

The gunman nodded, reassured.

They worked for the most powerful of Washington's drug barons. He had instructed them to cruise New York Avenue to look for a white four-door Chevrolet Caprice. When they found it, they were to kill its occupant. He was a heroin distributor who had cheated on his payments. He always used a hired car. The hitmen spotted Todd's car with its rental company bumper sticker after he had left Dr Barker. They had moved with their usual deadly skill.

By the time the Saab turned off, the fireball of Todd's funeral pyre was already subsiding. In the distance came the wail of fire trucks, and the strobe lights of police cruisers and ambulances.

They had been radioed by the FBI agents trailing Todd. He had known that the reporter was heading home. No point in getting closer. No point in chasing the hit team. People like that knew how to disappear.

Yaobang cycled onto Tiananmen Square, and once more glanced at his watch. For the second day running he was late for the transmission. His duties in the map room had delayed him. But perhaps David, or the person he had sent, would wait, somehow sensing how important his message was. Conscious of the heavy responsibility that was his, Yaobang pedalled with slow, methodical precision, listening to the patriotic songs in his headset. From time to time he heard a funny buzzing sound between the tracks. That would be the message being automatically transmitted.

David had said that the beauty of the system was its simplicity. All he had to do was to record what he'd wanted to say on the cassette. Its own inbuilt mechanics did the rest, turning his voice into encoded characters. Cycling over the paving stones, sweating a little more than usual from nervousness, he glanced from time to time at the foreigners. None of them was David. None looked like someone he had sent. Yaobang grinned sheepishly. What would someone like that look like?

When he heard the click in the headset which meant the transmission was over, he cycled out of the square into the anonymity of the nearest alley. Yaobang failed to notice the security agent reporting his departure into his lapel mike, just as a moment before he hadn't seen the agent photographing him.

Completely naked, Bud Emerson did the Ten Basic Exercises for Men in the living room of his suite in the Mandarin Hotel. The callisthenics were the start of his programme to recover from the long flight from Washington to Hong Kong.

He had decided to make the trip after his last call to Dame Lorna Ball in Manila. She had told him that her well-placed sources in Hong Kong had learned that Sir Alan Wingate, the Colony's Governor, had received instructions from his Prime Minister in London to host an extraordinary meeting between Tang Ming, China's nominated Chief Executive, and the President. That could only mean that Beijing and Washington were coming closer to being joined at the hip.

He began to rise and squat on his haunches, arms extended, neck rotating from side to side. The ache in his muscles fuelled his anger. First the Japanese were allowed to trample all over us. Now the Chinese were about to be invited to do the same, thanks to that liberal in the White House. Lying on his back, he started to bicycle in the air, driving his legs ever more rapidly, feeling his heart rate increasing and the sweat running down his body. He began to feel an old excitement, the memory of his last visit to Hong Kong when he had once more spent the night with Suzy. He still did not know her full name or anything about her. He did not want to. He needed nothing from her except his own physical gratification and her explicit recounting of her own sexual encounters with other men. That always further aroused him. In all his long and varied experience with women he had never known a woman who could do that better than Suzy.

They had first met when he had been visiting the Colony on a fact-finding mission. At the welcome cocktail party, she had told him she was an actress. He had listened politely. She had looked at him over the rim of her glass, taking long, slow sips. And he had known she was a whore and had smiled with relief. Only a whore would have that abandon all over her beautiful face. And only a whore would allow him to satisfy his appetites. An hour later he had been in her bed, throwing himself on her and pushing her firm thighs apart and beginning to thrust deep into her warm, moist body. She had stopped him, saying there was plenty of time, Buddy-boy.

He had not discussed her fee but in the morning had left a thousand American dollars in large bills on her bedside table before leaving her sleeping. That evening she had left a message at the hotel saying that the gift was acceptable. No thanks. No name. Just – acceptable. He had liked that. No commitment: just sex. Since then, whenever he visited, his first night in Hong Kong was always spent with her.

He had 'phoned from the airport and she had said to come round after dinner. Which meant she was in bed with some other man until then. The thought began to arouse him. Dressed in one of the lightweight suits and silk shirts he had purchased on his last visit, he went down to the hotel lobby and changed travellers' cheques into hundred-dollar bills. He used one to buy a large box of Swiss chocolates. Suzy could do things with a chocolate he had never imagined. He looked at his watch. He still had an hour to kill. He hailed a taxi and, ten minutes later, was outside the Government Information Service Library. It was open twenty-four hours a day, and on his first visit he had been made an honorary member. The flunkey at the door bowed when he produced his card. He did not mind that behind the man's smile was probably a Cantonese obscenity. It was another reminder of Suzy. Emerson went to the newspaper reading room, and began to work his way through back numbers of the *South China Morning Post*, and the less-reliable *Standard*. He gleaned a great deal of what was happening in Hong Kong.

Foreign investment had all but dried up, while the run of money from the Colony was like a race-tide. The brain-drain continued apace. The rich and powerful were fleeing in droves to their bolt-holes in Australia and Canada. Hong Kong was going to end up like Shanghai. Beijing would be happy to trade off the place. That made the deal the President was planning bad, bad news for America.

His eyes caught a report in the *Standard*. The Triads had killed no one for the past twenty-four hours. He shook his head in disgust. The whole place was already coming apart if that sort of thing warranted news space. The *Post* had devoted extensive coverage to the mainland's naval war games. A small boxed item in the middle of the story caught his eye. The paper's Guam correspondent reported that a Concorde was using the island for proving flights. He read on. In a column listing important visitors to the Colony he saw the name of Cyrus B. Voss. The tycoon had been spotted as he passed briefly through Hong Kong on his way from Beijing. Voss was the Administration's unofficial bridge-builder to Beijing. Like Topsy, this whole thing was growing all the time.

He frowned when he saw a large photograph of the *United States*, with a caption stating that the carrier would serve as the President's base in Hong Kong. Even given that there was no US Embassy in Hong Kong, there were ample fine mansions which could serve as a temporary White House. This way, the locals would feel snubbed. Another example of how this Administration fouled up. When he got back to the suite he'd called Todd Harper. There were some useful leads for the reporter to track down. He looked at his watch. Time to go.

The taxi dropped him outside Canton Mansions in Hennessy Road. At this hour the shopping arcades on the ground and first floors teemed. He had forgotten the insatiable appetite of the Chinese for shopping. He walked past the tailors and shirt-makers and the purveyors of plastic dolls, fake crocodile handbags and Rolex watches. The elevators were at the far end of the arcade. He pushed a button for the top floor. The elevator stopped immediately opposite Suzy's apartment. When she opened the door she was wearing a silk wrap and smelled of bath salts.

She reached up on bare tiptoe and kissed him on the mouth. He peeked down the top of her wrap, all the way down past her big firm breasts to her pubic hairs, a golden triangle against her darker tan. He wondered if she dyed those hairs or whether they were natural. Suzy looked at him and smiled, then reached down and brushed her hand against his crotch. Still without saying a word she led him into the apartment. She had lit his favourite joss sticks and they were burning in their holders on the god shelf in the hall. Carefully displayed on the narrow ledge were mandarin oranges and sweets between two statues. She had told him they were the goddesses of fornication.

'You like a drink, Buddy-boy?' she asked.

'How about later? Or do you need a break from the last one?' He smiled lasciviously.

'Always ready for you Buddy-boy,' she said, slipping off her wrap. She watched him studying her.

He stretched out his hand and slowly stroked her face, continuing to study her nakedness. She reached forward and whispered her first obscenity in his ears. Then she stepped back and glanced at the packet. 'Chocolates?' she asked.

'Yes. But not all for eating.' His voice had already thickened.

'I have a new wig, Buddy-boy,' she said. 'Maybe I wear it for the chocolates.'

'Maybe you wear it *with* the chocolates,' he whispered.

As he handed her the packet he stroked her beautiful triangle of golden curly hair.

Suzy removed the wrapping, dropped the paper and stuck-on ribbon bows on the floor. She opened the box and inspected the chocolates. She chose one and slipped it between his fingers buried in her triangle. He fell to his knees and began to give anguished moans of pleasure. She looked down at him dispassionately. *Waibin* could be such pigs. As he pressed his face against her skin, his tongue seeking the chocolate, she stepped back.

'Buddy-boy, let's get you to bed.'

Emerson looked up and she smiled teasingly. As he rose to his feet she turned and led the way to the bedroom, choosing another chocolate, this one to eat, using the muscles of her vagina to keep the other one in place. Only Tang Ming was as bizarre in his demands as this *waibin*. She had spent the afternoon once more standing over the Chief Executive-designate, performing a version of her profession's standard trick, the 'golden shower'.

Emerson saw that Suzy had changed the bedroom since he was last here. Gone were the rattan matting and Japanese paper concealing the futon, the mattress. The bedroom was now furnished like a Swiss mountain chalet: fake ceiling beans, ruffles on the shades and behind the heavy wooden double bed a blow-up of a verdant valley rising to distant mountains.

'You like it?' she asked.

'I like it.' He replied, his voice thicker.

Suzy put the box of chocolates on a side table holding styrofoam head shapes, each covered with a wig. As she went to remove a red one, he shook his head. 'No wig,' Emerson said.

She smiled at him, walked over to the bedside table and pressed buttons on a small control box. The room lights went out and suddenly the ceiling was a starlit sky. She lay back on the bed, spread-eagled, waiting, nibbling another chocolate, smiling wickedly. 'Get undressed – Buddy-boy,' she ordered, the American accent more pronounced.

Eyes never leaving her, he shucked out of his clothes. From her jet-black hair, breasts lolling magnificently, all the way down to her flat belly and that golden triangle, she was the incarnation of sensual depravity. Naked, he knelt on the floor and began to shuffle on his knees across the carpet to the bed, towards those long, widespread golden legs. As he reached her toes and began to lick them, Suzy arched her back and gave a convulsive jerk. The remains of the chocolate shot out and, as he had done many times before, he lunged forward, caught it in his mouth and swallowed it. Suzy gave him a mocking smile and grabbed him in a scissor-lock with her legs, dragging him onto her.

Dawn was breaking when Emerson emerged from Canton Mansions. He walked slowly, completely sated. In the darkness Suzy had whispered to him how she had spent the afternoon ... about some of the other men who had shared her bed since he had last done so. He had asked for names, and then physical descriptions, so that he could better imagine who they were and what they had done. He had been momentarily astonished when she had said that her previous client had been Tang Ming. Then he had once more buried himself in her body. As usual he had left his pile of dollar bills on the table beneath the god shelf before closing the apartment door behind him.

He hailed a taxi and twenty minutes later was standing under the shower in his suite, washing away the smells and traces of the night but not the memory. Wrapped in the hotel's complimentary bathrobe, he ordered breakfast and switched on the TV. He flopped in an armchair and used the zapper to locate the Cable Network News channel.

The third story was the death of Todd Harper. Pictures of the burntout car wreckage provided a macabre backdrop for a police officer's statement that the reporter had become another hapless victim of the internecine war between Washington's drug traffickers.

Emerson sat there, not touching his breakfast, ignoring the waiter who came to clear away the tray. The sun beat oily humid hot on the suite's windows. Outside the door, the floormaids vacuumed and went. Once, there was a tentative knock. Still he sat there, watching the regular reruns of the news. The sun was almost overhead when the 'phone rang. Eyes still glued to the screen, Emerson picked up the receiver.

'Bud Emerson?'

'Yes.'

'This is Bill Gates.'

Emerson forced himself to look away from the screen. The sun had warmed the room, but he felt suddenly chilled. How in the hell had Gates found him? And why? Was it something to do with Harper's death? Why was Gates calling him?

'Mr Emerson ... ?'

'Emerson gathered his thoughts, his mind racing. He was certain that Harper had not been wired during their meetings. And he had taken good care to ensure that the Bethesda report could never be traced to him. Maybe this was not about Harper.

'What can I do for you?'

'It's what you can do for the President, Mr Emerson.'

In Washington, Gates sat slumped in his chair, 'phone cradled under his chin, one hand hovering over a cassette player, listening to the faint hiss of atmospherics. It was something to do with the geo-positioning of the telephone company satellite.

'There's something in your tone I don't like, Mr Gates. And I really don't have time – '

'Hear me out, Mr Emerson. It may be the smartest move you've made in a long time.'

'What do you want, Gates?'

'I've got a tape here. I want you to listen to it.'

The player was connected to a speaker-phone.

Once the tape had arrived, the hardest part was tracking down the sonofabitch. It had needed the combined efforts of the FBI, airline security staff and the Agency's own man in Hong Kong to locate Emerson.

'What am I listening to – ?'

'Just listen, Mr Emerson.'

Emerson pressed the 'phone to his ear. Suddenly his hand began to tremble as a familiar voice came into his ear. 'You like a drink, Buddy-boy?' asked Suzy.

Emerson pulled the 'phone away from his ear as if the receiver had burned him. 'What the hell is this?' he shouted into the mouthpiece.

'Just listen, Emerson!' rasped Gates, his eyes on the revolving tape.

He had to give it to Morton's men. When they moved, they moved. Some time during the night, when Emerson had been performing like a stag running out of time, Hammer Force's Electronic Surveillance people had routinely sampled what was being recorded in the whore's apartment. A check with their voice library identified Emerson. The rest was simple. By the time this dumb cluck had left the girl's apartment, Electronic Surveillance had scooped up the recording of the rest of the night's shenanigans and made a copy which had been transmitted to Langley.

'You still there, Emerson?'

The sound of his and Suzy's love-making came clearly through the 'phone.

'Emerson?'

'What do you want?' He knew before he asked.

Gates straightened and used a hand to massage the tension in the back of his neck. 'You take the next 'plane out of there and come home and take a nice long vacation. I recall you have a place in Montana. The fishing's good at this time of the year – '

'And if I don't?'

Gates sighed. It was time for the wrap-up. 'If you don't Emerson, copies of these tapes go very public. To every radio and TV station. To every city desk and wire service. I shouldn't think her trick with the chocolate would go down too well with your colleagues on the Hill. But I can promise you it will get you more exposure than any of your President-bashing escapades. As of now they stop. You and they just became history. That way you can go on enjoying your sexual peccadillos. That's not just the best deal I can offer you, it's the only one, Emerson. You've got a minute to take it. Otherwise you're dead meat.'

Gates decided it was not only static but a sigh of defeat that came from the other side of the world.

Qiao Peng sat alone in his office studying the still wet prints an aide had brought. The older man in that expensive suit he knew. Danny Nagier wore that eye-patch with pride. With the physical resemblance, the younger man had to be his son. If Morton had sent them, did that mean he wasn't coming himself? The stogey rolled slowly across his lips as he picked up the third photograph. The print was a poor one, the agent not wishing to get too close. But there was no mistaking that familiar figure in a captain's uniform.

Qiao Peng spread the photos on the desk, as if they were playing cards, and did something he had not done for a long, long time. He smiled.

Sitting in a jeep on the tarmac at Guam, Morton watched the Hercules come in low and fast, the way Hammer Force pilots always flew. He waited until the aircraft parked just off the runway where a refuelling bowser waited, then told the jeep driver to take him there. Close up, the transport looked like any other Hercules, big and cumbersome, except that she was painted deep black, covered with the same radar detection-proof skin as a Stealth bomber. Her propellers and engine

241

cowlings were further protected against noise and flame emissions. Hammer Force had a number of these aircraft parked in various secure spots around the world, crewed and ready to go at a moment's notice. This one had come in from Wake, another of those pinprick American islands in the Pacific. A window on the pilot's side of the cockpit slid open and a bald head peered down.

'Clancy is waiting for you at the ramp, Colonel. Once we're tanked up, we'll be rolling.'

Morton nodded and walked to the rear of the 'plane. Clancy was standing at the foot of the ramp. It was hard to see how much of the dispatcher's bulk was muscle and how much the result of the heavily-padded overall he wore. An old-style flying helmet made the modern lip-mike appear incongruous. Foam rubber ear protectors were draped around his neck. He had another pair in his hand. Clancy thrust them at Morton, grinning.

'You'll need these, Colonel. Forecast's not too bad, but we're still expecting eighty knots. That'll make this crate sound like a banshee shrieking in hell!' Despite his name and Irishisms, Clancy's voice was authentically Texas. And his coal-black face was darker than any Kerry peat-bog.

'How'd you get to be called Clancy?' Morton asked as he followed the dispatcher up the ramp.

'They named me after the priest who ran the orphanage,' Clancy grinned over his shoulder.

Inside the fuselage Morton stopped. A couple of years ago he had attended the field trials at Edwards Air Force base in northern California for the microlite squatting on the rail track in the centre of the cavernous interior. It had been an extraordinary and thrilling experience to see the tiny 'plane shoot out of the Hercules high over the desert, the pilot strapped to its lightweight frame.

'We've made some adaptations,' Clancy said, leading the way forward. 'Before I explain, I'm supposed to read you the standard lecture on what to do if things go wrong.'

The dispatcher was silent for a moment then grinned even more broadly. 'I've just read it to you.'

'Thanks, Clancy.'

They stopped beside the microlite's port wing and Clancy began to point out the special features. 'She's Stealth-painted, of course. The engine's a built-in jet rocket that's self-firing once you're clear of the ramp. You'll have precisely forty minutes powered flying time. When the engine stops you'll have exactly one minute to leave the microlite before she turns into a firework display, literally.'

Clancy pointed under the stubby wings and to the 'plane's black frame. More fireworks were strapped to the wheels. 'To mark the end of their war games, the Chinese Navy put on their own firework display. From sea-level you'll look like part of those celebrations.'

Clancy pointed to a dull black suit and head visor hanging on pegs. 'Our pride and joy. We call it our now-we-see-you-now-we-don't outfit. Seen one before?'

Morton shook his head.

Clancy walked over to the suit and spoke like a salesman. 'Stealth-painted again and pressurised. She's got a built-in parachute. Twenty seconds after you break contact with the microlite the 'chute opens. It's also totally undetectable. You'll just drift down like a thought in the night.'

He lifted the head visor from off its peg. 'It's got built in oxygen and a head-up display which has already been programmed. The landing co-ordinates are also preset. You're dropping into the Yangzte Basin, south of Nanjing. From there on, as they say in all the best briefings, you're on your own – and good luck, Colonel!'

Morton smiled. A man like Clancy was a good one to have in your corner. Outside the Hercules he heard the fuel truck pulling away. The engines started and moments later the ramp began to close. There was still a gap when the Hercules started to roll down the runway.

For three hours Morton and Clancy sat on a pair of seats, facing aft, behind the flight deck. From time to time the pilot had kept them informed of their progress northwards across the Philippines Basin. Passing Okinawa, Morton put on the Stealth suit. It was like being draped in a feather-bed duvet. Then, helmet on his knees, he slept, oblivious to the wind howling on the other side of the aircraft's thin aluminium skin. The ear mufflers did not help much.

He awoke at once when Clancy nudged him and said they were coming up to the drop zone. A moment later the pilot's voice came over the intercom.

'We're well over the East China Sea and we've got one of their battle fleets heading back to Wenzhou. It's like fiesta time down there with those fireworks. Guess it's time to get strapped in, Colonel.'

Morton removed the ear mufflers and walked over to the microlite. He strapped himself into the bucket seat, bracing his feet against the rudder bar.

'It's simpler than driving a car,' Clancy said. 'You wanna go right, you press down right. Wanna go left, press left.'

Morton put on the helmet. There was a faint hiss as the oxygen began to flow. Inches before his eyes the configuration of the head-up display glowed.

'Just keep the centre arrow steady and you'll know you're right on target,' Clancy yelled, his mouth close to the helmet.

Morton raised a hand in acknowledgement and watched the dispatcher check that his own safety harness was securely shackled. Clancy pressed a button on a console bolted to a wall of the aircraft. A moment later the ramp began to open. The noise of the wind grew louder. The Hercules started to pitch and roll under the stress on its aerodynamics.

Clancy held up a finger. One minute.

The ramp continued to drop. When it was fully extended, the dispatcher pressed another button on the console. Under hydraulic pressure the rail track on the ramp extended into space to ensure that the microlite was ejected well clear of the underbelly of the Hercules.

Clancy formed a cross with two fingers. Thirty seconds.

Morton gripped the handlebars more tightly, crouching forward so that his upper body was almost parallel to the microlite's fuselage. The wind was howling around the inside of the aircraft. Morton closed his eyes. One way or another, it would be over in a few seconds.

Suddenly he felt a thumping sensation in his back, then the wheels of the microlite ran out of track. Seconds later it was moving forward under its own jet-propelled speed.

Morton opened his eyes and glanced back. There was no sign of the Hercules. He sat up and scanned the instrument panel. Clancy was right. The microlite flew itself. And it was like riding through the sky in a chair. You felt alone, but the view was spectacular. Rockets fired from the battle fleet continued to burst around him. But he was going too fast for their glare to catch him.

Forty minutes later the microlite's engine cut out. His air speed dropped and he felt the 'plane's nose dip. He released his safety straps, kicked hard left on the rudder bar and leaped sideways to his right.

He went into free-fall, arms extended, legs slightly spread to control his descent. Away to his left the night sky was once more brilliantly lit as the microlite put on its own firework display. He felt a wrenching tug between his shoulders. His rate of fall dropped. Above him he heard the wind filling the parachute canopy.

He drifted for a while until, below, he could see the faint line of surf breaking against the shore. The needle in his head-up display was steady. Thirty minutes after crossing the coast, he passed over the girders of a giant bridge. The railway into Nanjing. The city itself was where it should be, away to his left. Below Morton saw an expanse of water, the Yangzte.

Steadily losing height, he crossed the river, passed over a quilt of fields and finally landed close to a pair of water buffalo standing in amphibious lushness. They looked blearily at Morton and, with the same total lack of interest, watched him remove his suit and helmet. He rolled these with the parachute into a bundle. When he had done so he pulled a tab he had left exposed. When the acrid smell made his nose wrinkle, he turned and walked away from the bundle.

By the time Morton reached a nearby towpath the powerful acid the tab had released had completely dissolved the bundle into a pool of water. No one, apart from the water buffalo, knew that Morton was in China.

23

Shortly after dawn Igor Tamasara and his team returned to the bunker where the Gyroton tests were conducted. With them was Colin Baskin. The focus of everyone's attention was the squat black-painted box on a railcar. In shape and size it was no bigger than a family refrigerator. Technicians were aligning its snub-nosed barrel with a slit-like opening in the far wall. From time to time Igor Tamasara raised a powerful pair of binoculars slung around his neck to peer through the bunker's observation window. Soldiers were removing sandbags and barrels protecting buildings in the distance. Other troops were covering windows with black pieces of cloth, making the buildings appear increasingly ramshackle and sinister.

Igor Tamasara turned from the railcar, a rictus smile on his lips, his wig slightly askew, his coal-black eyes glowing with pride, as he beckoned to Colin Baskin. 'You won't see much back there, Professor! Come and have a clearer look.'

Baskin saw that the Gyroton's back panel was covered with dials and gauges, none of them familiar. But the calibrations on the barrel reminded him of the weapon he had constructed for his own experiments on lab rats. 'You're still using torque settings,' he said, managing to inject a degree of disappointment into his voice. The important thing was not to sound impressed by anything.

Tamasara frowned. The American could still surprise. 'Indeed so, Professor. But there's no point in changing something which works. And these settings are infinitely more sophisticated than the ones you would have used. With them, we can target individual parts of the limbic system.

'What you are looking at here, Professor, is the new face of neuro-behavioural control. With my Gyroton a man's mind is no longer his

246

own. His very thoughts can be reformed. He becomes a puppet and his brain an obedient servant of my Gyroton. With it many of the world's problems can be controlled, even solved!' As he spoke Igor Tamasara's voice had risen.

Colin Baskin remembered newsreels he had studied at Langley of Hitler and Stalin. They had displayed the same absolute certainty. But in the end they had been defeated by the very demagoguery which had sustained them. Perhaps Igor Tamasara would also destroy himself. If not, he had to be destroyed. If he had to die to destroy Igor Tamasara, it would be a sacrifice well worth making.

Dr Petrarova turned from the bank of wall-mounted monitor screens. 'Everything is ready, Igor Viktorovitch.'

Tamasara nodded, then continued to address Baskin. 'To make the experiment more interesting the buildings have been booby-trapped. The devices are not actually lethal, but more tests of nerve. Our Chinese hosts are very skilled at devising them.'

Again Baskin was assailed by a wave of nausea at the physical presence of such evil. 'And who is going to be put through this psychological obstacle course?' he asked at last.

'Come.' Igor Tamasara walked across the room.

After a moment's deliberate hesitation Baskin followed. At the window, Dr Fretov and the technicians made space for them. Several had field glasses to their eyes. Igor Tamasara snapped his fingers and spoke in Russian. A technician obediently handed over his binoculars to Baskin. He used them to study the expanse of ground between the bunker and the buildings.

'There! To the right of the last building on your left, Professor,' Tamasara said.

Colin Baskin spotted the man. A middle-aged Caucasian. He looked dishevelled and disorientated. Igor Tamasara turned to the technician at the controls of the Gyroton. 'Set for alpha-block at thirty-one point zero zero pulsing in fifteen seconds.' The technician acknowledged the instruction.

Baskin continued to focus. The man was pale-faced with pouches under his eyes and looked around uncertainly. 'What's he doing there?' he asked.

'Watch!' Tamasara commanded.

A moment later the technician reported that the Gyroton had pulsed and fired a fifteen-second burst of beam energy. Baskin saw the man suddenly straighten as if filled with a new resolve. From his pocket he pulled a hunting knife. Moving at a crouching run he entered a building.

'Excellent,' Igor Tamasara cried.

Dr Petrarova called, 'I have him on screen!'

Baskin glanced towards the monitors. He saw the man entering a room.

'Look there, Professor!' Igor Tamasara said, nudging him. 'To your right.'

Basking swung his binoculars to the far side of the buildings. A figure, half-hidden by shadow, crouched in the lee of some of the barrels. Only a woman would crouch like that. He heard Igor Tamasara give another order to the technician. Glancing over his shoulder, he saw the Gyroton's barrel traversing. He adjusted the focus on the binoculars. The woman was young and reminded him a little of Kate. She had the same look of steely determination.

A moment later the technician reported that the Gyroton had fired another pulse-beam.

'Now watch, Professor! You are seeing a moment of history.' Igor Tamasara was almost shouting with excitement.

Baskin saw the woman rise from the shelter of the barrels and stand defiantly. From her waistband she removed a short stabbing knife before she, too, ran into a building. Dr Petrarova reported that he had her on screen.

Igor Tamasara lowered his binoculars and tapped Baskin on the shoulder. 'Come. We can better follow on the monitors.'

They walked over to the screens. On separate ones the man and woman were clearly visible, the sound of their breathing audible. The man's was already laboured, but the woman's light and controlled.

'Who are they?' Colin Baskin asked.

Igor Tamasara gave a thin smile. 'I believe in your days at Langley they were called expendables. The man is an American who, I understand, had quite a sensitive position with your Navy in Washington. What he lacks in physical stamina he should make up for with his ability to reason.'

'And the woman?'

Igor Tamasara shrugged. 'She is an intelligence agent. Her training, in theory, should give her an advantage over the man. But he is physically strong and very cunning. It makes for an interesting confrontation, Professor.'

'Confrontation? What kind of confrontation?'

'Forgive me, Professor! I thought you would have understood.'

Igor Tamasara looked quickly at Dr Petrarova. Maybe Sergei was right and the American had outlived any further use. But that could be decided later. Nothing must overshadow this moment. He turned back to Colin Baskin. 'The scalar beam they have been exposed to carried pre-taped instructions. These are inaudible to the human ear. But once the beam penetrated their brains, the instructions will have been recognised by their amygdalas. The principle is rather similar to those subliminal advertising slogans you people in the West have made such a fuss about.'

'What are those instructions?' Colin Baskin asked in little more than a whisper.

Tamasara gave another brief smile. 'They have been ordered to behave completely out of character. They have never met each other. But they have been told that when they do, they must regard each other as a dangerous enemy. And, of course, that means they must each do their very best to kill the other. Let's see how well they manage.'

Igor Tamasara turned back to the monitors, completely absorbed in what was happening. On one screen Leo Schrag was now moving along a corridor, knife hand held high across his body, the way a street fighter would hold the weapon.

'His subconscious has reminded him how to do that, Igor Viktorovitch,' said Dr Fretov.

'Excellent, really excellent.'

On another screen Anna kicked open a door with a swiftness her Hammer Force instructor would have approved of. She, too, held her knife in an attacking position.

'Excellent,' Igor Tamasara repeated.

After Morton emerged from the architectural colossus of Beijing Central Railway Station he followed a pre-determined plan. Though it was barely dawn, the bicycle renters outside the concourse were already doing a brisk business. He hired a bike with no lamp, pump or gears, and pedalled into one of the alleys. A beret pulled low over his brow significantly altered his facial appearance. The rucksack he had bought in Nanjing marked him down as a cost-conscious tourist. China was nowadays full of them.

His behaviour for the next hour confirmed he belonged in their ranks. Only a *waibin* with limited means would eat a breakfast in an alley café of boiled rice and fish, washed down with cups of aromatic tea. And would ask for a cheap boarding-house instead of directions to the Great Wall Hotel or one of the other modern palaces where the price of a single whisky equalled a week's salary for the waiter who served it. Morton had gathered the names of a dozen hostelries where he could get a bed for a few yuan. It was important to seek such information. People would remember him as only another backpacker.

After breakfast he made his way to a public bath-house. For another hour he followed the slow self-broiling ritual of immersing himself in ever-hotter tanks of water. Glowing from the masseur's scouring, he emerged into the daylight and cycled on past the tiny factories and restaurants and shops, manoeuvring around handcarts stacked with produce as he pedalled through street markets, the air filled with the shrill of barter. Outside a marriage bureau, its tin door decorated with silver tinsel, he dismounted. Long ago he had discovered that there was a payphone in the bureau's entrance hall. He used it to make a call.

'Is the vacancy in your kitchen still open?' he asked.

'Yes, of course,' said the woman before he hung up.

She would do the rest. Tell Danny. Make sure Chantal knew. Send a message to the CCO on Concorde that he had arrived. They would all know what to do.

He remounted his bicycle and pedalled past the old men strolling with their bird cages and talking animatedly to each other. Occasionally girls with too much lipstick and old women walking arm-in-arm stared at him, not quite believing that a *waibin* had penetrated so far into the alleys. But for the most part he was ignored.

By mid-morning he had reached his destination, the city's Lama Temple. Once the largest monastery outside Tibet, it was now a tourist trap. Lining the road to the walled gardens and temple halls were scores of coaches bringing visitors to stand and gape. Morton parked his bicycle and walked through the portico. Danny waiting outside one of the old monk's cells which had been converted into a teashop. Tommy was acting as point man, over by a serving stall.

'Let's play tourists,' Danny suggested. 'I don't usually get much chance.'

As they strolled across the courtyard, Danny said there was still no news of Anna or the shooter. Nor had contact been made with Yaobang. He and Tommy were due to begin another sweep of Tiananmen Square in an hour's time. They joined the tail end of a line waiting to enter the first of the temple halls. Inside the door a pair of lamas, their scrawny necks jutting out of coarse-clothed brown habits,

250

held out begging bowls and chanted in unison for money for offerings. A small oil drum stood at their feet, half-filled with notes and coins. Morton dropped a few coins into the drum as they entered the gloom of the temple.

They were dwarfed by the towering altars, each a blaze of guttering candle-flame, and the godlings, demiurges and the demons of the underworld. Beneath magnificent tapestries suspended from the roof were great piles of conch shells, elaborate arrangements of peacock feathers and plastic flowers. In front of the altars were stacked gifts of cakes and sweets wrapped in plastic.

'This place makes Lourdes look positively spartan,' Danny murmured.

They walked past side chapels where statues of unfamiliar animals in mute slumber were waiting to be awakened by heaps of liturgical bells scattered around their deformed bodies. Morton quietly updated Danny on the lack of success in the searches for the *Rodina*, Colin Baskin and Leo Schrag. Crouching beside an offertory, a wizened priest proffered joss sticks to burn on a nearby altar. Danny shook his head and they walked towards a shrine.

Morton paused briefly to study a dog-headed divinity mounting a porcelain-faced goddess, her fingers clawing him in a mandorla of golden nails. He glanced over his shoulder. Tommy had stopped by the old priest to buy a joss stick.

'I'll go to Tiananmen alone,' Morton said. 'I want you and Tommy to go back to the Embassy and root out everything on file about the nuclear fallout system Mao ordered up.' Morton was referring to the network of tunnels and shelters beneath the city which Mao Tse-tung had built in 1969 when relations between Moscow and Beijing were at their nadir.

'Almost certainly one of those tunnels connects to that railway under Zhongnanhai. That's the way into Igor Tamasara's compound,' Morton said.

Danny shook his head. 'Even if we get in, what can we do?'

Morton smiled tightly. 'Let me get in there first.'

Danny did not bother to hide his surprise. 'You're going alone?'

'For sure. If anything goes wrong, you and Tommy will still be here to carry on.'

They walked in silence past more replicas of ugly demons and finally reached the temple's most imposing statue, the Buddha. It was carved from the single trunk of a sandalwood tree, and rose from its massive splayed feet, past strangely feminine thighs, to a navel the size of a

251

dinner plate, and on up a richly bejewelled body to the voluptuous negroish head lodged against the roof.

'He's seventy-five foot tall, the height the faithful believe you reach in paradise,' Morton said. He grinned at Danny. 'Not many people know that.'

They walked out of the temple into the sunlight. In a courtyard a monk was selling tiny prayer wheels. Morton bought one and shoved it in his rucksack.

'I'll give it to Bitburg for his next birthday,' he said, grinning again.

Leo Schrag peered into the gloom of the corridor, forcing himself to breath deeply and steadily to slow his heartbeat and calm himself. His head ached painfully and strange little lights bobbed and danced behind his eyeballs. They were driving him on to find the woman. She was here, in this building, where it was so easy to misjudge direction and distance, where his imagination threatened him with all the fears he had ever known. She was here, hiding and waiting to strike. *She wanted to kill him.*

He had no idea who she was or what she looked like. But her presence filled his entire mind. He could think of nothing else except how to find and kill her first. His grip on the knife handle was as real as the physical sensation of his surrounds: the foetid atmosphere, the clinging gloom, the chill which had not stopped beads of sweat breaking out on his forehead. Leo stood frozen to the spot, listening.

Something had moved halfway along the corridor. Among the shadows that shifted and bent and coalesced into insubstantial shapes, the way the darkness of his childhood bedroom had done, he had caught a glimpse of real movement. There it was again. A scurrying sound racing down the corridor. He glimpsed the red eyes and the sleek black body of the rat. Then the rodent was gone. He gripped the knife more tightly, the pressure on the handle reassuring. One of the soldiers who had brought him here had given him the knife. The man had said something in Chinese. Now he knew what the words meant. *Use the knife to kill the woman before she kills you.*

He could almost smell her presence in this building that was a honeycomb of cell-like rooms and long, dark corridors whose silent menace nibbled at his nerves. The ground floor was flagstoned. He had moved slowly over it, a step at a time, the sound of his shoes loud in his ears. He had paused frequently, uncertain where to go. The rooms were empty. Beyond the last one was a bare wooden staircase. His eyes growing used to the darkness, he had climbed the steps and emerged in this corridor. Now that the rat had fled, he let out a long shuddering breath and sucked in air one more time. Then, knife held high across his face, he began to walk down the corridor. He peered into a room. It was empty. He walked to the next door. It was almost closed. A floorboard squeaked under his footfall. As he pushed open the door he whirled, alerted by a sixth sense.

A crushing weight fell on his shoulders, driving him to the floor. He screamed and rolled free. Above him the trapdoor in the ceiling hung loose, flapping on its hinges. The body lay where it had dropped, legs askew, arms twisted, head turned grotesquely, only inches from his face. Leo screamed like an animal, teeth bared in abject terror. The top of the man's skull had been cut away; around the edges of the hole the blood had clotted and dried. He screamed again.

The woman would have heard. He forced down another scream. Scrambling to his feet, heart beating loudly, a throbbing in his temple, he reached down and retrieved his knife. He forced himself to crouch and look more closely at the ghastly skull. Had she done this? Surely no woman could have done this; the bone looked as if it had been sliced away with a surgeon's skill. But she could be a doctor! She could be armed with an arsenal of surgical weapons!

He touched the skin on the cheekbone. The flesh was cold but still pliable. He dimly remembered that rigor could be delayed for several hours. But that was only in cold weather. He poked at the clotted blood with the tip of his knife. Beneath the surface it was still moist. The man had only recently been killed. But how had she brought him here? If she had carried him, she must be a big and powerful woman. And how had she managed to get the body up into the ceiling cavity? Maybe there was somebody else helping her? But no: there was only the woman. His mind kept telling him that.

He began to walk slowly forward, knife extended, his eyes searching the vaguely shifting shadows, each with its own nightmare to be negotiated. Checking room by room he reached the end of the corridor. His clothes were damp with sweat. But the pounding feeling in his head drove him on as if some dark evil was loose in his brain.

In the bunker Igor Tamasara turned to those watching the monitors. 'Excellent, really excellent,' he said.

On the screen Colin Baskin saw that the man and the woman were in adjoining buildings. She was one floor above him.

*

Anna spotted the gap in the floor. Peering over the edge of the hole, she could dimly see the ground-floor flagstones a long way below. The man was somewhere down there. She had to kill him before he killed her. She peered once more into the void. She needed a rope. The building was hushed and still, as if it was waiting to see if she would find one.

Anna stood up, clutching the stabbing knife she had found in her cell after she'd woken. She had wondered how it had got there. That did not matter. All that mattered was finding a rope, then finding the man and killing him. She began to search the room. Behind each door lay an empty, crepuscular silence. The window in each room were draped on the outside with dark cloth. She was not curious; that part of her brain had shut down. She started to open another door. From the other side came a small creaking sound. She paused and held her breath. Was the man here, waiting in the brooding darkness? Had he somehow found a way to silently work his way up here to attack her? She pushed the door open a little further, knife held before her.

In the dim light she saw a body hanging from a rope tied to a hook in the ceiling. Nearby was an upturned stool. The rope made another creaking sound. She briefly closed her eyes, then opened them and stepped into the room. The body was dressed in the casual clothes of a student, its face towards the window. The rope once more creaked as the corpse began to turn of its own volition.

Anna stared into the remains of the face of Lilina. The skin and bone over her kidnapper's forehead had been cut away to remove Lilina's brain. The skull cavity gleamed wetly. Terror rushed up through Anna's throat, but the scream couldn't pass her lips. She stood there, petrified.

Standing below the review stands on either side of Tiananmen Gate, Morton watched the convoy of Red Flag limousines sweep past. Each contained a member of the Politburo on his way to attend the monthly meeting in the Great Hall of the People. As usual, a vast crowd was assembled for the occasion. The stands were filled with senior Army officers and Party cadres and their families.

On Tiananmen Square itself Morton estimated close to half a million men, woman and children were regimented. Among them were thousands of junior officers and soldiers leading the crowd in rousing applause for another rare public appearance of their aged rulers. Qiao Peng would have his agents there. But even they would not be able to constantly keep an eye on everyone.

As the cars parked outside the Great Hall the applause reached a climax. Morton watched the decrepit old men being slowly led by their nurse escorts up the steps of the building and disappearing through its towering doors. The crowd settled down on the ground to await the re-emergence of the Politburo. Only in China was such institutionalised sycophancy still part of daily life, Morton thought, as he crossed the broad expanse of Changan Avenue to the square. All around him people were talking loudly to each other. Loudspeakers relayed music interspersed with Party slogans.

Morton fished a cassette player and headphones out of his rucksack. When people said Communism was dead, they should see this. That brief bright moment in the spring of 1989, when Beijing's students had gathered here and dared to proclaim a vision of China's Camelot, had well and truly died in the massacre that followed on this same spot. He could understand why Yaobang was ready to risk his life to help bring about another change. These people were as oppressed now as they always had been.

Morton checked the tape. A tinny version of the music emerging from the loudspeakers filled his headphones as he began to stroll through the square. He reached the lines patiently waiting to enter Mao's mausoleum. There were hundreds of children queueing to file past the body of a tyrant whose policies had very likely condemned them to a life of semi-starvation. Would the deal America's President envisaged put an end to that? Provide sufficient work for unskilled hands? The deal would bring increased mechanisation. At its simplest, a tractor would do the work of fifty men; only one would drive, the others would go on the employment scrapheap. But they would still have to be fed.

Morton turned away and began to walk towards the Great Hall. All around him well-fed tourists were taking photographs and filming. He doubted if many of them knew, or cared, that with the present birthrate, the unemployed would reach three hundred million by the end of the century. How could any deal the President of the United States brokered resolve that? How could anyone?

The music in his headset suddenly stopped and there was a click. He felt a little surge of relief. Yaobang was about to transmit.

Morton looked casually around him. There was no sign of the young officer. But he was here, somewhere. Perhaps among the soldiers guarding the steps of the Great Hall. Or with those by the Monument to the People's Heroes.

A moment later came a second click.

Morton strolled on, hearing the hum of Yaobang's transmission. It would be encoded in the usual ten-letter blocks: 3,000 letters sent every fifteen seconds, all recorded in the spaces between the tracks on his cassette.

He began to count under his breath. Two bursts already. He changed direction, heading towards the underpass under Changan Avenue. A group of picnickers looked up smiling over their rice bowls. He smiled back. Another burst. He had told Yaobang never to transmit too long at any one time. The signal was loud. He must be close by. Morton looked towards where the Politburo limousines were parked. Their blue-suited chauffeurs stood smoking and talking among themselves, grand-standing for the onlookers, but totally ignoring them.

The signal suddenly stopped.

Morton waited, counting a full fifteen seconds. Only the sound of singing filled his ears. On the far side of the square there was a commotion. People were standing and pointing. There was some sort of struggle going on. Men were running towards the commotion.

A closed van drove onto the square, forcing its way through the crowd with its blaring horn. Morton walked steadily towards the underpass, the high-pitched singing still in his ears. He had stopped counting under his breath. There was no longer any point.

24

Lieutenant Tarinski had been fifteen hours at his navigator's desk in the control centre, plotting the *Rodina* to that point where the submarine was to surface on the edge of the Yellow Sea. There were dark hollows under his eyes and his teeth were stained from the flasks of borscht soup the ship's cook had regularly provided. Rings on the charts were from setting down his mug while plotting.

On the charts, the *Rodina's* track showed as a snaking blue line coming out of the Japan Trench, down past the shallow coastal waters of Yokohama to the shelter of the Ramapo Deep, another of those Pacific undersea valleys which extends for hundreds of miles. At its mouth Tarinski had ordered another course change, heading the *Rodina* towards China. He calculated he was still no more than a few cable lengths off track. Not bad after 7,000 kilometres, he told himself. Not bad at all.

His task had been complicated by other factors. The first was the need to maintain a course which kept them inside the echo of engine noise the sonar men had picked up. They had identified the steady thrumming as that of battleships and their destroyer escorts. The Chinese Navy was heading back to port.

Once more his eyes swept back over the track. They had made remarkably good speed. But they would still arrive too late to take part in the war games, the purpose of this mission. More puzzling, Marlo had not complained about this. Yet everyone on board knew he was once more waiting to pounce. A short while ago Yuri had thrashed the Captain at chess. Since then Marlo had prowled the boat looking for some imperfection upon which to vent his anger.

Tarinski could see Marlo out of the corner of his eye, leaning against a bulkhead, head cocked to one side as if listening for some mistake by the *Rodina* herself. But all that could be heard was the reassuring sound of the reactor's coolant pumps.

Tarinski reached for the flask to refill his mug. A hand stayed him. He looked up, surprised. Marlo was gripping his wrist. With his other hand the Captain took the mug and began to move it over the rings with deliberation as if it were a chess piece. 'Comrade Lieutenant Tarinski, how can you expect to navigate accurately when you damage your chart?'

Tarinski smiled wearily. 'We're right on course, Comrade Captain. See for yourself.'

Marlo swept his eyes over the chart. Nothing to complain of there. But these marks. No way this smartass would wriggle out of them! Holding the mug aloft for everyone to see, Marlo addressed Tarinski in a hectoring voice.

'What was the first thing you received when you volunteered for the submarine service, Comrade navigator?'

Tarinski frowned. What the hell was he talking about?'

Marlo moved the mug for emphasis as he continued: 'The very first thing! The one thing that makes it possible for us to work as a team! The one thing which allows us to know if we are performing our duties properly! Whether it's when to stand watch, open a valve or close off a pipe. The one thing that tells us when to check everything. The one thing, Comrade navigator! What is it?'

'I'm sorry, Comrade Captain – '

'Your rule book, Comrade Lieutenant!'

'My rule book?' Tarinski asked incredulously.

'Yes! Your rule book!'

With a small flourish Marlo produced his own copy from a breast pocket.

'Of course, Comrade Captain,' Tarinski's voice was husky from long hours of unceasing tension.

'And you forgot what the rule book says about this!' said Marlo emphatically, carefully placing the mug in a ring-holder fixed to the side of the chart table. 'All drinking utensils used on duty by the navigator must be properly stowed. See for yourself! Page nine, paragraph four!'

As Marlo flicked over a page, suppressed snickers came from the far side of the control room. He thrust the book under Tarinski's nose. 'The rule book, Comrade navigator! If you had read it we would not be having this conversation! When did you last read it?'

Tarinski glanced at the page, then at the Captain. 'I honestly can't remember, Comrade Captain.' Best to get this over with as quickly as possible.

Marlo closed the book with another small flourish. 'At least your honesty is commendable. But it is no excuse for lax behaviour. I expect my officers to set an example. Just as you will expect me to do so!'

'Of course, Comrade Captain.'

Marlo stared at the navigator. If only he would say something to justify himself! But there was nothing in the rules about punishing dumb insolence. Not yet, anyway. 'The rule book is clear. Careless damage to property by any member of the crew is punishable by a fine. Therefore, Comrade navigator, you will be stopped one day's pay for the damage to that chart. Any further infringement will lead to a more serious punishment.'

'Understood, Comrade Captain.'

The first thing he'd do when he got back to base was apply for a transfer. He'd rather spend the rest of his days on that damned ice-breaker than bust his gut trying to please this tyrant.

An hour later the navigator announced that they had reached their surfacing point. Marlo ordered periscope depth. Ten minutes later the *Rodina* was just below the choppy surface. The captain raised the periscope. There was nothing in sight.

'Surface,' Marlo ordered. The diving officer pushed buttons on his panel and the *Rodina* heaved herself above the waves.

'Bridge party into the sail!' the Captain ordered. An officer and two seamen look-outs scrambled up the ladder. There was the hiss of an airlock opening, then fresh sea air began to fill the control room. A moment later the officer reported no other ships in sight.

Marlo glanced at his watch. Five minutes on the surface. That's what the sailing orders said. It still made no sense. But the first thing they told you at *zampolit* school was never, ever, to query an order or fail to follow the rule book. 'Up aerials,' he barked into the 'phone. He did not expect any radio contact. But the book said always – always – put out your antennae when surfaced.

A voice came over the control room's internal speaker. 'Comrade Captain, incoming message. Prefix double R.' Marlo did not need the ship's radio officer to tell him that the prefix was an Eyes Only Captain signal.

The message was on the radio room's priority printer. The encoded preamble showed it was several days old and had continued to be automatically transmitted from Fleet Headquarters. Marlo fed the coded jumble of numbers and letters into the decoder. He inserted a key which only he possessed into the hole beside the machine's maw. There was a hum as the paper passed through the decoder and emerged through another slit-opening as printed clear text. He bent over to read the words.

'Vice-Premier Kazenko dead. Return immediately to base. Savenko.'

Marlo ripped out the paper and read it once more. Savenko. If anyone else had sent this he would not hesitate obey. But Savenko was a walking bundle of tricks! Somehow the bastard had managed to get hold of his prefix and codes. Savenko was running security checks all over the place. To radio for message confirmation would play into his hands. The rule book was clear: never break radio silence on a mission unless your boat is in a life-threatening situation. He dropped the message into the shredder. Responding to Savenko would be the quickest way to end up on the bench.

Back in the control room, Marlo ordered the bridge cleared and the diving officer to take them down to 1,000 metres. When that depth was reached, he picked up the microphone for the PA system. 'This is your Captain speaking. I want to inform you that we are on a special mission. We are to go to the Chinese Naval Port of Quingdao. When we reach there you will be briefed further.'

One hundred and ninety miles away, one of the electronics specialists on board Concorde checked the noise he had just recorded on his oscilloscope against the one he had obtained previously over the Kalin Peninsula. He turned and grinned wearily at the CCO. 'A perfect match,' the technician said.

'For sure,' the CCO said in a passable imitation of Morton.

The officer sat at his own keyboard and began to encode a message for the Embassy in Beijing reporting that the *Rodina* had been located.

To the south of Concorde's present flightpath, the cameras of an American satellite had filmed the submarine. The sat's computer identified it as a Typhoon class, the same as the three other subs photographed earlier in their newly-built pens at the Japanese port of Kagoshima. The pens were for the Typhoons Japan had recently purchased from Russia. The computer interpreted this latest sighting as further evidence of Japanese military moves in the area and transmitted the assessment to Washington.

Anna estimated that no more than fifteen minutes had passed since she had stood on the stool and unhooked the rope. Lilina's body had fallen to the floorboards with a shuddering crash which had sent Anna flying off the stool, hitting her head on the floor. She had scrabbled in the gloom for her knife. Rolling the body aside, she had found it. Forcing herself not to look away from that obscene face, Anna worked free the rope around Lilina's neck. Wincing from the pain of her fall, she strained to listen. There was nothing but silence.

Yet the man must have heard. The whole building seemed to have reverberated with the sound of the falling body. Rope in one hand and knife in the other, Anna desperately tried to think what she would do in his place. Wait. Wait for her to make the next move. Wait out there for her, hidden by the darkness.

Coiling the rope over her shoulder Anna crept back into the corridor, once more crouching at the edge of the hole, peering into the void. Her flesh crawled as she saw in her mind's eye the man waiting below for her to descend. But there was no other way. As she rose to her feet, she remembered that earlier she had brushed against something metallic. Hand groping in front of her, she located the ladder bolted to the wall. Securing the rope to the lower rung, she tested the knot by pulling hard several times. The rope held.

Anna returned to the hole and lowered the rope. As it disappeared into the darkness, a searing pain forced her to close her eyes. The agony eased and she opened them. She gave one final tug and then, hands clenched tightly around the rope, handle of the knife clenched between her teeth, she dropped down through the hole.

Igor Tamasara glanced away from the screen in the bunker at Dr Petrarova. 'Could that blow on her head affect her exposure to the beam, Sergei Nikolai?'

The neurologist pursed his lips. 'It really depends on how close it was to her amygdala. We'll have to wait a little longer to know one way or another.'

Tamasara turned to Dr Fretov. 'Sacha?'

'I agree. The blow is unfortunate, but nothing I've seen so far indicates that it has diminished her determination.' The psychiatrist nodded towards the screen where Anna was painfully inching her way down the rope. 'She's really remarkably resilient. I wish I could say the same for our American,' murmured Dr Fretov.

On another screen Leo stood in a corridor, his eyes staring about wildly, his breath coming in raucous gasps.

'The man's hyperventilating! For God's sake he needs help!' Colin Baskin cried.

'Professor, you really must stay calm,' Igor Tamasara said reprovingly. 'The American is just reliving old fears. They will pass soon.'

Dr Fretov pointed towards the screen. 'He's found the matches. It'll be interesting to see if he'll use them.'

Leo had stumbled across the kitchen-sized matchbox as he pushed open another door. The further he penetrated the building, the deeper became the darkness. It was like walking through a disused mine, with winding corridors branching off everywhere. The air was musty, leaving his throat sore and nose feeling blocked. He could not be sure from where the crashing sound had come from. That, too, had added to the horror of his surrounds. She could be around the next turn in the corridor, or lurking in one of the rooms he had to pass. He had given up trying to form a mental picture of her. All he could imagine was someone physically big and powerful. That meant she almost certainly was not Chinese.

Leo turned the matchbox over in his hands. He could light his way forward, spot new dangers, drive back those shadowy shapes that formed and reformed just beyond where he could clearly see. He opened the box, pulled out a match and lit it. It flared brightly. The room was empty. The match died more quickly than he expected.

He stepped back into the corridor and struck a second match. There was a wild flapping of wings and he glimpsed several furry creatures swoop past his head and fly down the corridor. Choking off a scream he dropped the match, grinding it out under his heel. Better the darkness than risk being attacked by bats panicked by the light. He dropped the matchbox on the floor and continued down the corridor, checking the rooms. Each was empty.

Something ahead made him stop once more and stare fearfully. He could just make out what looked like a snake twisting over a gap in the floor. Closer by came the sound of someone breathing. He whirled, teeth bared, knife hand extended, the other arm held protectively across his face. He must get close to her, smother her with his weight and size. The muscles in his arm were bunched in anticipation of the moment he would plunge the knife into her, turning it viciously in her flesh, widening the wound, draining her blood.

In that one moment her saw her face, bone white, the lips drawn back into a rictus of concentration and fury, the eyes blazing like an animal's. Even as he moved, she lunged, with speed and total lack of fear.

Anna felt no longer human, only dedicated to the total destruction of this shape staggering towards her. Her knife thrust plunged through his guard, catching him in the throat. The driving force of the blade jarred her hand as it entered gristle. She pulled out the blade and a dim memory came back. Strike the same spot twice. Oblivious to the terrible throbbing in her head, and to his warm, sticky blood beginning to spume over her, she drove the knife once more forward.

Leo was already swaying, one hand trying to staunch the blood fountaining from his neck, the other slashing wildly with the knife. But he couldn't see; his eyes were misting over. He vaguely saw the figure duck, then felt an intensely cold and momentarily indescribable pain in his throat. Then he felt nothing.

Anna saw the knife fly from his hand, followed a moment later by a crash even louder than that made by Lilina's body. The man lay inert at her feet, the only sound that of the blood gurgling out of his neck and mouth. She had never known blood could make such a truly awful sound. Then unable to control herself, she vomited over the body. Wiping her mouth, she turned and ran down the corridor from which Leo had appeared.

Igor Tamasara turned to the others. He was laughing in a way no one had seen him do before. 'It works! It really works!' he shouted.

Colin Baskin remained fixedly staring at the screen, watching the woman running down the corridor. Suddenly he felt a fierce, over-whelming need to protect her, the way he would Kate. He turned to Igor Tamasara. 'What will happen to her?'

Tamasara looked at him in amused surprise. 'Happen? Why, what happens to all our guinea pigs. She'll be shot. But this time we won't need her brain. My Gyroton works – '

'It's too soon to say that, Tamasara,' Baskin said as calmly as he could.

There was sudden and total silence in the bunker.

'What exactly are you saying, Professor?' Igor Tamasara asked softly.

Baskin deliberately watched the screen for a moment longer while he marshalled his thoughts. There would be no second chance. One wrong word and the woman and himself would be doomed. He turned and faced the group around Igor Tamasara. They were looking at him curiously, one or two in astonishment. His resolve grew. Igor Tamasara's coal-black eyes were staring impassively. But there was something else in them – the merest glint of doubt. It was enough.

When he spoke Colin Baskin's voice was filled with a cold certainty. He addressed only Igor Tamasara. 'The reason you had me brought here was because you didn't know all the answers. And you still don't.' He turned to the screen. The woman was racing down another corridor, pausing to check her bearings from time to time. He watched her for as long as he dared, remembering everything he had learned about body language indications at Langley. He turned back to the others.

'You saw how she reacted to killing him. Vomiting. That could have been an instinctive subconscious response, the beginning of a rejection of what she was made to do. Look at the way she moves. She's in shock. Look at the way she touches her knife. Guilt at what she's done? Or a readiness to kill again? Again, too early to say. But until you know for certain you can't say your Gyroton works.'

Tamasara glanced quickly at Dr Fretov. The psychiatrist looked thoughtful.

Baskin continued: 'She needs to be observed, her mood changes and behaviour patterns assessed over a period. You need to know exactly what she felt then, at the moment of killing, and what she will feel later. Then, and only then, will you be coming close to saying that your machine works with complete success.'

Once more silence returned to the bunker. Eyes turned from Colin Baskin to Igor Tamasara. He glanced again at Dr Fretov. The psychiatrist made a tiny head movement.

Tamasara looked at Colin Baskin. 'You do surprise me, Professor, after all.'

He turned to a technician. 'Instruct the soldiers to keep the woman alive.'

Baskin turned back to the screen to hide his relief. The woman had emerged from the building and was standing in the bright sunlight. The question now was how long could he keep her – and himself – alive?

The Ambassador had assured Morton that the small conference room in the rear of the Russian Embassy in Beijing was secure. Nevertheless Danny insisted on covering the room's one window with an invisible spray capable of deflecting the most sophisticated bugging device. He then hung the walls with tinfoil-lined blankets which were state-of-the-art soundproofing. The floor and ceiling had not needed attention: they were lead-lined.

Danny set up his equipment on the conference table. A small but powerful satellite-linked switchboard provided secure links to Concorde and Bill Gates in Washington. Two fax machines with built-in encoders provided an equally safe means to transmit and receive paperwork. A separate decoder and printer had transcribed Yaobang's tape and produced a transcript. Tommy had made copies of the document on a laser copier and sent them to Concorde and Washington, Geneva and the CCO on Concorde.

Before his transmission had abruptly stopped, Yaobang had managed to describe both the Gyroton and its present location and had gone on to provide the first news about Anna, Colin Baskin and Leo Schrag. They were all being held at the same location in a compound in the Western Hills.

Mention that Anna was alive brought a look of sudden hope to Tommy's eyes. 'Colonel – '

'Don't even ask, Tommy,' Morton said brusquely. 'I need to know a lot more before we can do anything.'

'I understand.' Tommy nodded faintly, a weary, defeated gesture, and turned away.

For a moment Morton wanted to take him aside, to tell him it wasn't only Anna's life, but Yaobang's too, that concerned him. But he'd always kept to himself these feelings each time he lost someone. More than mere pain, they seared his soul. Now he did what he had always done at such times, hid his feelings behind an icy control. It was the only way he knew of subsuming the hatred he felt, which must not be allowed to cloud his judgement during the difficult days ahead. But, as before, he could not quite banish the hatred – it had been nurtured for too long.

'David, I've got the Prof on the line,' Danny called out.

Morton picked up the 'phone. 'What have you got, Prof?'

The voice from Geneva spoke softly, steadily. 'Not much, I fear, not much at all. There are just too many gaps in Tamasara's personality to make a full value judgement on his psycho-profile. But there is one thing. If Anna's in his hands, he won't kill her unless he absolutely has to. From what I can make out, he's got a fear of women who stand up to him. And Anna will do that. Most certainly, most certainly.'

After he had told the others what the Prof had said, Morton stood at the window, his back to the room, this time allowing the anger and hatred to course through him. He could almost smell Igor Tamasara, that special stench of evil he had sniffed so often. He breathed slowly and deeply, sucking in the evil, then expelling it, the way he had always done when the time was close to engage the enemy and destroy him. After a while, completely calm again, he telephoned Gates in Washington.

'What's the position of your sub, the *Seattle*?'

'She's a good two hundred miles from the *Rodina*, David. Even if she goes like a bat out of hell, *Seattle* won't get to where your people spotted our Ivan for another four hours.'

'That could still be okay. Still nothing to show Tamasara's made a move?'

'Not a thing.'

'My bet is he'll wait for dark to get down on the coast. By then *Seattle* should be on station.'

'That's still a lot of coast for her to watch, David.'

'For sure. But we've got Concorde and your satellites.'

Morton put down the 'phone. Unspoken had been the one question. What to do if the Gyroton was on board the *Rodina*? Should *Seattle* force her to surface? Board her? Take her to the nearest US naval base? Supposing her captain refused? Things could get very nasty. It could lead to the kind of incident no one wanted.

Morton dialled a new number. The familiar voice of General Savenko answered in Moscow.

'Here's the problem ...' Morton began without preamble. When he had spoken for several minutes he asked one question.

'How far will you go with this, Yuri?'

The reply came without hesitation.

'All the way. If you have to, sink the *Rodina*. But just make sure there are no survivors. That could be embarrassing.'

'Thank you,' Morton said. He knew what it had cost Yuri to make that decision. The same as it was costing him now over Yaobang. He put down the 'phone and walked over to Danny, standing at the end of the room by an old-fashioned easel. Pinned to its blackboard was a blueprint. For a moment they silently studied the layout of the underground network of tunnels and bunkers which formed Beijing's old nuclear defence system.

'This is your best way in, David. Here.' Danny's finger indicated a circle above which were printed the words: 'Number One Chinese Hospital for Traditional Medicine'.

There were a number of identical circles on the blueprint.

'Hospitals. They have direct access to the bunkers. The idea was to get everyone to safety after a nuclear attack warning.

Danny's finger returned to the circle he had touched first. 'The network beneath Number One has direct access to Zhongnanhai. That's because it is the designated hospital for treating the leaders. If any of them get sick and need hospitalisation they are taken there underground. It's all part of their obsession with secrecy.'

Morton nodded. 'So what happens once I'm in ...'

'You go this way.' Danny's finger quickly traced a route from the circle to a small T-square. There were several of them on the blueprint. 'Junction points. This one is where the rail separates from Zhongnanhai. A spur leads to the hospital. Another to the Great Hall of the People. When he wants to surprise the Politburo by turning up unannounced, Chairman Hu uses it.

'And this – ' Danny indicated a third line leading from the T-square – 'is the rail track out to the Western Hills.'

He walked over to the table and picked up one of the satellite photographs which Gates had faxed. Back at the blackboard Danny held the photo up against the blueprint. 'Tamasara's compound is right here – ' he indicated a rectangle on the photograph – 'which is here on the blueprint.' Danny's finger stubbed another symbol, a small triangle. 'An access point. This one leads directly into the compound.'

Morton studied the sat photos. The buildings appeared foreshortened and the perimeter fence low enough for a child to jump. 'What's the security like?' he asked.

'Surprisingly light. No dogs, perimeter patrols. Nothing like that. No need to. The whole area is strictly off limits. Anybody who gets in is assumed to have clearance.'

He led them over to the table and laid out a selection of photos. As Morton studied them, Danny pointed to various features. 'Look at that rail spur. It's shiny. Which means it's in use. And those ground vehicle tracks. They're also fresh. See, they go from here, to here, to here.' Danny pointed to various buildings as he spoke. 'That could be a workshop. This, some kind of administration block or living quarters. Maybe that's where they're holding Anna.'

Morton grunted and pointed to another group of buildings on the edge of a large space.

'Look at the windows. All blacked out,' Danny said.

Morton pointed to a photo of a bunker-like structure, half-hidden by trees. A rail track ran from the building. 'What happened here? It looks as if the sat cameras went on the blink.'

Danny shook his head. 'The camera picked up some kind of heat emission from inside. You always get that burned-out effect with heat.'

Morton scanned the other photographs. There was no sign of a similar emission from any of the other buildings.

'Could be the Gyroton,' Danny said.

'Maybe.' He would know soon enough.

Danny pointed to the rail track. 'It connects to the national grid. Here.' He indicated a point on the photo where the tracks joined a spider's web of rail lines outside the compound. 'The place was obviously some sort of military storage depot from which they could move supplies quickly. Ideal for Tamasara's purpose,' Danny said.

'For sure.' Morton marked several of the prints and told Tommy to arrange for them to be further enlarged. The Embassy's all-purpose photographer would do the actual work.

Morton returned to the blackboard. 'Where exactly is this entry point in the hospital, Danny?'

Danny walked over with another blueprint and thumb-tacked it to the blackboard. His finger once more began to point as he spoke. 'Here's the main entrance. That's where the official reception committee will be. From there you'll all be taken to here, the main students' dining hall. Tea and cake followed by a lecture on traditional medicine. It'll be just about dusk when that's over.

'Then it's off to see the wonders of Chinese medicine actually at work. Various kinds of surgery first. The theatres are here, here and here – ' more finger jabs – 'then on to the wards. Here's where you stop playing curious Western doctor.'

Morton nodded. Danny had done wonders in the past few hours since returning from the Lama Temple. After discovering there was a foreign medical convention visiting the city he had arranged for the Ambassador to summon one of the Russian delegation to the Embassy. The doctor had been told just enough to convince him to give up an eagerly-anticipated visit to observe Chinese Traditional Medicine.

The doctor was now in the Embassy's guest quarters. He would wait there until the next morning before rejoining his colleagues. The photo on his convention badge had been switched for one of Morton. The doctor's features were sufficiently similar to pass all but the most careful inspection. Wearing a pair of the doctor's heavy-framed glasses and combing his hair differently would complete Morton's deception. The minimum of disguise was usually the most effective.

Danny indicated a spot on the plan. 'The door's just before you enter the first ward. There'll be a log-jam with everybody wanting to get up front to see better when they reach the beds. They'll probably be too busy to notice when you make your move.'

Morton glanced at Danny. They both knew it was never as easy as that.

'Beyond the door are elevators that lead directly down to the bunkers,' Danny continued, pointing again.

He picked up a textbook from the table. 'All you need to know about Chinese medicine, David.'

He handed Morton the book.

25

The chamber where Yaobang was being interrogated was in the basement of counter-intelligence headquarters, a short drive from Tiananmen Square. The windowless room smelled vaguely of chemicals and body odours. He stared at the light bulb swaying inches above his face where he lay, naked and securely strapped to a narrow wooden table. His head was positioned over a hole under which was a badly stained bucket. Yet he felt strangely calm.

The shock and fear following his arrest had been replaced by a conviction that if he co-operated with his captors he could still convince them he wasn't a traitor. He had begun to feel like this soon after one of the men had expertly injected him in the back of the hand as the van sped away from the square. After being strapped down he had been given a second injection and left to stare into the bright light. Now, when he tried to close his eyes, a voice ordered him not to. Yaobang heard a chair being sat down immediately behind his head, and sensed someone leaning forward close to his ear.

'I will expect you to tell me the truth, always. Please give me that assurance, Captain Cheng.'

The interrogator's voice was soft and almost sorrowful. The woman's breath smelled of dried fish.

'I promise to tell you the truth that I am no traitor,' Yaobang replied.

So it began. The interrogator's questions were precise and put in a non-threatening manner. And there was so much she knew: dates, places, moments Yaobang had all but forgotten. From the names of his schoolteachers, she moved to that of his first *danwei* leader and from him to his many Army instructors. Yaobang had the impression she was working down a list, checking his recall against it. Testing to see if he was telling the truth.

When she reached the name of the instructor who had taught him the intricacies of Special Signals, her questions became even more specific. What had they spoken about besides work? Had they met socially? Had he been to the instructor's home? Met his family? His friends? She asked about Captain Wong, whose place he had taken in the Operations Room. How had he managed that? From where had he obtained the contaminated food? Had Wong accepted it without demur? Could Wong have possibly suspected what was going on?

He answered truthfully, insisting Wong could have had no idea.

She asked questions about his family. Who was he close to? Had he spoken to anyone about what he was doing? The neighbours – was he friendly with any of them? Had he ever discussed with them his work? His feelings?

Again, he answered truthfully. He had spoken to no one about his work. He took her silence to mean he had successfully passed another test.

Her questions turned to his relationship with his father and moved rapidly to that day in Tibet when Lizhi Cheng ordered his troops to shoot the Lama monks protesting about China's occupation of their country.

'What did you feel about your father's action?' she asked.

He blinked his eyes. 'I felt many things. That this was not the way to show people they can learn from us. That what was done could seriously damage China in the eyes of the world. That made me very sad. And then I was angry. Many of those monks were my own age, some even younger. It seemed terribly wrong to kill them because of what they believed.'

'Did you tell your father any of this?'

'No.'

'Why not?'

He felt her breath once more on his skin.

'Because he ... was my father.'

'What does that mean?' she asked in little more than a whisper.

'My father murdered those monks. I had nothing to say to him!'

She reminded Yaobang that his father had been on his way back to Beijing to receive from Chairman Hu one of the country's highest decorations for his action when he was killed in the air crash. 'Do you still regard your father as a murderer?'

'Yes. He murdered not only those monks, but also this country's reputation.'

'You say that even though Chairman Hu awarded your father's decoration posthumously, an honour rarely given?'

'Yes.' Yaobang briefly closed his eyes. How could he make her understand? When he opened them he could hear the interrogator shifting on her chair.

'Did you discuss your father with the foreigner?'

'You mean David?'

'Yes. Did you discuss your father with him?'

'Yes.' The stark truth of David's judgement had led to everything.

Behind him someone was whispering to the woman. Then once more she was leaning forward. 'Describe the foreigner.'

Yaobang gave a description of Morton. A small sigh came from someone behind his head, a sound so small he couldn't be certain if it was from the interrogator or someone else.

'Did you see the foreigner as a replacement for your father?' she asked.

'No. David was very different.'

'In which way?'

'He was interested in my views. My father never was.' The one time he tried to discuss matters, his father had coldly cut him off. But David allowed him to share his love for China and his concern over the way the country was going.

'These views. Elaborate on them,' she said.

Yaobang did so without dissembling. The woman listened without challenging. Finally only the steady scratch of pen on paper punctuated the silence.

'Did the foreigner pay you money?' she asked at last.

'No. Never. If he had offered it, I would never have accepted. No one should profit from helping his country.'

'Where did you meet?'

'At the zoo mostly. Once we took the cable car to the top of Fragrant Hills. Sometimes we would just walk through the *hutongs*.'

'A tourist and his guide,' she murmured. 'How natural.'

Her questions continued. 'By then he had given you the recorder and tape?'

'Yes.'

'And explained its purpose?'

'Yes. But I was only using it to help my country. I am not a traitor –'

'How many times have you used it?'

'Before this time – once. To test it out.'

'What did you transmit for your ... test?'

A hint of a smile briefly crossed Yaobang's face. 'A summary of one of Chairman Hu's speeches. It was in *People's Daily*.'

'What was the speech about?'

'I don't remember ...'

'Why not?'

'I'd been ... drinking at the time.'

Her warm odorous breath wafted across his face. 'It's hard to remember when you've been drinking.'

David had once said it was another of China's many paradoxes that the authorities publicly disapproved of alcohol, yet its leaders often consumed copious amounts themselves.

'I hadn't drunk that much. Only a few beers. I think it was because I was nervous.'

The interrogator made another note on the pad on her knee. She wore a Mao jacket and trousers which disguised her figure. Thick pebble glasses made it hard to judge her age. 'Did you tell anyone about your friendship with the foreigner?' she asked.

'No. People would not have understood.'

She shifted in her chair. 'Perhaps to someone after you had been drinking? You could have done so then. And it would be quite natural to want to share your secret.'

Yaobang shook his head. 'I don't normally drink. It only happened that one time.'

The interrogator waited. Her job was to winkle out admission after admission. After a while her questions resumed. 'Did the foreigner ask to meet your friends?'

'No. Anyway, I don't have any special friends.'

'Did you meet anyone with him? Another foreigner, perhaps?'

'No. We were always alone.'

'Walking in the *hutongs*, eating dumplings or looking at the zoo animals. You talking, he listening,' she said softly.

'Sometimes David spoke too.'

'About what?'

'The change in the world. Our history, and how we could use it to play an important role in those changes. But first we had to change.'

The scratch of his words being written down was the only sound in the room.

'Did you always walk?' she asked.

'No. Sometimes we cycled.'

'Where did he get his bicycle from?'

'I don't know. But it looked like a rented one.'

'How could you tell?'

'It didn't seem very well looked after.'

'But you really don't know where he got it from?'

'No.'

The interrogator fell silent. She had managed to once more convey a sense of something being withheld. She leaned forward. 'He gave you a contact number.' A statement, not a question.

'Yes.'

'What was it?'

Yaobang repeated the number.

'What were your instructions about making contact?'

He told her about the advert for a kitchen boy.

The lengthening silence was broken by a whisper of voices, followed by the sound of chair legs scraping the floor. Then a new voice spoke in his ear – cold and distant and fearfully familiar.

'Did you see David in the square, Cheng?' Qiao Peng asked.

'Sir ... is that you?'

Qiao Peng rolled the stogey across his lips. The fool's reaction had been genuine. And surprise, like weakness, always showed itself; that was what distinguished it from strength. He continued to sit perfectly still in the chair the interrogator had vacated. She had done a good job. But unlike her, there was no need for him to lean forward. His very presence was usually sufficiently intimidating.

'Answer my question! Did you see him in the square?'

'No, sir.'

'When were you to meet him again?'

'I don't know, sir,' Yaobang whispered.

'Don't lie to me, Cheng!'

'I'm not, sir. I'm telling you the truth – '

'Did you recognise anyone else in the square?'

'No sir,' Yaobang's eyes began to glaze with tears. Why didn't they believe him? He had told them only the truth.

'Please, sir ...'

'Stop snivelling!'

Qiao Peng had seen this before, many times, when someone finally broke.

'Yes, sir,' Yaobang blinked back tears.

'Now tell me again exactly how you met the foreigner, what you said, what he said to you. Everything. Understand? Everything!' The effect of the drugs would last only a little longer.

'Yes, sir. It was the day, like I've said, I'd gone shopping ...'

Qiao Peng listened intently, his eyes fixed on the back of Yaobang's head. Morton would have briefed him well, telling him only what he absolutely needed to know, but never, for a moment, revealing his true purpose. Morton was like an animal, known only by his scent. But how much had he believed of what this traitor had transmitted? Much depended on that.

'How did he persuade you to betray your country?' Qiao Peng asked.

Yaobang felt tears on his cheeks. 'I never saw it as betrayal, sir. I only wanted to make China a better place.'

'Is that what he told you to say?' It didn't really matter.

'No, sir. It's what I believe.'

Qiao Peng stared pitilessly at the back of Yaobang's head.

'You are a traitor, Cheng.'

'I'm not, sir. Please believe me!'

Yaobang struggled to turn his head. He wanted to look into Qiao Peng's face, to show him he was telling the truth.

'What did he promise you?'

'Nothing, sir.'

'You are still lying!' That also really didn't matter now.

'No, sir! Please, you have to believe me ...'

The scrape of chair legs sounded unnaturally loud in Yaobang's ears. He heard whispers, then the sound of a door opening and closing. A moment later he smelled the fish-tainted breath of his interrogator on his face.

'Do you have anything else you wish to tell me?' she asked, almost gently.

'Only that I'm not a traitor! I know that in my heart!'

He heard a movement behind him.

'Please! Believe me!' Yaobang said again.

Something hard and cold was pressing against the nape of his neck. He shrieked. 'Please! Please – no!'

The woman pulled the trigger of her pistol, firing through the hole, then stepping quickly back as Yaobang's blood and brain began to drain into the bucket.

In the corridor Qiao Peng paused at the sound of the gunshot, then continued to walk towards the elevator. He never liked to witness an execution; it reminded him too much of his own mortality.

Minutes later, he settled in the back of the Red Flag limousine chauffeuring him back to Zhongnanhai. Cheng had unwittingly played his part perfectly. From the time he saw him copying down movements in the map room, he realised the truth. The discovery later of Cheng's cassette recorder and its tape, whose purpose Professor Wu confirmed, settled it. Wu's technicians had planted encoded data on the tape which would match that transmitted by Cheng. The traitor himself had been allowed to surreptitiously gather false information. It really had been quite simple. And there was no way that Morton would suspect that the entire operation in Tiananmen Square had been carefully orchestrated.

His own agents had failed to spot Morton in the crowd on the square. Yet he'd been there. Morton would not just have sent Nagier and his boy, not for something as important as this. The pair were now back in the Russian Embassy. But of Morton there was no sign. But he was still out there somewhere. He wouldn't be Morton if he wasn't. Yet to launch the usual search would be pointless for someone like him. Not that he needed to find Morton, not yet. Let him run a little more.

Qiao Peng glanced out of the tinted windows as another shoal of cyclists scattered before the speeding car. Evening fog, common at this time of year, was starting to cloak everything in grey anonymity. Passing Tiananmen Gate he could just make out Mao's portrait, its eyes staring with an intensity which seemed to send the mist swirling uneasily.

The broadcast from Japan was due in a few moments. He had arranged for one of his agents in Tokyo to pass on to the station – the authentic voice of the Japanese right wing – the tape taken from the American Ambassador's car by the Triad gang. Broadcasting the tape was guaranteed to inflame extremists against their Emperor and prepare the ground for Silent Voices.

He had no doubt now of its success. What the Russian had succeeded in doing to the minds of that man and woman, he would assuredly do with the mind of the President. This Gyroton was indeed a weapon like no other. And, in a moment of personal gratification, he would personally record the subliminal instructions for the President to order the launching of a pre-emptive atomic strike against Tokyo. The one doubt was how long both sides would sustain an all-out war; the one certainty that, when it was over, both sides would be so severely weakened that they would be in no position to stop China becoming the great new Empire.

Qiao Peng switched on the radio built into the veneered panelling. There was only the sound of static. Perhaps atmospherics were affecting the transmission? He began to retune, seeking another Japanese station. Radio Hiroshima came through clearly. Then a station from Kyote. But on the frequency for the radical Tokyo station there was still only static.

He was still searching when suddenly a voice announced that this was All-Nippon broadcast news, and that the top story of the day was that a police raid on an extremist radio station had uncovered important evidence about the assassination of Ambassador Lincoln. The station itself was off the air, its staff being held for questioning and all their broadcast tapes impounded.

Switching off the radio, Qiao Peng picked up the 'phone in his armrest. Glancing out of the window, his eye was caught by a banner welcoming the delegates to the medical convention. He began to dial a number.

Three hundred miles off the China coast the *USS Seattle* was racing west at 40 knots. In the submarine's attack centre, the Captain, Deke Edmunds, and his sonar officer, Chet Woodward, studied one of many screens. A tiny computer-created model showed the *Dallas*'s present position. Closer to the coast were scores of other blips, each one representing a ship of the Chinese Navy returning to port after the war games.

'That's our problem. Ivan bear gets in among them and he's safe, skipper,' said Woodward.

'Except for one thing, Woody. The Chinese haven't anything like a Typhoon. Our Ivan's engine noise is going to stand out like a calling-card in a Manila brothel.'

'What about those Typhoons the Japs just bought?'

The Captain grinned. 'If they're out there sniffing to see what the Chinese are up to, things could get really interesting.'

In the Oval Office everyone instinctively leaned towards the desk behind which the President sat. He, too, continued to listen intently to the amplified voice from the speaker-phone on the desk. The only movement was Madeleine Masters' hand noting down the words of the Emperor of Japan.

'Your Embassy here has confirmed that the voice on the tape that our intelligence agents recovered from the radio station is that of

Ambassador Lincoln, Mr President. I am happy to say the recording is also a completely accurate account of my meeting with him. But I would not have expected otherwise from your Ambassador. He was not only a credit to your diplomatic service, but to all the good things your country represents.'

'Thank you, Your Majesty.' The President inclined his head, touched by the Emperor's words. He glanced towards Gates and FBI Director Wyman. 'I'm glad our people over there were able to help stop that tape being broadcast.' The President was referring to the joint FBI-CIA team which had led Japanese intelligence to the Tokyo radio station. 'That would have been catastrophic,' he added.

'For both of us, Mr President,' the Emperor said gravely.

Alone in his study in the Imperial Palace, he sat before the scrambler satellite telephone which guaranteed his call could not be bugged.

'Although the physical violence has stopped, Mr President, the situation remains tense. But I am hopeful that the appointment of Mr Voss to be your next Ambassador here will help to calm things.'

The Emperor gave a gentle little smile. 'Perhaps we can learn from him.'

'He is a good man, Your Majesty. Anything he can do to help, he will,' the President said.

When he offered him the post, Cy had said he could take a year away from the office. His strong, visible presence in Tokyo could smooth over a lot of the bumps if the deal with Beijing went through.

'Nevertheless I am still extremely glad of this opportunity to speak to you personally about your forthcoming trip, Mr President.'

In the silence the President looked at the men seated before him. Thack, Bobby Collins, flanked by a couple of aides from States. The Secretary of Defense with his own note-taker, a Marine Major. The Chairman of the Joint Chiefs of Staff. Gates and Wyman. All good men. But in the end, as Harry Truman once said, the buck stopped this side of the desk. That's why he had agreed to the call.

'Mr President, I want you to know that I totally support, without qualification, your plan for helping China,' the Emperor continued with quiet determination.

'Thank you, Your Majesty.'

The President looked across the desk. Bobby's aides were making notes. The others continued to stare fixedly at the speakerphone.

'But for the project to succeed, it will be essential for it to also have

278

the support of your government and ultimately, of course, your people. Can you guarantee that?'

The Emperor sighed. Some of the government were harder, stronger men than him. He recognised that. Just as he also knew what he would finally do if all else failed. 'Mr President, I have made it clear to my Prime Minister that if he cannot provide full support for your plan, then I will give up my Throne. That will be the end of Japan as my people know it. But there will be no place for me in the new order of Bushido.'

The Emperor heard the gasps from the Oval Office.

In the silence the President tried to absorb this latest, unexpected piece of news. Then, slowly, his face changed, admiration replacing the astonishment. 'I don't know what to say, Your Majesty. I don't know if I could make such a sacrifice.'

'It is a small one compared to making sure your vision is a success, Mr President. And I hope I will not be forced into abdicating. I am still confident that once my government and people fully understand the great opportunities for them which will come with a strong and stable China, they will welcome wholeheartedly what you are doing. Realistically they cannot afford not to do so.'

'Why do you say that?' Relief mingled with the President's admiration.

In the Imperial Palace, the Emperor glanced at the fireplace. Flames danced in the hearth. Yet, despite the warmth of the room, he shivered. For a fleeting moment in his mind's eye he saw in the flames the face of Chairman Hu, as icy-looking as he had sounded during their telephone conversation. 'Success for your plan is important to Japan, Mr President, for one very good and simple reason. It would stop China from attacking us.'

The Emperor heard laughter, low and disbelieving, from the Oval Office. He could understand that response. Too often his people had cast themselves as aggressors. But not this time.

'Do you have reason to believe China will do that?' the President asked carefully.

The Emperor told him about his call to Chairman Hu. 'He left a great deal unsaid, Mr President. But what he did say contained an implicit threat, that China was no longer to be treated as the sick old man of the Pacific. I was left with the distinct feeling that the warning was directed at us. It is all the more reason for us to support your plan, so that your country can make sure that China's aspirations do not get out of hand.'

The President silenced the others with a glance. Yet, given what they all now knew, their reaction was understandable. He picked up the single sheet of paper Gates had given him earlier. The President glanced one more time at the words, and leaned towards the speaker-phone. 'Your Majesty, I have to ask you some very important questions.'

'I will answer them to the best of my ability.'

'They concern the three Typhoon class submarines your Navy recently purchased from Russia.'

The Emperor frowned. 'They were bought purely for their nuclear reactors. Our scientists believed they could be adapted to provide a safe and relatively cheap form of domestic energy. We have made no secret of that.'

The President moved closer to the speaker-phone. 'One of our satellites checked on those pens your Navy has built for the Typhoons. As you know, we are entitled to check on all nuclear weapon facilities, just as anyone else can check on ours.'

'My government was among the first to ratify that UN agreement,' the Emperor said quietly. 'But what exactly is your question about these submarines?'

'Our satellite photos show that those pens are now empty. Can you tell me where those submarines have gone to, Your Majesty? Given your concern over Chairman Hu's attitude, is it possible that your military commanders have decided to take some pre-emptive action? Those three submarines could unleash a great deal of devastation – a hundred times more than we did at Hiroshima.'

The Emperor felt his stomach tightening. Admiral Toshika was in charge of the Navy. He had been appointed on the recommendation of Ko Matzuda. Clearly the canker had spread this far. He would deal with Toshika later. The important thing now was to reassure the President. 'Wherever those Typhoons have gone to, Mr President, I will have them recalled at once,' the Emperor said tersely.

The Chairman of the Joint Chiefs was scribbling furiously on a memo pad. He tore off the page and strode over and placed it on the desk before the President. The General remained standing at the President's elbow. The President read the words, nodded, and turned back to the speaker-phone.

'Supposing they cannot be contacted, Your Majesty? I am advised that submarines on patrol normally maintain radio silence.'

'Mr President, you have my word that our forces will never attack anyone first – especially China. For us history is like an old man's memory. The past is often more vivid than the present. But here in Japan there are many who remember all too well the result of aggression.'

'I accept that totally, Your Majesty. But that still doesn't answer my concern about those Typhoons,' said the President.

The cramp in his stomach made the Emperor wince. 'What can be done, Mr President?'

The President glanced at the Chairman of the Joint Chiefs, who was once more scrawling on the paper. The President read what he had written the turned to the speaker-phone.

'I have no alternative but to order whatever measures will be necessary to deal with those submarines should they in any way pose a threat to what we both wish, Your Majesty.'

Morton followed into a toilet several doctors who needed to relieve themselves after the copious amounts of tea their hosts served before the hospital ward round. Like the others, he wore a white coat. A lapel badge displayed his convention ID as an urologist.

He waited in a stall until the others left, then walked back into the corridor. The tail end of the group was heading into the first ward. Morton stepped through the door Danny had shown him on the plan. The elevators were beyond. He entered one and descended into a concrete chamber. Facing him was a steel door with a bell-push. He pressed the button. There was a faint hiss and the door slid over. He stepped into a short corridor. The door behind him closed. For a moment he stood in the cold darkness, listening to a distant humming sound.

In the ceiling a low-wattage bulb came on. It probably worked on a timer, once the door closed. At the far end of the corridor another steel door slid silently back into the wall recess. Beyond was a tunnel. A rail track gleamed in the safety lights. Morton walked into the tunnel, his eyes growing accustomed to the strange shadow-filled light. He kept to one side of the track. At a bend in the tunnel he found the source of the humming: an air-conditioning plant.

Beyond was a large chamber with rows of benches, sufficient seating for hundreds. In one corner was a podium. Mao must have wanted his cadres to lecture the people on the virtues of Marxism while sheltering from a Soviet atomic holocaust. Leading from the chamber were other tunnels. This must be the junction point Danny had indicated.

Morton paused to take his bearings. The tunnel leading off to his left went to the Great Hall of the People, the one to the right to Zhongnan-hai. The one straight ahead had to go to the Western Hills. Danny hadn't mentioned the rail carriage standing at a narrow platform in that tunnel. Morton heaved himself up onto the platform and studied the carriage. The interior reminded him of the one he and Danny had ridden all those years ago when they'd gone to collect Tommy from school. This carriage had the same faded elegance as the Brighton Belle. He peered through the window of the driver's cab. It was completely automated. He remembered that Chantal had told him about this carriage: it was Hu's, the one that would speed him to an airfield in the Western Hills should the day ever come when the people would rise. At that time a driver could not be trusted to help the Supreme Leader escape.

Morton walked back along the carriage, recalling what else Chantal had said. The carriage was propelled by a gas turbine engine to avoid a problem with electrical failure. He peered through a window. On one wood-panelled wall was the control panel she had said allowed the carriage's destination to be automatically programmed. He walked to the closed double doors in the centre of the carriage. Chantal had been especially impressed with the carriage's security. The doors, like the windows and bodywork, were bomb-proof. But she'd also told him how rescuers could gain access in an emergency. He knelt down and felt underneath the running board. His hand found the button. He pressed it and the doors silently slid open.

The moment he stepped into the carriage a number of things happened. The doors closed behind him. The carriage's lights came on. The wall panel lit up. From the cab came the hum of power. Morton stood for a moment looking around him, marvelling at the simple efficiency of everything. Hu could operate this himself; a child could. He walked to the control panel. It was laid out like an underground train system, the rail lines blue, the stations marked in red. Above each station was a small light bulb. Only one was lit at the moment, a tiny pinprick of green. Morton guessed that that marked the carriage's present position. Beneath each station was its name in Mandarin and Russian. The carriage must have been another gift from Moscow in those days when the Kremlin was still trying to buy favours from Beijing.

He traced the line with a finger. The longest one ran out to a station simply marked 'Air Base One'. The end of the bolt-hole. A couple of stops before was one marked only with a red star. It had to be the exit point for Igor Tamasara's complex.

Chantal had said everything was literally touch-button. Morton pressed a finger against the bulb above the star. Again several things happened simultaneously. The bulb above the star glowed green. A loud speaker in the ceiling hissed and a man's voice announced that the destination was 'Research Complex'. A moment later the carriage started to move. Morton sat down in a pullman chair, his eyes never leaving the control panel.

A mile away, in a corner of the Zhongnanhai compound, the chief technician in charge of the underground rail network watched the light move across the grid covering the entire wall of the control room. He still could neither quite believe what was happening nor what he had been told to do. Normally, at the sight of this unauthorised movement of the Chairman's carriage, he would have pressed the alarm buttons connecting the room to Public Security Headquarters and that of the Beijing garrison. Thousands of security men and troops would by now be pouring into the tunnels and blocking off all the overground exits.

Yet he had been expressly forbidden to trigger the alert. Instead, he was to make a 'phone call to the number he had been given. It was like no other he had ever dialled – three digits. Once he had assured himself of the carriage's destination, the technician picked up the 'phone on his desk and dialled the number. 'The destination is the Research Complex,' he said.

In the back of the Red Flag, Qiao Peng put down the 'phone without acknowledgement, leaned forward and ordered the driver to go directly to Air Base One.

26

Morton felt the carriage slowing and, moments later, it emerged from the tunnel and stopped at a deserted platform. He peered through the windows, but there was nothing to indicate where he was. The loud-speaker recording announced, first in Mandarin, then Russian: 'Research Complex'.

The doors opened and he stepped onto the platform. At regular intervals there were lights in the arched roof, tiled white like the walls, producing watery pools of light which made the shadows seem more uncertain. Halfway along the platform was an opening. Behind him the carriage doors closed with another pneumatic hiss followed by the car's power supply dying as suddenly as it had come on. He walked towards the opening, pausing when a whisper of a breeze came from the darkness of the tunnel and was gone. Another train? Or a surface wind which had somehow found its way down here, into this cold and oppressive place? He walked on, his steps echoing flat and lifeless on the concrete.

Inside the opening was an elevator door. With one hand he moved his gun from the small of his back to his hip for easier reach under his doctor's coat. With the other hand he reached forward and pressed a button to open the door. The cage was made of polished walnut. He had seen elevators like this before in Moscow, in all those places where Russia had liked to impress foreigners. He stepped into the elevator, almost having to duck to avoid touching the chandelier. Beside the control panel were stuck hand-printed notices in Russian: 'Laboratory', 'Workshop', 'Administration', 'Staff Quarters'. Morton pressed the button marked 'Test Area'.

The door closing was followed by the soft whine of the elevator cables. When the door opened, Morton found himself facing a passage with closed doors on either side. The heavy hand of Soviet interior design was visible in the dark wood panelling of walls and ceiling and coarse-woven carpets. Perhaps Igor Tamasara had been homesick? At the far end of the passage was a small window set in yet another door. Through the glass the daylight was fading.

Morton walked to the nearest door and, without knocking, thrust it open, the way a Russian would. The store's floor was littered with earthenware vats. He examined the labels. Russian chemicals of various kinds. He closed the door and walked to the next one. In the centre of the room was a large rickety wooden table covered with cheap plates and mugs. A mess hall.

He checked other rooms. Each was empty and smelled of damp from the patches of mould on the walls and ceilings. Morton reached the door with the window. Beyond was an expanse of open ground about the width of a couple of football pitches and several times longer. Away to his left, barely visible in the dusk, was a low, squat building half-hidden by trees. On his right were a number of derelict-looking buildings.

He fished under his shirt and pulled out the enlargements of the satellite photographs the Embassy photographer had provided. From a pocket he removed a pair of goggles, not unlike a welder's. They had been developed by Technical Services to provide perfect vision under any conditions. He put them on, making adjustments by turning a screw on either side of the eye-pieces. The microchip-powered computer built into the frame did the rest. He began to compare the buildings on the prints with those he could now clearly see.

The structure to the left was the bunker from where the sat cameras had picked up the heat emission. The rail track would be at the back. He panned his head slowly across the buildings to the right. The windows were covered with what looked like black sacking. Danny had suggested that this was where Anna could be held. Possibly Baskin and Schrag, too. Yet there were no guards, no one in sight at all.

Morton turned back to the bunker, adjusting the focus to increase the definition. Its one window seemed to be made from refraction-free glass. But it was the narrow slit in the wall to one side that he concentrated on. The heat emission must have escaped through that. He began to quarter the ground methodically in front of the bunker. Nothing caught his eye.

Shoving the photographs back under his shirt, he tested the handle. The door opened to his touch. He was about to step outside when a dull metallic sound came from beyond the bunker. The noise came again. The trees made it difficult to judge distance but there was no mistaking the sound of a rail car being coupled up. Some things just stuck in your mind.

Morton removed his doctor's coat, rolled it up and tossed it into the nearest room. He fished inside his shirt once more, removing and shaking out the one-piece overall. He put it on. Technical Services had demonstrated that the material made anyone virtually invisible to infra-red detectors or any other form of night scope. From a small tube already packed into the overall pocket he squeezed a dark paste and rubbed it on his face, neck and hands to conceal his scent from a guard dog. After tightening the strap on his goggles, he began to walk purposefully towards the bunker.

Reaching the shelter of the trees he stopped. About half a mile beyond was the train; an engine, half a dozen box and flat cars, and a solitary carriage. Soldiers were milling around a flat car on which a number of white-coated civilians were supervising the positioning of a black-painted box-like structure. The train was at maximum range for the goggles, the faces of the civilians and soldiers merely blobs under the sodium lights. With the overall came a gadget the size of a TV-zapper. Attached to it was a pair of headphones. He placed them over his ears and then held the voice transponder towards the train.

A faint and indistinguishable babble filled Morton's ears. On the transponder's small fluorescent screen a command appeared: 'Spec Trans Lang'. He pressed a button to specify that he wanted translation from Russian and Mandarin into English. The transponder's powerful miniature parabolic mike began to gather up the distant voices for its small but equally powerful miniature decoder to translate. The civilians on the flat cars were speaking Russian. Igor Tamasara's men.

'I thought the tests were over. Now we have to go to Luda,' one grumbled.

There it was! The Gyroton! So tantalisingly close! But it could be a million miles away for all the chance he had of destroying it. Those soldiers would cut him to pieces. He felt defeat rushing through him, threatening to enmesh his resolve. He struggled with it silently, fighting himself clear of its deadly embrace by concentrating on the voices in his headphones.

'I hear he wants to test his Gyroton out over water,' one said.

'Why?' grunted a third voice.

'Who knows? I didn't even know Luda existed until an hour ago,' said a fourth Russian.

Morton continued to listen intently. Luda was China's northernmost naval sea base in the Gulf of Bohai. Geographically it was in a direct line with Manila, a couple of thousand miles to the south. But for the Gyroton's beam distance would be no barrier. Like the click of a well-oiled lock slipping home, it all fell into place. He knew – oh God – he knew. The attack against the President would not be in Hong Kong, but in Manila.

He began to work out distances and time in his head. The train would get to Luda well in time for the Gyroton to be positioned to strike the President when he arrived in Manila.

Morton moved the transponder to a group of soldiers. Enlisted men's talk. What the food and girls were like in Luda. He panned across to the rail carriage. The voices from inside were indistinct. He panned back to the flat car. The technicians had covered the Gyroton and soldiers were clambering up to squat around the tarpaulin. The remaining troops were boarding the box cars.

Moments later the train began to pull out of the siding. Watching it go, he checked the compass on his wristwatch. Holding the transponder firmly in both hands he pointed it skywards and began to press keys. Several thousand miles in space the Hammer Force communications satellite would cone up the transmission and simultaneously relay it to Hammer Force Headquarters. From there it would be sent to all those who needed to know the Gyroton's destination.

Morton turned towards the bunker, walking along the rail track. Set in the bunker's main sliding door was a smaller one. Through gaps around its frame came a bluish light. Morton pressed an ear against the door. Silence. He tried the handle and the door opened inwards. The hard, steely light came from the bank of flickering monitor screens on one wall. He stepped inside, closing the door behind him.

The bunker was larger than he had thought, about the size of a squash court, with rough bare concrete walls ending in the window and the slit-like opening on one side. The rail track ran to the centre of the floor. Scattered around the area were work benches with various items of equipment. He recognised the oscilloscopes and phase testers. But there was no clue as to the actual purpose of the other pieces. It did not matter. This was where Igor Tamasara had fine-tuned the Gyroton.

Morton walked over to the monitors. They offered various views of cell-like rooms and corridors. Most of the rooms were deserted, but in one or two he could see what looked like sleeping figures. On one screen a rope descended from a hole in the ceiling. Nearby lay another inert figure. Watching, Morton felt almost a sense of intrusion.

He went over to the window. The buildings were on the far side of the open expanse of ground. He studied them carefully, his skin crawling as realisation dawned. The emission the sat cameras had picked up was the Gyroton's beam being fired. Almost certainly the figures on the screen were some of Igor Tamasara's victims.

Morton turned and ran towards the door. Outside it had started to rain. By the time he reached the buildings the storm was lashing the walls, the sheer force of the downpour tearing the black cloth from the windows. Though the overall was waterproof, he felt chilled to the bone. As he stepped through a doorway the downpour stopped.

Adjusting his goggles, he began to explore the rooms, gun in one hand, loosely at his side. The rooms were empty. He reached a staircase at the end of the corridor. The storm had left the atmosphere heavy and oppressive. He climbed the stairs to the next floor. The same brooding silence lay here. Halfway down the corridor, immediately beneath a gaping trapdoor in the ceiling, lay the body of a Chinese man, face upwards, legs and arms twisted inhumanly.

Morton walked down the centre of the passage and stood over the body. No fall could have done that to the man's head, severing the top of the skull and leaving a dark empty hole. Some dark evil had done that.

He continued down the corridor, checking rooms. Their empty silence seemed to grip him like a hand. Rounding a bend in the corridor he spotted the spent match. He picked it up and sniffed. It had been used recently. A few yards further on was the matchbox itself. As something fluttered above his head, he instinctively crouched and brought his gun to bear. He relaxed. Bats. There was a small colony of them clinging to the ceiling. Someone had struck the match, disturbed the bats and dropped the matchbox in panic. That didn't sound like Anna.

Morton walked on. He had gone about thirty paces when he saw a dark stain on the floor. He crouched and touched the stain. It was wet to the touch. He sniffed his finger. Fresh blood. He stood up. Holding the gun in both hands in front of him, he followed the stain around another bend in the corridor. A man's body lay slumped on the floor. The blood, clotted and dried now, made the gaping hole in his throat seem even more obscene.

Morton crouched beside the body, ignoring the open eyes staring at him, dull, but still somehow startled at the savagery of the manner of death. The man was Caucasian, big and flabby, in his middle years. Morton inspected the ghastly wound. Whoever had done this had been taught to kill professionally. Anna?

He checked the man's pockets. Empty. He examined the maker's label in the jacket seams. To finally make sure he worked the jacket free of the shoulders. On the inside collar tab was a name. Schrag.

Stepping away from the body, Morton searched the remaining rooms on the corridor. They were empty. He reached the gap in the floor and the rope descending from the ceiling. He peered up. The rope disappeared over the edge of the hole and had begun to fray where it had rubbed against the edge. He tugged on the rope; it seemed securely fixed. Shoving his gun into his overall pocket he climbed the rope, using his hands and feet to control its snaking and twisting. He reached the hole and pulled himself over the edge. Rising to his feet he took the gun out and continued searching.

In a room he found a woman's body lying face down beside an upturned stool. There were burn marks around her neck as if she had been throttled to death. He turned over the corpse. Hair still clung to her forehead which had been sliced away, leaving the woman's mouth wide open, as if she was screaming in the silence. Another of Igor Tamasara's experiments?

Morton froze. Out of the corner of his eye he caught a glimpse of brief movement under the woman's skirt. There was a rustling sound, faint and almost inaudible even in that silence. Another movement disturbed the cloth taut across the woman's thighs. Out of the gap between her legs darted the rat. It scurried across the floor and out of the door.

Morton continued his search. There were no more bodies. And no sign of Anna or Colin Baskin. He left the building the way he had come, crossed the open ground and returned to the wood-panelled passage. The elevator door was still open.

He went to the room into which he had tossed his doctor's coat, stripped out of his overall, refolded it and put it back inside his shirt. Once more placing his gun in the small of his back, he put on the white coat and walked to the elevator. When he reached the platform the carriage was where he had left it. He opened the door and pressed the bulb on the control panel marked 'Military Hospital Number One'. The doors closed and the loudspeaker confirmed the destination. Thirty minutes later Morton was back where he had started from.

He walked out of the tunnel and entered the hospital elevator. It brought him up to the corridor leading to the wards. A nurse emerged from a side room and looked curiously at him. She pointed down the corridor. He nodded and smiled. Moments later he joined the rest of the delegates emerging from a final lecture on Traditional Medicine.

An hour later Morton was back in the Embassy conference room briefing Danny and Tommy on what had happened.

Captain Marlo stood at the back of the rail watching the bridge crew going about the business of reaching *Rodina*'s berth. He could not fault them. In the half-hour since surfacing Quingdao had come steadily closer; now he could pick out individual lights in the myriad of pin-pricks in the hills behind the port. The seaway itself teemed with boats of all shapes and sizes. Few of them bothered with navigation lights.

For'ard of where the Captain stood, Tarinski continued to call out course changes that would take the *Rodina* across the bay to the pen which had been assigned by Quingdao Navy Headquarters. Without charts of the local hazards, the navigator was depending on the voice in his headset. The Chinese officer on the shore spoke passable Russian and had boasted that he had done this several times. That would be in the days when Typhoons had made regular voyages into these waters. But Tarinski knew there was no such thing as taking anything for granted, especially when docking in a strange port. He had ordered another course change to avoid an old freighter which had passed to port, her broad bow forging a bulging wave despite her slow speed. He had called down the change a full minute before the voice in the headset told him to do so. The Chinese was slow as well as cocksure.

So far he had not acknowledged the presence, about a half-mile in front, of a tanker. Tarinski studied her through his binoculars. She was low in the water, which meant she was fully laden. And that bow-wave showed her picking up speed. Even as he watched, the curved front of the tanker's bridge grew larger.

He swore softly. If she was going to pass him to port – as she should – he should be seeing that curve grow smaller. The damned thing was heading directly towards them! He called over the bridge telephone: 'Increase revolutions one third.' The water began to stir beneath the *Rodina*'s spherical bow.

A moment later the Chinese voice was in his ear. 'Maintain present course and position.'

'We've got a tanker directly ahead,' Tarinski said into his lip-mike.

'She has been ordered to change course,' came the reply.

Tarinski raised his glasses. Marlo was at his elbow.

'Comrade Captain! The tanker's bearing is a collision situation!'

In the binoculars the oncoming bow was surging.

'Starboard twenty,' Marlo ordered.

As the seaman moved to pick up the bridge 'phone to relay the order, Tarinski stopped him and turned to the Captain. 'We'll never get out of the way in time, Comrade Captain! She'll catch us side-on in the turn! Our one chance is to race past before she can hit us.'

Marlo glanced at the navigator then swung his glasses back on the tanker. She was awfully close. 'Maintain present course,' he ordered.

The submarine began to roll under the increase of engine revolutions. On the bridge every man was staring towards the tanker. 'Lamp her,' ordered Marlo.

'No point, Comrade Captain. Chances are no one on that bridge reads Russian,' Tarinski replied brusquely.

'Then tell that fool in your headset to do something!'

Tarinski cupped his hand over the lip-mike. 'It'll only confuse him.'

Behind the binoculars all eyes continued to watch the tanker.

'Tanker reversing!' yelled one of the look-outs.

'Reduce your speed,' came the voice in Tarinski's headset.

'Two thirds full ahead,' Tarinski ordered.

Marlo looked at the navigator but said nothing.

His eyes glued to the oncoming bow-wave, Tarinski spoke again. 'Her engines are going to thresh enough water to drive us under unless we get well clear.'

The onrushing tanker's bow-wave was less than three hundred yards away. The flare of its bow seemed to block out everything else.

Two hundred yards. That huge anchor was large enough to crush the *Rodina* with one blow.

'All full ahead!' Tarinski yelled.

The *Rodina* began to rock from the wash created by the tanker's bow-wave, which drove great surges of water over the submarine, soaking everyone on the bridge.

'What are you doing?' demanded the petulant voice in Tarinski's headset.

Tarinski ignored the question. The tanker's bridge was now abeam. Faces were peering down. The turbulence from the ship's threshing screws continued to rock the *Rodina*. But the gap between them was narrowing all the time.

'She's turning away,' Tarinski yelled.

Either that stupid Chinese bastard had given the tanker a new course change or her pilot – if there was one aboard – was taking his own evasive action. The huge vertical side of the tanker continued to slide past. But the gap was continuing to narrow.

Marlo stood, open-mouthed, as if frozen by the approaching collision. Tarinski grabbed the mike of the ship's electric loudhailer and yelled with all his strength. 'Tanker bridge! Put your rudder to right full!'

The water between the tanker's hull and the *Rodina* was foaming in a turmoil of its own.

'Tanker! Right full rudder!' Tarinski could feel his neck muscles straining with the repeated yelling.

Fifty ... forty ... thirty feet separated them from the towering steel cliff.

'Her stern's abreast!' yelled the look-out. 'Passing – now!'

The tanker's fantail passed the spot where a moment before the *Rodina* had been. The water churned furiously beneath the tanker's rusted plates. The *Rodina* began to lurch back on an even keel as the water's threshing was reduced. The danger was over.

Marlo picked up the bridge 'phone. 'This is the Captain. We have narrowly escaped being run down by a tanker ...' He paused and looked at Tarinski. Then he continued, 'Prompt action by Comrade navigator Tarinski saved the day.' The rule book was clear: you acknowledged good seamanship.

From the control room the silence was followed by a rousing cheer. Tarinski looked in stunned amazement at the Captain. Marlo certainly knew how to surprise.

In the headphones the Chinese voice was demanding querulously, 'Why you not obey orders?'

Marlo reached for the lip-mike of Tarinski's headset. 'This is the Captain of the *Rodina* speaking. When I come ashore my first task will be to ensure that you will never navigate anyone ever again!'

He turned to Tarinski. 'Take her in, Comrade navigator!'

For the first time Tarinski could remember the Captain was smiling. The navigator was certain there was nothing in the book about that. In the moonlight he could see the entrance to the submarine pens. From below came reports of no damage.

27

Five floors beneath the Oval Office the President sat halfway along the conference table in the White House War Room. Teak-panelled walls, beige-coloured ceiling and matching carpet gave the room a soothing atmosphere. The only clock on the wall showed Washington time. The psychologist who advised on such matters said that that was important for decision-making.

Around the President sat key members of his Cabinet and the Defense Chiefs. By custom the Vice-President sat at one end of the table, Thack at the other. Gates stood immediately behind the President. Military uniformed or soberly-suited aides stood along the walls. Conspicuous by the gap around him in the otherwise crowded room, was Satchel, with his bag, the Football. Beside him stood Dr Barker.

On separate screens were the Prime Minister in London; Sir Alan Wingate, the Colony's Governor, in Hong Kong; the President of the Philippines in Manila. Morton was in the conference room in the Russian Embassy in Beijing.

Before coming down here Thack had informed the President about an earlier meeting between the Vice-President and the Chairman of the Joint Chiefs of Staff. The President had not realised that the Chairman of the Joint Chiefs was such a scheming dinosaur. But Thack had advised against direct confrontation. Instead he'd said to wait until after the Far East trip: if all went well, he would be in a far stronger position to see off the Vice-President and his allies. In the meantime, it would be best to bring into the loop everyone who now needed to know the score.

The President began by saying that he would explain what had happened since he sent Cy Voss to Beijing with the plan. He paused while the new Ambassador solemnly distributed copies. It was a measure of his own oratorical skills that, after glancing at the document, everyone continued to listen intently rather than study the written version of his vision for China.

He told them about Chairman Hu's response, why he was going to Hong Kong, and what he hoped to achieve there. Next he described his telephone call from the Emperor of Japan. Then after glancing quickly at Morton's screen, the President revealed everything he had been told about Igor Tamasara and the Gyroton. He cut short astonished murmurs and described Colin Baskin's earlier research for the CIA. Once more he waved for silence before revealing just what he had learned about the secret voyages of the *Rodina*, the links between Qiao Peng and Vice-Premier Kazenko and those between Leo Schrag and Li Mufang.

The President said that more would no doubt emerge following the arrest that morning of Li Mufang by the FBI.

The Director inclined his head. Morton's news that Schrag was dead and Colin Baskin no longer at the research complex meant no further need to allow the Chinese intelligence operative to remain free. A rummage squad was tearing apart Li Mufang's bar and apartment while the FBI's most experienced interrogators began to question him.

After the President had said that there was still no trace of the three Japanese Typhoons and had confirmed that the train was still heading for Luda, he looked around the table. 'I think at this stage it's going to be helpful to get some answers from Colonel Morton.'

All eyes turned to the screen linking the War Room to Beijing.

'Colonel, as I understand it, you saw nothing in that complex to show that the Gyroton is actually operational?' asked the President.

'No, sir.' There had been nothing. Plenty of clues but nothing to show the machine was fully functional.

'And those bodies ... ?'

'They were victims of Tamasara's research, Mr President.'

'But the technicians said they were going to Luda for more tests?'

'Yes, sir.'

The President half-turned in his chair. 'Has your satellite over Luda come up with anything, Mr Gates?'

'Nothing at all so far, Mr President. But it's smack bang over their naval facility and will spot anything.'

The President nodded and turned back, lost in thought for a moment. When he spoke again his voice was sombre as he addressed Morton. 'You think any attack will be launched from there?'

'Yes, sir. Luda's in a direct line with Manila.'

The President sighed. 'In a sense, it won't matter then. The important decisions will have been made in Hong Kong. I will make sure nothing will undo them no matter what may happen to me in Manila.'

He glanced to where the Vice-President sat.

'Let those who would criticise me for acting alone and not revealing most of this until now remember one thing. Everything I did was done for the same reason that still makes me proud and humble to hold this office. My every action was done to serve the people the best way I can.'

The Vice-President flushed but said nothing.

Morton sensed the tension in the War Room. He knew the reason, just as he knew there was nothing he, or anyone else, could do. This was a battle the President must win for himself. But he was lucky to have Thack in his corner. The President was speaking again. 'The issue is very simple. Nothing I have been told directly points a finger at Hu or his government. They may well be unaware of any treachery that is being prepared. What we have here could well be no more than the maverick malevolence of China's intelligence chief and his aides.'

The President looked at the London screen. 'I'm sure none of us would be unduly surprised to discover that an unelected spymaster has tried to usurp the role of government.' He knew that Britain was still reeling from the discovery that MI5 had been plotting to bring down a Conservative government which it perceived was going soft on Northern Ireland.

'Indeed not, indeed not,' murmured the Prime Minister in that classless accent which made it that much harder to know what he was really thinking.

'What do I do? Pick up the 'phone and call Chairman Hu and say "I know what's going on – I *think*"? The chances are he would hang up. And I couldn't blame him. Almost certainly we're a long way from a smoking gun.'

The President sat back. Out of the corner of his eye he saw Thack tug on an earlobe. A signal that the snipers were moving into position. He smiled tightly. He had certainly given them something to fire at.

The first shot came from Manila. The President of the Philippines was a pug-faced gnome with a smoker's voice.

'Mr President, I think you must reconsider the wisdom of attending our Non-Aligned Conference.'

The President smiled wryly. 'I don't think some of your fellow leaders would take kindly to missing out on another chance to tell me how to run things.'

He glanced at the adjoining screen, where Sir Alan Wingate was already speaking.

'... from what you have said, Mr President, I gather any threat from this ... this beam machine, is now minimal, at least as far as Hong Kong is concerned. Can I therefore suggest that instead of staying on board your carrier, you stay at my residence?'

The President gave another little smile. He understood perfectly well the Governor's motives. He wanted to be close to the action, for himself and for Britain. Nothing new in that.

'I appreciate your offer, Sir Alan –'

'Mr President! I strongly oppose any change of plan!'

All eyes swung to the Chairman of the Joint Chiefs. He continued to address the President. 'Not only can we better protect you on that carrier, but there's even more at stake here.'

'Such as?' asked the President.

'It boils down to this. Who do we believe? The Emperor when he says there's no way to contact those Typhoons? Just because he says his Navy chief committed hari-kiri? Very convenient!' He glanced around the table. The Vice-President was nodding.

'Go on, General,' the President said.

The Chairman of the Joint Chiefs looked at Gates. 'Your people in Tokyo pick up anything about that Admiral's suicide?'

'Nothing confirmed, General. But there are persistent rumours that he did the only honourable thing open to him after the Emperor forced his resignation. The Admiral was a real Knight of Bushido –'

'Meanwhile his subs are somewhere out there! And no one in Tokyo seems to know where or why. Well, I've got a pretty damn good idea!'

The Chairman of the Joint Chiefs looked across the table at the other three Service Chiefs. They began to nod.

'Our collective military consensus is that the Japanese could be about to launch a pre-emptive strike. Either against the Chinese or us,' he said.

'The CIA has nothing to support that,' Gates snapped.

'That doesn't surprise me,' the Chairman of the Joint Chiefs said witheringly.

'General, Mr Gates. I don't have time to listen to internecine war. Let's just stay with the facts.' There was a hardness in the President's voice not there before.

The Chairman of the Joint Chiefs cleared his throat and looked around the table. 'The only one that matters is that we have a pack of hostile subs on the loose. Between them they could do more damage than all our subs did in World War Two. The question we have to answer, Mr President, is not what you should tell Chairman Hu, but what you should say to the Emperor to make him understand that we'll dump all hell on him if he unleashes a first strike – '

'You forget that the Emperor gave me an absolute guarantee, General, of Japan's peaceful intentions,' the President said coldly. 'I still believe that.'

The Chairman of the Joint Chiefs shook his head. 'When President Roosevelt sat in your chair in 'forty-one, the Japanese made him a similar promise. That was twelve hours before Pearl Harbour.'

'That's not a valid comparison.'

'Let me show you something, Mr President. All of you.'

The Chairman of the Joint Chiefs turned to a backlit display panel. He nodded to a Marine colonel, who began to clip satellite photos onto the opaque glass. As the Chairman of the Joint Chiefs continued to address the room, he indicated the prints. 'The latest sat photos of that train. But even our cameras can't tell us what's under this rail car's cover. So what are we to believe? That this ... Gyroton weapon is on the way to kill you, Mr President? Yet Colonel Morton says he doesn't even know if it's operational!'

Morton remained silent. He really wasn't going to get drawn into this dog-fight.

'What are you saying, General?' the President asked.

'Just this, sir. We *are* being made to look the other way while the real attack could come from elsewhere. From those subs!'

'You got anything to back that up, General?'

'Hear me out, Mr President! We've all heard a great deal about this weapon. But it's all theory. Your scientific people can't say, for certain, it will *ever* work. Nor can the CIA. No one, not even Colonel Morton, has actually seen it in operation. All he has are a couple of bodies with their brains cut out!'

The Chairman of the Joint Chiefs grinned wolfishly. 'The Chinese eat monkey brains, I hear. Maybe they've got a taste for the human kind as well.'

'General, you're out of order,' sighed the President.

He looked across the table, at each face in turn, continuing to weigh what he could see there. When he spoke, quiet resolution and determination were once more in his voice. 'Nothing I have heard convinces me I need to change my plans.'

The President looked at the Chairman of the Joint Chiefs. 'You have the means to protect me, General. I shall expect you to use them to the full. But I don't want our people starting anything. They watch, but do nothing about those subs, Japanese or Russian, until there is no doubt, no doubt at all, of their hostile intent. Then you go in – hard. But I will give that order and no one else. As far as this train goes: it also remains under surveillance. But no more. We're not going to go in there and take it out. Because I agree with you on one thing. There's just no proof it's carrying a threat. Tomorrow, next week ... maybe in a month, things could be different. But by then we'll have hammered down the bones of our deal with Chairman Hu. One of them will give us inspection rights over what Professor Tamasara has been up to. If we don't like what we see, we take it to the United Nations. Just as my predecessor did with Saddam Hussein's arsenal. But right now I don't want to rock the boat with Chairman Hu. Or with the Emperor.'

The President stood up and looked at Thack. 'I've got a 'plane to catch.'

As the President walked out of the War Room, Morton saw the Vice-President and the Chairman of the Joint Chiefs of Staff exchange quick looks. But he couldn't tell from where he sat if they signified acceptance.

In the sonar compartment of the *USS Seattle* one of the row of technicians scrunched his eyes to listen better to the faint low-frequency rumble in his headphones. He opened his eyes and made an adjustment on the sonar board connected to the pressure sensors on either side of the hull. Once more he closed his eyes to better concentrate on the sound. 'Come on, you sonofabitch,' murmured the technician. 'Come to me, little baby.'

The desk before which he sat was no bigger than one in a school classroom. But its dull metal surface hid a computer that cost over three million dollars, and could run up to 60,000 operations a second with its 64-bit chips. Its memory stored every submarine engine noise not only the *Seattle* but all its sister boats had ever recorded since being commissioned. The technician listened for a moment longer then turned to his Watch Supervisor. 'I've got a second one, Matti.'

'Bearing?' asked the Watch Supervisor. He plugged in his own 'phone to the jack which allowed him to listen in to all the workstations.

'Zero-three-zero. Speed thirty-plus.'

'Confirmed,' said the Watch Supervisor. He tapped the mouthpiece of his headset. 'Conn, sonar. We have a third contact. Another Typhoon class.'

Moments later Captain Edmunds and Sonar Officer Woodward appeared in the sonar room. 'How close, Matti?' demanded the Captain.

'Right out on our rim, skipper,' said the Watch Supervisor. 'Like she knows we're here and is keeping her distance.'

'And the others?' asked Woodward.

'Same. Faint but steady.'

The two officers turned to a plotting table where another technician was checking a paper trace. 'We know this bear too,' he said, not looking up. 'We came across him about a year ago in the South Atlantic.'

He turned to a binder folder that lay open on the table and ran his finger down a column of abbreviations. 'Like the other two bears, she was sold to the Japanese by the Russians three months ago.'

The technician turned back to the trace. 'From what I can tell they're keeping an old-fashioned triangle watch, Captain.'

'Let me know if there's any change,' Edmunds said as he led the way back to the attack centre. He and Woodward went to the monitor with its computer-enhanced display. There was no sign of the triangle – only scores of blips from the Chinese Navy warships.

Woodward grunted. 'Our Nippon bears know their business, merging with those Chinese ships, skipper.'

'Which means if they're not running surveillance then who are they waiting for?' asked the Captain.

Woodward grunted again. 'No guesses, skipper. It's got to be our Ivan bear.'

Qiao Peng glanced out of the aircraft window. They were crossing the Yellow River, the divide between plateau and plain. His ancestors had come from the plateau side, from the land of agricultural hardship and insufficiency. Not like those Russian *waibin* and the other foreign men and women. They were from a softer world. He had seen that when he boarded the 'plane at Air Base One. He ignored them all, even Igor Tamasara, and made his way to the forward cabin, drawing the curtain behind him.

Since take-off he had run over everything. Once he'd realised that Morton could still be in Beijing, everything else had fallen into place.

Leading him to the complex, allowing him to see the train depart and to discover those bodies. Morton would have seen just enough to confirm his suspicions. This time, though, the surmise and informed conjecture which in the past had enabled Morton to draw facts out of darkness would fail him. Like those Japanese submarines. He had arranged their despatch with Admiral Toshika. He had been cultivating the Admiral for years, promising him a place in the new order. The only surprise was that Toshika had committed suicide when his Emperor demanded he resign.

Morton would want to find out more about those submarines. More about everything. He had allowed for that. Like calculating that Morton would have the train watched by a satellite. Indeed he was banking on that. Convincing the arrogant Russian to co-operate had been simple. He had offered him a further five million American dollars. For that Igor Tamasara had built a replica of the actual Gyroton and briefed his lower-echelon technicians to take it by train to Luda. The dummy was no more than one of the discarded casings built when the Gyroton had been scaled down.

In the greatest secrecy, the actual machine – together with the Russian and his senior aides – had been taken by underground train to Air Base One and loaded into the hold of this 'plane. The only hiccup had been that fool of a Commander in Chief of the Beijing garrison who had queried the need for so many of his soldiers to die. There had been no point in arguing that that was a small price to pay for the success of Operation Silent Voices.

Qiao Peng looked at his watch. The train should now be close to the river crossing watched by one of those American satellites. His prodigious memory had recalled that the bridge was one of those weakened by the lash of the typhoon the Americans called Cindy. Such a strange thing, to classify an evil wind by the female, Yin. A typhoon was Yang. That was the trouble with *waibin*: they always thought they could improve on things.

He reached into a jacket pocket, removed the audio tape and pressed seat call button. A moment later the senior of the security agents accompanying the flight arrived. He told him to fetch Igor Tamasara. 'Please sit over there,' ordered Qiao Peng, motioning Tamasara to a seat across the aisle. There was something about a *waibin*'s body odour he found repellent. 'The American – what have you learned from him?'

Igor Tamasara considered. To say that the American had been very helpful could diminish the importance of his own work, reduce the prospect of that extra ten million dollars he planned to ask for when this was all over. The American's real skill had been the brilliant way he had interpreted the woman's response. Even Sacha had been astonished.

'Professor Baskin has confirmed some of what we already knew,' Igor Tamasara finally said.

'And the woman? How has she responded?'

'Really very well. She appears to have fully accepted the false story we transmitted to her brain comparator. She believes now that what happened to her was really no more than a confused dream.'

'You are certain?'

'Of course,' Igor Tamasara said sharply. 'Would you like to see her?'

'No.' To discuss the woman was not the reason he had sent for this insufferable Russian. He held out a bony hand with the tape. 'As you requested.'

'I would like to hear it,' said Igor Tamasara, taking the cassette.

After a moment's hesitation, Qiao Peng pressed the seat call button again. When the agent arrived he told him to bring a tape player. When he had done so, Igor Tamasara inserted the cassette. A moment later the slightly metallicised voice of Qiao Peng began to speak.

'I know the Japanese are treacherous. That's why they have sent those submarines. Not only to destroy my plan – but to also destroy all I am pledged to defend. They did that before to us at Pearl Harbour. This time, though, we will strike first. I will now authorise a nuclear air strike against Tokyo ...'

Igor Tamasara rewound the tape and removed it from the player.

'Perfect,' he said at last. 'There will be no way the American President will be able to realise he is acting on anything but his own volition ...'

28

Driven by a powerful tailwind, Air Force One headed westwards at a speed close to sound.

Outwardly, the most luxurious passenger 'plane in the world looked like any other stretch-Boeing. But the legend 'United States of America' emblazoned in gold lettering on a blue background along its fuselage, together with its red-painted engine pods and a five-figure tail number, indicated that it was the personal flagship of the President. A hundred-plus tons of gleaming machinery powered by Pratt & Whitney engines, it had exquisite appointments, high-tech air-conditioning and sound-proofing.

The President and his immediate party had boarded by the front ramp. Marty Fitzpatrick had shepherded the White House press corps up the rear steps. The mood among the reporters was subdued. They had come straight to Andrews Air Force Base from the funeral of Todd Harper. When they settled in their seats for the long flight, stewards brought them drinks in glasses bearing reproductions of the gold Presidential logo. Forward, the emblematic theme appeared on the wall of the various state rooms, on the Presidential pillowcases, the crockery and in the centre of each telephone dial.

The 'phones were connected to the communications centre immediately behind the flight deck. The size of a closet, the shack housed ten million dollars' worth of electronic gear, including fax machines, a hooded cryptographic encoder/decoder and a switchboard linking the 'plane to the Secret Service network on the ground. Among the many duties of the two technicians squeezed into the shack was maintaining constant contact with the chain of checkpoints along the entire route. At each ground station was a mobile rescue unit. Out over the Pacific were US warships and rescue aircraft stationed all the way to Hong Kong.

Standing in the door of the shack, Gates heard the station in the Panhandle sign off with news that there was a rainstorm lashing the prairies. At this height, nearly nine miles straight up, the sky was blue and serene. The next check would be over the Rockies. Then just before they crossed the coast, north of Los Angeles. After that it would be the ships.

Before leaving Washington, Gates had spoken to Morton. They agreed that the chances of the Gyroton being able to focus its beam on Air Force One, given that its flight plan was a classified secret, were small. Nevertheless they arranged to stay in touch during the trip. Gates turned to one of the technicians. 'I want to open a link with Colonel Morton.'

He glanced at a wall clock. Like all the others on board it showed Zulu time, Greenwich Mean Time. 'He should be back in Hong Kong in a couple of hours. He can be patched in through the *United States* Command Control Center.'

'No problem,' acknowledged the technician. No problem was the unofficial motto of the Signal Corps.

With nothing to do for the moment, Gates wandered back through the 'plane. In the galley the chef and his assistants were preparing dinner. Next door the purser and a steward were selecting wines from the well-stocked liquor pantry.

'A drink, Mr Gates?' asked the purser.

'A spritzer.' It was going to be a long night.

Glass in hand, Gates strolled into the area known to everyone on board as Madeleine's Kingdom. It contained groups of pullman chairs set around desks with electric typewriters. Here Madeleine Masters and her team of secretaries dealt with the President's paperwork.

At the moment Secretary of State Bobby Collins was dictating to a secretary. Madeleine herself was over by her window desk, reading. At another window seat sat Satchel with the Football at his feet. On the far side of the cabin Dr Barker had tilted back his chair and, mask covering his eyes, was already asleep.

Madeleine looked up and smiled when Gates strolled over. 'Don't you love this feeling of being up here away from it all? I just adore these long flights!'

'You're a romantic, Maddy.'

'I wish. But ever since I was a schoolgirl I've been in love with aeroplanes. And wasn't it Gann who said that flying is a healing lacuna under the moon?'

303

'Except we're going the wrong way, racing away from the night,' grinned Gates.

He glanced through the window. Behind them the magenta twilight had turned to dusk. At this time of the year the over-mantling sky was brilliant. The Big Dipper kept watch over Chicago; Arturus hovered over Kansas; Cassiopeia and the bright square of Pegasus floated many millions of miles above the Mississippi. But to the west, towards the Rockies, the sunlight glimmered, its rays beckoning them forward. Maybe this sort of thing brought out the poet in everyone.

Gates straightened and glanced towards a closed door, adorned with a golden eagle and thirteen gold stars. Beyond was the President's on-board office. From there came his halting voice reading aloud in an unfamiliar language. Gates looked quizzically at Madeleine.

'He's working on his speech in Mandarin. Thack says it did wonders for Nixon, being able to say a few words in their language.'

'Where's Thack now?'

'Taking a shower. He's ordered a tray supper and plans an early night. He's told the President to do the same.'

She nodded towards the corridor that led to the President's private quarters. A bedroom with a full-sized bath. Beyond that was Thack's altogether smaller bedroom, with its shower stall in one corner, and a bunk bed against a wall. There were three similar cubicles, reserved for other ranking aides. Next came the cabin for the Secret Service detail. Gates had a seat back there. Behind that was a second galley that handled the needs of the press corps.

He looked at Madeleine. 'You free for dinner?'

'I'm not going anywhere,' she said.

Gates grinned. The last time they had dined together on board had been on the South Africa trip. They'd drunk a middling amount of wine and discovered a lot about each other. When they reached Johannesburg they had shared adjoining rooms on the first night and the same bed on the second. Maddy had revealed unexpected skills as a lover. But on their return to Washington she had turned away all his invitations, pleading pressure of work. Perhaps she only broke out when she got away from the place. Suddenly he couldn't wait to get to Hong Kong.

The last thin rays of sunlight were fading when Colin Baskin and Anna climbed down the ladder inside the sail of the *Rodina*. Behind came

Qiao Peng. He had still not spoken a word to either of them. They had passed Igor Tamasara and his team on deck manoeuvring the Gyroton through a hatch into the submarine.

The seamen in the control room looked at Anna and Colin Baskin curiously. A tall and tired-looking young officer turned from his plotting table. 'My name's Tarinski. I hope you don't find my cabin too uncomfortable,' he said in English, smiling.

She smiled back. Tarinski sounded friendly. There could be others like him on board. But certainly not the older man with simian features whose eyes had flicked sideways at Tarinski's words. He spoke sharply and Tarinski turned back to his plotting table. She saw Qiao Peng walk over to him and murmur something. Tarinski shrugged then buried himself at his charts.

The older man stared at them for a moment. 'I am Captain Marlo. Follow me.' He turned and led the way out of the control room. Moving through the submarine's central passageway, Anna glimpsed a galley and a small mess hall. But all the other compartments seemed filled with machinery. The walls and ceiling of the corridor were festooned with pipes.

Colin Baskin recognised the low humming sound. Years ago he had gone on a mission aboard one of the first American 688 class nuclear submarines; somebody at Langley had asked him to run a study on the psycho-stress factor that constant noise created in people confined in an enclosed space. The one sound that had remained with him was the humming of the reactor.

Marlo stopped before a cabin door. 'You will remain in here.' He opened the door and motioned for them to enter. They heard the door being locked behind them and Marlo's footsteps receding.

Anna looked around her. The cabin was small and smelled faintly of oil. Most of the space was taken up by a bunk bed. Storm weather clothing hung from a peg. Sea boots stood in a corner. 'Our navigator's a tidy man,' she said.

'Think he can help us escape?' Colin Baskin asked. He had thought of nothing else since coming aboard. There had to be a way out of here – a way to warn the world about what Igor Tamasara was going to do. The man was more than mad – he truly saw himself as the heir to ultimate power.

'I need to escape as much as you,' she said quietly. 'But you've got to remember we'll almost certainly only get one chance so let's not rush into anything.'

He looked at her quizzically. 'That sounds like a very professional opinion.'

'It is.'

Anna came to a decision. Her initial instinct to trust him had been reinforced by the memory of what she had read in the paper Morton had circulated. It had included a reference to Kate Baskin's own work in electromagnetism. There had been time before flying to Hong Kong to check the reference books. Kate was doing good work. A man with a daughter like that had to be okay. Everything he had said so far confirmed that, and given their situation, she had no option but to follow her instinct and trust him.

'Our Captain looks a nasty piece of work, but he's not as dangerous as that Chinese,' Anna resumed.

Colin Baskin looked at her curiously. 'Why do you say that?' On the 'plane she had been more anxious to listen to what he had to say, rather than reveal what she knew.

'His name's Qiao Peng and he runs the Chinese Secret Intelligence Service,' Anna said, walking over to sit on the bed.

'My God.'

'Now come and sit here and tell me everything else you know,' she ordered.

After a moment he sat beside her. There was a quality about this woman which made him want to continue sharing with her all he knew. And, in a situation like this, two heads were always better than one. The only way was to tell her everything. Anna listened without interruption, fitting what she was hearing into what Morton had told her. When Colin Baskin finished she turned to him.

'Will Igor Tamasara be able to fire this Gyroton from under the sea, Professor Baskin?'

'Call me Colin. My daughter, Kate, does. It makes me feel younger.' He smiled.

Anna grinned. 'Okay – Colin. Now can they launch underwater?'

'There's no way he'll want to do that. The refraction from even a few feet below the surface could bend that beam way out of true. They'll need to surface and get fairly close to the target. From what I've seen, a mile or so is the optimum effective range. But that's assuming a clear shot. Look what happened to you. Being inside those buildings diminished the beam's potency. So they'll need to make sure when they launch they have the target in clear view.'

Anna nodded. 'Which means there's just a chance they'll be spotted. That's all my people would need.'

Once more he gave her a curious look. 'Your people? Who are they?'
She told him about Hammer Force and Morton.

He began to nod, remembering. 'We used to say at Langley God help anyone who came up against him. That guy could think faster than a computer.'

'That's Colonel Morton,' Anna said.

Colin Baskin looked at her with even more respect. 'And here was I thinking I had to take care of you!'

Anna smiled. He reminded her of her own father, the same old-fashioned courtesy and values. The smile went as a new thought struck her. 'Supposing they tried for a shot some distance from the target? Could the beam still make someone do something they didn't want to do? Not for long, just long enough, like it did to me?'

He considered. In theory the quantum physics said it was impossible because the force-field magnitude would be too weak. But supposing Igor Tamasara had managed to in-fold the stress-energy so that it was only released in a pre-calculated target area? That would be an extension of Tesla's old theory about the transmission of energy at a distance without loss. But that theory had been well and truly knocked by the mainstream of Western science. And there was nothing he had heard or seen to suggest that Tamasara had resurrected it as the basis for his scalar interferometry.

'I don't know, Anna. I just don't know if that would work or not,' Colin Baskin said.

A rumble of engine noise began to fill the cabin. From outside the door voices were giving commands. Then came the first faint movement.

Baskin spoke to Anna in a low and urgent voice. 'You're only alive – we're both only alive – because I convinced Igor Tamasara that he could still learn from your responses. You've got to show from your behaviour that he may not have got it quite right. That could make all the difference.'

'What do you want me to do?'

He squinted at her. 'You ever seen anyone who's had electro-shock treatment?'

'A cousin of mine had it. It was terrible. She kept saying her mind felt like a blurred, pounding emptiness. For weeks she walked around like a zombie,' Anna said.

'That's what Igor Tamasara hopes has happened to you. But he isn't absolutely certain. So what you've got to do is behave something like your cousin. That may confuse him just enough. Think you can do that?'

Anna nodded. 'I'll give it my best shot. The problem is he kept looking at me in the 'plane. I must have appeared perfectly normal then, otherwise he'd have said something.'

Baskin smiled encouragingly. 'He's a scientist, Anna. That makes his mind ready to accept changes. And I've told him enough to plant the idea that in your case it could come on quite suddenly. We've got to keep him guessing!'

Anna stood up and turned her back to him, remembering how her cousin had looked. When she turned to face Colin Baskin her mouth had slackened and there was a dull, listless look in her eyes. Her very posture had altered, so that her shoulders drooped and her fingers moved restlessly.

Colin Baskin nodded approvingly.

'What I don't understand is that I don't feel any after-effects from that beam,' Anna said.

'You're young and healthy. That undoubtedly helped your brain to recover more quickly. But in an older person ... someone like me ... it could be different ...' He squinted at her. 'I should have asked you this before. Do you know who could be the target?'

She stared at him for a long moment. 'Yes. The President of the United States,' she finally said.

The colour drained from Colin Baskin's face. 'Oh my God,' he whispered. 'Oh my God.'

It was early evening in Hong Kong when the US Marine brought Morton into the Carrier Command Control Centre on board the *USS United States*. Known as the Four Seas – a play on the initials CCCC – the compartment was two decks below the carrier's island superstructure. After the Marine left, Morton stood inside the door for a moment, getting his bearings, mindful that even in the eerie green light from the scopes, he must look an incongruous sight in his off-the-peg blue serge Russian suit.

It belonged to the Russian Ambassador in Beijing. He had loaned it to him after a telephone call from Savenko, ordering him to also provide a diplomatic passport for Morton to leave China. After Danny and Tommy had caught a scheduled flight to Hong Kong, the Ambassador had driven Morton out to a Tupelov cargo-freighter waiting at Beijing Airport. Savenko had ordered the 'plane to divert on its way from

Moscow to Singapore to pick up Morton. Three hours later he landed at Kai Tek, and a US Navy helicopter had brought him out to the *United States*.

The Marine had led him through a succession of pale blue passageways at a smart trot. More than once Morton had been forced to duck to avoid the maze of pipes above their heads. Every thirty feet or so his escort had paused to open another large steel door. The Marine had explained that there were 3,000 such doors on board, designed to seal the ship into watertight compartments. It was the only information he volunteered.

The Four Seas housed radar displays, communications equipment and rows of scopes. In addition to Navy personnel, a score of men wearing sound-powered telephone headsets were positioning equipment around the floor. They wore Army fatigues and an air of quiet confidence – they knew what they were doing, and no one was going to stop them doing it. In a room already crammed with electronic gear they were finding space for more.

A burly figure in a Navy commander's uniform saw Morton and came over. 'Colonel Morton? Robert Porter, Operations Officer. I'm supposed to run this madhouse. But not any more. And you'd better call me Look-out.'

He smiled ruefully and turned and pointed. 'Welcome to the Hong Kong branch of the White House communications agency. They're calling this place Stopover. That I can just about accept. But Look-out ...'

One of the signalmen with a headset drifted over. 'You gotta be Colonel Morton, right? Warrior in the Eagle wants to speak to you. They're south of Hawaii so no reception problems.'

Warrior was Gates; the Eagle, Air Force One.

The signalman turned and strolled back to a bank of telephones linked to a console. He punched buttons, listened for a moment, then picked up a receiver and handed it to Morton.

'Hello,' said Morton.

'Is that you, David?' asked Gates.

'For sure.'

'You heard about that train?'

'I just got here.'

Relief mingled with excitement as Gates spoke. 'A bridge collapsed as she was crossing. Our sat people saw it live on screen. Engine, box cars, the whole damned lot dropped a couple of hundred feet into a river. On some of the photos there's a clear view of the Gyroton breaking free of its moorings. The cameras followed it right down to where it smashed against rocks. What's left got washed away. The river was in full spate.

'I guess, David, that's that. As far as any threat goes its back to the drawing-board for Igor Tamasara.'

'So it would seem.'

Morton stood perfectly still, a towering presence that transcended his mere physical stature.

'It's really over, David,' Gates said reassuringly. 'All we've got to do now is to make sure Tamasara doesn't get a second chance.'

'For sure.' The rigidity refused to leave his shoulders.

There was a moment's silence before Gates spoke again. 'Something still bothering you?'

Behind him Morton could hear Porter and the signalman debating where to position yet another telephone console that would provide a direct satellite back-up link to Washington for the President when he was on board. Porter was asking if this was really necessary.

'Mistah,' said the signalman, his Texas accent thickening. 'You ain't seen nothin' yet. By the time we've finished here, this place is gonna be filled with back-ups for back-ups. We're dealing here with Laser.'

'Laser?'

'The President o' the United States. From now on he's Laser. Just as you're Look-out, Mistah.'

After a moment, Morton asked Gates a question.

'You got anything new on those Japanese subs?' He could feel a deep well of strength and certainty beginning to fill him. It was as though it had been produced expressly for this moment, for what still had to be done.

'The *Seattle* picked them up a little while ago. They're lying doggo in the old textbook dog-in-the-kennel position.'

'And the *Rodina*?'

'Not a thing.'

Morton asked a further question. 'When your people spotted her, how far was she from that bridge?'

There was a lengthy silence on the link with Air Force One. Then Gates was back. 'Give or take an inch or two, she was about a thousand miles away.'

'And what's the nearest Chinese Navy facility to her last-known position?'

This time silence was shorter. 'Quingdao.'

'I'd like you to get your satellites down there as fast as possible,' Morton said.

'Any special reason, David?'

With anyone else, Morton would have ignored the question. But then, no one else but Bill would have asked. He hunched himself over the console before he spoke. 'Right now it would suit Qiao Peng to have Igor Tamasara out of the way. That way he can stay squeaky clean. And later he can always bring Tamasara back.

'So maybe the *Rodina*'s come to pick him and his team up and take them to some place where they lay low. South America. Cuba. Or one of those African countries where China's got a foothold. There are plenty of people who would gladly take him under their wing just to win brownie points with Beijing.'

'Those sats are on their way,' Gates said.

Morton put down the 'phone and turned to the signalman. 'Any chance of getting a local call out of here?' he asked politely.

He needed to get Danny and Tommy running surveillance on Tung Shi, Supreme Dragon head and leader of the Triads in Hong Kong. The certainty now filled him almost to the brim.

'Your Majesty – ' the Prime Minister of Japan's voice was hoarse after many hours of unceasing tension – 'those Typhoons are armed. I have discovered that Admiral Toshika made it a condition of the sale that the Russians provided a full complement of weapons.'

The Prime Minister, a puckish figure in formal morning dress, glanced down at the briefing paper in his hand, then looked across the desk at the Emperor. When he spoke his voice was little more than a whispered croak. 'Each submarine has torpedos, mines, anti-ship rockets and fifteen long-range ballistic rockets with multiple atomic warheads. Each one of those Typhoons could devastate the entire seaboard of China or reduce Hong Kong to radioactive rubble for a thousand years – '

The Emperor lifted one hand to silence the anguished voice. 'But nothing has been found in Toshika's office to indicate what orders he gave to the Typhoon captains?'

'No, Your Majesty. Nothing. All our security people have been able to discover is that before they sailed each captain was personally verbally briefed by Toshika.'

There was silence in the study. The Emperor looked across the desk at the bowed and deeply troubled face of the Prime Minister. Then he turned to the satellite 'phone console. 'I will call Chairman Hu. He must alert his naval forces to take every possible step to destroy our Typhoons. And if needs be, he must ask the Americans to help him.'

As the Emperor began to punch buttons on the console, the stricken voice of the Prime Minister across the desk stopped him. 'Your Majesty, I implore you to reconsider such an action. It could precipitate the very terror we wish to avoid. I am advised that the nature of their method of operation ensures that not only are those Typhoons designed to disappear, but that even if one, two or even three of them are destroyed, there would still be time for the fourth to fire its missiles.'

'Then what –' the Emperor broke the terrible silence at last – 'then what can we do?'

'We must do nothing, Your Majesty. There is nothing we can do,' said the Prime Minister.

Inside the back of the van parked opposite Canton Mansions on Hennessy Road it was stiflingly hot and cramped for Danny and the two shooters. They all wore headsets which were plugged into a large metal box with a face resembling a small switchboard and the guts of a Packard computer. The scanner had a capability of simultaneously handling up to five hundred separate telephone conversations. Danny was certain there were not that many telephones in the apartment block.

'Tommy's going in now,' called out the shooter behind the wheel, watching Tommy disappearing into the shopping arcade on the ground floor of Canton Mansions.

Tommy wore a sweatshirt and jeans. Taped to his skin beneath the shirt was a small transmitter whose aerial ran down the inside of a trouser leg and linked him to the scanner.

After Morton's call, one of the shooters had rented the van. He'd haggled over the price because he was expected to, but finally settled for a rental of twenty Hong Kong dollars an hour. The scanner costed out at a couple of million US bucks, and couldn't be rented. Not only would it isolate the contents of any of those calls – you just programmed the computer and it did the rest – but the scanner could guarantee to trace a call to its source up to a thousand miles away. Beyond that it got a little problematic.

Tommy was really a walking telegraph pole, the conduit through which the transmitter gobbled up all the telephone calls in the block and relayed them to the scanner for assessment. Hidden beneath the collar of his sweatshirt was a diode mike, the size of a dime, taped against the lower end of his windpipe. It enabled him to communicate in short sentences with the van.

'Reached elevators,' Tommy reported.

A short while ago he had watched the nondescript Chinese, a cloth cap obscuring most of his face, make his way through the evening throng in the arcade to the elevators. Tung Shi had taken one to the upper floor. He hadn't changed from those police pictures he'd studied when he'd flown a helicopter for the force. Hard to believe he was the godfather of all the local godfathers.

'Going up,' Tommy murmured.

In the van Danny began to jiggle keys on the switchboard.

One of the shooters lifted his headset from his ears and made a face. 'This woman's got a voice like a chainsaw.'

As Tommy rode the elevator he continued to pick up 'phone calls on each floor.

'Top floor,' he finally murmured.

The elevator opened and he found himself facing the closed door of an apartment. He stepped out into a small hallway. The place was exactly as the Colonel had briefed him.

'Got him,' said Danny softly, 'loud and clear.'

The two shooters nodded. A moment ago they had all heard the dialling sound, then in their headsets Tung Shi's voice on the 'phone inside the apartment.

'Sonofabitch,' breathed Danny. 'Sonofabitch.'

He picked up a handset and dialled the number Morton had given him to ring into the Four Seas.

'Look-out,' announced a clipped voice.

'I wish to speak to Colonel Morton.'

'You mean ... Anvil ...?'

'Whatever. Just get him on the 'phone,' Danny said crisply.

A moment later Morton was on the line. 'Yes, Danny.'

'He's talking to someone on a boat that's going to rendezvous with the *Rodina*.'

'You got a fix?'

Danny glanced at a dial on the scanner. It showed the signal strength of a call in fifty-mile multiples.

'It's somewhere between, two, two-fifty miles from here.'

'Hold a second, Danny.'

Morton turned to Commander Porter in the Four Seas.

'You got a map of the mainland coast?'

313

Porter grinned. 'Better yet, we have it three-dimensional on screen.'

He pointed to one of the scopes before which sat a Chief Petty Officer.

'I need a two-fifty-mile view from here,' Morton said.

The operator worked the scope's keyboard. On screen came the outline of the Chinese coast, south to the Gulf of Tonkin and north to Sandu.

'Forget the south. Give me a closer look between here and Sandu.'

The operator did as ordered.

'The Chinese Navy has half a dozen major bases between here and Sandu. You looking for anything in particular?' Porter asked.

Morton turned from the display. How long would a Typhoon take to come from Quingdao down to this area, Commander?'

Porter pondered for a moment. A Typhoon had the same turn of speed as an attack class sub. 'Flat out – about eleven hours,' he said.

'Thank you.' Morton spoke into the 'phone. 'Danny, I reckon we've got a few hours yet. Try and pin down that boat's position.'

But Danny had a more immediate concern. A moment ago Tung Shi had ended his 'phone call. There was the sound of a door opening. The Triad leader emerged from the apartment and stared uncertainly at Tommy. 'Who you?' he demanded.

'I'm looking for Suzy,' Tommy said. The Colonel had briefed him on her as well.

'You client?'

'Not yet, but a friend recommended me.'

'Suzy not here.'

'Okay. I'll come back.'

'No. Wait,' insisted Tung Shi.

In the van the two shooters were removing their headsets while the driver was already striding up the pavement towards the apartment block.

'I'll come back,' said Tommy more firmly.

He and Tung Shi looked silently at each other.

29

'Dive!' ordered Marlo, crouching at the periscope. The hull began to fill with the continuous shrill of the diving alarm. Seamen spun wheels and reported that the lights on dials and gauges were changing from green to red, from idling to action. There was a rushing noise of air as the ballast tanks filled with water.

'Scope down,' Marlo said.

The periscope slid into its pod bolted to the deck of the control room. Qiao Peng heard the hull begin to groan under the pressure of the water. Some of the crew were glancing surreptitiously at him. When he had decided to come, he had read all he needed to know about submarines. This creaking was normal even if it sounded unsettling. He fished in a pocket and clamped a stogey in his mouth.

'Smoking is only permitted in the wardroom, Comrade Peng,' Marlo said reprovingly.

Qiao Peng looked hard at the Captain. It had been a long time since anyone, let alone a *waibin*, had spoken like that to him. 'I am not smoking, only chewing. Or is that forbidden too?' There was a chill in Qiao Peng's voice which made the others in the control room look away.

Marlo stared at Qiao Peng. Normally he would have ordered any passenger out of here – even off his boat – who dared to be so supercilious. But his sailing orders said that he must do nothing to offend this visitor. He made an attempt at a conciliatory smile. 'Some of our instruments are sensitive to smoke, Comrade Peng. Would you like to join your colleagues in the wardroom? We have vodka – '

'This is not a cruise, Captain.'

'Of course not.' He tried not to let the irritation come through in his tone. This Chinese was an easy man to upset. He turned to the control room officer. 'You have the conn, Comrade Lieutenant. Ahead two thirds.'

Marlo turned back to Qiao Peng. There was something about this Chinese he increasingly found unnerving. But this was still his ship and there were some things he would insist on knowing. 'Can you tell me if Comrade Vice-Premier Oleg Kazenko is dead?' he asked.

Qiao Peng listened a moment longer to the watch officer giving orders. This was a good crew. They deserved better than this *waibin*. But best not to antagonise him, but not while he needed him. 'Yes. He was killed in a 'plane crash.'

Marlo stood silent for long moments. Savenko's signal had not been a trap. But with Oleg dead, what would it mean for him? Would Savenko have him stripped of his command for disobeying the order to return? Worse, have him posted to some land station in the depths of Siberia? Savenko could do anything. The realisation brought a slight tremble to Marlo's lips when he finally spoke. 'The Vice-Premier was my father-in-law. We were very close ...'

Qiao Peng nodded, a quick, perfunctory nod. He hated sentimentality of any sort. 'Your orders remain unchanged,' he said in a thin voice.

'I have received an order to return to base at once, Comrade Peng.'

Qiao Peng's face remained impassive. He had long ago perfected the art of not showing surprise.

'From whom?' he finally asked.

'Comrade General Savenko.'

'I have spoken to General Savenko. He has agreed to cancel it.' It was always easy to lie to a *waibin*.

'But I have received no confirmation, Comrade Peng.'

'General Savenko asked me to inform you. He felt that should be sufficient. However, if you doubt my word – '

Marlo shook his head. 'No, no of course not.'

'Good.' Qiao Peng said in a voice that settled the matter.

With the pressure against the hull stabilising, there was no need for Marlo to raise his voice when he next spoke. 'My orders state I am to be briefed fully by you on this mission, Comrade Peng.'

Qiao Peng considered. He needed this *waibin* a little longer. And telling him would make no difference. 'Comrade Captain, you have been entrusted with a mission that will guarantee you a role in history ...' Qiao Peng began. Quickly, but leaving nothing out, he described the purpose of the Gyroton and revealed its intended target.

Marlo looked at him with growing, stunned amazement. No wonder Savenko had cancelled that order! And more important – far, far more important – here was a glorious opportunity for him to redeem himself in Savenko's eyes! To be entrusted with such a mission must surely guarantee his future in a Navy that would once more be powerful enough to face any challenge.

'The American President,' he breathed. 'What you are describing will lead to the rebirth of Marxist Socialism. I had no idea, Comrade Peng. No idea at all ...'

'Go about your duties, Comrade Captain,' Qiao Peng said softly.

The words were a reminder to Marlo. 'Comrade Peng, there is a tradition that before every mission I inform the crew ...'

Qiao Peng sighed. He could imagine what this fool of a *waibin* would tell his crew. But that also didn't matter.

'Very well, do it.'

With a mounting sense of excitement, Marlo walked back to his cabin. He needed to be alone to prepare what would undoubtedly be the most momentous address to the crew he had ever given.

The shooters came out of the elevator with guns drawn. Tung Shi stared at them in stunned disbelief for a moment. Then instinct took over. He backed into the open door of the apartment, reaching for his own weapon.

Tommy dived forward, catching him above the knees, sending the Triad leader skeetering into the apartment's hallway with such force that the offerings on the god shelf fell on Tung Shi's head. An overripe mandarin squelched down his face. Tommy yanked Tung Shi to his feet and shoved him hard against a wall, grabbing the Supreme Dragon head's gun with the other hand.

The shooters followed and closed the door. Guns drawn, they searched the apartment and reported that it was empty.

'Everything under control,' Tommy announced through the throat-mike to Danny in the van.

Tung Shi looked at him in relief. 'You police? Then all okay. You call Superintendent Kowloon side. He tell you. All okay.'

He began to brush himself down, more aggrieved than angry as he continued to speak. 'Why you here? Money already paid to Superintendent this month.'

Tommy ignored him and spoke into the throat-mike. 'We're bringing him down.'

'Where you take me?' demanded Tung Shi.

Tommy looked at him. 'First we go for a little ride. Then a little boat trip. Then, who knows? But I can tell you this. There are people in Washington for a start who would like to ask you a lot of questions about your drug operations. Meanwhile, I've got a question for you.'

Tommy described Anna and asked Tung Shi if he knew where she now was. The Triad godfather looked at him. 'No know this woman.' Now he knew what all this was about. Qiao Peng's people must have snatched another of those women narcotic undercover agents the *waibin* were increasingly using.

Tung Shi's mouth began to work. 'You DEA? FBI?'

'Whatever you like us to be, we are,' Tommy said softly.

'You no take me,' Tung Shi blustered. 'I no leave here!'

'You leave here and I take you,' Tommy replied in the same calm voice.

There was the sound of a key turning in the apartment door. The shooters crouched in firing positions. Tommy placed Tung Shi between himself and the opening door.

Suzy stood there. One of the shooters grabbed her and slipped a hand over her mouth even as she reacted to the situation and was about to scream. 'Don't make a sound,' the shooter whispered, once more closing the door.

She nodded, her eyes still wide with panic.

Tommy spoke to Suzy. 'He's going to take away his hand, do you understand? Don't yell or do anything foolish or I'll have to stop you. Do you understand?'

She gave another frantic nod. The shooter removed his hand and she breathed in deeply several times, then started to tremble, a reaction to the shock.

'No one's going to hurt you,' Tommy promised. 'Are you Suzy?'

'Yes,' she whispered.

'It's time for you to leave,' Tommy said. The Colonel had said that she should be offered the opportunity.

Tung Shi stared at Suzy in disbelief. He spoke to her in Cantonese. 'Who is this *waibin*?'

Suzy ignored him and turned to Tommy. 'I must get a few things.'

Tommy shook his head. 'No time for that.'

She took a quick breath and wiped her eyes. She was beginning to calm down a little. Who were these people? What were they doing here? She spoke to Tommy. 'Are you friends of David?'

318

'Yes.'

Tung Shi lunged towards her. Tommy pulled him back, roughly.

'Don't ever do that, not ever again,' Tommy said in perfect Cantonese. For the first time he saw fear in Tung Shi's eyes.

Tommy spoke into the throat-mike. 'We're coming down. One hostile and one friendly.'

He turned to Tung Shi. 'You've got two choices. You either come quietly. Or I shoot you here. Right now I'm not really bothered which choice you make.'

Tommy placed the barrel of Tung Shi's gun in his ear, moving it about. At training school the instructor had said that that could be an especially terrifying sound.

'I come with you,' whispered Tung Shi.

Tommy tucked the gun in the waistband of his jeans. Then, arm clapped over Tung Shi's shoulders, he moved to the door. 'Remember, pal, we're supposed to be buddies. So smile. If it'll help, I'll tell you all the jokes I know in Cantonese,' he grinned as they stepped out of the apartment.

In the sonar room of the *USS Seattle* Captain Edmunds and Sonar Officer Woodward plugged in headsets. The other technicians were fine-tuning their sets to follow what was happening.

'First there was one little bear. Next there were two. Then we had three. And now there are four. All gambolling together. And all that's missing is Goldilocks!' murmured the Watch Supervisor. Goldilocks was a mother supply ship.

Edmunds turned to the plotting table. 'Do we know this fourth bear?' the Captain asked the technician.

'We know him, Cap'n.'

The seaman nodded at the open binder folder. 'It's the *Rodina*. She used to be on the Atlantic run. The guys in Washington got a fix on her there a little while back. Now she's here, digging big holes in the water. She's up to thirty-five knots and still stomping on the gas. The Japanese bears are keeping pace with her. One each to port and starboard, the third up her tail.'

'Prisoner and escort,' Woodward murmured.

The Captain slipped off his 'phones and looked at the Sonar Officer. 'I think it's time to tell our masters, Woody, about this teddy bears' picnic.'

*

Forbes, the President's valet, knocked on the door and walked into the President's bedroom on Air Force One, carrying a tray holding a cup and saucer. The President was already dressed and was sitting on the edge of his bed. Spectacles perched on the edge of his nose, he was studying cables marked 'Eyes Only President' which had come into the communications centre while he had slept.

A Treasury report saying there would be more cutbacks next quarter, accompanied by a gloomy forecast on trade links with Europe. A State report predicting a new famine in Africa, on which the Vice-President had written, 'recommend we do not intervene'. Typical. What are we supposed to do? Sit back and watch another million starve while their leaders try to kill each other? He'd scratched through the Vice-President's words and wrote: 'Send more aid and the forces to make sure it is properly distributed.' His predecessor had made it work in Somalia.

Putting aside the paperwork the President smiled at Forbes. 'A nice cup of tea would be very welcome,' he said in carefully-enunciated Mandarin.

'Very impressive, Mr President,' beamed Forbes. 'Whatever you said, it sounded just dandy to me.'

'Thank you, Forbes. Let's hope our hosts are as impressed.' The President glanced at the tray. 'What have you come up with this morning?'

'Rosehip and lemon. The Chinese say it's the best way to keep Yin and Yang in harmony all day,' Forbes said, handing over the cup.

The President began to sip the scalding drink as Forbes left the cabin. He could get to like this stuff.

Moments later Thack stuck his head around the door. 'I've got Colonel Morton on the line. It's about those Japanese subs.'

The President put down his cup and turned to the bedside 'phone console.

In the torpedo storage compartment where the Gyroton was housed, Igor Tamasara found the low thump of the pumps, water continuously coursing through the pipework and the hum of electric motors curiously soporific. He leaned against a bulkhead, arms folded, watching Dr Fretov and Dr Petrarova completing a careful inspection of the Gyroton to ensure that it had suffered no damage while being on-loaded.

They had served him well. But soon it would be time for them to move aside. There was room only for one star. And he was that star: the creator, begetter and deliverer of something so truly awesome that nothing, and no one, would be able to stop it. In the very different world which would emerge afterwards he was certain of one thing. As a scientist he would be above all others, respected and courted. His old colleagues at Postbox 97 and elsewhere would recognise his achievement as returning science to where it belonged: in the hands of the scientists. For too long science had been under the control of the generals and the politicians. Decisions had been taken from their standpoint. But soon that would be a thing of the past. Soon science would subsume all else. And, because of his achievement, he would be the scientist to whom all the others would turn. Even those who would hate him for what he had created would then fear him.

The hatch to the torpedo room swung open and Qiao Peng came into the storage compartment. He stood for a moment, his face ghostly in the hard inspection lights. It was cold in here. The doctors had said that any sudden change of environment could affect his body, hasten his end. But he would still live to see the beginning of Operation Silent Voices. That was what mattered. The rest would follow naturally, as Yin followed Yang.

'Is all well?' he asked Igor Tamasara, managing to keep his voice pleasant. This *waibin* was still important.

Tamasara asked the inspection team to report.

'The machine is fully operational,' Dr Fretov stated.

From his pocket Qiao Peng produced the cassette tape he had let Tamasara listen to in the 'plane. 'I wish to insert this personally.'

Tamasara smiled briefly. 'Come and leave your mark in history,' he said in a voice tinged with amusement. Who would have thought there was an ounce of sentimentality in this cadaver?

Qiao Peng looked at the Gyroton curiously. This was the first time he had seen it since the modifications. He walked slowly around the machine, peering closely at the snub barrel, the inspection hatches on the side, the controls at the back. It really was hard to believe that this could achieve all he had planned for. Yet in a way the proof it would work was here on this very boat. He turned to Igor Tamasara. 'I've just seen the woman. She appears to be in some kind of mind regression. When I questioned her, she was unable to give me any proper account of what had happened to her.'

Igor Tamasara glanced at him in surprise and irritation. 'Why did you question her?' His voice had a sharp edge to it now. No one spoke to any of his guinea pigs without his permission.

Qiao Peng looked at him. Right to the very end this *waibin* was being insufferable. But now was not the moment to deal with that. He took a long, deep breath, held it a moment, then let it out slowly. 'I was curious to see the effect the beam has had.'

'And?' Igor Tamasara fought down his anger.

'It's what I would expect. Nevertheless, I have instructed the crew doctor to examine her – '

'Why? Why have you done that? Who said you could?' Igor Tamasara's fury had returned.

Qiao Peng raised the hand holding the tape. This *waibin* had better understand a few things. 'Calm yourself, Professor. First, I do not need your authority to do anything on this boat. Everyone here, including you, is under my direct control. Remember that. Second, there is no harm in obtaining a second and independent opinion as to her medical condition. If the woman is hiding anything, it will be easier for a doctor used to dealing with the human condition to detect it, perhaps, than for a pure scientist like you.'

Igor Tamasara stared at him wordlessly.

Qiao Peng waved the tape. 'Now where do I put this?'

Tamasara pointed to a slot, still not trusting himself to speak. As Qiao Peng stepped back after inserting the tape, a loudspeaker in the wall came alive.

'Comrades! Officers and men of *Rodina*! Distinguished guests! This is the Captain.'

In the control room Marlo paused for a moment to consult the notes he had written. Then he continued to use the boat's public address system. 'We are now embarked upon a momentous voyage. It is the fitting climax to all the previous ones when we brought our distinguished scientists out of Russia, Comrades Tamasara, Fretov and Petrarova. I am certain you must have wondered about the purpose behind what we were doing. I will now tell you.'

Surgeon Yuri Borikov looked up at his cabin loudspeaker in astonishment. First that old Chinese had ordered him to examine the woman, and now Marlo was on a roll of his own! The Captain's voice continued to boom.

'We have on board a weapon like no other! It will be used against a target like no other! He is the leader of all the forces opposed to those of us who wish to see the return of Marxist Socialism, of our Party, our creed, of all we believe in ...'

322

In a thunderous voice Marlo announced that the target was the American President. 'Comrades! We have been chosen to deliver the weapon that will strike this first blow that will see our nation, our people, our very beliefs rise once more!'

In Tarinski's cabin Colin Baskin listened to Anna's simultaneous translation. He stared white-faced at her. Holy Mother of God, this sonofabitch sounded as if it was really going to happen.

'Comrades! Our enemies with their spy satellites and reconnaissance 'planes will still be watching. They will be doing the same down here. But we shall evade them! We must evade them!'

In the torpedo compartment the technicians around the Gyroton looked at Igor Tamasara in awe. From the speaker the voice roared on. 'But go about your duties secure in the knowledge that you are not without help. You will remember our three sister ships that were sold to Japan. What you did not know then was that they had been purchased for the purpose of protecting us when we needed help. Even now as I speak, they are out there, on our flanks, protecting our stern ... making sure that no one can attack us while Comrade navigator Tarinski takes us to our rendezvous ...'

In the control room Tarinski stared fixedly at his charts. So much now made sense. And yet he was filled with a sudden sinking sense of dread, not least because of the role Marlo had cast for him.

'When we have transferred the weapon and distinguished visitors to the boat we shall rendezvous with, we shall retrace our course until we are safely under the polar ice. We shall remain there until the Americans and Japanese have finished with each other. Then we shall return home, to help build the new Russia with our Chinese compatriots.

'Comrades! In the years to come, your children and your children's children will say that never in the history of our glorious Navy was so much achieved by so few. Do your duty! Obey all orders! Remember you are sailing into history. That is all.'

Marlo lifted his thumb from the switch and returned the mike to its cradle.

Throughout the *Rodina* there was only stunned silence.

Morton had requested from the Captain of the *United States* a compartment sufficiently large and secure to serve as a Hammer Force's on-board operations room. The Captain – a Rear Admiral who had led the coalition naval task force in the Persian Gulf War – had a reputation for having a short fuse. Morton hadn't given him a chance to light it.

He'd called on the Captain in his day cabin, explained exactly what he needed, and why, and the Rear Admiral had been co-operation itself. He led the way into a compartment that could have been the board-room of a Wall Street law firm. The walls were covered with expensive panelling, the floor in a thick blue shag carpet, and the furniture was a tasteful blend of European and American. Only the ceiling, festooned with exposed pipes, indicated that this was part of a fighting ship: the Rear Admiral's staff conference room.

The centre table could seat fifty. Along the walls were a similar number of chairs. Every one was now occupied and every eye focused on Morton. Danny and Tommy and the shooters sat in one group. With them were Kate and the CCO from Concorde. The 'plane was now parked at Kai Tek. Another group consisted of the Presidential advance party: Secret Service men, junior White House aides. With them was FBI Director Wyman. He had flown in a couple of hours ahead of Air Force One. A third group was made up of Governor Sir Alan Wingate and his senior staff. They were attired in formal morning dress, ready to welcome the President. British officers from the Col-ony's military garrison and the Royal Hong Kong Police Force formed a solid phalanx at one end of the table. At the far end sat the Rear Admiral and a cluster of flag officers.

Morton had spoken without notes, in a flat and controlled voice. What he was saying did not need embellishment.

He had begun by saying that Tung Shi had been brought on board in one of the carrier's cutters and was now in the lock-up beneath the flight deck. Nodding towards Wyman he added that the FBI were arranging to fly the Triad leader to Washington to face charges of wholesale drug-running into the United States.

'Those are simply holding charges,' Morton continued. 'There is every likelihood that Tung Shi is implicated in this plot to kill the President.' He paused and looked around the table.

'Here is where we are right now. Five hours ago, the USS Seattle signalled the position of the three Japanese Typhoons and the Rodina. They were then about nine hours north of here. More precise informa-tion is not available. The seas are deep and a number of underwater valleys make close surveillance difficult. The Seattle has been instructed by PACSUBCOM' – he glanced quickly at the Governor and his aides – 'that's Pacific Submarine Command, to maintain watch, but to take no further action pending the outcome of further discussions the President is having with the Japanese Emperor.'

He waited for his words to take effect. Then he told them what he had told the President. 'We know those Japanese Typhoons are fully armed. Even if they were all sunk before they launched an attack, we could still face an unparalleled ecological disaster. Between them those subs carry sufficient nuclear material to pollute almost the entire Pacific for centuries to come. The whole industry and lifestyle of the area would be destroyed. The President has accepted that before we do anything we must be absolutely certain that attacking those submarines is the lesser of two very great evils.

'As far as the *Rodina* goes, we know from General Savenko that she is unarmed. Why she is being shadowed by those Japanese submarines is unclear. The message from the *Seattle* suggested the Japanese were acting as a sort of bodyguard. It's an interesting theory, but no more. It is just possible that the Japanese are there out of curiosity as to what exactly the *Rodina* is doing.'

Once more Morton paused. Then he continued in a low but implacable voice. 'My communications people monitored a telephone call Tung Shi made shortly before he was arrested. It indicated the *Rodina* is to rendezvous with a boat. So far, despite every effort, the location or purpose of this rendezvous has been impossible to ascertain.'

Morton looked towards the Rear Admiral and his staff. 'However, this now raises two further possibilities. Firstly, that the *Rodina* will be transferring Igor Tamasara and his team onto that boat so that they can escape elsewhere. But that seems unlikely. If they were going to run, they would run all the way in the *Rodina*.

'That leaves the final possibility. Igor Tamasara and his people will use that boat to mount some kind of attack against the President. The Hong Kong Harbour Authority tells me that at any given hour, day or night, there are up to ten thousand boats in their jurisdiction alone. Between here and the Chinese coast there could be close to a hundred thousand out on the water. To stop and search them all is a physical impossibility. And all that would do would be to alert Igor Tamasara. The chances are that even if we mobilised the entire Seventh Fleet we still couldn't mount a totally effective surveillance operation.'

Morton paused again briefly. He knew exactly what he had to say. 'I am now proposing the following course of action.

'One. The *United States* will take every defensive measure it can to create a protective shield around itself. I understand that it has such a capability.'

The Rear Admiral nodded.

'Two. The hunt for this boat will be the sole responsibility of Hammer Force.'

For the first time there was an interruption. A red-tabbed General with a Sandhurst haircut turned to Morton. 'Dryhurst, C-in-C British Forces Hong Kong,' he introduced himself. 'How exactly do you intend to find this boat?'

'By going after them the way they won't expect, with a small task force. But your people can help. I understand you have a couple of Cobra Kings?'

Dryhurst nodded. His Cobra Kings were the latest off the assembly line, finished in the same anti-radar-detection paint as Stealth bombers.

'I need them both,' Morton said.

'Agreed,' Dryhurst said promptly.

Morton looked to where Tommy, Danny and the CCO sat. 'Danny, I want those emission tracers transferred from Concorde to the choppers. Tommy, you'll fly the lead one. Danny you'll be with me.'

Sir Alan Wingate had a question. 'What exactly does an emission tracer do?'

'They'll tell us if there's a second Gyroton,' Morton said.

30

In the *Rodina's* control room, Tarinski ticked off their position on a chart, turned in his chair and announced that they were approaching their rendezvous. They had held this course and speed for the past seven hours. In that time he'd taken a short break to go to the sick bay, telling Marlo he needed something from Borikov for a headache. In truth, he'd wanted to see whether Yuri felt like him about the man and woman locked in his cabin. That they were being held prisoner almost certainly meant that their lives were in danger. Yuri had agreed that the old Chinese standing in a corner of the control room was capable of anything. He had also agreed that most certainly the couple were not part of this terrible madness Marlo had described, this insane plot to launch an attack on the American President which would assuredly drag in Russia, drag in everyone. He'd told Yuri that if they couldn't get near that infernal weapon in the torpedo room there had to be a way of helping the man and woman. Yuri had outlined his plan.

Surgeon Borikov stood unobtrusively in a corner of the control room, still thinking hard. Boris was right. The couple were in danger. He'd known that ever since he'd examined the woman. Mentally there was nothing wrong with her. Mind you, her posture would have fooled most doctors. It just so happened, he'd told her, that at Navy medical school he'd written his thesis on the pros and cons of electro-shock treatment. There had been silence in the cabin after that. Then the man – who said his name was Colin – had spoken.

Borikov suspected that even now, if Marlo had not made that extraordinary speech, what Colin had said would still be just too incredible. And perhaps he had not told him everything. But he had said enough to convince him that he spoke the truth. No one could have made that up. Besides, in describing what had happened to Anna and himself, he must also have known he was taking a risk, that what he said could be reported to Marlo or that Chinese. That Colin had been prepared to do so weighed further in his favour. And, even in a place like Gremikha, there had been whispers of experiments going on in secret establishments out on the steppes. Not just the usual medical abuse of dissidents, which for so long had been a shameful part of Soviet medicine. But something altogether more sinister. Academician Tamasara and his colleagues remained part of that; what they had begun in Russia they had perfected in China.

When Colin had finished, Borikov had felt an unaccustomed anger welling up at what other doctors had done. When Anna asked him, he instantly agreed to help, explaining that she was his patient and he had a solemn duty to protect her from further harm. Somehow he had to keep them on the boat. Maybe later, he could arrange for them to use the radio to speak to someone. Sasha, the radio officer, was a decent man; he could be persuaded to help.

Borikov watched Marlo straighten from the plotting table. 'All stop,' the Captain ordered. 'One third speed astern.' The submarine's movement fell away until the *Rodina* came to a halt. Marlo looked towards the sonar compartment. 'Report.'

'Surface noise, Comrade Captain. Bearing two-four-zero. Sounds like a diesel engine,' an operator called out.

Marlo turned to the diving officer and ordered periscope height. The *Rodina* rose slowly until she hovered ten feet beneath the surface of the South China Sea. 'Up 'scope,' Marlo ordered.

He placed his eye against the rubber shield and began to scan slowly. Halfway through the movement Marlo adjusted the viewfinder. After a moment he stepped away from the periscope and motioned to Qiao Peng.

'Is this your junk?'

Qiao Peng pressed his eyes against the shield. In the dark of the night it looked like any other junk, cumbersome and low in the water. But inside that caulked hull were powerful engines and a lot of other surprises. He stepped away from the periscope. 'That's her.'

'Stand by to surface. Blow all ballast tanks,' Marlo ordered.

With a rush of water being expelled, the sail broke the surface and the upper hull rose out of the sea. 'Bridge party report,' Marlo said.

The bridge officer reported by 'phone that the junk was stationary about a quarter-mile on the port side. Beyond was the darker mass of the Chinese mainland. 'Any other ships?' Marlo asked.

'None in the immediate vicinity, Comrade Captain. But a number of lights further out.'

Marlo nodded. They would be the Chinese Navy warships Qiao Peng had mentioned. He'd said they would be positioned all along their track to help deter surveillance. This was also one of the most secure military zones on the Chinese coast. 'Handling crew to the foredeck,' he ordered.

Seamen began to hurry through the control room and climb up to the bridge. From there they would descend to the flat missile deck.

'Junk approaching, Comrade Captain,' reported the bridge officer.

Marlo dialled a number on the control room 'phone console. 'Prepare for transfer.'

In the torpedo storage compartment a seaman spun a wheel to open the deck hatch. Two of the handling crew grabbed its lugs and pulled the hatch back on its hinges.

In the control room Borikov knew he had little time left to help Anna and Colin. He looked at Tarinski who nodded. They'd do what they could.

'Radio to conn.'

'Status?' asked the Watch Officer.

'No submerged contacts.'

Marlo grunted. Those Japanese subs would be keeping radio silence. He'd have done the same in their place. It was good to know they were there, keeping their protective watch.

'Radar to conn.'

'Report.'

'Chinese radar. Shipboard and land side.'

Marlo gave another satisfied grunt. Those Chinese radars would have laid down a grid over hundreds of square miles of sea. Not even the Americans would be able to slip through it to search for them. Outside the hull came the steady throb of powerful engines. The *Rodina* began to roll gently in the surge they created.

'Junk alongside,' called down the bridge officer.

'Coming up,' Marlo replied.

He put down the 'phone and turned to Qiao Peng. 'Can you assemble all those being transferred?'

Borikov stepped forward. 'The woman and the American should remain here. They are my patients and need proper medical care.'

Qiao Peng turned and looked at Borikov. He asked no questions. But behind those eyes Borikov once more saw a quick intelligence evaluating the information it received.

Marlo shrugged. 'They're not really our responsibility, Comrade Surgeon – '

'They go with us, Captain!' said Igor Tamasara. He stood in the hatchway of the control room. Behind him were Dr Petrarova and Dr Fretov.

'If they need any medical attention, we can provide it!' Igor Tamasara said angrily, stepping through the hatch. His face continued to darken. First this damned Chinese had dared interfere. Now a pup of a doctor was trying to do the same!

He spoke witheringly to Borikov. 'Comrade Surgeon! I don't know where you qualified. But one thing is clear. You have attended none of my classes. If you had, you would have known better than to speak with such temerity!'

'Academician Tamasara, I did not mean to offend you,' Borikov said quietly. 'But I have examined the woman – '

'And what did you discover?' Igor Tamasara was almost shouting.

'She appears to have undergone electro-shock therapy – '

'For her depression,' Dr Fretov said quickly. 'I was treating her before she came on board.'

'Nevertheless, Comrade Professor, in my judgement she is not fit to travel,' Borikov said. 'She can remain on board, and I can assure you that she will receive proper medical care until we reach land – '

'Have you forgotten that your Captain said you will be spending a considerable amount of time under the polar ice before you return home?' asked Dr Petrarova icily.

Borikov spoke in the same steady voice. 'Her companion is a doctor. He can assist me – '

'Enough!' Igor Tamasara shouted. 'These people are not your concern.'

Qiao Peng had listened impassively. Why was this ship's doctor so keen to keep them on board? It had to be foolish humanity. He turned to Marlo. 'Have the woman and the man brought on deck.'

'Comrade Captain,' implored Borikov. 'Please let them stay.'

'The matter is closed!' snapped Marlo.

In the silence Igor Tamasara and the others began to climb the ladder inside the sail. Having ordered a crewman to fetch Anna and Colin Baskin, Marlo and Qiao Peng followed.

From the junk's stern projected the jib of a small crane. Igor Tamasara stood by the open hatch, peering down at the technicians in the torpedo room securing a loading net over the Gyroton. When they had done so,

330

he turned and made a hoisting motion to a Chinese deckhand at the junk's stern.

The man started up the winch. With two of the technicians clinging to the net, the Gyroton emerged from the compartment and rose slowly above the missile deck before being swung on board the junk.

Qiao Peng climbed down from the bridge and walked along the wide missile deck. Dr Petrarova and Dr Fretov followed. They joined the technicians and the Chinese security men who had climbed out of the torpedo room. From the junk a gangway was lowered to the missile deck.

When Colin Baskin and Anna arrived in the control room Borikov walked over to them. 'I'm sorry. There was nothing I could do,' he said in a defeated tone.

'Do they suspect I'm faking?' Anna asked in a low voice.

'I don't think so,' Borikov replied.

'Is there any way you can get a message to the outside world, warning what's going on?' she asked.

'I will try,' Borikov answered without hesitation.

They were silent now, staring at each other, then the surgeon continued, 'I still can't understand why they need to take you.'

Colin Baskin spoke quickly. 'As well as everything else, Tamasara's on an ego trip. He wants to show me the end result. The Nazi doctors were like that. They used to make their prisoners watch their experiments.'

'Do you think this weapon can actually affect the American President's mind so much that he will attack Japan?' Borikov asked.

'Who knows? But I still hope that I can somehow throw a spanner in the works.' Colin Baskin felt cold and functional. Ready to do anything. Ready to die to succeed. He turned as Tarinski joined them. 'This may be better than a spanner,' the navigator said. Turning his back so that none of the crew could see, Tarinski produced his service revolver and handed it to Colin Baskin.

'But won't you – get into trouble ... ?'

'It's okay,' Tarinski smiled tightly. 'Now that our Captain's cast us in the role of the stone that launched the avalanche, I don't think I'll need it.'

Colin Baskin handed the gun to Anna. 'You're probably better trained to use it than I am.'

As she shoved the revolver inside her dress, Marlo called down from the bridge. 'Send up the foreigners.'

Impulsively Anna reached up and quickly kissed Tarinski and Borikov on their cheeks. Afterwards Colin Baskin shook their hands. Then they climbed the ladder.

Seventeen nautical miles away, the Japanese Typhoon class *Hiroshima* hovered with only its radar antennae protruding above the surface. 'Targets separating,' called out the radar officer, bent over his 'scope. 'The junk's bound inshore. The Russian is submerging.'

Commander Yoshio Yamakama nodded. The time had come. He began to give orders. He knew that identical orders were being given on board the Typhoon class *Nagasaki* and *Kyoto*. Like his own, their names had been chosen by Admiral Toshika as a reminder of the terrible atomic destruction visited upon Japan in 1945. Kyoto had been spared from the holocaust. 'It is better to die than face the disgrace of surrender ever again,' Admiral Toshika had said after he briefed them.

Yamakama knew the maxim would guide him and his fellow captains in what they must now do.

The President sprawled in a chair in his state room on Air Force One, reading the revised draft of his speech in Mandarin which Madeleine Masters had typed. He glanced out of the window. The daylight was once more fading. Over the port wing a waif of a moon hung ghost-like near the horizon. They would be landing in the dark. Gates said it made for better security.

The President sighed and turned back to his speech. He'd used the Chinese *pinyin* system of romanticising Mandarin, but he'd decided against calling Hong Kong Xiang Kang. That could send the wrong signal to Beijing. What he was proposing was a partnership, not a takeover.

There was a knock and Thack poked his head around the door. 'Governor Wingate's people say Tang Ming will be on the tarmac to greet you. They want to know if you're going to invite him to chopper out with you to the *United States*?'

'Invite him along. If nothing else it'll be useful to test the temperature with him.'

In the sonar room of the USS *Seattle* Matti, the Watch Supervisor, turned from his board and looked at a rating. 'Sonofabitch,' they said in unison. 'Sonofabitch.'

'Oldest goddamn trick in the book,' murmured Matti.

'But it still works,' said a sonar man.

Woodward joined them, listening through his 'phones. 'The U-boats used to do this in the Atlantic when they were convoy hunting. In the end it was the only way they could get in close,' he said.

He reached for a 'phone and dialled the attack centre. 'Skipper, our three Nippon bears are running flooded down. Not an electronic peep out of them. It's pure luck that we got an echo bounce.'

The Japanese Typhoons were travelling with their missile decks awash and only a few feet of their sails above water. They were navigating by periscope and had killed their radios.

'Where are they?'

Woodward glanced at the plotting table where a technician was making another computation. 'Bearing zero-six-zero true, range thirty-two thousand yards,' Woodward announced.

'And Ivan bear?' asked Edmunds.

'We have a submerged contact, bearing seven-zero-four true, range thirty-four thousand, speed approximately sixteen knots, depth three hundred feet.'

Edmunds growled. Just over a mile apart. 'Woody, either our Ivan bear is feeling supremely confident or he's about to get the shock of his life. I'll signal PACSUBCOM.'

It took four minutes for the communications rating to encode the characters on tape, then transmit the encrypted signal to Pacific Submarine Command Headquarters with details of the position of all four Typhoons.

Two minutes later the bell marked 'incoming' rang in the *Seattle* radio room. The radio man ran the tape at high speed to decode the message and took it to the communications officer in his cubby-hole. After reading it, he strode to the attack centre and handed it to Edmunds. The message read: 'Keep distance. Do not repeat not intervene unless directly attacked.'

Morton's task force, Concorde and the two Cobra King helicopters, were parked in a corner of Kai Tek. For the past thirty minutes the airport had been closed to all traffic pending the arrival of Air Force One. Now, caught in the blaze of light from the ground, she was skimming past Kowloon's high-rise apartment blocks to make a text-book touchdown on one of the most difficult runways in the world.

At the end of its roll-out Air Force One turned and trundled to where the official reception committee waited. Through his night glasses Morton could see the Governor standing beside the squat figure of Tang Ming. An hour ago Morton had sent him a copy of a recording Electronic Surveillance had made in Suzy's apartment, together with a note asking Tang Ming to call a number after he'd listened. The telephone was in the Concorde communications centre. When he had called, Morton had told Tang Ming that he could guarantee that a copy of the tape would be in Chairman Hu's hands by morning. Everyone knew that in sexual matters Hu was something of an old-fashioned moralist. Tang Ming's choice was either ending his career, or answering a few questions. Playing dirty in this business went with all the other things no one liked doing.

What little he had learned had only convinced Morton he was on the right track. He turned to the small group around him. 'Time to go,' he said.

Kate was the only woman among them. After he had finished his briefing on the carrier, she had taken him aside and spoken with a simple eloquence. If her father was still alive, there was every chance he was with Igor Tamasara. In the dark, in the heat of battle, it would be easy to make a mistake and kill her father. By being there, she could help avoid that, because only she knew what he looked like. And, almost certainly, they would need a doctor if people were going to get hurt. Finally, she'd said that if he wouldn't take her along, she'd damn well charter her own chopper to go and search for Dad.

He'd smiled at that. She really knew that smile by now. Morton had said okay – they needed a medic.

Hefting her first-aid box, Kate followed him to one of the Cobra Kings.

Entering the Formosa Strait, Marlo ordered speed increased to 35 knots. They were two hours into their long run north. He wanted to be well clear of Japanese waters before the Amerikanski launched their first attack after their President suddenly went crazy. He still did not understand the science involved. But that look in Igor Tamasara's eyes as he'd turned at the top of the junk's gangway and given a clumsy salute said it all. A man like that wouldn't fail.

He was wrong about the Japanese Typhoons. He had assumed they would continue to escort the junk. Sonar reported that they were still out there and matching his increase in speed. He debated whether to have Tarinski awoken. An hour ago he'd given him permission to go off duty. He'd need him fresh and alert for the long run north after they'd lost their escort.

Marlo walked over to the sonar status screen. The three blips which, when he had last checked, were close together, had now separated. Right on the very edge of the screen was a fourth blip. That had to be the Amerikanski sub.

He reached for the mike on the PA system. 'Rig ship for ultra quiet!'

No activity that would generate unnecessary noise would be allowed. In the galley the chefs stopped preparing a hot meal; the sound of metal pots grating on burners could be picked up by that Amerikanski sonar. Instead helpings of black bread smeared with pork fat were prepared and served on plastic plates, together with paper cups of milk. For the next hour the crew received and acknowledged commands in whispers. Everyone knew the slightest unnecessary noise would attract the wrath of the Captain. He would punish them later: that would be the worst part, waiting to see what form it would take.

In the meantime he was obsessed with running from the Amerikanski, constantly asking the sonar men for the sub's speed and bearing. Time and again Marlo put on headphones to listen to the sounds of the Amerikanski and the Japanese Typhoons.

'Why don't they beat her off?' the sonar chief croaked.

Marlo guessed that the Japanese were waiting until they were clear of the strait: they'd have more room in open sea to manoeuvre. Now, the sonar chief reported that the other Typhoons were bearing down so that their bow-mounted sonar pointed almost directly at them. Marlo took a pair of 'phones to listen once more to the engines storming through the water at flank sped. 'I want Comrade Lieutenant Tarinski here!' he shouted, ending the silent-ship routine.

Aboard USS Seattle, Captain Edmunds studied the computer display on the screen in the attack centre. The three Nippon bears were continuing to close at an oblique angle on Ivan bear. The attack centre 'phone pinged.

'Ivan's no longer playing possum. He's going like a bat out of hell, and to hell with the noise!' reported Woodward.

'Start taping, Woody,' Edmunds said tersely. From now on the Seattle would record what was happening.

Tarinski arrived in the control room in his old-fashioned long underpants and vest. The Rodina vibrated beneath his bare feet. Marlo seemed not to notice the navigator's flagrant breach of the rule book's dress code. 'Give me a course for Fochan,' he ordered. 'We may have trouble with the Amerikanski.'

Fochan was the headquarters port of the Chinese Navy in the South China Sea. Tarinski went to his table and bent over his charts, wondering whether Marlo had correctly read the situation.

The *Seattle* attack room 'phone pinged again. 'Skipper, our Nippon bears have primed!' Woodward reported.

A moment ago Matti had picked up in his headphones the unmistakable sounds of hydraulics lifting torpedos off their racks, followed by tube doors opening. Edmunds reached for the squawk box. 'This is the Captain. Now hear this. Go to action stations. Prepare for attack.'

Throughout the *Seattle* men moved in grim and almost silent speed to their battle quarters.

Marlo stood over Tarinski. 'How long?' he asked hoarsely. If the Typhoons were going to attack the Amerikanski, the sooner they were out of here the better.

The navigator finally looked up. 'Two hours to Fochan, Comrade Captain.'

The sonar chief called out urgently, 'The Amerikanski is now arming, Comrade Captain.'

Two hundred feet forward of the *Seattle*'s attack centre in the torpedo launch compartment two enlisted men sat side-by-side with headsets. One confirmed to the attack centre every move the other man made.

'Arming circuit opened.'

'Inertial guidance system activated.'

'Trigger mechanism set.'

The checks continued at the same swift, relentless pace.

Commander Yamakama stood directly behind the officer at the fire control panel in the *Hiroshima*'s command centre. At this precise moment the Captains of the *Nagasaki* and *Kyoto* would be doing the same. They had rehearsed every measure, anticipated every move that would be made to try to stop them. 'Russian Typhoon changing course, Captain,' reported a sonar man.

Even those without headphones imagined they could hear the distant sound of coolant pumps being driven flat out and the peculiar swish a submarine prop makes at maximum revolutions.

'And the American, sonar?'

'Armed and closing, Captain.'

Yamakama watched the red lights blinking on the panel. Each one indicated that a sub-killer torpedo was armed.

It had been agreed that he would fire first. Then, if there was a need, *Nagasaki* would unleash a fusillade, followed by *Kyoto*.

Almost total silence had fallen over the attack centre in the *Seattle*. Officers and men tried not to look at Edmunds. He, and he alone, would have to decide whether to launch. He sat absolutely immobile in the Captain's chair, blind and deaf to everything except the continuous flow of reports in his headset from Woodward in the sonar compartment.

Yamakama tapped the fire control officer on the shoulder. 'Open muzzle doors on tubes one, two and three.'

The officer depressed a switch to allow sea water to rush into the torpedo tubes. Yamakama asked for the latest position of the *Rodina* and *Seattle*. When he received them he gave a further order to the fire control officer. 'Set for minimum spread.'

The officer punched a command into his console. Its computer fed the information to the guidance system on each torpedo.

'Fire one, fire two, fire three,' Yamakama said clearly.

By the time the officer had punched the last red button, the first nine weapons had exited the angled bow tubes and were streaking in a close pattern. Tube three's two larger torpedoes set off after them.

'She's fired, skipper!' yelled Woodward, his ears filled with the sound of the high-pitched whine from electric motors driving the torpedos.

'Hard port! Go deep,' Edmunds said. He was committed now.

Marlo heard the blind terror in the sonar man's voice, saw his chief push the youth aside, heard the chief yelling the range, speed and course of the torpedos. All this he heard as he reached up and hit the alarm button. Klaxons began to blare throughout the *Rodina*, turning her into a sonic beacon for the noise-and-heat guidance system in each oncoming weapon.

In one blinding, searing second Marlo knew the terrible truth. He had been wrong! It wasn't the Amerikanski hunting him, but those Japanese! Right to the very end he had been tricked!

The first four torpedos struck *Rodina* amidships, near her greatest source of heat, her reactor. Half a ton of high explosive tore through the outer pressure hull. The impact ruptured the inner hull, allowing water to cascade over the reactor's heat exchangers. Instantly super heated, the force of the steam completed the work of the salvo by blowing out bulkheads, killing everyone it touched.

Two more torpedos penetrated the control room, instantly killing everyone. Three weapons crushed the aft hull. One moment it was a still recognisable shape, the next it was fragments. The two heavier torpedos fired from tube three hit the bow section, destroying it totally.

In no more that twenty seconds, every trace of life on board the *Rodina* had been extinguished.

'Holy Christ,' breathed Woodward.

'Amen,' said Edmunds.

They were the only words spoken in the *Seattle*.

A moment later Matti reported: 'Nippon bears picking up speed and moving away. The two who didn't fire are unloading.'

On the attack room screen Woodward could see for himself that the three Typhoons had changed course and were heading north towards Japan. He went to the communications room to draft a signal to PAC-SUBCOM.

Ten miles clear of the attack area, with no sign of the American in pursuit, Yamakama ordered the *Hiroshima* to once more run just below the surface so that he could raise his radio mast. Then he ordered the communications room to send a pre-taped message that had arrived on board shortly before the mission.

One hundred and fifty miles to the south, the radio man in the junk's state-of-the-art control centre had been waiting for the past hour for the message. It was short and explicit. 'Silent Voices has begun.'

The radio man picked up a 'phone, called the wheelhouse and repeated the message.

Qiao Peng, as usual, did not acknowledge receipt of the words he had drafted. He walked out onto the deck. Destroying the *Rodina* had been the first step in removing any evidence that would link him – and China – to what was about to happen.

338

For the first time in months he lit the stogey in his mouth, and began to savour the pungent smoke. That, too, would make no difference now. He stared out over the sea. From all directions the other junks were heading south towards Hong Kong, as he had ordered.

31

The Cobra King swept along the edge of the international shipping lane and past the outlying islands which fringed Hong Kong. The pilot had just reported that he had spotted two more junks. 'We'll have to refuel afterwards,' he added in Morton's headset.

'Understood,' acknowledged Morton. He was squatting on the floor of the cabin in the helicopter in front of the emission tracer. The size of an overnight suitcase, the tracer had been developed for the Persian Gulf War as a means of detecting the start-up emissions from Saddam's Scuds. Danny's technicians had refined the tracer so that its oscilloscope could detect the heat from a car exhaust a mile away.

Most of the remainder of the cabin was filled with equipment for Morton to communicate securely with the ops room on the *United States*, Tommy's Cobra King and Concorde itself. Danny and his technicians operated the equipment.

Kate sat on her first-aid box in a corner of the cabin. Like everyone else she wore a Stealth overall and boots. Faces and hands were covered with a cream to eliminate the risk of an infra-red scanner detecting body heat. Clipped in wall racks were weapons, each coated with a paint to make their metal undetectable to radar. Near the cabin door were coiled ropes shackled to bolts in the fuselage. They had been similarly treated.

The Cobra King displayed no navigation lights and its engine mounting was heavily baffled to reduce rotor clatter. The blades were coated with the same radar-repellent covering as the rest of the chopper. Window perspex was anti-reflection. Pods of cluster bombs and rockets were fitted to the outer fuselage.

Inside the cabin the low mush of radio traffic was the only sound. The *United States* had announced the arrival on board of the Presidential party, which included Tang Ming. Concorde had completed a sweep over the area where the *Rodina* had sunk, and had monitored a transmission from the *USS Seattle* confirming its order not to pursue the Japanese Typhoons. They were now well on their way home.

A few minutes earlier Morton had received another brief message that Tommy's Cobra King had refuelled and was once more heading north. Tommy's chopper was carrying an identical consignment of men, equipment and weapons. 'He's doing a good job,' Morton murmured to Danny.

Tommy's father smiled proudly and turned back to his equipment. A while later he looked up at Morton. 'Concorde says it's like some kind of junk olympics down there. They're still pouring out of the mainland towards Hong Kong and those radar jammers over there are making it hard to keep track of all the movements.'

'Tell Concorde to back off, Danny,' Morton said. The chance of Concorde picking up anything now was small. But Igor Tamasara and the others had to be down there. Qiao Peng wouldn't have gone to all this trouble otherwise. But knowing and finding that junk were still a long way apart.

In his headset came the double click from the flight deck. 'Junk coming up,' the pilot said.

Eyes fixed on the oscilloscope, Morton could imagine how startled its crew would be as the chopper suddenly appeared overhead. Around him the shooters tensed, hands ready to release safety belts and grab guns from the racks.

'We're right over their stern,' reported the pilot. 'Starting to crab now.'

Morton could feel the helicopter slowly moving towards the junk's bow. The oscilloscope showed boat engine emission traces. But nothing else. 'Crab completed,' said the pilot.

'On to the next one,' Morton ordered.

The manoeuvre was repeated above the second junk. Again, nothing. The Cobra King climbed away and headed in the darkness towards the lights of Hong Kong.

Several minutes later the oscilloscope filled with traces. Danny glanced at the screen with professional interest. 'They're using that new interferometer system that's designed to deflect laser beams. Plus every other gizmo they've got on board,' he said.

In his headset Morton heard the pilot curse softly: the *United States'* electronic defences would be playing havoc with his instruments. But the pilot had shown that he was good enough to bring them in manually.

Within a few minutes the carrier loomed like a brightly-lit cliff out of the water. Her bow faced directly out to sea, presenting a smaller target. Spread out on the surface was a semi-circle of police boats. They cruised slowly back and forth. The carrier's own helicopters were continuously flying across the harbour. Beneath the surface submarines of the Seventh Fleet formed an additional defence shield.

The Cobra King dropped onto the carrier's flight deck, close to where the refuelling crew waited. With them was Gates.

Igor Tamasara had designed the control room beneath the junk's wheel-house so that it resembled the one in the bunker in Beijing. He knew familiarity would reduce the tension his team must feel as they made their final preparations. For once he did not chivvy them: what they were doing now they had rehearsed many times.

At the far end of the room was a closed hatch in the bow of the junk. Before the hatch was the Gyroton. Dr Petrarova and Dr Fretov worked at a status board, constantly updating information. Each wore a sound-powered headset so he could communicate with them directly from his console at the back of the room.

To one side of the console were Anna and Colin Baskin. They were guarded by the one agent Tamasara had allowed into the control room. He had told Qiao Peng that the presence of his other operatives would make his own men nervous. To further reassure them he had pointed out the control room's lead-lined walls and ceiling which allowed them to work undetected by any hostile surveillance system. Nevertheless, several technicians now glanced up anxiously at the sounds from the deck. Tamasara turned to Qiao Peng. He stood on the other side of the console, arms folded, eyes half-closed. 'What are they doing up there?' he demanded irritably.

Qiao Peng glanced up. His agents were placing their explosive charges and inflating the rubber boats in which he and they would return to the mainland. The others would die and sink with this boat when their work was finished.

'They are only doing their work,' Qiao Peng finally said.

Aboard the *United States*, the Rear Admiral's spacious day cabin had become the President's temporary Oval Office.

'Some more tea?' the President asked courteously in Mandarin, point-ing towards the tray.

Tang Ming shook his head. 'Thank you, no. I see you speak our language well,' he said in passable English.

The President smiled. 'Not really. Just a few words. I fear I'm a little old to learn a new language fluently.'

'Chairman Hu speak English perfect,' Tang Ming said formally.

Out of a corner of his eye the President saw Thack run a finger down his nose. They'd worked out the system. Thack's nose touch meant it was time to move on. To hell with trying to loosen up this guy. In the end, only Chairman Hu really mattered.

'One of the things I hope my plan does is to encourage our own Chinese to re-invest in your great country,' the President began.

Seventy miles to the north of Hong Kong, Tommy's helicopter swooped towards another junk. Nothing. Thirty more so far on this run. How many more were out there? After the pre-mission briefing, the Colonel had taken him and Dad aside and said the chances were that Anna and Colin Baskin were now dead. The Colonel had looked at him and said he was old and wise enough to know that revenge was the most pointless and bitter of all human excess; that the only way to avenge Anna was to deal with Igor Tamasara with a total lack of emotion.

Nevertheless Tommy knew that every nerve and muscle in his body was clinging to the hope that she was still alive. Was she somewhere down there?

On the radio came a report from Concorde. No contact. He could hear in his headphones the steady breathing of the operative crouched over the tracer in the cabin. His hand nudged the stick slightly towards him. He felt the muscles in his buttocks tighten involuntarily again and he rose a fraction in his seat, the way he had in the simulator. *Go, go, go!*

On the carrier flight deck Morton and Gates watched the crew finish refuelling the Cobra King.

Gates nodded thoughtfully. 'Tang Ming seemed somehow different to what I'd expected. And a little nervous, too. Like he was struggling with something in his own mind. Maybe he's debating whether to go to Hu and make a full disclosure about that tape.'

From the cabin door of the Cobra King Danny called that it was time to go.

In the junk's control room a radar technician spoke quietly into his lip-mike. 'We've started to pick up the carrier's defence systems. They're broad spectrum.'

'Range?' demanded Igor Tamasara.

'Twenty-seven miles, Professor.'

Tamasara punched a button on his console and told the helmsman in the wheelhouse to maintain their present course and speed.

Colin Baskin turned to Tamasara. 'You really think your Gyroton will work from out here?'

Igor Tamasara smiled enigmatically.

When the President had finished speaking, Tang Ming abruptly stood up and walked over to the cabin's large window. Below on the flight deck a helicopter was lifting off. There was something strange about it. Then he realised: unlike the other helicopters he had glimpsed landing from time to time, in a clatter of rotors, this one displayed no navigation lights. And made no sound. A nation that could produce a machine able to fly silently in the dark was indeed a powerful one.

And this imposing man who had spoken so knowledgeably about China – often using the right Mandarin words to emphasise a point – was a fitting leader for that nation. The President had not been at all what he had imagined. Not bombastic, like so many *waibin*. Not arrogant, like the British Governor and his minions. Instead the President was quietly confident about all he said. And much of it indeed made a great deal of sense. That had been perhaps the most surprising thing of all.

The President had understood so much. That for China the speed of the introduction of democracy was a strongly contentious issue, but not its inevitability. That unlike Russia's, China's Communist Party would not disappear overnight, but must be allowed to gradually fade away. The President's plan would guarantee political stability in this necessarily slow period of change. The great gap between rich and poor, old and new – the cause of so much resentment in China – would be narrowed without the national chaos that in the past had accompanied a clamour for change. There was something for everyone in the President's plan.

Tang Ming blinked his eyes. There was something almost shocking in him even thinking like this. Was he only being carried away by the charisma of this imposing figure he could see watching him in the window's reflection? In the distance were the lights of the New Territories. Tang Ming turned and smiled for the first time at the President.

'You speak well. But you must have more than words. You must smell and breathe China.'

He motioned towards the window. 'Come, let us walk on your American flight deck and absorb something of my country's culture simply by standing there.'

The President glanced at Thack and smiled. They'd been wrong. This guy was human after all. 'I'd be glad to, Mr Tang,' the President said.

Colin Baskin glanced towards the radar screen displaying the traces from the carrier's electronic defences, then turned once more to Igor Tamasara. 'There's enough energy there to send your beam all over the place.' If only he could unsettle Tamasara just enough to force him into a wrong move.

Igor Tamasara forced down his own sudden anger, knowing that Qiao Peng was listening and would expect an answer. But he was disappointed in the American. First he had tried to pretend to know more than he did. Now he was treating him like a fool in saying such a thing.

Tamasara smiled quickly at Qiao Peng then spoke to Colin Baskin. 'Those defences are primarily intended only to protect the carrier and those on board as long as they remain inside,' Igor Tamasara said.

'In that case the President is beyond your beam's reach,' Baskin replied.

Anna listened in silence. She knew what he was trying to do. But this was a waste of time. Taunting him was not going to shake Igor Tamasara's superiority.

'Why don't you just wait and see, Professor Baskin?' Igor Tamasara asked. He pressed a key on the console that connected him to the room's PA system. 'Fifteen minutes to transmission time,' he announced in a calm, confident voice.

Qiao Peng glanced at a wall clock. By now Tang Ming should be walking with the President down the flight deck to the carrier's bow.

Morton and Gates huddled around the oscilloscope as the Cobra King once more soared away from a junk. 'He's down there somewhere,' Morton said.

Moments later Danny turned from his equipment, a surprised look on his face. 'Carrier Ops are reporting that the President and Tang Ming are out strolling the flight deck.'

'Patch me into Ops, Danny,' Morton said urgently. He heard a new voice in his headset. He told the voice to put Thack on the line. 'I want them off that deck now,' Morton said to Thack.

'I'm not sure – '

'Do what I say, Thack. And do it now,' Morton said, even more urgently.

All around the flight deck the lights of Hong Kong and Kowloon sparkled; the swell was ripping spindrift from the top. Back along the deck the Secret Service men stood patiently. Once, when they had come too close the President had waved them back. He wanted no one, not even Thack, to intrude on these moments with Tang Ming.

They stood for a moment longer in silence, staring out towards the mainland of China. Then, without trying to hide the emotion in his voice, the President spoke. 'One of your philosophers once said that a journey of a thousand miles starts with a single step. Tonight the steps I have taken here are the beginning of my journey towards your people. I want you to go back to Chairman Hu and tell him that the United States is the future of China.'

Tang Ming looked away. Could this *waibin* really be telling the truth? And could China really risk opening its doors? Or would China once more become a land of disparate warring tribes? He honestly did not know. All he knew was that he had not expected to feel like this.

'*Ku-hai yu-cheng*,' Tang Ming said softly.

The President looked quizzically at him. 'What does that mean?'

'It is an old Buddhist saying about survival in a time of uncertainty.'

'You are not certain my plan will work?' the President asked gently.

'I am not certain of anything, Mr President.'

Tang Ming turned to the President and gave a little shiver. 'Let us go inside.'

Even now he did not really understand why Qiao Peng had ordered him to find an excuse to bring the President out here. All he sensed was that in remaining here he was somehow jeopardising the life of this man who clearly had China's interests at heart. Suddenly, no matter what it meant for his own future, he was no longer prepared to play any part in harming the President. To do so would be to harm China – to destroy its one great chance to find its rightful place in the world.

Whether he would be allowed to have a voice in shaping this bright new era would not be for him to decide. There was much in his past that this silent figure beside him would, no doubt, find unacceptable. Yet to promise he could give up all his ways would be unrealistic. He would always need a Suzy. But in so many other ways he could help. He now understood the people of Hong Kong. They were not like the main-landers; and they were fearful that they faced an uncertain future. He could help take that uncertainty away by convincing Chairman Hu that the President's plan was good for everyone.

'Come, Mr President,' Tang Ming said, more insistently this time. 'I think you are needed.'

Thack was running down the flight deck.

In the control room Igor Tamasara ordered the junk's engines to stop and the bow hatch opened. A patch of night sky appeared and the junk began to pitch gently in the swell. 'Cut all power,' Tamasara ordered. Screens and equipment fell silent to reduce the chance of discovery.

'Start up beam,' he commanded.

As Dr Petrarova and Dr Fretov walked to take up their positions at the Gyroton controls, Anna moved. Shoving Colin Baskin to one side she pulled out Tarinski's revolver and thrust it against Igor Tamasara's head. The guard stared at her in disbelief.

'The first one who moves dies,' Anna shouted.

Over her shoulder she spoke to Colin Baskin. 'Get out of here!' As he ran for the door, Qiao Peng broke the silence.

'Shoot her!'

Even as the guard reached for his gun, Anna pulled the trigger, and then rammed the barrel against Qiao Peng's head. On the floor Igor Tamasara twitched and lay still.

'Shoot her!' Qiao Peng screamed again.

The gunfire, when it came, was from the decks, and was followed by a splash.

'Bogey!' Tommy yelled, breaking radio silence. Outside the window there was nothing except a blue-black void.

'Confirmed!' Morton acknowledged.

He stared for a moment longer at the oscilloscope. Only machine-gun fire produced that trace. He jumped to his feet and reached for a weapon from a rack. Around him the shooters were doing the same. In his headset, he heard Tommy's throat clearance, then: 'Let's make it a good one, Colonel. Let's go up, up and away.' Just like the simulator.

One of the soldiers pulled open the cabin door and began to pay out the ropes. Morton and Gates grabbed one and dropped down from the chopper, swinging in the darkness above the waves with weapons clipped to their safety harnesses. The shooters were emerging from the cabin and dropping down beside them. Soon there were a dozen men swinging precariously above the sea.

Both Cobra Kings raced towards the junk.

'Shoot her!' Qiao Peng screamed again in the control room. 'Start the beam!'

As Dr Petrarova jumped forward to press the lever on the Gyroton, Anna's shot caught him in the neck. Before he hit the deck, she had the revolver back against Qiao Peng's head. 'Next time it's you,' she grunted.

She had four bullets left. What did she have to hit to knock out that machine?

'Have bogey visually,' Tommy said into his mike. 'Starting attack run now!'

Danny glanced at the oscilloscope and ran forward to the cabin door. Behind him a technician was reporting what was happening to the carrier's ops room.

Leaning out of the door Danny yelled down. 'There's a new trace. He must have activated the Gyroton.'

Beneath the Cobra King Morton raised a hand in acknowledgement, then gripped the rope once more. All around him men were holding on grimly to their ropes.

In the wheelhouse of the junk Qiao Peng's agents, crouching behind machine guns, stared in astonishment. One moment the sky had been empty, the next shadowy figures suspended beneath a helicopter were racing towards them. They raked the darkness with gunfire and saw the splash of bodies hitting the water.

As Tommy's helicopter veered away, there was a resounding crash on the wheelhouse roof. Morton and Gates burst into the wheelhouse, firing as they came, killing everyone inside.

In the door of the helicopter, Kate watched the shooters tumbling down the rope and spreading out across the deck. The sounds of battle were intensifying. Danny pushed past her with a field radio pack on his back. He grabbed a rope and shinned down to the junk. She reached for a headset. 'Get as close to the deck as you can,' Kate ordered the pilot.

The Cobra King began to descend.

*

The gun battle on deck finally galvanised the technicians in the control room into action. They began to dive through the hatch into the sea. Dr Fretov joined the scramble.

Suddenly, catching Anna by complete surprise, Qiao Peng rammed his elbow into her stomach with such force that her gun hand flew in the air, the weapon clattering to the floor. Still moving, he chopped her viciously in the throat and ran towards the Gyroton. There was still time!

Scrabbling across the floor, half-choking and dizzy with the pain, Anna found the revolver. She struggled to her feet and fired. The bullet smashed into a monitor.

Qiao Peng plunged on across the room.

Anna felt something claw at her leg, sending her off balance. She looked down. Igor Tamasara's fingers once more tore at her. She kicked his hand away. She fired at Qiao Peng, and again missed.

He'd reached the controls. His eyes swept over the panel. The *waibin* had said everything was preset. A child could fire it.

Anna's next shot caught him in the shoulder. He felt the bone shatter and his arm go numb. But the hatch was clear! One burst. That was all he needed. One burst!

Anna fired her last bullet, shattering another screen. As she began to stagger towards the Gyroton the control room door crashed open.

'Down, Anna!' yelled Morton.

He fired a sustained burst at the Gyroton.

For a moment Qiao Peng was pinned by the impact against the shattered controls. Then he sank to the deck. From within the Gyroton Qiao Peng's metallicised voice began to speak.

'I know the Japanese are treacherous ...'

Morton walked over to Anna. 'Are you okay?' he asked.

She nodded.

'I will now authorise a nuclear air strike against Tokyo ...' said the disembodied voice.

From the doorway Gates asked in an awed voice: 'Jesus H. Christ. Do you think he triggered it?'

Behind him Danny arrived with the radio set. 'Carrier Ops have just reported that the President was safely back inside ten minutes ago. His doctor says he's performing perfectly normally.'

'Jesus H. Christ!' Gates said again, this time in relief.

On deck the shooting had stopped. In the near silence Kate's voice could be heard. 'It's my Dad. They've killed him,' she sobbed.

349

'He was the first we pulled out of the water,' Danny said quietly.

'We lose many?' Morton asked.

'Five shooters from Tommy's chopper. All recovered. But we pretty well wiped them out. Those we didn't get, the sharks will.'

Gates pointed to the deck. 'This whole tub is wired like a time bomb. Shall I tell your people to dismantle?'

'No,' Morton replied.

From the deck the sound of Kate's sobbing continued.

'I'll go to her,' Anna said. As she turned to leave Danny said he would go up top to arrange the final clean-up.

Morton walked over to the Gyroton and hit it with the butt of his Usi. The voice finally stopped. Gates looked at the shattered Gyroton. 'You think it would really have worked?'

'Who knows?'

Gates glanced around him, 'You thinking what I'm thinking, David?'

Morton nodded. 'Lets go do it.'

On deck Morton and Gates walked to where Anna knelt with Kate beside Colin Baskin's body. Gates gently reached down and pulled Kate to her feet. 'There's no easy way to say what I have to. We can take your father's body back with us. But that could raise questions, open old wounds. Not everybody would understand why he was here. They'd dig into his past. Pull out enough to hurt. He was part of this, Kate. Only in the beginning, maybe, but still a part.'

'I see,' Kate said in a small, tight voice. She looked at Morton. 'What do you say, Colonel?'

'A lot of things died here tonight. A lot of bad things, and one good man – your father. When we sink this tub it's your choice whether you take him or not. But with what little I know of your father, I can't help feeling he would have liked to have ended it here.'

She turned away, nodding, the tears running down her face.

Fifteen minutes later Morton, Danny and Gates were crowded behind Tommy on the flight deck of his Cobra King. From there Morton had radioed a report to the carrier. It was prefixed 'Eyes Only President'.

Tommy had grinned foolishly at Morton. 'And Anna's absolutely okay?'

'Not a scratch. Now just concentrate on what you've got to do,' Morton shook his head wearily.

'Will do, Colonel, will do!'

Morton smiled in the darkness and this time it was not an on-loan smile.

The cockpit radar showed the junk as a blip five miles away in an otherwise empty sea. Choppers from the *United States* had cleared the area of all other boats, warning everyone the junk contained explosives. A medi-evac helicopter had flown Anna and Kate and three wounded shooters to the carrier. All the bodies had been recovered and laid out on the junk's deck. They included Dr Fretov and Dr Petrarova. Colin Baskin's body and the dead of Hammer Force had been kept separate from the others. When they had volunteered, Morton had told them that, should they die in action, they would have to be buried where they fell. Hammer Force was not in the business of State funerals.

'Strike. This is Control,' Morton said quietly into his mike. 'Commence attack.'

Tommy pushed the commit button on his stick to arm the rockets. The helicopter swept towards the junk. In silence the others watched Tommy's gloved hand moving in a continuous fluid motion. The armament panel lit up. 'Going ... now,' Tommy called out.

The rockets were released, and with a quick series of thuds they left their pods.

Tommy banked the chopper hard left.

A moment later the night sky erupted in a glow of fire as the rockets struck the junk. The fireball grew and blossomed, brightening the sea all around. Then it faded as swiftly as it had appeared.

'That's it,' said Danny quietly.

'For sure,' added Morton.

Tommy turned the chopper towards the lights of Hong Kong. No one spoke.

Two hours later Morton was escorted by a Marine to the floating Oval Office. The soldier once more saluted perfectly, knocked and opened the door.

The President rose from his chair and walked across the room. 'Hello, Colonel Morton,' the President said, shaking hands and leading them back to their chairs. 'I've seen your radioed report. Now just tell me the rest,' the President said.

When Morton had finished the President was silent. It was a solemn moment and neither spoke for long seconds. Then the President stood up. 'You did well, Colonel. An hour ago, after Tang Ming sent the details to Beijing about the deaths of Qiao Peng and those Russians, he had a long talk with Chairman Hu. Then the Chairman called me. We also had a good talk. He's coming over here in the morning. And so's the Emperor. Hu's certain that between us we can make my plan really work.'

'For sure, Mr President,' Morton said, as they once more shook hands.